SLEIGHT
OF
HAND
A Hart & Drake Thriller

CJ LYONS

ALSO BY CJ LYONS:

Lucy Guardino FBI Thrillers:
SNAKE SKIN
BLOOD STAINED
KILL ZONE
AFTER SHOCK
HARD FALL
BAD BREAK

Hart and Drake Medical Suspense:
NERVES OF STEEL
SLEIGHT OF HAND
FACE TO FACE
EYE OF THE STORM

Shadow Ops Covert Thrillers:
CHASING SHADOWS
LOST IN SHADOWS
EDGE OF SHADOWS

Fatal Insomnia Medical Thrillers:
FAREWELL TO DREAMS
A RAGING DAWN

BORROWED TIME
LUCIDITY: A GHOST OF A LOVE STORY
BROKEN
WATCHED
FIGHT DIRTY

Angels of Mercy Medical Suspense:
LIFELINES
WARNING SIGNS
URGENT CARE
CRITICAL CONDITION

Caitlyn Tierney FBI Thrillers:
BLIND FAITH
BLACK SHEEP
HOLLOW BONES

PRAISE FOR NEW YORK TIMES AND USA TODAY BESTSELLER CJ LYONS:

"Everything a great thriller should be—action packed, authentic, and intense."
~#1 *New York Times* bestselling author Lee Child

"A compelling new voice in thriller writing...I love how the characters come alive on every page." ~*New York Times* bestselling author Jeffery Deaver

"Top Pick! A fascinating and intense thriller." ~ 4 1/2 stars, *RT Book Reviews*

"An intense, emotional thriller...(that) climbs to the edge of intensity." ~*National Examiner*

"A perfect blend of romance and suspense. My kind of read." ~*#1 New York Times* Bestselling author Sandra Brown

"Highly engaging characters, heart-stopping scenes...one great rollercoaster ride that will not be stopping anytime soon." ~Bookreporter.com

"Adrenalin pumping." ~*The Mystery Gazette*

"Riveting." ~*Publishers Weekly Beyond Her Book*

Lyons "is a master within the genre." ~*Pittsburgh Magazine*

"Will leave you breathless and begging for more." ~Romance Novel TV

"A great fast-paced read....Not to be missed." ~4 ★ Stars, Book Addict

"Breathtakingly fast-paced." ~*Publishers Weekly*

"Simply superb...riveting drama...a perfect ten." ~Romance Reviews Today

"Characters with beating hearts and three dimensions." ~*Newsday*

"A pulse-pounding adrenalin rush!" ~Lisa Gardner

"Packed with adrenalin." ~David Morrell

"...Harrowing, emotional, action-packed and brilliantly realized." ~Susan Wiggs

"Explodes on the page...I absolutely could not put it down." ~Romance Readers' Connection

This book is a work of fiction. Any references to historical events, real people, or real locales are used fictitiously. Other names, characters, places, and incidents are the product of the author's imagination, and any resemblance to actual events or locales or persons, living or dead, is entirely coincidental.

SLEIGHT OF HAND
Copyright 2011, CJ Lyons
Edgy Reads

Cover art: Cory Clubb

All rights reserved, including the right of reproduction in whole or in part in any form. This book, or parts thereof, may not be reproduced in any form without permission in writing from the publisher, Edgy Reads. The scanning, uploading and distribution of this book via the Internet or via any other means without the permission of the publisher is illegal and punishable by law under the U.S. Copyright Act of 1976.

Please purchase only authorized electronic editions, and do not participate in or encourage electronic piracy of copyrighted materials. Your support of the author's rights is appreciated.

Library of Congress Case # 1-804387036

SLEIGHT OF HAND

A Hart & Drake Thriller

CJ LYONS

EDGY READS

CHAPTER 1

THE LAST TIME Dr. Cassandra Hart entered Pittsburgh's Three Rivers Medical Center she was covered in the blood of the man she had killed.

Not to mention bits and pieces of his brain and skull.

Now, forty-one days later, Cassie halted beneath the large marble angel that stood near the doors of the ER. Her palm grew clammy as it gripped her cane, her fingers digging into the rubber handle. Once upon a time, Three Rivers Medical Center was a second home to her, one of the few places where she felt comfortable, safe even. Today she looked at the door and fear churned through her gut, a counterpoint to the throbbing in her ankle.

The last time she crossed this threshold she'd come not as a physician, but as a patient. A victim.

She swallowed hard, forcing down bile as she remembered the expressions of her colleagues that night. First came surprise, then pity, and finally—when they learned what Cassie had been forced to do, trapped in a cellar with a killer—fear.

Her eyes squeezed shut at the memory. What if she couldn't handle it? What if she'd lost her edge? People's lives were at stake. What if she made a mistake, hurt someone? Once begun, the treadmill of anxiety revved into overdrive. She could take more time. Her boss and doctors had wanted her to. They'd said she was coming back too soon.

Cassie opened her eyes and realized she was hunched over, leaning on the cane. Her gaze fixed on the concrete walk splattered with mud from April showers. Both hands now pressed on the cane as if the thin cylinder of metal was the only thing keeping her on her feet.

She hated the damned cane.

Lashav. She borrowed one of her Gram Rosa's favorite gypsy curses. Shameful. She could damn well stand on her own two feet.

Forcing herself upright, she faced the doors emblazoned: EMERGENCY DEPARTMENT in blood-red letters. She took a deep breath, and balanced without the cane. Turning her gaze to the marble angel, she sent a quick prayer for hope, strength—for whatever it would take to get her through this day.

Cassie walked the remaining ten feet to the entrance. She threw the cane into the garbage can. The sliding glass doors swished open, and she crossed over.

※

"THIS DOCTOR, CASSANDRA Hart, she almost got you killed, didn't she, Detective Drake?"

"Yes. No!" Mickey Drake pulled his gaze away from the view of Pittsburgh's PNC baseball stadium and turned to face the departmental psychiatrist.

Noah White was his name, although the man had one of the darkest ebony complexions Drake had ever seen. White's accent was a soft, southern syrup. Better to sooth the jagged nerves of men who carried guns and knew how to use them.

"No, you don't understand. She saved my life."

"But you wouldn't have been there, you would not have gotten shot if not for her, correct?"

Why did shrinks have to twist everything? They were bad as lawyers that way. Drake spun away, clamping his jaws shut before he said something stupid. He needed White's recommendation to the OIS team to allow him to return to duty. The Officer Involved Shooting team was breathing down his neck because he'd canceled this psych eval twice already. Three strikes and he was out.

Drake's hands clenched into fists as he paced the room. Damn, his leg ached. The surgeons said the wound was healed, but there was still a knot where the bullet had torn through his thigh muscle.

"Detective?" White's voice brought Drake back to the subject at hand.

"No, I wouldn't have been there if it weren't for her," Drake admitted, running a hand through his hair, tugging on dark strands past due for a trim. He found himself back at the window, avoiding the shrink's hyper-vigilant gaze.

The Northside office building had a great view down into PNC Park. The grass in the baseball stadium shone with a rich viridian hue. April, home games, bright sunshine. Damn, he missed Three Rivers Stadium where his dad used to take him as a kid. Drake remembered clutching his glove, anxious for any chance to catch a fly ball as he and his dad hung out over the railing beyond third base.

Drake shook his head, turning his back on the springtime antics of Pittsburgh Pirates' baseball. He faced White once more.

"We also wouldn't have found the killer without her," he reminded the shrink, trying to steer him away from the subject of his relationship with Hart. A relationship that both confused and frightened Drake. No way in hell was he gonna let any head-shrinker start dissecting those feelings.

"Stress debriefing" the Pittsburgh Police Bureau called it. Bullshit was more like it. What good would come of sitting around talking about things in the past? What he needed was to get back to work.

"You sound like you feel angry. Is that because Hart was a civilian doing your job for you?" White's voice was bland as he probed, searching for the weak spots in Drake's psyche.

Drake was silent. He imagined he could hear the crack of the batter connecting with a pitch far below. It wasn't so different from the sound a tire iron made when it cracked a human skull.

"Or because you almost died because of her?" White continued.

The roar of the crowd was a distant rumble as runners rounded bases. To Drake it sounded like the thunder of gunfire in close proximity. Sweat gathered at the back of his neck, slipping under his shirt collar as he tried to block out the memory of the bullet tearing through his chest, collapsing his lung, and the certain knowledge that each breath would be his last.

"I'm not angry with Hart," he told his reflection in the window.

"No? Then tell me what you feel."

Fed up to here with shrink talk, Drake whirled on White, ignoring the twinge in his still-healing thigh.

"You're the one with all the answers. You tell me. What should I feel?"

White curled a corner of his mouth into a disappointed frown. It was an expression Drake was well acquainted with. His dad had often used that same look, that "I expected better of you" look. Drake never had the right answers for him either.

He sighed and sank into the overstuffed chair farthest from White. The only way he was going to get back on the streets was to play by White's rules.

"I'm angry with myself," he said, the words almost catching in his gritted teeth. Damn, he hated talking about this shit. "I'm a cop. I should have protected her, should have been the one . . ."

His voice trailed off, a haze of blood floating over his vision despite the sunlight streaming into the office. He blinked and it was gone, leaving only White, his face neutral, waiting for Drake.

"You know she killed a man that night?" Drake continued. "Caved his head in with a tire iron."

Another cheer rose from the crowd at the ball game, it made for a bizarre punctuation to his words.

The shrink nodded, folding his hands over his ample belly. With his bald head, rimless glasses and full beard, he resembled a dark-skinned Santa Claus. Drake could only hope that White had an early Christmas present for him—a chit back to the streets.

"And you blame yourself that she was forced to such extremes?"

Drake nodded, his gaze never leaving the Karastan rug beneath his feet. "She's an ER doc. There's a Latin term, an oath doctors take—"

"*Primum non nocere,*" the shrink supplied. "First, do no harm."

"Yeah, whatever. Anyway, things haven't been the

same between us since then." Drake closed his eyes. He would never have been here if this wasn't the only way to get back on the job. But this wasn't helping. He felt worse now than he had before.

"After all that happened, you're still interested in pursuing a relationship with her?" White sounded surprised.

Drake's eyes snapped open. "Of course I am."

"But she's reluctant?"

"She's been hurt before. Her ex-husband was abusive. But she got out. In fact," he smiled at the memory, "one time he came after her, and she gave him a black eye."

The shrink was silent. Drake wished he'd never said anything about Hart's ex, Richard King. Even though the man was now confined to a wheelchair, he and his lawyer brother were still around to cause trouble. They blamed Hart for the accident that ended King's career as a surgeon.

"It was in self defense," he added lamely. White remained silent. The only sound in the room was the infuriatingly slow ticking of the clock. "It's not like she's a violent person. She's passionate, that's all."

"Passionate about her ex-husband?" the doctor asked in a bland voice.

"No. That's over." Drake returned to his feet, prowling the room once more. Judas H, how the hell had they gotten onto this subject? "She's passionate about everything. This whole thing started because she wanted to help a patient. She latches onto something or someone and suddenly she feels responsible for everything that happens. And she won't let go, won't stop until everything's right."

"Dedicated," White suggested.

"Driven is more like it. Reckless, relentless. And

stubborn as hell. Christ doc, you don't know stubborn until you've met Cassandra Hart." Saying Hart's name aloud wrenched something deep in Drake's gut. He sucked his breath in, turning away from the shrink to hide it. Hart's face filled his mind, her porcelain skin with exotic high cheekbones, dark hair, and eyes a man could drown in. He took a deep breath and steadied himself, turning back to face the doctor.

"Speaking about Dr. Hart seems to disturb your equilibrium."

Understatement. "Guess she kind of threw me off balance."

"Why do you speak of being with her in the past tense?"

"It's not Hart that's in the past." Drake fumbled to explain. "It's just that overwhelming passion—you know what I mean. That feeling like you're drowning in a whirlpool that sucks you under, but you're too far gone to even care. That's what is past."

White cocked his head. "But isn't that what most people find exciting about being in love? Doesn't that passion drive the relationship forward?"

"Maybe. But that passion made me drop my guard. That feeling almost got Hart killed."

"And what about your Dr. Hart? Does she agree with this new philosophy of yours?"

"Guess that's enough for today," Drake said in a casual tone as if they'd been talking about the Pirates' opener.

He and Hart hadn't exactly talked about things since he got back from his mother's last week. At least not important things. Like the way his heart about jumped out of his chest every time she got too close. Or the way his throat closed tight and he broke out in a cold sweat when he watched her move, her natural grace impeded by her healing Achilles' tendon, reminding him of what he'd almost lost. "Time's up, right?"

The shrink didn't even glance at his watch. "No," he said. "We've a few more minutes. Sit."

Drake took his seat once more, perched on the edge, hands hanging between his knees.

"How would you categorize your relationship with Dr. Hart?" White persisted in his torture.

Drake swallowed his groan and hung his head. There were no words for the way he felt about Hart. Why waste time trying to find any? Besides, they were supposed to be talking about the shooting, about getting Drake back on the streets where he belonged.

The silence lengthened, but the shrink did nothing to alleviate Drake's discomfort. Finally, the clock chimed the hour, and Drake popped from the chair like a schoolboy released for the summer.

"I can get back to work now, right?" he asked, hands clenched at his sides as he waited for White's reply.

"Desk duty." Came the grudging answer. "I want to see you tomorrow morning, Detective. We still have a lot of ground to cover."

Drake said nothing, only nodded. He had to restrain himself from slamming the door behind him as he left the office. He moved down the corridor, his gait unbalanced. Not from the leg injury, but from the weight missing on his hip. Amazing that thirty-four ounces, the weight of a fully loaded forty caliber Glock-22, could make such a difference.

It made all the difference in the world. A cop without a gun, chained to a desk—what good was he to anyone?

CHAPTER 2

CASSIE MADE HER way to the ER's locker room, changed out of her jeans and into scrubs. She was glad there was no one there to watch her sit on the bench to maneuver her legs into her pants. This shift was going to be long enough, no sense allowing stubborn pride force her to put more stress on her ankle.

Her hands moved in a familiar routine, clipping her name badge to the top pocket, checking the trauma radio and fastening it to her waistband alongside a pair of hemostats that held a roll of tape. The short-sleeved scrub top revealed the jagged scar that ran down her left forearm, and she debated on a lab coat to cover it.

Let 'em stare, she decided. They'd have to get used to it sooner or later.

The first person she encountered at the nurses' station was Rachel Lloyd, the day shift charge nurse. Rachel stood several inches taller than Cassie's five-four stature, and looked down on her with dark brown eyes set in even darker skin. Her hair was arranged in an intricate coiffure of braids perched high on her head, not a strand daring to leave its designated position. A definite contrast to Cassie's own frizzled curls, which resembled a wet mop struck by lightning.

"Good to have you back, Dr. Hart," Rachel said in her clipped Caribbean accent. Her tone was neutral as if she didn't care whether Cassie succeeded or failed. Either way, Rachel would be there to witness and document it for the record.

Nice to know some things didn't change. She and Rachel shared a mutual respect for each other's skills combined with a mutual disapproval of the other woman's methods. This morning Rachel's look held the same frosty regard as it did six weeks ago. Without a trace of pity, which Cassie was grateful for.

Because she refused to be a victim—ever again.

"Ready for your first patient, Dr. Hart?" Rachel asked, holding a clipboard out to her.

Cassie tried to act nonchalant, ignoring the sudden clenching of her stomach as she took the chart and headed into exam room five. Waiting for her was a young black woman cradling a toddler on her lap. They both looked up when Cassie entered, the woman's expression tired and anxious. The toddler's face was tear stained. He took one look at Cassie and threw his arms around his mother's neck, hiding his face.

"Is this Antwan?" Cassie asked, reading the name on the chart. *Antwan Washington, age three, chief complaint ear pain.* No fever, vitals normal, no complicating past medical history according to the nursing notes. Looked like Rachel had picked out an easy one for Cassie's first patient back.

"I'm Dr. Hart." Cassie sat in the rolling stool and wheeled her way across the room, stopping as soon as little Antwan's shoulders hunched. "What brings you here this morning?"

"It's his ear," the mother replied. Cassie snuck a quick peak at the demographic sheet; so many mothers had different names than their children. Tammy Washington. "I don't know what's wrong, he took all the medicine the clinic gave him, but all weekend he's been complaining and last night it hurt so bad he was up all night crying."

"Do you remember what medicine he was on?"

"The pink stuff." Tammy shifted in her seat, rearranging Antwan's weight. Cassie took the opportunity to inch closer, watched as the toddler slit one eye open but didn't pull away.

"Amoxicillin?"

"Right. He took ten days, finished it last week. I tried to wait until the clinic opened, but he was crying so bad."

"It's all right, Ms. Washington. Hey, Antwan, I need you to give your mom a really big hug, all right?" Cassie warmed her stethoscope between her hands then slid it under Antwan's t-shirt. "Okay, big breaths now. Good job, that's perfect. How about if you turn around so I can listen to your heart?"

Still wary, Antwan obeyed, even smiling when Cassie pretended for a moment that she couldn't find his heartbeat. As she maneuvered through the exam she asked his mom more history but found nothing worrisome. Finally, it was time. A big challenge for any toddler, but especially one whose ears were already painful: the ear check.

Cassie wrinkled her face in a mock expression of disbelief. "I think there are kitty cats in your ears, Antwan." His eyes grew wide and he shook his head, almost smiling, but uncertain. "Let's take a look. We'll start with the one that doesn't hurt first. Okay, hold still and listen for the kitty cat." She gently positioned the otoscope. "Meow."

"Hey, momma, I got kitty cats!" No longer suspicious, he eagerly bounced forward on his mother's lap so that Cassie could check the other ear out.

"He's right," she pronounced after finding another kitty cat, as well as a rip-roaring otitis media. "That ear is fire engine red and bulging with pus. I'm going to get him some pain medicine and the first dose of antibiotic before you leave. We're going to use a stronger medicine. It may give him diarrhea, so lots of yogurt, okay? Schedule an appointment with the clinic for an ear check, but if things aren't getting better in two days or if anything gets worse, he needs to be seen."

"Yes ma'am. Thank you."

"No problem. Hey, Antwan, you take all your medicine and don't you drive your momma crazy, okay?" Cassie fished out a Sponge Bob sticker and handed it to the little guy. He beamed with delight.

"What do you tell the nice doctor?" his mother prompted him.

"Thank you," he chimed out.

Cassie left the room still smiling. She loved it when kids weren't too sick. The radio on her belt squawked. "Dr. Hart to Trauma One, stat."

She limped down the hall, trying to restrain herself from running as the familiar rush of adrenalin humming through her veins. It felt good to be back.

· ⚙ ·

EIGHT HOURS LATER, by the time her shift was over at four o'clock, Cassie was wishing for the cane once more. Not as a crutch, although her ankle now screamed with the ferocity of a toddler in the midst of a tantrum. If she'd brought the cane she could use it to fend off the awkward glances and whispers of her co-workers. Whispers that scurried underfoot like rats in the sewer, ambushing Cassie when she rounded a corner or entered a room.

With the cane Cassie could announce her presence, and salvage some pride, instead of flushing as people became silent and adverted their eyes from her, uncertain how to label her now that she was back at work: resilient victim, tough as nails survivor, or flavor of the month gossip.

Finally, she'd retreated to the sanctuary of the dictation desk at the nurses' station and waited for her replacement. She eased her left leg out, stretching it gingerly.

"Someone help me!"

The woman's cries reverberated from the tile walls of the ER. Her high heels skidded on the white linoleum as she ran toward the nurses' station.

Cassie jumped up from her chair. Too fast, her leg shrieked. Her vision blurred with pain for one brutal moment. She grabbed the counter and steadied herself with a quick breath, then moved to intercept the frantic woman.

"What's the problem?"

"My baby, my baby." The woman's purple designer suede jacket flew open, and Cassie could see that beneath the empire-waist silk dress, she was pregnant. Very pregnant. At least seven months or so.

"Are you having contractions?" Cassie began to usher her down the hall, but she pulled away.

"You've got to help my baby!" The pregnant woman whirled, looking behind her. The ambulance bay doors slid open once more, and a security guard came running through, his arms filled with an ashen-colored toddler.

"Room one." Cassie hobbled ahead to hold the door open. The hysterical mother followed. "I need some help here," Cassie called over her shoulder into the nurses' station.

The guard almost tossed the baby onto the bed, immediately backing away, his own face flushed and sweating. Cassie began to undress the small boy, ripping apart snaps and buttons. The boy's arm was still jerking, and his eyes were deviated to the right; he was in the midst of a seizure. "What happened?"

"I don't know, he just started seizing—the monitor never went off—is he going to be all right?" the woman said. Cassie assumed she was his mother.

Cassie stripped the boy to naked skin. A wide belt bristling with brightly colored wires encircled his chest. It was an apnea monitor designed to alert parents to breathing problems in their premature infants. But she'd never seen one used in a child as old as this boy, who appeared to be at least fifteen months. Grabbing an oxygen mask, she stretched it over the boy's thick blonde curls, and listened to his chest. Breathing was fair, heart sounded good.

"When did the seizure begin?"

"About two-thirty, I had just put him down for his nap." The mother clasped her purse to her chest. She was taller than Cassie, with blond hair styled in a neat bun and grey eyes framed by meticulous makeup.

"Why didn't you call 9-1-1?" She bent over to examine the child. Rachel Lloyd rushed in before the mother could answer.

"What do you need?" Rachel saw the boy on the table. "Charlie." She turned to the mother. "Virginia, what happened?"

"Rachel, he's had a seizure. I didn't know what to do, so I brought him here."

"Of course. We'll take care of him, everything will be all right."

"Help me get an IV," Cassie interrupted their reunion. If the boy had been seizing for over an hour, then Cassie was already out of time. If she didn't stop it soon, he could suffer permanent brain damage.

"Of course, Dr. Hart." Rachel moved to Charlie's side and began to search for a vein. "Dr. Hart, this is Virginia Ulrich. Charlie is her son." Rachel made the introductions while trying without success to start the IV.

"What kind of medical problems does Charlie have?" Cassie asked the mother, continuing her examination.

"Dr. Sterling follows him for apnea."

"Has he had seizures before?"

"After his pertussis shot."

"Damn," Rachel swore under her breath. Cassie looked up at that. She'd never heard Rachel swear before. "I can't get a line."

"I'll take a look." She searched for a likely vein, but the prolonged seizure had collapsed all of them. "Set up for an IO," she ordered after her own failed attempt.

The mother moved closer, rubbing her belly with slow, rhythmic movements as she watched Cassie work on her son. Rachel stopped what she was doing to stare at Cassie. "Don't you mean you want me to call Peds to come start an IV? That's what we usually do."

"We don't have time to wait for them. An IO is faster."

"But Dr. Sterling doesn't like us to—"

"Sterling's not here. Charlie's my patient. I'll do what is best for him."

Rachel glared at her, then turned to get the proper

equipment. Cassie straightened and placed a hand on Virginia's forearm, drawing the mother's attention away from Charlie. "Mrs. Ulrich, Charlie is still seizing and he's in shock. We can't get an IV started, so I'd like to insert an intraosseus line. That is a special needle that will go into his lower leg bone, then we can give him the medicine he needs. We'll take it out as soon as we can. The main risks are damage to the bone and infection, but we do it under sterile conditions."

"That's fine, do it." The mother was amazingly composed for someone who had basically just been told that they had to drill into her child's leg bone.

"You might want to step outside. It's not a pleasant thing to watch."

"No, I'm fine. I want to stay."

Cassie didn't have time to argue. She turned back to Charlie, mentally visualizing the intraosseus procedure as she prepped his shin with Betadine.

"Our usual protocol when we can't get a line on a child is to call Peds." Rachel's tone was one of a schoolmarm instructing a recalcitrant student.

Cassie said nothing. Rachel was an excellent nurse, but if she had her way, every patient would be handled according to a cookbook of procedures, each accompanied by the necessary paperwork in triplicate.

Cassie reached for the sterile bone marrow needle. She placed the needle against the skin and bore down, leaning her weight on the thin dagger of metal until she felt it break through the bone. The resulting crack echoed throughout the room. She winced, hating that noise, then looked up and saw Mrs. Ulrich at the head of the bed, watching closely.

"There's good flow," she told Rachel as she secured the needle into position. "Push a milligram of Ativan. Get me a blood sugar, chem panel, CBC, and blood culture."

Cassie combed her fingers through Charlie's thick golden curls as she waited for the medication to take effect. Slowly, his limbs relaxed, and the seizure activity faded. She bent over him, flicking her light into his eyes, and then examined his mouth with a tongue depressor.

She frowned. That was strange. The inside of Charlie's upper lip was bruised, and there were tiny broken blood vessels on his face.

"Have you noticed these little red dots before?" she asked Mrs. Ulrich.

"The petechiae?"

The mother surprised Cassie by knowing the medical term. "Yes."

"A few days. You can check his chart, we were here last week."

Charlie's color was finally improving, Cassie noted with satisfaction. "Who's on for Peds?"

"Dr. Sterling." Rachel replied.

"Thank God," Virginia gushed at the mention of the Chief of Pediatrics. "Dr. Sterling will know what to do. He always does."

In her two years as an attending physician at Three Rivers, Cassie had only spoken with Karl Sterling on the phone a handful of times and had yet to meet him in person. Since most of his time was spent in administrative duties, Sterling rarely took call and only cared for a small, select group of patients.

"Give him a call and tell the Peds ICU that we have a customer for them." She'd finally get the chance to see the renowned Dr. Sterling in action.

Mrs. Ulrich looked up at that. "You're going to admit him? Can't I take him home?"

Cassie swiveled her head to look at the mother in surprise. "I'm afraid Charlie is going to be here for a while. We need to find out what caused the prolonged seizure and those petechiae. The Pediatric ICU doctors will be down to talk to you more."

"No, I want Dr. Sterling involved. He's cared for Charlie all of his life. No one knows him better."

"Certainly. I'll call him myself," Cassie said. "But you'll still have to talk to the ICU doctors."

Virginia frowned. "All right. But I'm not going anywhere until Dr. Sterling says it's okay."

· ⬩ ·

"ANY MESSAGES FOR ME?" Cassie asked the desk clerk after she alerted Sterling that he had a patient. The clerk shook his head in time to the Godsmack playing over his headphones. Cassie tried to ignore the knot of disappointment that tensed her shoulders. She'd hoped Drake would call. He knew it was her first day back.

She wished she understood what was going on with him. He hadn't touched her since the shooting almost six weeks ago. Forty-one days ago to be exact. And Cassie was definitely counting the days.

Why was he acting like this, holding her at arm's length?

Was Drake merely biding his time, waiting for her to get back on her feet again before he called it off? After all, she had saved his life—he couldn't just dump her like a hot potato, could he?

Next time she saw him, she'd find out. She needed to know where she stood.

Thrusting aside all thoughts of Drake and her life outside the ER, Cassie gave the physician replacing her a quick sign out, then returned to the critical care room to check on Charlie Ulrich.

Rachel had found a rocking chair for Mrs. Ulrich

and was helping her into it. By the time the Peds residents arrived, Charlie's color had improved, and there was no further seizure activity.

"Dr. Sterling is on his way," Cassie told Charlie's mother.

"Oh, thank goodness. He'll know what to do. He's a brilliant man. If it wasn't for Dr. Sterling, Charlie wouldn't be alive today."

"Do you want me to place a central line?" Cassie asked the pediatric residents.

"No, I think you've done quite enough, Dr. Hart," came a deep voice from behind her. Cassie turned, and Karl Sterling was there. A tall man with silver hair and pale blue eyes, the Pediatric Department Chairman resembled the stereotypical Norman Rockwell portrait of everything a physician should be. A full professor with tenure, he had an established reputation in SIDS research.

"Was an intraosseus absolutely necessary? If you can't get an IV in a child, I'd rather that you called us to come down and do it for you." Sterling's tone was mild, not condemning, and he tempered his words with a fatherly smile. "After all, that's what we're here for."

Cassie bristled at the pediatrician's indictment of her and her department's skills, but tried not to let it show. She couldn't tell if Sterling was being sincere or patronizing. Besides, with the mother in the room, this was hardly the time to be arguing about procedures.

Sterling moved to take Virginia Ulrich's hand. "How are you holding up?" he asked, his voice gentle.

"I'm so glad you're here, Dr. Sterling. I don't know what happened. Everything was going so well—"

"Don't worry, Virginia. We'll work it out. Let me just examine Charlie now." Sterling donned his stethoscope and bent over the little boy on the gurney.

Cassie left. The story was puzzling, but the pediatric residents and Karl Sterling could sort it all out.

She headed down the hall to the security office inside the ambulance bay. Video cameras were positioned in all of the critical care rooms, the tapes used for quality assurance and educational purposes.

At least one good thing had come from Charlie's resuscitation. Cassie was preparing a teaching video of emergency procedures. If the video from Charlie's IO looked good, she would include it.

"You mind making a dupe of the video from Trauma 1 for me?" she asked the security guard monitoring the surveillance. It was the same man who had brought Charlie in. "I only need the last hour or so."

"Sure thing, doc."

"Thanks. Just drop it by my office when it's ready."

"I sure am glad the kid's gonna be all right. The way that mother was shrieking, I thought he was dead already."

Not bad for her first day back, Cassie decided as she headed back to her office. Her ankle was hurting, but nothing she couldn't handle. And, despite the awkward encounters with her co-workers, it felt good to be back in the ER—like coming home.

Her office was behind the nurses' station, a windowless cement block cube that had been a broom closet in its previous incarnation. The narrow confines barely held her bookcases, desk and two chairs, but, since Cassie was junior faculty, she wasn't complaining.

She opened her office door to find Drake lounging in her desk chair, long legs stretched out before him. A beautiful bouquet of exotic flowers graced the desk. White orchids glowing against the green florist paper.

So, he hadn't forgotten after all.

His eyes were rimmed by tiny worry lines that hadn't been there six weeks ago. He climbed to his feet, still a little stiff. She knew he had no idea how lucky he was that he'd recovered so quickly. It didn't matter to Drake—all he wanted was to get back to work again.

"How was your first day back?" he asked.

Cassie shrugged. She was exhausted after her encounter with Sterling's patient, but that was the last thing he needed to hear about.

"These are beautiful." She dipped her face into the flowers and inhaled a deep lungful of the sweet fragrance. Drake wore a flannel shirt over jeans with no telltale bulge of a gun, so she guessed his day had been worse than hers. "What did the psychiatrist say?"

He winced, and she knew she'd been too direct. She couldn't help it—she just wasn't any good at this give and take stuff relationships were made of.

She pushed the door shut, and noticed the way he tensed at the sudden bang. The small room overflowed with everything unspoken between them.

"Can you go back to duty?" she asked, her face tilting up to meet his gaze. She moved toward him, their bodies almost touching until he stepped out of reach. His avoidance of her flared her anger further. She couldn't stand this limbo any longer. She needed to know one way or the other how he felt.

"He wants a few more sessions, but he said I could return to desk duty tomorrow."

Enough small talk. Cassie took another step, forcing Drake back against the edge of the desk. Before he could say anything more, she reached up, her fingers fisting in his hair, dragging his face down to meet hers.

She enjoyed his startled gasp as she pressed her lips over his. He flinched, but she gave him no maneuvering room, and after a long moment, she felt his body respond. His hands moved to rest on her hips, she could feel their heat through the thin cotton of her scrubs.

Yes, she thought as his lips parted, allowing her to plunge deeper into the kiss. *This is right; this is how it's supposed to be.*

He closed his eyes. She felt his inhalation echo through his chest. Then his eyes snapped open and he pushed her away. Cassie drew her breath in, swallowing her disappointment.

"What's wrong?" she demanded, hands on her hips, hoping he didn't notice the tremble in her voice. She'd screwed up. Again.

He seemed fascinated with the hospital issue linoleum as he spoke. "I don't want—"

"You don't want to be with me? Is that it?" Her words tumbled over each other as her worst fears were confirmed.

That was why he didn't want to touch her; he was trying to find a graceful way out of this. What a gentleman, he even brought flowers with him to cushion the blow.

Might as well beat him to it. Less painful that way.

"Why didn't you just say so? I don't need you hanging around out of pity or duty or whatever." She flung the door back open. He opened his mouth, began to speak, but she steamrolled over his words as the sucker punch of hurt and humiliation spiraled into her gut. "You don't have to pretend anymore. Take off, get back to your life. Get out of here."

CHAPTER 3

DRAKE STARED AT Hart, her small frame silhouetted in the light from the hall, long, dark hair bouncing in frizzled curls, anger hunching her shoulders. The color in her cheeks glowed against her pale skin while her eyes blazed with fury.

Christ, he wanted to shake her. Why did she have to always rush into everything?

"Just go," she repeated, gesturing to the open door.

Heat flooded over Drake. He moved to the door, but instead of going through it, he reached above her and slammed it shut. Caging her with his arms, he pressed her body back against the door, even though he knew she despised being trapped, confined in any way.

"I was trying to say—" He placed one finger over her lips before she could protest. "That you are too important. There's no need to rush. I was trying—" He lowered his head so that his forehead rocked against hers as she caught her breath. "To tell you that I'm not like your ex-husband, and I'm not going to force you into anything."

Her gaze rose to meet his. She glared up at him, crimson flushing her face. Drake saw a glint of humor enter her eyes and felt a surge of relief. One thing about Hart—she had a temper but never held a grudge.

"I'm so sorry," she said in a voice dripping with sarcasm. "Were you going to inform me about this 'slow and easy' plan of yours?"

He opened his mouth to answer, but she hooked her good leg behind his recuperating one and pivoted him into the chair. His breath emerged with a whoosh of surprise. Then her body was straddling his.

"What if I don't want to go slow?" Her hands tugged at his shirt while her mouth buried his.

He struggled for a moment, just enough to sooth his dignity, then allowed himself to answer her passion with his own. With his eyes locked onto hers, drowning in their dark depths, it was almost as if the shooting had never happened. His heart geared down from panic to the steady thrill of arousal.

"I guess we can discuss it," he said when they parted for air.

She slid one hand around to the small of his back, her fingers working their gypsy magic. They found their target, the sensitive area at the base of his spine where her touch could make his blood boil. He closed his eyes against the surge of pain and delight that resulted.

"Discussion's over," she announced, nipping at his earlobe.

Drake had to agree.

A loud rapping on the door echoed like gunfire from the concrete walls. Drake's heart slammed against his chest. He almost dumped her on the floor as he leapt to his feet. The sudden movement sent a wrenching pain through his thigh muscles.

Hart pulled her top back into place and opened

the door. Drake heard a male voice. His hand moved to his right hip. But of course his gun wasn't there. His world teetered off balance, his heart raced out of control. He sank back into the chair, rubbed his sweaty palms against the coarse denim of his jeans, trying to relax the clenched muscles of his thighs, and forced himself to breathe.

"Dr. Hart? I have that tape for you," the unseen man said.

"That was fast. Thanks."

Hart closed the door, tossing a video onto her desk with a clatter that made Drake jerk. He had a hard time meeting her gaze, certain that she too was overcome by memories of the awful night when he couldn't protect her, when he was forced to watch, helpless, while she confronted a killer.

"You want to tell me what the problem is?" She leaned against her desk and looked down at him.

A jagged length of pink-tinged flesh extended along the inside of her left arm. His eyes followed the length of the scar, then squeezed shut as he remembered the others she carried from that night. None of it would have happened if she hadn't rushed into something she had no business being involved in . . . No, Drake quashed that thought. *He* was the one who had gone in blind.

His feelings for her had superseded everything: his training, his good sense, and his judgment. He should have known better. It was his job to know better, to stay in control.

He would not allow anything like that to happen again. He couldn't let the passion Hart aroused in him to overwhelm his judgment. Never again.

He rubbed his eyes with the heels of his hands. When he opened them again, Hart was still there, watching him, a frown creasing her forehead.

"You're angry with me. You blame me for what happened—"

"No, of course not," he protested. He pushed up to his feet, ignored the pain in his leg. "I'm just tired, that's all. I'd better go. The shrink wants me in for an early session tomorrow."

"We need to talk."

He said nothing. He made his way to the door and was through it before he could change his mind. Before he allowed the truth of how he felt to spill out.

･⦿･

RICHARD KING WHEELED his way towards Ella's office. He couldn't think of her as Cassandra Hart—to him she would always be his Cinderella.

He stopped as a tall, dark-haired man emerged. The man was a cop, Richard remembered, the one whose life Ella had saved. He felt a surge of anger, and knew he hadn't liked the man even before his accident had stolen parts of his memory and scrambled the rest. Drake, that was the cop's name.

Richard leaned back, bouncing the front wheels of the wheelchair, his new favorite thinking position. The rhythmic movement soothed him, allowed him to get past the tsunami of emotions that sometimes threatened to engulf him.

Ella emerged from the office carrying a videotape, and he could see even from this distance that she was flushed. Had she and Drake been doing it right there in the office—while he watched?

The thought was maddening. Richard rammed his chair into the tile wall. Something had to be done. It wasn't fair. Here he was, trapped in this metal prison, while she strutted around making love to strange men in his place. He'd lost everything—and it was all her fault. That much he knew.

The most important thing he remembered, what filled his days and nights as he tried to piece his life back together, was that he'd been happy when Ella had been his. Richard had a favorite photo, one that he kept coming back to over and over. He wasn't certain exactly when it was taken, so he spent hours staring at it, recreating the scene, spinning tales of romance everlasting.

In the photo, he and Ella danced on the deck of a boat, the *Riverstar*. City lights glittered behind them, cascading them in color. She smiled at him, a smile that promised him the world.

Richard would do anything to go back to a time where Ella would always be his. That hope was the one thing keeping him sane.

⁂

"ELLA!" A VOICE called from behind Cassie.

She whirled as a blond man in a wheelchair approached. Richard. What was he doing here? Looking down on her ex-husband brought back a rush of memories Cassie thought she'd left behind in her nightmares.

Although Richard had caused his share of suffering, she hated to see him a prisoner of his disabilities. After spending two weeks in a coma, the once-talented surgeon now had limited use of his right side and suffered from cognitive defects as well.

"Ella, Ella!" he repeated loudly, using the nickname Cassie despised.

Instead of the designer Italian suits she was

accustomed to seeing him wear, he wore baggy sweat pants and a T-shirt. Around his neck hung a bib to catch the drool slipping from his mouth. His speech was slow and hesitant, but understandable. He whirled the wheelchair in a reverse three-sixty, and then came to a stop in front of her. "How do you like my new toy?"

"Nice wheels," she said, uncertain of how to deal with this new Richard. "What do you want, Richard?"

"Hey, where's your ring?" He grabbed hold of her left hand.

Her ring? She hadn't worn a ring on that hand since the night she'd left him almost two years ago. Then she saw he wore a familiar gold band on his left hand. Surely he didn't think they were still married?

"You didn't lose it, did you? Don't worry, Cinderella, your Prince Charming will buy you a new one." He beamed up at her with a happy grin, and the knot of apprehension in her gut tightened.

She crouched down so that she was level with him. "Richard, we're not married anymore. Not for over a year and a half."

Richard blinked, trying to process her words. And then he frowned. His grip on her hand tightened painfully.

"No. I remember. You promised to love, honor and—" He groped for the word, then finished triumphantly. "Cherish for the rest of your life. That means for always, forever and ever, amen."

He squeezed her wrist so hard her bones began to grind together. She tried to pull away, but he leveraged her closer to him.

"You can't break your promise, Ella," he told her, tiny bubbles of saliva spraying as he hissed the words.

Cassie knew the look in his pale eyes now. Richard's fury was an old familiar friend, and the reason she'd left him. She thought she'd closed this chapter in her life, had shelved it away under painful lessons learned. But here she was again.

"I'm sorry, Richard. It's over. It's been over for a long, long time. You just need to get used to it, that's all," she said in as gentle of tone as she could manage. She wrenched her arm free and stood.

His gaze locked with hers. "No. You're my wife, 'til death do us part." Tears welled in his eyes as his mood shifted once more. "Please, Ella. Give me a chance."

Cassie watched tears slide down his upturned face and felt even worse. Richard had lost everything important to him—his career, command of his own body, and apparently a large chunk of his memory. "I'm sorry, Richard," she said in a low voice, "I can't."

"You bitch! You think you can run out on me just because I'm in this?" He slammed the wheelchair with his fist, his raised voice capturing the attention of the rest of the ER staff. She looked around, searching for a graceful way to disengage herself from the confrontation.

"I have to go now," she said.

"You don't go anywhere until I say so!" He moved the wheelchair forward, pinning her against the wall.

Angry now, she glared at him. There'd been no damage to Richard's narcissistic ego. That, combined with his new lack of impulse control, made him as volatile as a cornered junkyard dog. Or, given Richard's blue-blooded pedigree, a pure-bred Rottweiler.

Cassie awkwardly stepped over the footrest of the wheelchair, very aware of the audience behind her watching their little drama.

"Good bye, Richard."

She stepped into the nurses' station where his chair couldn't follow, and walked back to the staff lounge, shutting the door behind her. She took a deep breath, but her nerves still buzzed with adrenalin after the encounter. Would she ever be able to face Richard without churning up all the anxiety that came with those past memories? She'd made bad choices, terrible choices—how long would she be punished for them?

Collecting herself, she shoved the tape into the VCR and pushed the play button. Nothing happened. She ejected it and tried again. Still nothing.

"Damn it!" She pounded the machine with the flat of her palm.

"Yeah, that'll teach it." A woman's voice came from behind her. "Is this a private tantrum or can anyone join?"

She turned to Adeena Coleman, a social worker at Three Rivers and her closest friend. "I can't get this stupid machine to work."

"That's all? I thought it might be something to do with Drake. I passed him in the parking lot, and he looked like he'd just lost his best friend."

"If he did, it's his own damn fault!" Cassie stabbed play once more. Still nothing.

Adeena moved over to the machine, reinserted the tape, and then hit rewind. A whirling noise rewarded her actions. "Want to talk about it?"

Cassie glared at her friend's superior technical mastery of video equipment. Why couldn't the hospital go digital like the rest of the world? She and Adeena had gone to grade school together at Our Lady of Sorrows. Both outcasts, the plump black girl and skinny white girl forged an ironclad bond.

Adeena was known as the good girl, never in trouble, levelheaded, able to talk her way out of any situation. Cassie had been the troublemaker, constantly conspiring against the nuns' authority, getting into fistfights, and teaching the other children swear words and the real facts of life when she should have been studying her catechism.

Together they had made an outstanding team, able to outwit and out maneuver teachers and students alike. Cassie sighed at the memory and hoped Drake wasn't only a memory as well.

"He won't talk to me," she confessed. Adeena poured them both cups of coffee. Cassie took a sip of hers and stared down into its depths.

"You've both been through a lot," Adeena said. "Drake came close to dying—"

"I know that!" She softened her voice. "Sorry. I understand what he went through. I know he's upset he's still not back at work. But I was there too. I wouldn't have made it without him. So why won't he tell me what's going on, let me help?"

"Everyone heals in their own way." Adeena delivered the cliché as if it were a novel idea. She held her hand up, cutting off Cassie's protest. "You go into solitary confinement when you can't deal with things."

Cassie shrugged. "Sometimes I need time by myself to work things out, to think things through."

"To an outsider, the way you handle things appears self-destructive, a form of depression, even."

"It's not! And you know that. It doesn't mean I'm crazy just because I need to shut out the rest of the world for a while."

"That's your style of coping." Adeena dropped into her clinical mode. "What do you think Drake's is?"

"I don't know," Cassie admitted. "At first he seemed fine, last week when he came back from his mother's."

She smiled, remembering how great it had felt to have Drake back in her life. He'd painted a watercolor for her, a portrait of her parents that she'd hung in her living room. They'd talked about everything—school, family, friends, work—everything except the shooting. Or their relationship. Whenever she tried to get close to him, he made it very clear that other than casual handholding and the occasional hug, deeper intimacy was off limits. "I think he felt like he was somehow rescuing me."

"But you left him to come back to work early."

"I couldn't let him keep taking care of me. I was being smothered. I wasn't rejecting him—"

"Maybe Drake's way of coping with this is by doing, keeping busy taking care of someone, so he doesn't have to think about that night or face his own feelings."

"But why won't he touch me?" Cassie asked, desperate to understand. She hung her head. "I even tried to seduce him earlier," she admitted. "I felt him respond—I know he wanted to—but then, nothing. He just left."

"Why don't you give him some space?" Adeena suggested. "A little time to sort things out for himself. Maybe you need more time yourself as well. You look exhausted."

The VCR clicked as it finished rewinding. Adeena hit the play button, and a picture filled the screen. "Is that Virginia Ulrich?" she asked. "Is Charlie sick again? I thought he was doing better."

"They came in today. How do you know her?"

"I've worked with her before. Both with Charlie and her other son, George. Before George died." Adeena shook her head, her bead-festooned braids clicking together. "I can't imagine what that poor woman has been through. Losing one son is bad enough, but then finding out the other has the same illness. And she does such a great job taking care of everything."

"What's their diagnosis?"

"There's been about two dozen different ones. I think the current thinking is some rare genetic defect that affects their muscles."

Cassie considered that. Made sense. Muscles lined the respiratory tract, if they weren't working properly, she could understand the breathing problems. But it didn't explain the seizure or the petechiae.

"Virginia's a wonder," Adeena continued. "Somehow she's even found time to volunteer with the Children's Coalition. It's an activist group trying to get support and funding for children with rare, debilitating diseases. You might have seen her in their TV commercials."

"Here comes the intraosseus." Cassie focused on the image on the monitor.

Adeena made a face. "I'm out of here. Think I'll run upstairs, say hi to Virginia and Charlie. You—go home and get some rest, all right?" She quickly left before the video revealed the painful procedure.

Cassie watched the IO insertion. Textbook. She rewound the tape and played it again. Then she frowned, ignoring the procedure and focusing on Virginia. Cassie watched once more in slow motion. At the moment her son's bone was drilled into, Virginia Ulrich appeared to be smiling.

Cassie leaned back, freezing the image. The mother's expression appeared grotesque as it spread over the TV screen. Was it a smile, or a grimace? Maybe Virginia Ulrich was simply relieved that her son would be out of danger.

Or maybe she enjoyed seeing her son suffer?

Cassie shook her head. She was trained to assume

the worst and hope for the best, but even so, there was nothing in Virginia Ulrich's actions to condemn her as an abusive parent.

Even abusive parents did not enjoy their children's sufferings. Most of the abuse Cassie had seen occurred from a lack of impulse control rather than a lack of caring. She thought upon her own experiences with Richard. He'd been violent only when drunk or high on drugs. And she was certain in some warped fashion he had loved her—and loved her still, despite everything that had happened.

She was just tired. She was looking for demons to fight because she couldn't confront Drake.

※

VIRGINIA ULRICH SLID her hand out from under Charlie's head and shook the blood back into it. He was finally asleep, thank goodness. She stood, stretched, and kneaded the sore muscles in her lower back. The baby was kicking a lot lately. Maybe little Samantha was worried about her big brother. She headed over to the nurses' station. There, her nurse, Emily, sat charting.

"He's asleep," Virginia told her. "I'm going to go call his father. Will you keep an eye on him?"

Emily looked up at that, a small frown creasing her brow. She was new, and had never cared for Charlie or George.

"I never leave him alone," Virginia explained. "He's been through so much. And accidents do happen. His brother, George—" She cleared her throat. Emily made a small noise of sympathy. The other nurses or Dr. Sterling must have filled her in on what happened to George, saving Virginia the need to re-open those wounds. "George was here a lot, too. He almost died when a nurse gave him too much potassium."

Emily nodded her understanding. "Of course. I'll sit by him while I catch up on this paperwork."

"Thanks, Emily." Virginia reached out and squeezed the nurse's shoulder in gratitude. She always appreciated it when she found a healthcare professional willing to go the extra mile to protect one of her children.

She took a long look back at her son, and then left the Pediatric ICU. People didn't understand how stressful it was to have a child as sick as Charlie, especially if you had to protect him from the doctors and nurses who were supposed to be making him better. It forced her to maintain a constant state of vigilance, but she wasn't going to take any chances.

She went into the parents' lounge across the hall from the PICU. There she found fresh coffee and a quiet corner to sit and call Paul. She knew all the books said to drink decaf when you were pregnant, but she couldn't stand the taste. Besides, she'd drunk coffee and the occasional glass of wine during her previous pregnancies without any problems.

Virginia eased herself down into the low-slung vinyl chair. She cradled the phone on her stomach and leaned back, lifting her feet onto the coffee table. Her feet were swollen and the veins on her legs looked like ugly blue worms crawling under her skin. She hated this part of being pregnant. She couldn't wait until the baby was delivered and she could go back to being a person instead of an incubator. But it was nice the way they spoiled you after a baby came—the steak and champagne dinner at the hospital, all the flowers and visits to see how the new mother was doing.

As she dialed, she looked out over the familiar

landscape. This side of the hospital faced the old cemetery. Behind wrought iron gates and between the silhouettes of still-leafless maple trees, white marble memorials shimmered in the sunlight. Virginia quickly found the large angel she considered her guardian. How many times before had she and that angel sat vigil?

Paul answered the phone after four rings. "Yes?"

"It's me. They admitted Charlie to the Pediatric ICU."

"Why? What happened? I thought you said he was fine and you were just taking him in as a precaution."

"I know, but when I got to the ER the doctor said he'd gone into seizures and shock. They kept sticking him over and over for an IV. They couldn't get one, so they had to put one into his bone. It was awful!" She finally allowed herself to cry, remembering the sound of Charlie's bone breaking.

"Why couldn't they get the IV?" Paul demanded. "They've never had trouble before."

"I don't know. The doctor in the ER didn't seem to know what she was doing."

"Did they call Sterling?"

"I begged them to. They finally did, and he got Charlie up to the ICU. He's all right now. They pulled the IV out of his leg and put one in through his femoral vein. He's finally asleep."

"Jesus, Virginia. It's Georgie all over again." George, their first son—they'd been in the hospital with him almost a dozen times before he finally died.

"I know, I know. But Dr. Sterling is working on it. He's doing everything he can."

There was silence for a moment. Virginia knew how frustrated Paul was. He was a man unaccustomed to feeling helpless. As an attorney, he preferred to take control of a situation, not sit by and watch helplessly. Especially when his son's life was at stake. But she also understood his fear of hospitals. It seemed that every time he visited George or Charlie they would take a turn for the worse. That was why he relied on her, with her medical knowledge, to deal with the medical professionals.

"You want me to come in?" he finally offered.

"No. One of us should get some rest tonight." They'd developed their own system over the years, first with Georgie, now with Charlie. "Just bring me some clothes in the morning, okay?"

"I'll see you then. And Virginia—"

"Yes?"

"Get me the name of that ER doctor. I think Sterling should speak to her or her department head."

"It was Hart. Cassandra Hart."

There was a long pause. "Did you say Cassandra Hart? She's Alan King's ex-sister in law. You know, the one involved with those drug thefts in February."

"The woman who almost got Richard King killed?" Virginia asked.

Suddenly the doctor's antipathy toward her made sense, despite their never meeting in person before. She'd probably recognized Virginia's name.

"Paul," she hated to voice her fears, "what if she did something wrong, something to hurt Charlie? She'd know that you're partners with Alan and that we're friends of Richard. What if . . ." Her voice trailed off. It was too terrible to even imagine anyone intentionally harming her beautiful little boy.

"Don't worry about it," he reassured her. "I'll talk to Sterling, make certain that everything is taken care of."

"Okay, honey. Love you."

Virginia thought about the dark-haired ER doctor. She hadn't liked Dr. Hart, the way she questioned everything Virginia told her about Charlie. She understood now. Cassandra Hart was covering up her own incompetence by questioning Virginia's. The newspapers had made Hart out to be some kind of hero, a brilliant doctor who helped the police solve a big drug investigation. But Virginia was a friend of Richard King, had visited him while he was in a coma when he was suffering from a drug overdose that Cassandra Hart had claimed was accidental.

Richard had almost died. Even now, almost two months later, he was a warped shadow of the vibrant man he'd once been.

She'd seen Dr. Hart's handiwork firsthand. Somehow, Virginia had to make certain Cassandra Hart never had a chance to treat her son again.

CHAPTER 4

Before going home, Cassie decided to join Adeena upstairs in the Pediatric ICU. She needed to quiet this niggling feeling that there was something more going on with Charlie, maybe something she'd missed. And she wanted to get another look at his mother. After watching the video several more times, she couldn't decide what the fleeting expression on Virginia Ulrich's face meant.

The PICU was quieter than the other units. A perpetual twilight surrounded its small patients who balanced between life and death. Everything in here seemed muted, surreal, as if to avoid jarring patients and their loved ones into the harsh reality of their existence.

Like the ER, it was a place where battles were waged. But, unlike Cassie's territory, there was no atmosphere of chaos and frenzy. Rather, it had an anxious undercurrent evident in the quick footsteps of nurses and the strained faces of parents keeping vigil over their children.

The laughter at Charlie Ulrich's bedside was a garish contrast.

Cassie looked over, surprised to see Karl Sterling laughing as he held Virginia's hand and patted it.

"No worries now. I'll have Charlie good as new in no time," he promised the mother. Around him, beaming and nodding residents clustered, a flock of white geese surrounding their gander.

Charlie must be doing better, Cassie thought as she grabbed his chart and sat down at the nurses' station with it.

According to the progress notes, he was. There had been no further seizure activity, and Charlie was now awake and acting appropriately. She turned to the history section of the chart.

Virginia Ulrich's story had changed somewhat. She'd told the pediatric residents and Sterling that the seizure began a few minutes before she arrived in the ER and that everything had started with an episode of abnormal breathing. The only consistent fact was the delay before bringing him into the ER. Virginia explained this was because an ER doctor, Ed Castro, did "nothing" when Charlie had a similar episode last week and had berated her for coming in when he wasn't sick enough.

Cassie tapped her finger against her lips. Everyone lied when they came to the ER. In fact, the first rule of emergency medicine she taught her residents was to trust no one, assume nothing.

Had Virginia been so intimidated by Ed Castro during her visit last week that she waited at home for almost an hour before bringing Charlie in today and then lied to Cassie about the timing of his seizure? She doubted it. Ed had six kids of his own and was much more sympathetic with over-anxious parents than any of the other Emergency Department attendings.

"Can I help you, Dr. Hart?"

Cassie looked up, startled by Virginia's voice. She sounded so comfortable, as if Cassie was the outsider here, the stranger who needed guidance.

"A bit far from the ER, aren't we?" Karl Sterling asked as he joined Charlie's mother at the nursing station. Both of them looked down at Cassie.

"Just checking on my patient." She wasn't sure why, but she felt as if she needed to straighten her posture, that she was being judged. She closed Charlie's chart, then stood, leveling the playing field.

"You mean *my* patient," Sterling corrected her, increasing her irritation. His tone was friendly, jocular even, but Cassie found herself frowning. "Did anything in particular interest you? I've been following Charlie since he was a newborn. And of course, his brother before him."

Sterling obviously had no concerns about Virginia's history. Cassie glanced past them to Charlie's bedside. The small boy was surrounded by white-coated figures. "I was interested in the discrepancies in the history I received from Mrs. Ulrich."

"Surely you aren't implying—" Sterling started, but Virginia Ulrich interrupted him.

"Now, Karl. I'm sure Dr. Hart isn't accusing me of anything but being a distraught and overwhelmed mother." She smiled at Cassie. "You'll excuse me if I was confused. It's just that Charlie had been doing so well lately, I dared to hope—anyway, I apologize."

Cassie was taken aback by the mother's gracious concession. She had no choice but to accept it. "Of course. I just wanted to be certain that I hadn't missed anything important."

"No," Virginia Ulrich continued, her smile unchanging, still wide, exposing perfectly aligned white teeth but without wrinkling or marring her makeup. "You were concerned about my son and wanted to be certain that I hadn't misled you."

"Virginia, you don't have to explain yourself. We all understand what a strain you've been under." Sterling placed an arm around Virginia to steer her away.

"It's all right, Karl." With a regal shake of her perfectly coifed hair, Virginia straightened to her full height and looked down, meeting Cassie's eyes. "You see, Dr. Hart, it's happened before. Charlie had a brother, George, who died. Early in the course of his illness a well-meaning but misguided nurse reported me to Children and Youth. They investigated fully, we even spent time in Room 303 on Peds—you know, the room with the video surveillance.

"I was upset, of course, at the allegations that I could be capable of doing anything to harm my child. But I knew they were just trying to do what was best for my son. I even volunteered to go away and leave George in the hands of you people here at the hospital."

"Do you have children, Dr. Hart?" Sterling asked Cassie.

"No." She focused on the pediatrician. What did that have to do with anything?

"Then you can't begin to understand the sacrifice Virginia was prepared to make for her son. Trusting him to the care of strangers. I'm just thankful it never came to that." He patted Virginia's hand.

"I would do anything in my power to help my son," she went on. "I would have left. But then that same nurse gave George the wrong medication, and he almost died."

"Thank God you were there for him," Sterling said.

"So you can understand why I might seem hypervigilant about my son's care," Virginia finished. "I'm sorry if my anxiety caused you concern. But I appreciate your efforts on my son's behalf."

Cassie noted that a small crowd of residents and nurses had gathered around them. If Sterling was the King of the PICU, then Virginia Ulrich was the current Queen of the realm.

She looked past the flock of white coats to the little boy lying in the bed across from the nurses' station. He met her glance and smiled faintly.

"If you'd excuse me, I'd like to return to my son." Virginia Ulrich moved to join Charlie.

Sterling tapped his pen on the desktop, pulling Cassie's attention away from the little boy and his mother. He gestured for her to join him in the dictation alcove behind the nurses' station.

"I know we've never worked together before," Sterling started, his voice mellow but with that same hint of condescension that had irritated Cassie earlier. "But I hope you've learned something today, young lady, about a mother's love for her child and—" He straightened, snapped his brilliantly white lab coat shut. "About pediatrics in general. Our patients aren't just small adults. They need special care."

Cassie stared up at the older man. She fought to keep her voice down, and lost the battle. She wasn't about to be patronized or have her skills criticized by anyone, not even the Chief of Pediatrics. "What are you trying to say? That I made a mistake starting the IO? He'd been seizing for over an hour, his veins were collapsed—"

He held up a hand. His voice remained civil, gentlemanly, as he continued. "All I'm saying is that if you'd followed protocol and called me, I might have been able to save a very sick little boy who's been through more pain and suffering than either of us can imagine from another painful procedure."

"He needed the IO. I don't know what she—" Cassie jerked her head toward the alcove's opening, indicating Virginia Ulrich, "told you, but if she hadn't waited so long—"

"Virginia explained that already," Sterling interrupted her, his voice now revealing a trace of steel. "You have no idea what Virginia and her family have been through. I've been doing this for over thirty years and it still amazes me how well she's been able to cope with her sons' illnesses. A lesser woman would have been devastated."

He paused, and laid a hand on Cassie's arm. She shook it off. "I know about you, Dr. Hart. What you've been through."

"Dr. Sterling." Cassie's fingers curled into tight fists as she tried to keep her composure. There was no door on the alcove. Everyone at the nurses' station could hear them. "This isn't the place—"

"I'm concerned about you, Dr. Hart. Have you considered that perhaps you returned to work too soon?"

Cassie snapped, her patience at an end. "That's none of your business."

Sterling grew rigid, his expression now remote. He took a step back, as if Cassie somehow threatened him. "All I'm asking is that if you're ever faced with a patient of mine again, you'll do me the courtesy of calling me first before you perform any painful or dangerous procedures."

Before Cassie could reply, Sterling backed out of the alcove and was gone. She took a step after him, determined to defend herself further, but pulled up short when she saw the faces of parents, nurses and residents staring at her. Including Adeena, whose expression was one of incredulity.

This wasn't the time or the place, Cassie told herself as she struggled to master her anger. She glanced once more at Charlie Ulrich, now huddled against his mother's shoulder. She had done the right thing for him, she was certain.

But that was cold comfort as she walked through the sliding doors of the PICU. Disapproving stares following her.

Adeena joined Cassie out in the hallway. "Sterling was only trying to help. And you—you practically accusing Virginia of child abuse. If you had any idea what that woman's been through—"

"I thought I was doing what was best for her son," Cassie protested. Adeena's indignation hurt more than Sterling's accusations of incompetence. She turned away and walked toward the stairwell, her ankle yammering at her, punctuating Adeena's words.

"I know you, Cassie. Once you get into your crusader mode it's impossible to stop you. But, trust me, you're wrong this time. I was with Virginia after Georgie, her first son, died. I'm surprised she survived it. Then Charlie was born, and Sterling watched him like a hawk, hoping he wouldn't follow in his brother's footsteps."

Cassie leaned against the concrete wall of the stairwell, her head bowed as she listened. To watch your child die—how terrible would that be? She thought of her own mother and her choice to sacrifice herself rather than risk any harm to her unborn child.

Was that the kind of mother Virginia Ulrich was?

"Then Charlie got sick. For Virginia it was like losing Georgie all over again. But she got through it. Somehow all this has made her stronger, given her the energy to care for Charlie and reach out to help other families in need. To tell the truth," Adeena continued, her tone softer as she lay a hand on Cassie's arm, "Virginia has always reminded me of you in some ways."

"Me?" Cassie asked with a frown. She'd never had the responsibility of caring for an ill child day after day. Even the thought of raising a healthy child filled her with apprehension.

"You." Adeena smiled. "You're both strong willed, relentless, stubborn. And you would sacrifice anything to help the people you love."

"Trust me," Adeena continued, "I've known Virginia for years. There's no way she could ever harm her son. And even though Sterling can be a pompous ass, he really is the best. I guess he's a lot like you, too—he gets over-protective of his patients."

Cassie was happy to be wrong. That meant Charlie was in no danger. But something still didn't feel right.

Adeena shook her head, her braids jangling in impatience. "Isn't it about time that you concentrated your energy on what's really important?"

"Like what?" Her work had always been the center of her life.

"Like Drake. You finally found a man who truly cares for you. Are you going to let all that just slip away?"

"It was so much easier when Richard and I met," Cassie muttered, remembering the dazzling way Richard had romanced her. Their first date he'd hired a boat to take them on a moonlight cruise along the Monongahela. They'd danced all night. She'd almost forgotten that. Sometimes it was so easy to forget that there ever had been any good times with Richard.

Adeena scoffed. "That was lust, not love. You have to work hard for the real thing."

That coaxed a reluctant smile from Cassie. "Now you sound like Rosa."

"Your grandmother was a very wise woman, so I'll take that as a compliment."

"Anyway, I'm not in love with Drake. I just don't want things to end like this . . ." She trailed off, her conflicting emotions confusing her. How would she know love, anyway? Maybe Drake was right to want to go slow.

"Were you worried about Virginia's treatment of Charlie when you first met her in the ER?" Adeena asked. Cassie looked up in surprise. "You weren't, were you? I know you. Things start to go badly with Drake, so what do you do? Find the first lost child that needs help, a cause you can throw your energies into, anything easier than dealing with Drake."

She stared at the linoleum, reluctant to admit that Adeena might be right.

"Go home. Get some rest. You look like you need it. I'll keep an eye on Charlie, and let Sterling know you only had his best interests at heart." Adeena pushed open the door leading back to the ICU corridor.

Cassie continued down the steps and paused at the door leading to the ER. Usually she'd give her boss, Ed Castro, a heads up when she upset someone like Sterling. But Ed was in Washington, trying to raise funding for a community clinic that he was setting up in Drake's building in East Liberty.

The building was the former home of the *Liberty*

Times newspaper, back when the Pittsburgh neighborhood had rivaled Harlem during the jazz age. Drake was slowly rehabbing the sorely neglected building and had given Ed the space for free, but Ed still needed a large chunk of change before he could start.

She stopped, her hand frozen against the doorway. Ed was meeting with a bunch of politicians during his trip to DC. One of them was the senator from western Pennsylvania, George Ulrich.

Had to be a coincidence. It couldn't be the same family, could it? Ulrich wasn't that uncommon of a name. There was also a lawyer in Richard's brother's firm named Ulrich. Cassie went through the door, oblivious to the chaos swirling through the ER as she made her way to the woman's locker room. Had her impetuousness endangered the clinic, a life-long dream of Ed Castro's?

The sunshine ambushed her when she emerged outside. April had just arrived, and Pittsburgh was celebrating with a glorious succession of mild, sun-filled days. Cassie turned her face to the sun, squinting at her guardian angel beside the entrance. She'd hoped she'd be having a celebration dinner with Drake. Peace and quiet, a little wine, a little conversation—about something more important than the weather or baseball.

That wasn't happening anytime soon. She blew her breath out in exasperation. If she hadn't over-reacted, and misinterpreted his words earlier, she could be with him right now, his arms wrapped around her, sharing their strength . . .

Standing around never solved anything, she thought, mimicking Gram Rosa, and started down Penn Avenue.

A few blocks away, between Three Rivers Medical Center and the precinct house Drake worked out of, was the Blarney Stone, a bar owned by Drake's first partner. Andy Greally was tending bar himself when she entered.

"Why, it's the good Dr. Hart." He guided her to a bar stool with a jovial smile. "It's nice to see you again. You doing all right?"

"Fine, thanks," she replied, gratified by his warm greeting. She hadn't been here since the shooting and wasn't certain how Drake's comrades would accept her presence. Her gaze darted around the brightly lit space with its dark oak and brass trimmings.

"DJ's not here," Andy told her. Drake had joined the force while his father was still working and so was known throughout the police bureau as Drake Junior or DJ. "But Tony Spanos is in the back room playing pool." He leaned across the bar toward her. "Don't go leaving on his account. I'd throw that bum out before I'd let a pretty girl like yourself leave." He patted her hand. "Now, what can I get you?"

Cassie debated leaving anyway. Spanos was a uniformed cop who'd made a pass at her, and she'd let her temper get the best of her. Unfortunately, she'd also humiliated Spanos in front of other police officers and made an enemy of the man.

"That's all right, I'm good," she told Andy.

"Well then, if you're not drinking, you have to try my new recipe." He moved his bulk into the kitchen before she could demur. A minute later, he returned with a plate of heavenly smelling meat garnished with fresh asparagus.

She sniffed in appreciation. In the excitement of her first day back at work, she'd forgotten to eat lunch. The rumbling in her stomach decided for her as he placed the plate in front of her with a flourish.

"Spring lamb with fennel and rosemary. My cousin's wife in Killarney mailed me the recipe last week."

She took a first succulent bite. Andy nodded with a smile as she rolled her eyes in appreciation.

"Now, you want to tell me why I've the pleasure of your company this fine evening?" he asked when she came up for air. "Not that I'm complaining, mind you. Everything all right with DJ?"

Trust Andy to get right to the point. She shrugged. "The psychiatrist said he could return to desk duty." She hoped she wasn't revealing any confidences.

He nodded. "Jimmy Dolan told me when he was in earlier." Jimmy was Drake's partner on the Major Case Squad. "Said Miller would have DJ cleaning out the fridge—guess she's still pissed."

Commander Sarah Miller led the Major Case Squad and had not been pleased two months ago when she learned about Drake's involvement with Cassie, a witness in a homicide case.

"Clean out the fridge?" Cassie asked.

"Cold case files. You know, ones that have stumped everyone, but no one has the heart to bury them. They're stored in a closet at the House, and every once in a while someone gets assigned the thankless job of going through them, looking for any new leads."

"But if they're older cases, isn't it more likely that you have less information as witnesses forget or move on?"

"Sometimes with new technology like DNA testing, you catch a break. And," he brightened, "once the shrink clears DJ to return to active duty he can get back on the streets where he belongs."

"He's good, isn't he?"

"Of course. I trained him, didn't I? He's the best I've seen," he went on, "when his head's in the game. Got a mind like a freaking camera—remembers everything. The way he reads a crime scene, it's like he sees something different than the rest of us."

She nodded. Drake's painting was like that. He seemed to see beyond the superficial to what lay beneath. "He'd be on the streets now if it weren't for him getting shot—because of me."

"You're good for him," Andy assured her.

"I just don't know how to—what to—" she stammered, unable to finish. She couldn't believe she was discussing her private life here in a public bar. "What does he want? I feel like I've done something wrong and I don't know what."

Andy cleared her dishes and swiped at the bar with a wet rag as he thought. "DJ's never been easy. Sometimes you just have to give him time to come to his senses." Cassie nodded, that was the same advice Adeena had given her. Then Andy looked up and grinned. "But don't give him too long to sulk," he went on. "Sometimes what the kid needs most is a swift kick in the butt."

"Thanks, Andy." She placed a ten-dollar bill on the bar. Andy pushed it back at her.

"You know your money's no good here."

She slid off the stool, refusing to argue with him. He took the bill and dropped it in a large jar with the words Children's Coalition emblazoned on it. Cassie froze, looking at the photo below the words. Virginia Ulrich, smiling as she cradled Charlie in her arms.

"Do you know Virginia Ulrich?" She gestured to the jar brimming with contributions.

"Sure. Her husband, Paul, grew up near here. I remember when his father ran his first campaign for

City Councilman. George has gone a long way, a Senator now. It's sad about his grandkids being so sick. Just breaks my heart every time Virginia comes around."

Cassie nodded absently as he spoke, her focus on the photo. Virginia smiled for the camera, her hair perfectly coiffed, makeup in place, the image of the loving mother. But Charlie stared out at the camera, lunging, as if desperate to escape his mother's arms.

"Your money's going for a good cause," Andy assured her. She looked at the photo again. Surely Charlie was only squirming like a normal toddler?

What if he wasn't? Cassie felt like she was sinking, mired in quicksand that was closing fast over her head. What if everyone was wrong about Virginia Ulrich?

CHAPTER 5

"Hey pardner, how's it going?" Jimmy Dolan called out as Drake entered the squad room on the fourth floor of the Zone Seven station house the next morning. "Good to have you back."

Drake winced at his partner's bonhomie. Because of him, Miller had both of them working cold case files, obviously not trusting Drake to go it alone. By rights Jimmy should be pissed as hell for being taken off the streets and forced into babysitting duty.

Instead, Jimmy wrapped his beefy ex-marine's hand around a dusty homicide binder and handed it to him. "This is the one we should be working."

"You've already gone through them?" Drake had expected to take at least a day combing the files, seeing which cases had any viable leads worth following.

"Didn't have to. I've been wanting another crack at this one for a long time."

Drake opened the murder book. The seam of a manila envelope had worn through, and crime scene photos spilled out. He spread them over his desk.

Jimmy leaned back in his seat, hands behind his head. "Me and your dad worked that one, nine years ago now, right before he made sergeant."

Drake nodded, his attention riveted by stark black and white photos of the body of a young child. A girl, maybe four or five, garroted, and left on a muddy patch of grass. She wore a pale flannel nightgown bordered with ruffles and lace.

"Sofia Frantz. We kept coming back to her over and over, but we never got anywhere with it. Your dad thought it was the work of a serial, and tried to tie it in with several other murders, but got nowhere."

"You try VICAP?" Drake asked, his eyes raking quickly over the photos, absorbing every detail. The FBI violent crimes database was supposed to pick up on patterns left behind by signature killers. He turned to the next photo, a more distant view of the crime scene, and was surprised to see that the muddy lawn was actually a playground.

"Yeah, more than once. But they couldn't find any pattern. Want to see the others?" Jimmy slid a stack of photos across the desk. "Two girls, one boy, and one woman. The oldest goes back eleven years, the most recent four years ago."

He looked up at that. His father had died seven years ago, so Jimmy must have continued working the case afterwards.

Jimmy read his thoughts and nodded. "This one's a ball buster. Might want to think twice before you dive in."

Too late. Drake sorted through the photos, taking the crime scenes one by one. Frantz was the second, nine years ago now. Two years before her was an older boy, Adam Cleary, six, found in identical circumstances but this time in the front of the Phipps' Conservatory, a well-traveled and well-lit area that attracted crowds of school tours and tourists every day.

"All in public places?" he asked without looking up from the boy's bloated face, Cleary in his pajamas also.

"All but the woman, Regina Eades."

"Guy probably lives in the city proper, comfortable with the roads, knows how to get in and out of potentially congested areas fast." Drake continued cataloguing the carnage, turning to the next victim. A woman in her early thirties, killed fourteen months after Frantz. Nothing for four years, then another girl, Tanya Kent. This one was African American and the youngest so far, just a toddler. Body found in the playground at the Highland Park reservoir, just like Frantz's.

"You sure about the woman?" he asked Jimmy. "She's not in her night clothes like the children are. And crossing races, sexes and ages—not typical for a signature killer. The long delay before the last bothers me too. What cooled him off? Unless he was picked up for something else."

"Your father decided on the first three based on the scenes and the autopsies. I'm not certain about the woman. She was the only one restrained, taken near her work, and killed right away. He might have been wrong about her," Jimmy said this last as if it was a remote possibility.

"She's the only one large enough to pose any threat." Drake shuffled the photos as if they were poker cards. Placed side by side, the children's crime scenes appeared almost identical. An unholy flush. He had to agree with his father, something seemed to link them, they felt like they belonged to the same actor. "No leads?"

"Nothing that panned out. What'd you say we take a crack at them?"

"I'm in."

"All right then, grab that fancy camera of yours and let's go."

They spent the morning on a tour of the crime scenes. Drake took his time. One good thing about cold cases, no one was breathing down your neck, forcing results.

There were three sites used to dump the four bodies. Part of the signature, or just convenient? The first was Adam Cleary's, age six, found dead in the lawn in front of the Phipps Conservatory. Jimmy drove, edging the unmarked white Intrepid into an empty spot between the two traffic lanes in an island of parking spaces reserved for conservatory volunteers.

A jogger passed them on the crest of the hill opposite, following one of the many paths in Schenley Park. Two elderly women sat on one of the benches that lined the stone wall while an Asian couple maneuvered, vying for the best possible photo of the sprawling Victorian edifice of metal and glass.

Drake had always loved the conservatory—so many colors and textures, light bending in a dozen delightful ways as it reflected through the multitude of glass panels and onto glistening leaves of plants from all over the world. To him the Phipps was an oasis of quiet, muted footsteps, hidden alcoves revealing exotic treasures of silken orchids, tangled vines, and colors that challenged his imagination.

His mother brought him here often, bemused by his fascination. Drake Sr. hadn't been as impressed by his son's passion for color and texture. He insisted on dragging Drake across the bridge to the Carnegie natural history museum with its dinosaurs. Or better yet, to a Pirate's game where he would pin Drake between himself and the railing, positioning them to catch a fly ball.

Jimmy slammed the car door shut and Drake blinked, remembering the crack of a bat connecting, the surge of the crowd around him, everyone scrambling for the ball hurtling in their direction.

He stepped out of the car, and crossed the street without looking, hypnotized by the memory of reaching out, almost toppling over the rail in his quest to catch the ball just as his father had taught him. But at the last moment the missile racing directly at his face had proven too much and he had shied away. The ball landed with a hard slap of leather against flesh in his father's outstretched hand.

Not even the roar of the crowd could drown out the look of disappointment as Drake Sr. dropped the ball into his son's forgotten mitt.

"Right here," Jimmy said, pulling him back to the present. "These bushes and stuff weren't here back then," he added after consulting the crime scene photos. "I didn't work it originally, your father brought me here after we partnered up. We came back whenever things got slow and we had time to work it again, but—" He shrugged, obviously embarrassed by his and Drake Sr.'s failure.

Drake stepped back, observing Adam Cleary's final resting place. It was now a nicely mulched plot curving from the curb to the front entrance. Rhododendrons with glossy leaves lined the route, interspersed with budding azaleas, holly, and low growing juniper. An exotic appearing tree that appeared out of harmony with the rest of the landscaping stood in the center of the plot. Right where

Cleary's body laid, Drake realized after glancing at his father's sketch of the crime scene.

He stepped into the mulch, taking care not to disturb the plants anymore than necessary and leaned forward to read a small, brass plaque at the base of the tree.

"Beloved son, never forgotten," he read aloud.

"Kid was dumped here," Jimmy said. "We never did find the actual killing ground—not for any of them except the woman, Eades."

"Who found him?" Drake asked as he picked his way through the shrubs back out to the paved path.

Jimmy nodded to the park across the street. "Jogger—not even light out yet. He worked over in Bellefield Towers and was jogging to work. He checked out. Didn't see anything, just stopped to tie his shoe and saw kid's pajamas. Took another step and saw there was a kid still in them. He lost his breakfast, then called us."

"Eleven years," Drake muttered as they headed back to the car. He turned around one more time, marveling at how much seemed unchanged from the Phipps of his childhood. But, for Adam Cleary and his family, everything had changed. "Helluva long time."

"Yep," Jimmy said, leaning across the roof of the Intrepid, his gaze fixed on the graceful curves of the conservatory. "Might help if we could figure out why here. And why he never came back after the first one."

Drake frowned and opened the car door. "After this long, we might never learn anything."

※

SITUATED IN THE basement of the main building, the medical records department was about as close to the

Underworld as you could get at Three Rivers Medical Center. Even the morgue was upstairs with the pathology labs.

Most of the recent records were computerized, but there still existed hard copy backups. Cassie liked being able to look at the complete chart instead of one page at a time on the computer. Especially at times like this when she had no idea what she was actually looking for.

She stumbled as she crossed the entrance, her coordination hampered by a lack of sleep. A perpetual problem ever since what happened two months ago. Last night Cassie had almost been tempted to take a few of the Percocet her orthopod had prescribed, and which still sat un-opened in her medicine cabinet.

Every time she did fall asleep, each groan and creak of her old house transformed into a killer's footsteps. A killer waiting to pounce on her, beat her unconscious, drug her, and leave her helpless to warn Drake as he walked into an ambush.

Ed and Adeena had hired a cleaning company that specialized in crime scenes to deal with the mess left in the wake of the killer's attack. It had taken days to scrub her oak floors clean of the dried blood, to clear the air of its stench, to vacuum and erase all the fingerprint dust and Luminol.

The worst had been finding the blackened, wilted and crushed remains of the roses Drake had brought her that night—only to confront a killer in her living room instead.

She yawned, covering it with the back of her hand. Last night had been particularly bad, the now-familiar scenes of that night six weeks ago mingled with Charlie's resuscitation yesterday. In the end it had been Drake staring up at her from the gurney, his blood covering Cassie's hands as his life slipped away.

There was only one clerk this early in the morning, and he seemed less than thrilled to be working, favoring her with a glare designed to send lesser beings skittering away to seek comfort above ground. Cassie met his gaze, undaunted. After the hell she'd been through, the dour-faced, pasty-skinned denizens of medical records failed to intimidate.

She wrote down George Ulrich's name and date of birth on the request slip and handed it to the clerk. The paper crackled between his fingers as if his touch might set it on fire.

"No medical record number?" the clerk asked in an annoyed tone as dry as the paper he handled.

"I don't have it."

He sighed, rolled his eyes, and punched the information into the computer. "Why didn't you tell me the patient was expired?" he snapped. "It'll be a minute. Wait here." He rose and left the desk, disappearing into the shadowy stacks of musty medical charts.

He returned in a few minutes and dumped three thick volumes onto the counter, releasing a small wave of dust. Cassie took them over to one of the dictation cubicles that lined the room.

The manila covers were printed with Charlie's older brother's name, date of birth, medical record number, and the Three Rivers logo, as well as a confidentiality disclosure. Stamped overtop all the printing was "Expired" in large red letters.

Expired. Medical records term for dead. Cassie hated it. It made the often messy process of death seem sterile and uncomplicated. What was wrong with good old-fashioned dying? Why was everyone so frightened by the word? After all, it was something that happened to them all, no avoiding it.

If anyone knew that, it was Cassie. She closed her eyes briefly, willing the image of Drake, covered in his own blood, away from her mind. It was painfully obvious that something she'd done was keeping him at a distance. If she just knew what it was, she could fix it.

She pulled her attention back to the chart before her and the lost child whose story it told.

George's chart was thick for someone who died at such a young age. Cassie thumbed through the indexed tabs and counted nine admissions and at least twice as many ER visits interspersed with clinic notes.

She grabbed a piece of the ubiquitous hospital notepaper and started on the first volume. George's birth was unremarkable. Full-term, no complications. But things quickly changed. His first ER visit was at three weeks of age for a blue spell. He was admitted and evaluated for possible sepsis as well as cardiac problems, but no cause was ever found.

It was then that Karl Sterling got involved. He invited the Ulrichs to participate in a study of children with "near miss SIDS" or Apparent Life Threatening Events. He would provide free care and a monitor for George. The parents were both trained in CPR as well as the monitor use, and George went home after a week in the hospital.

The very next day Virginia Ulrich brought him back into the ER for another blue spell. She reported giving the baby CPR for several minutes before he responded. He was admitted again.

And so it went.

By the time he was a year old, George had spent more time in the hospital than out of it. Nursing assessments and social work notes described Virginia as a devoted, concerned, intelligent mother who would do anything to make her baby healthy.

George stopped growing and a feeding tube was placed. Then he developed an intolerance to his feeds and experienced such profuse diarrhea that a central line was inserted near his heart so that he could receive nutrition intravenously. The IV became infected, he was treated, it again became infected, he was treated a second time, and then evaluated for an immunodeficiency.

It was during this admission that a nurse named Sheila Kaminsky documented that she'd found Virginia Ulrich holding George with his IV line open, dripping blood.

Virginia claimed that it had come loose when her husband had placed George into her arms, but Kaminsky reported her suspicions to Children and Youth.

Notes from the correspondence section of the chart documented Karl Sterling's rabid defense of Virginia. Then came a notation that Children and Youth, after an exhaustive investigation, had found no evidence of abuse or neglect.

Cassie skimmed through George's next admission, this time for breathing problems, and found a medication mishap form. George had apparently received more than ten times the dose of potassium in his IV fluids. A nurse who prepared the bag of fluid was blamed. She raised her eyebrows when she noted the nurse's name: Sheila Kaminsky. Coincidence?

Dr. Sterling's notes detailed more and more exotic possible causes for George's illness, each hypothesis tested for and rejected in turn. Cassie could detect his growing frustration as he documented consultations with colleagues throughout the country, each with more ideas but no one with an answer. She sympathized with Sterling as he investigated every possible avenue, trying to find a cure for his patient. She would have done the same thing.

Sterling's spidery handwriting blurred before her as her eyelids drooped.

"When's the last time you slept?" Adeena's voice jerked her back to attention.

Cassie rubbed her eyes, swallowed a yawn as Adeena pulled a chair up beside her. "What? You mean like all night?" She tried to joke away Adeena's look of concern.

Adeena's frown deepened until parallel furrows divided her forehead. "I can't believe you're going to treat patients in this condition. Cassie, you have to take care of yourself." Then her gaze dropped to the chart in front of Cassie. "George Ulrich. I had a feeling you wouldn't let go so easily."

Cassie shrugged, looked away. "I couldn't stop thinking about Charlie."

"Is that what kept you awake all night?" Cassie was silent. "Let me guess," Adeena continued. "You're dreaming about the shooting. Want to tell me about it?"

Cassie touched her lips with her finger and looked away. No, she didn't want to talk about it. She didn't want to let her fears control her waking hours as they did her dreams. Not dreams, not nightmares—night terrors. Filled with images of blood and death. The man she'd killed with her own hands. Drake, lying still as death, staring at her with unblinking eyes.

Then came the worst part. Drake would morph into her father. She'd hear her father's voice, his last words. "Be strong, Cassie. I need you to be strong."

On some nights, history would rewind itself and Cassie's twelve-year-old self would trudge through the snow, scrambling to find help in time to save her father. Sometimes the entire car accident would play itself out, the lurching sensation as they bounced off the mountain, the sickening wrenching feeling when they'd become airborne, plummeting through the air.

The deafening crash of pain when they'd finally hit the ground.

She'd see her father hopelessly pinned in the wreckage. Hear his words. Feel the snow slipping over the tops of her boots, the cold biting the bare flesh of her hands as she climbed back up the mountain.

When she returned with help, she'd tasted the salt of swallowed tears, the bitter knowledge that she'd failed her father choked her into a strangled silence.

These dreams were familiar ghosts, haunting her sporadically in the eighteen years since the crash. But now as she floundered through the snow to the wreckage, it was Drake staring out at her, his eyes dull with death. She would flee her dreams, heart slamming against her ribs with the certain knowledge that she'd killed Drake.

She'd reach out for him, the empty bed beside her opening up like a dark, bottomless abyss—and he wouldn't be there.

Cassie hunched her shoulders, still not meeting Adeena's gaze. "It's not so bad," she lied. "Getting better. I'm fine."

Her voice was leaden and she knew she fooled no one, much less her best friend.

"Right," Adeena said. "That's why you're spending your free time digging up the ghost of a dead little boy. Because your life is just so very *fine*."

Cassie turned to Adeena, her palms flat on George's chart as if daring her friend to take it from her. "There's something going on here. I can feel it."

"I'm surprised you can feel anything right now. You're a walking zombie." Cassie was silent. Adeena shrugged one shoulder, setting her braids jangling. "All right, then. You want to know what happened to Georgie, I'll tell you."

She pursed her lips, blew her breath out and started. "He was twenty-two months old. But he weighed less than what an average twelve month old should. He didn't crawl or walk, could barely sit up and his only words were 'mama' and 'no' which he'd cry anytime one of us got close to him. He couldn't go anywhere without a special stroller equipped with IV pump, cardiac monitor, and a bag for his medications.

"It was a beautiful fall day—bright sun, not too cold yet. Virginia was taking him outside to the children's area in the ground floor atrium. It was change of shift, no one was there but her and Georgie. She was pushing him in his stroller, round and round the tiny space that was the entire outside world to him.

"He was smiling, actually reaching for the bright leaves that she plucked off the trees to show him. His monitor lead became dislodged, but she didn't want to undress him to replace it—he was having so much fun, it was the first time she'd seen him laugh in weeks, so she didn't take him back inside.

"There are wind chimes scattered on the tree limbs, but there was no wind that day. Virginia left his side to run from tree to tree, setting them singing for Georgie. At first he clapped his hands and cooed. So she kept racing, keeping the magic music flowing."

Adeena grew silent, her gaze fixed on the shadows hiding below the desk. "Then she realized he'd stopped laughing. She ran back to him. He wasn't breathing. She started CPR, called for help, but by the time anyone got there, it was too late.

"He died in her arms. Sterling had to sedate her, she was hysterical. She wouldn't let anyone take the body from her, crying that it was her fault. We all knew that he'd been going down hill—Sterling was surprised that he'd lived as long as he had—but Virginia had actually been planning for his second birthday. She never gave up hope, never. Not until then. And once Georgie was gone, it was as if part of Virginia died with him. She was admitted to the hospital, placed on suicide watch. If it wasn't for Charlie, I'm not sure she would have ever snapped out of it."

Cassie closed her eyes, wincing at the pain in Adeena's voice. How awful, to have your child die in your arms. She chewed on her lower lip, imagining herself in the mother's place. Virginia Ulrich had gone through so much—how could Cassie suspect her of harming her own child?

"Satisfied?" Adeena asked, swiping her tears. "Get what you came for? Are those really wounds you want to reopen? You think it's going to help Charlie by dragging this up again?"

Cassie clutched the top volume of the chart to her chest, hugging it as if she could still feel the heartbeat of the little boy whose life it chronicled.

Adeena sniffed and then laid a hand on Cassie's shoulder. "You need to talk to someone, Cassie. Get some help. Before it's too late. You can't keep on like this. You know damn well it has nothing to do with Virginia or Charlie."

Cassie bowed her head, was silent. What was wrong with her? Why was she here reading the chart of a dead baby? Adeena was right, she had come back to work too soon. Maybe she was the sick one, not Virginia Ulrich.

"I'm here if you need me," Adeena said as she scraped her chair back and stood. "Think about what I said." Then with one final squeeze of Cassie's shoulder, she was gone, leaving Cassie alone with the ghost of George Ulrich.

Cassie shook her head. She took a deep breath and began to stack the charts back together. This was dangerous, she wasn't going to go any further with this delusion. She would end it now, start her shift, and forget about the Ulrichs.

She returned the volumes of charts to the clerk. She had a stack of notes written in her cramped printing. She slid them into the wastebasket, and then added the copies of Charlie's ER visits that she'd retrieved from the computer.

She watched the sheets of paper swirl down to the bottom of the black metal basket. Instead of feeling better, she felt worse.

She took a step away from the basket, heading for the exit, but stopped. She turned, scooping up all of the papers. Cassie spread them out on the counter, ignoring the jaundiced stare of the clerk, and examined them once more.

That was it. She traced a finger over the date of George's death with one hand and the date of Charlie's birth with the other. Charlie had been born only five days after George died.

CHAPTER 6

CASSIE'S VISION DARKENED. She gripped the counter's edge with sweaty palms.

"Hey, if you're sick, the ER's one flight up," the clerk said, his voice sounding more annoyed than concerned.

"I'm okay," she mumbled, rolling her papers into a cylinder and shoving it into her coat pocket.

She stumbled out of medical records, her vision clear—too clear. The thoughts that rushed through her mind disgusted her, but now she understood.

Virginia had no need to keep George alive when she had Charlie coming in a few days. And it would be a burden to care for both infants at the same time.

Cassie wanted to scream, to cry—she didn't want to understand this madness.

But somehow, it all made sense, in some twisted, grotesque way. She pictured George and his mother out on that empty playground. She could see Virginia look at George, and it wasn't a mother's love that she imagined in Virginia's face. Then a hand reaching down to the little boy, so defenseless as the hand slowly pressed over his nose and mouth.

No! Cassie forced the image from her mind. She stopped when she found herself in the stairwell. She sat down on the grey concrete steps and tried to still the surge of anger that overwhelmed her. Pounding her fist against the rough cinder block wall was the only thing that kept her from racing up the steps to the PICU and confronting Virginia Ulrich.

They'd think Cassie was the madwoman. She looked down on her scraped and reddened hand. Who would blame them? She still had no tangible evidence. Just an intuition, a feeling that twisted her gut with the force of a knife blade. If experts like Sterling and Adeena believed Virginia, what could Cassie do?

"WHY'D YOU WAIT so long to tell me about these cases?" Drake asked Jimmy as the older man drove them to the next scene in Highland Park.

Jimmy cleared his throat. "Truth is, after Sophia and Cleary went unsolved, your dad got kind of obsessed. Threatened to leak it to the media that there was a serial killer loose in Pittsburgh. Then Eades was found, and he was certain it was the same actor. He wanted to work the case himself."

"Who caught it?"

"Miller. When she got promoted it just sat collecting dust." Jimmy grunted. Commander Sarah Miller had leapfrogged through the ranks with a speed that put her on track to becoming the first woman police chief in Pittsburgh history. "Right before he died, your father thought he'd found a connection between the cases. Not a suspect, but maybe something to get them reopened."

"What kind of connection?"

"Dunno. He never said, never wrote anything down. A lot like you that way."

Drake smiled. He never made any notes until he was certain of their importance to his case. He loved it when defense attorneys invoked Rosario and subpoenaed his notebooks. All they ever got for their trouble were pages of doodles and a few cryptic words left as reminders.

"Think he told Miller about it?"

"He was campaigning to get the case reopened, even sent to Quantico for the Feds to look at it. That's why she was riding with him—" Jimmy stopped, cutting his eyes over to his partner.

"The day he died," Drake finished slowly. He forced himself to relax his clenched hands. He'd wanted to ask Miller about those last few hours his father spent alive but never found the courage.

He'd always assumed that his father had died needlessly, racing on foot after a suspect merely to impress his female supervisor. But maybe it was this case that had killed Drake Sr. This case had driven him to the heart attack. He wished his father had talked to him about it. But Drake's father never talked about his work. At least not with his son.

"Miller never said anything?"

"No." Jimmy pulled off Washington Boulevard and into Highland Park. He followed the curving road past the zoo and up to the reservoir. "Sophia Frantz and Tanya Kent were both found here. Both killed right away but dumped forty-eight to seventy-two hours after death. Like the others, strangled. No signs of sexual activity or any other wounds."

"Still, it's about sex," Drake muttered. Weren't they all? Just had to figure out what fed this particular bastard's sick fantasies, gave him the illusion he was in control.

They trudged through the grass to the playground across from the reservoir. Drake blinked in the bright sunshine. The temperature was in the fifties, and mothers and their children had flocked to the park, escaping their winter hibernation. A school bus pulled up, releasing kids in bright-colored jackets who raced to and fro like flower petals scattered on the spring breeze. Field trip, he guessed, watching three teachers huddled together, comparing notes and glancing at their watches. Letting the kids run off energy before herding them down the hill to the zoo.

He kept the photos in a manila folder, referring to them frequently as he oriented himself, trying to block out the laughter of the children around him. They squealed with delight at the play area built to resemble a medieval castle, each fairy-tale spire hiding another sliding board or monkey bars.

He didn't need the murder books for the details—for those he had Jimmy. The gruff former Marine had a way with witnesses and could remember interviews he'd performed years ago.

"Right here, this is it," Jimmy told him, squatting down in the wood shavings that now covered a patch of hard-packed dirt. "Sophia Frantz."

Drake looked up, more interested in what the killer had seen than the victim's perspective. He turned around in a full circle, slowly, absorbing each view.

"When?" he asked.

Jimmy reached a hand out, gently patting the ground where the dead girl had laid nine years ago. "May," he told his partner. He pivoted ninety degrees and paced about four feet towards the road. Then he squatted once more. "Tanya was here. Five years later and the bastard still found almost the exact same spot."

He looked up at the two stone obelisks that guarded the entrance to the park. On top of each was a statue depicting an angel holding a lantern aloft, two small children clutching her skirt, seeking protection.

Drake looked away when Jimmy crossed himself and continued his circling. He took the small camera out and snapped photos of the panorama that surrounded them, and then paused, staring down the hill into the thick woods.

"There are some rocks, pretty slippy. It gets steep between here and the zoo—tricky at night," Jimmy answered his unasked question. "Could have come through the tunnel down there," he nodded to the stone tunnel that led under the road and protected a paved path that continued down to the zoo. "But only if he came on foot."

"May. Nights getting warmer." Drake looked over at the silhouette of the apartment building a few blocks in the distance. Its blue-tinted glass and steel facade reflected the morning sun, transforming the rays of light into spun copper that danced with the movement of the clouds. "I'll bet this is a popular spot at night."

"You'd think. No one ever came forward who saw anything."

"Anything to connect either victim to here?"

"Neither had ever been here according to the families." Jimmy closed his eyes, remembering. "It was a heat wave—windows open that week. Actor slit the screen and bundled Sophie out of her Northside apartment without waking a soul. Two days later, she was found here. Autopsy showed she'd been killed the same night she was taken, though. Same with Tanya—

only she lived in Homewood."

A loud whistle split the air and the children came to an abrupt halt. Drake watched as they left their amusement to line up before the teachers.

Drake froze. His stomach clenched as he realized what the killer needed, what thirsted for more than the death of his victims.

"He wanted kids to find them. That's why he changed from the Phipps. He thought it would be kids who found Cleary, not the jogger."

Jimmy's gaze was also fixed on the wide yellow bus.

"Yeah," his voice was low. "I think maybe you're right."

Drake left Jimmy and prowled the area, ignored by the children climbing back onto their bus. He circled back and forth, taking photos from every angle. Sonofabitch. It took an effort to maintain his professional demeanor as his anger simmered. It wasn't enough to watch the kill, not enough to turn the families' grief into a public spectacle by delaying the dumping of the bodies, this actor wanted other children to live with the horror of finding the bodies.

Now he moved with intent. He would bet any money that their man watched, concealed, as the bodies were discovered. There was a large grove of bushes at the edge of the trees, before the terrain dropped off. It would make for excellent cover. He broke into a jog even though he knew there could be no evidence left. Sidling between branches of sumac, he settled himself down and turned his head.

A front row seat to where the bodies had been discovered. Drake closed his eyes and held his breath for moment, trying to absorb any essences the killer had left behind. *Where are you now, you sick bastard?*

Finally he stood and returned to where Jimmy waited by the car, talking on his cell phone.

"You're right. They've been doing field trips here for the past fourteen years," he told Drake when he hung up. "And the schedule is posted on the public information bulletin board at the zoo's entrance."

"I think that's where he camped out to watch." Drake gestured to the bushes. "Don't suppose they collected evidence from there in either case?"

Jimmy frowned and shook his head. He ruffled through the pages of Frantz's, then Kent's murder book to be certain. "They looked but didn't find anything."

"I'm not surprised. This guy's too cool to leave any part of himself behind." He got into the car. "Where's the last one?"

"Eades, the oddball that doesn't fit the pattern. Found in an alleyway off of Forbes."

"Let's go."

Jimmy pulled out of the parking lot, and they headed through Shadyside into Squirrel Hill. He parked illegally in front of a loading dock. They walked to the back door of a photographer's studio.

"The place used to be Eades'," Jimmy told him. "She'd just locked up for the day, and was taking out the trash when he got her. Left her here beside the dumpster. Her son found her."

Drake glanced up at that. "Her son?"

"Yeah, he goes to school over at Davis, it's only a few blocks away. After school he'd come here, do his homework, go home with mom."

"Why was he late getting here that afternoon?"

"He had a speech therapist he worked with after school on Tuesdays and Thursdays."

Drake prowled the alley, squinting up, searching the walls for a vantage point. He pushed the dumpster five feet over, vaulted onto the lid.

"There's an air shaft back here," he explained as he climbed down, brushing grime from his jeans. "Perfect view."

"We need to talk to the son," Jimmy said.

"Right. Damned certain his routine wasn't posted on any bulletin board." They returned to the car and headed back to the station house. "Did you question the therapist?"

"Just to verify the kid's story. She didn't know anything."

"Be nice to track her down, too."

"Yeah, just remember it's been seven years. People move around a lot," Jimmy reminded him.

His words of caution couldn't dampen the thrill of anticipation that raced through Drake. Even without his gun, he was still a cop—*the* cop to nail this bastard.

CHAPTER 7

Every ER had its Morris. A frequent flyer, usually homeless, psychotic, addicted—or any combination of the three—who adopted the Emergency Department as his own.

Despite the fact that Morris couldn't manage life in the "real world", he was smart enough to work the hospital system to his advantage. He knew to check the schedule to see which attending was on duty, knew which symptoms they would have to take seriously but not seriously enough to warrant any painful procedures, and knew what the cafeteria would have on its menu.

No one was sure where Morris spent his time outside of the ER. Cassie had once passed him on the steps of the Carnegie Library. He cursed and spat at her as if she'd invaded his privacy, overstepped her bounds. She guessed Morris was about thirty, he never gave the same name or birthday when asked. He was tall and built solidly. Some of the staff said he'd been in the military, a boxer said others, but Cassie thought he was then just what he was now: a bully, accustomed to getting his own way and not afraid to use his fists to achieve it.

The first time Cassie met him he tried to sweet talk the new "lady doctor." She'd called security to remove him. He came in a few more times while she was on duty, but never got what he wanted: drugs and a free bed for the night.

This morning it seemed Morris had gotten both elsewhere. Two uniformed officers brought him in, obviously intoxicated. Blood from a deep gash in his scalp smeared his face and he had other lacerations on his hands and forearms, probably defensive wounds. One of the officers handcuffed him to the gurney, shook his head and left the room, wiping saliva from his uniform.

"Watch him, he'll try to bite," the second officer warned Juanita, the nurse assigned to Morris. The officer stopped short when he saw Cassie, stretching himself to his full six foot four height.

Tony Spanos. First Morris, and now Spanos. What more could go wrong today?

"Of course, that wouldn't scare Dr. Hart," Spanos continued, his voice brimming with sarcasm. "She'd probably just bite him right back." He leaned into the room. "Hey, Morris, you had your rabies shots?"

Cassie met Spanos' smirk with a glare but said nothing.

"Isn't that right, Dr. Hart? You're the kind of gal who likes it rough, aren't you? C'mon, Johnson, it's time for our break." Cassie had the feeling that she'd be the main topic of conversation between the two. "Call us when you're ready for us to take him in."

"Yeah, right," Juanita answered without

enthusiasm. "I'm not going in there by myself," she told Cassie.

Cassie sighed. This wasn't her idea of a good time either. "Grab some Haldol and etomidate and meet me in there." The two drugs ought to be sufficient to chemically restrain Morris in order to examine him and repair his lacerations.

She entered the room where Morris lay, his right arm secured by the handcuffs. Cassie cursed. Spanos hadn't taken the time to notice that Morris was left-handed. Okay, they were just going to have to do this the hard way.

Morris stopped thrashing long enough to give her a long, venom-filled stare. She could tell by his pinpoint pupils and the way he smelled that he'd binged on crack. It wasn't a hard guess; it was Morris' favorite pastime when he went off his meds.

"So they persecute me further by sending in the Queen Bitch," Morris said, his voice level, almost rational.

"Morris, I need to examine you, fix those cuts," she kept her own tone even.

"Yeah, whatever. I just need me some rest." He closed his eyes with an exaggerated sigh.

Cassie remained in the doorway. Maybe he was starting to come down or maybe he was faking. Either way she wasn't getting closer without some help, handcuffs or not.

"Hey, Cassie," one of the residents called from the nurses' station. "Help me with this X-ray, will you?"

She left Morris and joined the resident at the X-ray view box.

"I don't see anything," the resident told her. "Is it okay if I discharge them home?"

"Look again. See the posterior fat pad there?" She

pointed to the suspicious area of tissue surrounding the elbow joint.

"Damn, you're right. There's a break there. I'll call ortho."

Cassie saw Juanita go into Morris' room and went to join her. She sped up when she heard a muffled cry and the clash of metal on metal. She reached the doorway and froze.

Morris held Juanita in a chokehold with his left arm. She was struggling, but he leveraged her neck against the bedrail. Juanita's eyes were bulging with terror but Morris smiled, baring his teeth as he squeezed harder.

Cassie checked her instinct to rush inside. She'd only make things worse, fuel Morris' rage.

"Morris, why don't you let her go?" she said in the calmest voice she could manage.

Juanita's face turned red as she struggled to breathe.

"Why don't you play nice Doctor Bitch and ask me what I want?"

"Let her loose, and I'll get you whatever you want."

"Don't try to jive me. I don't mind killing this one and then I'll start in on you if you cross me."

Juanita was now turning an alarming shade of purple.

"Let her breathe, otherwise you'll be holding a corpse!" She moved forward to help her nurse.

"Freeze, bitch!" Morris shouted, but he did loosen his grip enough so that Juanita was able to gasp for breath. "This one can live if you do what I say."

Cassie held her distance. "What do you want?"

"Go get the keys to these bracelets." He rattled the handcuffs. "And I want some of that coke you people keep around here. I hear that stuff is 100% proof."

"We don't keep cocaine down here in the ER." She thought fast. "We do have morphine, though. You want some of that?" She thought she remembered heroin on the list of drugs that Morris abused.

Morris shook his head, but his eyes were alight with the possibilities. "No, none of that morphine shit—that other stuff, the funforall or whatever it's called. I heard that's the biggest rush ever."

"Fentanyl. Yeah, I can get you some of that, I guess." She tried to make it sound like it would be more difficult than it was.

"Okay, go get it—some for here and some to go. I'll give you five minutes, or this one gets to see how long she can hold her breath." Cassie turned to leave the room. "And don't forget the key to these fuckin' cuffs!"

She ran through the crowd gathering outside in the hall.

"Who's got narc keys?" she shouted.

Rachel Lloyd was talking to Virginia Ulrich at the nurses' station, but left to join Cassie at the computerized medication dispenser. Cassie wondered why Charlie's mother was down here in the ER, but didn't have time to ask. "Someone go tell Spanos his coffee break is over."

Rachel punched in her code, and then used her key to unlock the drawer with the fentanyl.

"Give me two vials," Cassie said. She twisted the plastic lock off the crash cart and grabbed a bottle of succinylcholine and a pair of syringes.

"Here," she handed a syringe to Rachel. "Empty them and waste the fentanyl. We'll replace it with succ—"

"Are you sure? What if he suspects?"

"Insert the needle right at the edge of the seal. He won't notice a thing." She demonstrated with the vial she held.

"But what if he doesn't use it here?" Rachel continued to argue. The charge nurse had a soft spot for Morris—she'd even gotten him into detox once. "He'll die if he injects that without medical help nearby."

"A chance we'll have to take." She finished replacing the contents of the fentanyl vial and took the one Rachel held.

"He's your patient. You can't just let him die. Our job is to help people, not to gamble with their lives."

"I don't intend to. I also don't intend to allow him to hurt Juanita or let the police start a gun fight in the middle of my ER." Cassie turned and left.

The two cops, the younger one looking more than a little sheepish, stood outside the doorway to Morris' room. They had their guns drawn and had moved the spectators back.

"Give me the key to his handcuffs," she demanded.

"Sorry, doc, no can do," Spanos told her, muscling his bulk between her and the room. "Don't worry, the SWAT guys are coming."

Exactly what Cassie was worried about. A bunch of gung-ho cowboys shooting up her ER, with her nurse caught in the crossfire.

"We don't have time. He's going to kill her if I don't get back in there." She held her palm out for the key. "If anything happens to Juanita, I'll make sure the entire city knows it was your fault."

Spanos' glare had no effect on her. He lifted his shoulders in a dramatic shrug. "You want to play hero, go ahead," he said. "But if I get a clear shot, I'm taking it. So you'd better stay out of my line of fire." His eyes narrowed. "Or not. No matter to me."

"Just give me the damned key." She knew Spanos was merely posturing, being his usual idiotic Neanderthal self, but this wasn't the time. Her five minutes were almost up. He slapped the key into her waiting hand, and she rushed past him back into the room.

"Okay Morris, it wasn't easy, but I got the fentanyl from the pharmacy." She pretended to be out of breath, hoping that her notoriously poor acting skills were up to the task.

Morris had relaxed his hold on Juanita enough so that he could wrap his arm around her and fondle her breast. Cassie almost wished she had let Spanos shoot him. Or at very least Taser him. She forced herself to stay calm and not lash out at the addict.

"First, unlock these." He jangled his handcuffs.

Cassie showed him the key. "You'll have to let her go, so that I can reach them." She slowly moved toward the two.

"Think I'm a fool?"

Instead of releasing Juanita, Morris grabbed her tighter, hauling her over the bedrail so that she now sat on top of him. He adjusted his grip, his arm returning back around her throat. Cassie tried to ignore the huge biceps and bulging veins as he slowly began to squeeze. She rushed forward and after fumbling with the key, released the handcuff from Morris' right wrist.

Morris sat up and lowered the bed rail. He swung his legs around, Juanita still on his lap. "That's better."

"Let her go."

"Not until you give me my stuff."

Cassie thrust the two vials at him. "Here. Now, let her go."

Morris took the vials with his right hand and scrutinized them. He nodded. "Might as well use a clean needle, right doc? Wouldn't want to catch the virus or nothing." He extended his arm. "You shoot me up."

She shook her head. "Not until you let Juanita go."

"She can go. Long as you stay." Morris stared at Cassie with eyes filled with anger and loathing. She knew that if she remained with him, he would kill her.

And if she did nothing? Morris could easily kill Juanita before the cops stopped him.

This was a bad idea. A very bad idea. But what other choice did she have? She nodded. "Deal."

CHAPTER 8

CASSIE GRABBED A syringe and tourniquet, holding them up, a peace offering. Morris stared at her for a long moment, then grabbed her by the arm as he released Juanita. The nurse's legs buckled, and she gasped for breath. She looked up at Cassie with tearful eyes and hurried from the room.

Morris' grip on her wrist was bone crushing. Cassie bit her lip with the pain but said nothing.

"Okay, bitch, just you and me. Go ahead and give me the good stuff." He held out his arm, releasing his grip on her wrist and grabbing a handful of her hair instead.

Searing pain raced across her scalp, bringing tears to her eyes. She applied the tourniquet, drew up the drug and quickly injected it. He wrenched her head back when she finished.

"Now you and me are walking out of here," he said, rising to his feet. "We'll find someplace quiet and have ourselves a little party."

Succinylcholine had been around for years. Cassie

had never seen it fail. She prayed this wouldn't be the first time.

"How long before this stuff starts to work?" he asked.

She said nothing, counting the seconds in her head. Just about . . . *now*.

"Whoa, I feel a rush coming on already—" His voice faltered. He stopped, slumping against the gurney, pulling her down to the floor with him. Cassie reached up and pried his fingers from her hair. Now paralyzed, unable even to blink, Morris watched her with reproachful eyes.

"I need some help in here!" she shouted, going for the oxygen.

Quickly, the room swarmed with medical personnel and police. "Get him up on the bed, set up for intubation."

She began to use the bag-valve mask to force oxygen in and out of his lungs. Morris' eyes remained open, staring at her as he lay helpless on the gurney.

"Hey doc, that's good stuff—how long does it last?" the younger cop asked as he applied handcuffs to both of Morris' arms.

"Long enough for him to have brain damage if we don't breathe for him," she snapped. "Get that pulse ox and monitor on him. Let's go people!" She looked up to see Rachel frowning at her from the doorway.

Cassie felt a twinge of guilt. What she had done was in violation of the Hippocratic oath and principles of medical ethics. Her job was to heal, not to harm.

She focused on her task, quickly intubating Morris and ensuring that he was getting oxygen. Once Morris was stabilized and headed up to the ICU, she went out to the police officers.

"He'll be here overnight, then he's all yours," she

told them.

In truth, they could have allowed him to wake up and extubate him in the ER, but she didn't think it was fair for her staff to have to deal with Morris anymore. Let the ICU handle his crap.

"Not bad for an amateur, Hart," Spanos told her grudgingly. "Still, it would have been easier just to shoot him."

"Not in my ER. Next time you guys might want to notice if a guy's right handed or left handed when you cuff him."

She ran her fingers through her hair, massaging her sore scalp. Her hands were trembling, but she'd be damned if she'd let Spanos see that.

Johnson, the younger one, looked down. "That was on me. It won't happen again. He seemed so out of it—"

"Just do me a favor and make sure that he stays locked up for a good, long while this time, okay?"

The two officers headed toward the elevators leading to the ICU. Cassie went back into the nurse's station and handed Rachel the remaining vial of succinylcholine.

"You want to dispose of this for me?"

Rachel took the vial with a look of distaste. "Certainly, Doctor," she said in a frosty voice.

Damn, here we go, Cassie thought. Confrontations with nurses were bad enough, but if you get on the wrong side of a charge nurse you were in for hell.

"Want me to call the Critical Incident Team?" Cassie asked, referring to the multi-disciplinary team that helped to defuse the stress of traumatic events on medical personnel. It might be helpful. Lord knew, she was feeling pretty shaky after her confrontation with Morris. Contrary to popular media images, having your life threatened was not an ordinary part of working in the ER.

"I don't feel that is necessary," Rachel replied.

"It might help Juanita and anyone else to talk about things, review security procedures so this doesn't happen again, vent any feelings—"

"Don't you dare try to blame this on my nurse!"

"I'm not. I just thought—"

"That's the problem, you didn't think, Dr. Hart. You rushed in to play hero, totally ignoring the fact that you were placing my nurse and your patient in jeopardy. I hold you responsible for everything that happened today and don't you think for a minute that I won't report your actions to Dr. Castro and administration. Your callous disregard—"

"If you had a better idea, you should have said something!" Cassie snapped, her temper flaring now. "I had less than five minutes to come up with a plan that wouldn't get anyone killed."

"And did you ever consider the consequences if your plan hadn't worked? We're here to serve our patients, to help them get better—whatever their illness or injury. I took an oath in nursing school: First do no harm. Tell me, Dr. Hart, what about your oath?"

Cassie was silent. Rachel had hit a nerve with that one, but what else could she have done? Stand by and let the police handle things? The outcome could have been bloody.

Or everything might have been fine. She should have trusted the police to do their job. They were trained for these things, she wasn't. She'd overstepped her bounds and in doing so, she had violated one of the fundamental principles of her profession.

She started to apologize to Rachel, but the charge nurse turned her back and walked away.

"Hey, Drake. Got a case for you."

Drake looked over as he and Jimmy moved through the front lobby of the station house. Tony Spanos leaned against the desk, talking to a girl about ten and a younger boy who clung to her hand.

Behind Spanos, his partner had the thankless task of writing up a report.

"Here you go, folks," Spanos said. "This is Detective Drake, he specializes in your kind of case." Spanos moved away, leaving the two children with Drake.

He sent a glare toward the uniformed officer. Spanos returned it with a mocking salute. Then Drake crouched down so he was at eye level with the kids. "Hi, guys. What can I do for you?"

"Will you help us?" The girl was the spokesman for the duo. Drake watched as she looked over her shoulder at a man who stood just behind her. Their father, Drake guessed, nodded his encouragement, and she turned back.

"First of all, what's your name?"

"I'm Katie Jean and this is my little brother, Nate."

"Pleased to meet you, Katie Jean and Nate." Drake extended his hand and shook Katie Jean's. When he offered it to Nate, the boy flinched away, moving so that his sister shielded him. "And is that your dad?"

The man moved closer and took Drake's hand. "John Trevasian." He looked down on his daughter. "Go on, Katie Jean."

She straightened and stared up at Drake with an intense expression that reminded him of Hart. "It's my job to talk to you, 'cause Snickers is our responsibility."

She stumbled on the last word, and he realized she had rehearsed the speech. "We need you to help us find him. Nate drew pictures and we left them all over, but no one's seen him and he's just a puppy and what will happen if no one knows how he likes his belly rubbed or what kind of food to get him?" The last came out in an explosion of fear.

Drake rocked back on his heels. He could hear Spanos' laughter from behind him but ignored it. Katie Jean sniffed back her tears and tried to continue.

"Anyway, Daddy always says the police are here to help us, so I asked him to bring us here today. So will you? Find Snickers and bring him home? Please?" She looked up at him with an earnestness that was mirrored on her brother's face.

How could he say no? He nodded solemnly. "I'll do my best," he assured them. "You said you have a picture?"

Katie Jean turned to her brother who withdrew a sheet of paper from his pants pocket and silently offered it. Drake unfolded the paper and smoothed it. He glanced up at the boy in surprise. It was a detailed rendering of an Australian Shepherd done in pencil except for two blue smears of crayon for the eyes.

"Did you draw this?" he asked Nate who merely shrugged. The boy looked to be only eight or so, but the artwork was that of an advanced talent.

"He drew it 'cause we didn't have any new pictures of Snickers, only when he was a baby," Katie Jean continued her role as spokesperson. "Nate draws lots of things."

"I'll bet he does," Drake told her. "You kids wait here a minute while I talk to your father, all right?" He glanced over at Spanos who was still lounging nearby. "Officer Spanos will get you both some honorary police badges." Spanos looked up at that, but it was too late, Katie Jean had already marched over to him and began tugging on his arm.

"Thanks for talking to them, Detective," John Trevasian said. "I know there's nothing you can do, the dog's probably long gone. But Katie Jean was determined." His voice trailed off as he looked over at his children.

Drake smiled. "I can see that. You've got a couple of great kids there, Mr. Trevasian. Did Nate really draw this by himself?"

A cloud passed over the father's face. "Yes. Since Snickers disappeared, drawing has been his only form of communication. He loved that dog so much."

"He's very talented. You should look into classes for him. Maybe it would give him something to concentrate on now that Snickers is gone."

"Yeah, that's what the people at school say. We don't know what to do. He refuses to talk to anyone—not even Katie Jean. First the school said he was hyperactive and needed medication, then once he started taking the drugs he got moody and sullen. And since Snickers has been gone he hasn't said a single word, not to anyone. We even have the school psychologist working with him."

Drake turned and watched the boy clutching his sister's hand. "What's your address?"

"It's on the back of the picture. You're not really thinking you can find Snickers, are you?"

"I told Katie Jean and Nate that I'd do my best. Let me talk to some of the guys who patrol near your house. Who knows, maybe we'll get lucky."

Trevasian smiled and took Drake's hand once more. "Thank you, Detective. I—we—really appreciate this. Come on kids, it's time to go."

Drake watched the family leave, ignoring Spanos' approach. He remembered being a shy kid, his only solace the pictures he'd draw, scribbling over any scrap of paper he could find. But Nate seemed more than shy, the boy was lost somewhere, wandering alone without comfort.

"Figured you're the only one not actually doing any real work around here so you had time to tackle a tough case like that. By the way, I just got back from seeing your girlfriend," Spanos told him, a sneer twisting his mouth. "Guess she learned better than to try to do a cop's job."

Drake narrowed his eyes at the patrolman. "What are you talking about?"

"You haven't heard? Me and Johnson took this crackhead over to Three Rivers, and he got hold of a nurse. Hart went in and almost got herself killed."

"Is she all right?" Drake felt his fists clench even as he fought to keep his voice level. "What was she doing in the middle of a hostage situation? Why didn't you follow procedure?"

Spanos shrugged as if they were talking about the weather. "Hart's fine. She pulled rank—said it was her ER and she knew what she was doing. What was I supposed to do, shoot her?"

"You were supposed to do your job!" Drake started toward the door.

As much as he disliked Spanos, he felt certain that the patrolman was telling the truth—it was exactly what Hart would do. Rush in, not think twice about the consequences, or the fact that someone else might be better equipped to do the job. Why could she never learn to stand back and observe from the sidelines where she'd be safely out of harm's way? It was just like last time, just like before. Sooner or later, someone was going to get hurt.

"At least I'm allowed on the streets with a gun," Spanos shouted at his back.

Drake slammed the door behind him, tried not to flinch at the sound that reverberated through his memory like a gunshot.

CHAPTER 9

Cassie pulled her yellow Tyvek trauma gown closer around her, shading her eyes from the bright April sun. She heard the ambulance before she could see it. The constant howl of the siren was punctuated by a screech of brakes and scream of a horn as they reached the intersection. Med Five was bringing in an unresponsive child, Code Three, no other report given.

The guys working Med Five were good; time-tempered pros who'd seen the worst the streets of Pittsburgh could offer. If they were too busy to call in report, there was reason for her to worry.

Time to rock and roll.

The squad pulled into the Emergency Department's drive and quickly backed up. Cassie already had her staff preparing the resuscitation room, but she preferred to meet critical patients herself. It gave her precious extra seconds to assess her patient.

When Med Five stopped moving, Cassie rushed forward to open one of the rear doors. "Glad to see you, doc," the medic said, jumping down and pulling the gurney forward.

"What've you got?"

"Three year old, healthy until Sunday when he complained of cold symptoms, ear ache and low grade fever. Developed progressive fever and vomiting. Today was unable to retain any fluids. Mother found him unresponsive this afternoon. Responds only to pain for us, went apneic in route, so we started to bag him." He gave her the bullet as they hurried down the corridor into the critical care room.

She focused on her patient. A skinny little boy, his pulses weak, abdomen distended from the oxygen forced down his throat, eyes wide open but not focusing on anything.

"Let's move him, gently now," she instructed her team. "Set up for intubation, five-oh ET tube. Two of Versed and give him two grams of ceftriaxone."

Cassie assessed her patient from head to toe. His neck was rigid, his pupils sluggish but equal. Other than the abnormal vital signs, the only other finding was a ruptured right eardrum with purulent material coming from it.

"Foley, monitor, he'll need a head CT. Let's draw a CBC, blood culture, lytes, glucose and call for a chest X-ray. Who's on for Peds today?"

"Sterling again."

Oh great. Another chance to irritate the patronizing department head. Well, she wasn't going to give him anything to complain about with this resuscitation. "Call him."

She moved to the head of the bed and prepared to insert the endotracheal tube. Cassie hated it when kids were this sick—it just didn't seem natural. He was a cute kid, too.

Then she looked again and realized she

recognized him. Antwan was his name. He had smiled when she gave him a sticker yesterday morning. He'd been her first patient of her first shift back.

Could she have missed something? Her stomach dropped as she remembered Adeena's warning that she wasn't in any shape to be caring for patients.

Cassie glanced away, trying to regain her perspective, to slow her racing thoughts. Focus. She raised the bent metal blade that would hold Antwan's tongue out of the way while she intubated him. Before she could proceed, a banshee's wail came from the hall.

"Antwan!" a thin woman in her early twenties screamed as she rushed in. "My baby!" She tried to go to her son, but Jason, the ward clerk, intercepted her.

"Please, Mrs. Washington, you have to let the doctors work on him." He tried to gently move her from the room, but she refused to leave.

Cassie tried to make her voice as firm and level as possible. "Mrs. Washington, Antwan is very ill. We're doing everything we can for him, but we need a few minutes before you can see him. Go with Jason down to the family room, and we'll let you see him as soon as possible."

"My baby, take care of my baby," the mother sobbed, as she allowed Jason to move her.

"I'll call social services," Jason said over his shoulder.

Cassie merely nodded; she didn't have time for anything else. She quickly pulled the oxygen mask off Antwan's face and inserted the metal blade. Cassie held her breath. It wasn't as easy as it looked on TV, especially in kids. They tended to have big tonsils that could bleed easily. And lots of secretions, like now.

"Suction," she called. She cleared the mucus from Antwan's airway and his vocal cords popped into view.

Cassie slid the silastic tube through them into his trachea. The respiratory tech secured it and took over ventilating him.

"Get a gas in five minutes," Cassie ordered. She glanced up at the monitor. Heart rate was up, blood pressure was down, all good signs. She checked his pupils again, much more reactive now. "Did he get the antibiotics?"

Rachel nodded. "And CT is ready anytime you are."

"Let's get a chest X-ray first. I'll go talk to the mom. Let me know when that's back."

Cassie moved down the hall to the family room. She paused before entering, trying to squelch the churning in her gut. What had gone wrong? Why had this happened? When she'd seen Antwan on Monday morning, he'd been a happy boy with a cold and ear infection. How could he be lying in her ER now, fighting for his life?

She took a deep breath and pushed the door open. The family room was a tiny, claustrophobic space containing four chairs, their upholstery peppered with cigarette burns, and a telephone. There wasn't enough room to pace, but this forced people to sit while speaking with staff—a simple intervention designed to prevent violent outbursts. The room was soundproofed to give grieving family privacy, but there was also an emergency panic button tied directly to security. You never knew what might happen in here where circumstances forced people to extreme emotions.

Over the years Cassie had noticed that no matter what the outcome for the patient, there were always two dominant emotions in their family members: guilt and anger.

Adeena was already there, trying to calm Mrs.

Washington. Both women looked up when Cassie entered.

"Is my boy okay?" Mrs. Washington asked, her voice strained and cracking with tears.

Cassie pulled a chair close to the mother and reached over to touch her hand. Mrs. Washington was young, but her face had a pinched, guarded look that told Cassie that she'd already been through a lot.

"Antwan is very, very sick," Cassie started. "I think he has a serious infection called meningitis. It's an infection of the tissue around the brain, and sometimes the brain can swell because of it. This can be very dangerous."

"Is he going to be all right?"

"The next few days will tell. One way to treat the brain swelling is to put a tube into Antwan's lungs and breathe for him, so that he doesn't have to work so hard. That's what I just finished doing. We're going to take a CAT scan to look at his brain and then he'll be going to the Pediatric ICU."

"Is he brain damaged?" Mrs. Washington gasped.

"I don't know. I can't answer that yet." Cassie paused to see if the mother had any other questions. She hesitated to ask about what was on her mind. The lawyers would surely advise her not to, but she had to know. "Mrs. Washington, do you remember me from yesterday? I saw Antwan for his earache."

Mrs. Washington looked at Cassie, and then nodded. "Yeah, you gave him medicine and a Sponge Bob sticker."

"Did Antwan take his medicine? It was called Augmentin, he was supposed to take it twice a day and see his doctor if he wasn't better."

The mother looked at Cassie and then Adeena, her eyes filling once more with tears. She bowed her head so that Cassie could barely make out her next words.

"I couldn't afford it," she whispered. "I made his appointment at the clinic, but their first opening was in two weeks. He felt better after that ibu medicine that you gave him. I gave that every eight hours, just like you said, until he started to throw up." She looked back at Cassie, her eyes pleading for understanding. "What else was I supposed to do?"

Cassie wished she had the words to comfort the mother. She grasped Mrs. Washington's hand, noticing that the woman had no wedding band and that her hand was roughened and calloused. What could she say to this hardworking mother who made too much money to qualify for free care, but too little to afford a two hundred dollar prescription?

"I'm going to check on Antwan," she said. "Then we'll try to get you down to see him, okay?"

The mother nodded, wiping her tears with a torn tissue.

Cassie returned to the critical care room. Karl Sterling was there, completing his assessment of Antwan. She told him what she'd learned from Mrs. Washington.

"I'll pull the chart from Monday for you," she finished.

Sterling tapped his pen against the X-ray view box. Antwan's chest looked fine, but Sterling continued tapping an irritating rhythm, scowling into space. It was obvious that Karl Sterling was not happy with this case.

"CT is ready," she reminded him. "I'll go get the mom, so she can go up with you."

Sterling turned his gaze onto her. "I really don't want to see the mother right now," he said in a tight voice. "I'll have Adeena notify CYS when we get upstairs."

"Children and Youth? Dr. Sterling, this mother loves her child, she never meant to harm him."

The department head sighed. "Cases like this make my job as a pediatrician very difficult, Dr. Hart. But no good comes of ignoring the situation. You know the law as well as I do. Any suspected case of abuse or neglect must be reported. It's not up to us to decide anything—but in my mind this is a clear-cut case of medical neglect."

"At least talk to the mom before you decide. She was doing the best that she could."

"Well, that wasn't good enough, was it?" He gestured to the comatose child on the gurney. "It's my duty to protect that child, whatever the consequences for the adults involved. And if I were you, I'd prepare for a lawsuit. After all, you did see him yesterday."

Cassie glared at the pediatrician. "What are you trying to imply? He was fine—just a cold and an ear infection. No signs of meningitis."

Sterling shook his head in disbelief. "You really are naive, aren't you? Believe me, I've seen cases like this before. You should thank me for calling CYS. If they find the mother guilty of neglect, it will take you off the hook."

"I'm not on the hook, I did nothing wrong. And that's no reason to threaten a mother with taking her child away. Dr. Sterling, don't rush into this—"

"I'm taking my patient up to CAT scan now. Your services are no longer necessary, Dr. Hart. Thank you." With an imperious wave of his hand, Sterling led the way from the room.

Cassie watched as the nurses pushed the gurney out the door. She balled her fists in frustration, clamping her teeth together to avoid screaming. There was nothing more she could do. Sterling had his mind made up and nothing she said would change it. She blew her breath out. She'd talk to Adeena, she'd know how to handle it.

She opened the door, never noticing the chaos that swirled outside of the now silent critical care room. It all seemed ordinary to Cassie.

DRAKE PARKED THE Intrepid in one of the restricted spaces in front of the ER entrance. He ignored the security guard as he stalked through the ambulance bay and into the tile-walled corridors that framed Hart's world.

An old man dragged his IV pole with one hand and held his gown closed with the other as he shuffled down the hall. In the curtained alcove beside the nurses' station a college-aged girl vomited into an emesis basin as a friend held her hair back from her face. Clorox and Betadine fought to overcome the smell of dried blood, vomit and urine—one of the never ending battles fought on this ground.

He ignored all this, his vision tunneled to a form about five-four and slight of build, not looking left or right until his gaze locked onto Hart. She was leaving one of the resuscitation rooms, her gait heavy and slow compared to her normal rapid stride. One hand pulled her hair back out of her face, the barrette that restrained it long lost. She froze when she saw him, hand still tangled in her hair, mouth open like a small child caught in a forbidden act.

Drake inhaled deeply, imprinting the image on his mind—he would paint it later, he was certain—and moved to her. He took her arm, pulled her past the gawkers at the nurses' station and into her office, closing the door behind him.

"What the hell do you think you're doing?" she flared before he could say anything. Her eyes blazed as her unfettered hair fell around her shoulders. "Get out of my way, I've work to do. I'll deal with you later."

He leaned against the door, determined not to give in to her.

She shifted her weight into a fighting stance. He almost smiled, would've smiled, if not for the rage and fear that had been building ever since he left the House. Anger at her reckless behavior, fear that she wouldn't listen to him, that some day it would be Hart lying on a bed up in the ICU. Or worse, on a slab at the morgue.

"I have a job to do also, in case you haven't noticed," he told her, his voice raised but steady. "A job I left to see if I could talk some sense into you."

She narrowed her gaze. "Let me guess, Spanos told you about Morris."

"Morris?" Now his voice was almost a shout but he couldn't help it. His vision reddened with anger. "Morris is a stone killer—every cop in the Zone knows it."

"I don't care what Spanos told you," she continued, her voice loud enough to bounce off the concrete walls. "Your people," she hurled the last at him, lumping him in with incompetent cops everywhere, "put one of my nurses in danger through their stupidity. No way in hell was I going to let them turn my ER into a shooting gallery! Is that your answer to everything? Go in with your damned guns blazing!"

"You can't just rush in! Look what happened the last time you got mixed up in something you shouldn't—" His words came as rapidly as machine gun fire, trying to hit her before she moved out of range. "Are you trying to get someone killed?"

Silence. Head tilted up so that she could meet him eye to eye, she opened her mouth, then closed it again.

The slap came from nowhere, stinging across his face.

"How dare you! Don't ever—how could you even think—" Her words tumbled over themselves. Drake lost most of them as she buried her head in her hands. Then she looked up. "God, I'm sorry. I can't believe I did that."

"Why the hell can't you trust anyone?" he asked, the bitterness in his voice betraying his true question: *why couldn't she trust him?*

The haunted look in her eyes told him everything he needed to know. Everyone she'd ever placed her trust in had abandoned her.

Her mother sacrificed herself to save Hart's life when she was a newborn, she'd watched helpless as her father died when she was twelve, the grandmother who raised her had died mere weeks before she had married Richard King. And King—the worst betrayal of all. He'd devoured Hart with his love, whittling her down until her universe had shrunk to include only him, and then he'd returned her love with violence.

Two months ago, Drake had saved her life, now he had to earn her love. And harder still, her trust.

"Just leave," she said, her voice strangled with unshed tears. "I don't want to talk about it."

"Of course not," he replied, holding his ground. "You never do." Action before words, always Hart's way. He rubbed his cheek, looking down on her. "Maybe that's part of the problem."

Then he left. Got the hell out of there before he said something he would regret. Something they might both regret.

CHAPTER 10

CASSIE DIDN'T KNOW whether to cry or scream. What she wanted to do was throw something, break something, hit anything. But the nearest thing to hand was the plastic pitcher that held the orchids Drake had brought her yesterday. Her fingers brushed against their delicate petals, showering them to the floor.

Damn. She collapsed in her chair, and focused on breathing. Something so simple even she couldn't mess it up.

How dare he come barging into her ER, make a scene, and judge her without hearing her side of the story? Worse, how could he take Spanos' side over hers? She hugged herself, blinking hard. Cassie didn't cry. Not easily and never at work.

God, had she really slapped Drake? Maybe she had come back to work too soon. Maybe she had missed something yesterday with Antwan Washington, had mishandled the incident with Morris. Maybe everyone was right, she did need help.

Drake had once trusted her with his life. If that trust was gone...

She shook her head. The prospect was too much to face. He was upset about Morris, and he had a right to be. She should have called him. Only she had no idea of what to say, had put it off.

She'd give him time to cool down, and then would explain what really happened with Morris and Spanos.

AFTER HER SHIFT, Cassie found Antwan in a private alcove in the side hallway of the Pediatric ICU. His mother was asleep in the chair beside the bed, one hand covering his.

Cassie noted by the bandages around his head and the wave tracing on the monitor that they'd inserted an intracranial pressure monitor; a small computer chip on top of his brain that recorded the pressure around it. The reading was high, but according to his bedside chart it had improved dramatically since admission. His blood pressure and pulse were better also, although she saw that he had had several seizures. That wasn't so good.

As she was leafing through the bedside chart, Antwan's mother stirred. Cassie looked up, then moved to the chair beside her. Mrs. Washington said nothing, merely looked at Cassie with eyes that held fear and distrust.

"I'm sorry I woke you," Cassie told her. "I just wanted to stop by and see how Antwan was doing."

"You tell me, you're the doctor," Mrs. Washington replied in a frosty tone.

"What has Dr. Sterling told you so far?" Cassie wondered if Sterling was the reason behind the mother's sudden hostility.

"Nothing! No one will tell me nothing. They made me wait outside while they took those pictures of his brain. Then all the sudden there's thirty people racing down the hall, all pushing into the room where they got Antwan. I try to go in and they shove me out but not before I see he was having a fit of some kind. Then we get up here and all they do is ask questions—what kind of home do we have, where do I work, what hours—I ask them what's this have to do with Antwan being sick, but nobody will tell me nothing!" Her rage vented, the young woman seemed to collapse back into herself, sinking into the chair. She looked frightened by her own indignation.

Cassie took her hand. "How about if I try to answer your questions, Mrs. Washington?"

Antwan's mother stared at her with suspicion, and then gave a small nod of acquiescence. "You call me Tammy," she said. "You know as well as me there ain't no Mr. Washington. Makes me think you're talking to my mom."

"Right, Tammy. The doctors here did a procedure called a spinal tap where they took a small amount of fluid from Antwan's back. I'm sure they talked about that with you, asked for your consent?"

"They shoved a bunch of papers in front of me to sign before they'd let me come back. I didn't know about any needle in his back—but look at him, they've got needles and tubes in him everywhere."

"Well, this fluid showed that Antwan does have the infection I was telling you about, the spinal meningitis. In his case it looks like it was caused by a certain bacteria called pneumococcus. It's common in children, causes everything from ear infections to pneumonia to infections in the blood, and occasionally meningitis. It's so common that we've found that many children fight it off without even needing medicine, just with their own immune system. Kids also get shots to prevent it nowadays."

Tammy frowned. "There was a shot the health clinic wanted to give him a while back, but they were out of it both times I went. Why can't he fight this off? Was it because I didn't give him that medicine or get him that shot? Is it my fault?" Tammy leaned forward, her eyes locked with Cassie's.

Cassie sighed. The easy answer was yes, but medicine often had no easy answers. "Maybe—I can't tell you for certain. You see, there are some types of pneumococcus that don't respond to the antibiotics given by mouth and the new shot doesn't prevent. If that's what Antwan has, then there's no way anyone could have prevented this—"

Tammy took a deep breath and rolled her eyes heavenward. "Oh thank you, God," she whispered and collapsed back in the chair. "I was so worried that I did this." She gripped Cassie's hand again. "I love my boy, doctor. He's all I've got. You've got to make him better."

Cassie gave her a tiny smile. "We'll do everything we can. Now you try to get some rest, okay? I'll stop back tomorrow and see how you're doing."

"Thank you, Dr. Hart."

As she left the darkened PICU, she noted that Charlie's bed space was empty. Probably getting another test.

She entered the bright and noisy world that was the rest of the medical center. But even as she traveled through the hospital back down to the ER, she could feel the atmosphere of the PICU cling to her like a fine coat of sweat.

Tammy Washington didn't deserve to have her

child taken from her—and she certainly did not deserve to be kept in the dark about the care her son was receiving. Cassie returned to her office in the ER and paged Adeena.

· ⚙ ·

DRAKE SQUEALED INTO the Zone Seven parking lot, braking hard as he pulled the Intrepid into its space. He sat in the car, trying to calm down. His head was pounding, his chest clamped tight by a vice grip that refused to let any air through.

Hart could have been killed today.

A feeling of overwhelming doom settled over him. Suddenly he was back, on the cellar floor, pain lancing through his chest and leg, his breath coming in ragged gasps that sent fire through his lungs, sweating with the effort to push a tire iron inches across the floor to Hart's hand. He closed his eyes against the vision, leaned forward against the steering wheel.

His fingers and face grew numb. God help him, he was dying. He was having a heart attack, right here in front of the House. As he struggled to breathe, slumped in the driver's seat of a beat up city vehicle, his mind was a prisoner of time, trapped in that godforsaken cellar, fighting for his and Hart's life with every ounce of energy he could summon. Crimson flares of color danced across his vision. What if he hadn't been able to get the tire iron to Hart? What if she hadn't used it?

What if Morris had hurt her today? What would she rush into tomorrow?

Infinite possibilities of calamity spun out before him, sucking him into their vortex of darkness. He was dead, Hart was dead, everything was lost—and it was all Drake's fault. He should have known better, should have called for backup, should have found a way out before anyone got hurt, should have never gone in, should have been better, faster, smarter—

Laughter sliced through the roaring in his ears. Drake took a deep breath. Gradually, the red haze that clouded his vision cleared. The pressure lifted from his chest, and he looked around. Two uniforms were laughing as they walked down the steps.

He wasn't back in the cellar, he wasn't dying. Judas H, what was he doing sitting here, clammy with sweat when he had work to do?

Hart's face, flushed with anger right before she'd slapped him, filled his mind. He pushed it away along with the memory of her passionate embrace from yesterday. Lots of work. That's what he needed. Enough to drown out all thoughts of Cassandra Hart.

Because if this was the kind of effect she was going to have on him, they were both better off taking time apart, getting some perspective. Breathing room.

Maybe once he got a handle on this case . . .

Drake shrugged thoughts of his personal life aside. He wanted to get through the case files and make a list of priority interviews for tomorrow. Maybe start working on more similarities between the victims, get an idea of the actor's mindset, however warped it might be. There was something nagging him about these cases, if he could just put his finger on it—

Maybe there were more cases that Jimmy and his father had missed. It would take a solid week to go through all the unclosed homicides, but it might come to that.

He left the car and inhaled deeply. Pittsburgh in springtime. A possible signature killer on the prowl. What more could a cop ask for?

CHAPTER 11

"Got your message." Adeena balanced a large stack of folders in her arms. Sometimes business was just too good.

"Did Sterling talk to you about a CYS referral for Mrs. Washington?"

She slumped into Cassie's spare chair. "Yes he did. He's pretty adamant about it."

"What did you think?"

"I'm not entirely sure. I get good vibes from Mom. I think she's caring and really invested in Antwan, but the household sounds rather chaotic. She's worried about losing her job—said they already almost fired her because she mixed some chemicals while cleaning. She's doesn't want to go on welfare, that's something she was very clear about. But she has no idea how she's going to pay for this hospital bill or what she'll do if Antwan is permanently disabled. I think we have a long road ahead of us whatever we decide." She watched as Cassie frowned at her words.

"Can she read?" Cassie asked.

"She's a high school graduate, for what that's worth. But I didn't ask her about her reading skills." Patience, Adeena counseled herself. But she sensed another of Cassie's crusades coming on. Why couldn't she just learn to leave work at work like everyone else? Why did she always have to borrow trouble?

"Maybe she can't read. That would explain her mixing the wrong chemicals together at work, what if she thought the ibuprofen samples we gave her were the same as the Augmentin?"

Adeena shook her head. "I don't think so. I think you want to let her off the hook because you like her."

"I just think she's a caring, hard-working mother and I don't want to see her child taken away from her, that's all. I'm not saying she didn't make a mistake."

"I like her too, but I have to be an advocate for Antwan. I don't think removal is the best answer, but I do think that support services are necessary. And I think very close supervision will be needed, especially if Antwan requires any long term care."

"So you're going to call CYS."

"Yes. That's the best way to get the services that Antwan and his mother will need."

"Just because Sterling asks you to, you're going to ruin that woman's life."

Adeena watched as Cassie blew out her breath, got to her feet and began to pace the cramped office like a mother lion protecting her cubs. A lion itching for a fight. Right now, Adeena was happy to oblige.

"You know better than that," she snapped. "Stop pissing off everyone and start living in the real world. Either that or take more time off, and get your head on straight again."

"Can't you ever cut anyone a break?" Cassie asked, her voice taking on an edge.

Adeena dropped her stack of charts on the desk with a loud thud. "Now you're going to do my job, too? What the hell's gotten into you? When did you start to think that the M.D. after your name stands for Major Deity?"

"That's not true, and you know it. I just think—"

"No, that's the problem. You're not thinking. You're reacting. And you of all people should know that the ER is no place to rely on instincts."

"But—"

"But, what? I shouldn't do the job that I've trained for and have been doing for eight years now? Karl Sterling shouldn't believe Virginia Ulrich because you don't like the way she looks? The police should give you a Junior Marshall Badge and you can do their job for them, too?"

Cassie flinched. Adeena gave her one of her best face-the-music stares. Cassie surprised her by looking down, and then she sank into her chair and was silent.

Adeena sighed and lowered her voice. "Face it, you made a mistake. You've been traumatized. You're overreacting, imagining dangers that aren't there. You shouldn't have pushed yourself to come back so soon. You weren't ready. Maybe you should take more time off."

Adeena knew what she was asking of Cassie. But she was more worried about Cassie's future, about the damage she was doing to herself by pushing herself to the edge like this.

"Just think about it, all right? And remember, I'm always here for you."

·⚙·

VIRGINIA ULRICH RAN her fingers through her son's

curly hair and smiled at her husband. "He looks just like you when he's asleep," she told him.

The nurses had found her a glider rocker so she could hold Charlie without straining her back. Not that she had much of a lap left to hold him on, but he was tiny for his age. And if he died before Samantha was born, it might be Samantha's only chance to be near her big brother. "Certain you don't want to hold him?"

Paul flinched and shifted his weight away from them. "No. Remember last time?"

"That wasn't your fault," she assured him. "He had a choking spell, that's why he stopped breathing, you know that."

Her husband hunched, his hands in his pockets of his designer suit, safely tucked away where they could do no harm. His eyes widened as he took in the dizzying array of medical equipment.

Lights of every color blinked and swirled, mysterious numbers comprising an alien language flashed above them. Virginia prided herself on being able to interpret all the medical technicalities, it was important to know what was going on every second in a place like this. But she understood how overwhelming it could be for Paul.

"Better safe than sorry," he said. "I talked to Sterling about Hart. He said he'd make certain that she stayed far away from Charlie."

"Thank you. I know how busy you are."

"Alan King is going to talk to his brother, see if Richard might know anything useful about her as well."

"I might call Richard myself," Virginia said, although she dreaded the thought of seeing the once-vibrant man reduced to such a weakened state. "I want to see how he's recovering."

Paul glanced at his watch. "I've got to get going,"

he told her, leaning down to kiss her forehead. Gingerly, he patted Charlie's blonde curls, taking care not to disturb any of the medical apparatus. He bumped into the IV pole as he turned to leave, tripped, then swore as he righted it once more. He practically ran from their bedside.

"Good night," Virginia said, returning her attention to Charlie.

She didn't disturb the IV tubing as she rocked him. Charlie moved slightly, and the monitor alarm sounded. Damn thing was too sensitive, always going off at the slightest movement. Virginia reached up and turned it off.

Charlie needed his sleep after everything he'd been through; all the poking and prodding. More blood work, another chest X-ray, an orthopedic resident manhandling him, and placing a splint on the leg where Cassandra Hart had drilled into his bone.

At least the nurses were nice. They let her give Charlie a sponge bath and showed her how to change the dressing on his leg so that no infection would creep into his bone.

Maybe later today they'd let Charlie eat. She had that much to look forward to. Little enough, but it would be a comfort for Charlie.

Of course they still had no answers. Even Dr. Sterling seemed disappointed. He'd scheduled more tests—a MRI of Charlie's head and another EEG. More doctors would be visiting also: neurology, pulmonary medicine, and a new specialist in metabolic diseases.

She'd have to tell Charlie's and George's stories over and over again, each doctor asking the same questions. After everything that had happened with George, she doubted that they'd have any answers for her, but she was willing to try anything.

God, she was so tired. If she could just rest her eyes for a moment.

Charlie's jerking startled her. He was having a full-blown seizure this time, his lips and face a dreadful shade of blue.

"Someone help me!" Virginia called out. Immediately the curtain that gave them what little privacy they could get was pulled back and Gail, one of the day shift nurses, was there. Virginia thrust Charlie's tiny body at her. "He's having a seizure."

"It's okay, Virginia, we'll take care of him," Gail said as she slid Charlie onto the bed and grabbed the oxygen. "Page the resident, stat! And get me respiratory, he's gone apneic," she called over to one of her colleagues.

Virginia turned the monitor back on and hovered near the head of the bed. "Is there anything I can do?"

"How long ago did the seizure start?"

"I called you right away. I've never seen anything like this—please help him. Someone call Dr. Sterling, please!" Virginia pleaded, rubbing her belly. Samantha was kicking like crazy, agitated by what was happening to her brother, no doubt.

The resident arrived and took over. "I'll call him right now, Mrs. Ulrich," she told Virginia. "You'll have to step outside for a moment."

The ward clerk ushered Virginia through the sliding doors that guarded the entrance to the PICU.

Virginia looked back through the glass doors, frustrated that she couldn't be with Charlie. She ought to be used to it by now. How many times had they kicked her out of the room when George was taking a turn for the worse? She just wished that the doctors and nurses realized how awful it was for family to be shunted aside at the very times when their children needed them most.

She sighed. She could only hope that Charlie was in good hands.

Virginia walked across to the family waiting area. For once the telephone was available so she called Paul on his cell phone.

"Yes?" he sounded annoyed and tired.

"It's me. Can you come back to the hospital?"

"What happened? How's Charlie?"

"Not so good. He had another seizure. They're putting him on the ventilator."

Silence. She could picture his jaw tightening. Paul was a man of few words, but strong emotions.

"I'll be right there, I just have to get Thayer to take over this depo." He hung up.

Virginia slumped down in the chair. The father of one of the other children in the PICU came in. He looked even worse than she felt, unshaven with that panic-stricken gaze of a parent about to see his child leave this earth before him. Virginia nodded to him but he ignored her, just stood by the window, looking out with unfocused eyes, his posture one of defeat.

She stood and left the room. She'd seen that look too many times before, parents too wrapped up in their own situations to interact with anyone else. But she needed to talk to someone, someone who could help her understand what was going on with Charlie. Ignoring the signs asking her not to use her cell phone, Virginia dialed Richard King's home number.

⁂

"Zone Seven, Major Case Squad, Detective Wallace speaking. Hi, Mrs. Drake. Yes, he is. Oh yes, we're very pleased to have him back with us." Wallace waggled his fingers at Drake and propped his feet on Drake's desk as he spoke. "Oh no, Mrs. Drake, we're not overworking him. No ma'am, wouldn't dream of it."

Wallace held the phone away from Drake, swiveling out of reach. Drake lunged for the receiver, yanking it from the other detective's hand.

"Don't you have work to do?" he asked, sliding into his desk chair once Wallace leveraged his bulk out of it. "Mom, why are you calling me here?"

"Is that anyway to greet your mother?" Muriel Drake demanded.

"Sorry. Hi, Mom, how are you? How's the weather?"

"I'm fine except for worrying myself sick about you. You weren't at home when I called, three times. I knew you went back to work too soon, you're working yourself too hard—"

"Take a breath, Mom. I'm fine. I just came in to get caught up on paperwork, you know how that is."

"The doctors said you shouldn't push yourself too hard."

"Mom, the doctor cleared me for duty, said I was fine."

"Still." Muriel paused, and Drake hoped she'd run out of steam. "I think I should come up there, you need someone to look after you. There's a flight," she paused, "Thursday. It gets in at four-twenty."

"How do you know that?" Drake had long ago accepted that his mother was omniscient in many things, but airline schedules?

"Just got that high speed Internet. And a new computer to go with it."

Great, just what the world needed, Muriel Drake had entered the information age. "Really Mom, there's no need—"

"It's no problem at all. Maybe this trip I'll be able to meet that doctor you've been talking about."

Drake rubbed a hand over his cheek, remembering the sting of Hart's slap. He looked down at the murder books scattered over his desktop and decided to change the subject. "Did Dad ever mention a case he was working, back before he was promoted?"

"Your dad never talked about his work, Remy, you know that," she said, using his childhood nickname. "Maybe if he had, he would have lived longer. You remember that when you get married."

"Yes, ma'am." Married? Rate he was going, he might never *date* again. The thought left him feeling empty. He shrugged it aside. He and Hart would work things out—they just needed time, that's all. Time and space.

And trust. A little communication wouldn't hurt. And the ability to be in the same room without arguing.

Damn, this was going to be a lot harder than he ever imagined. Was it worth it?

Muriel's voice pulled him back to the present. "Fine. I'll see you in two days. You'll pick me up, won't you?"

"Yes."

"Bye then."

Drake hung up and ran his fingers through his hair. What had he done to deserve this? First Hart was pissed at him—and she had no right to be, because he was right. Now his mother was coming for a visit. And he needed time to go through these case files in detail, see where the next step led in tracking a killer.

He gathered the papers together, and then spotted the sketch of the Trevasians' dog. He'd promised the kids he'd take a look. Wouldn't hurt to swing by on his way home.

Drake lifted the hefty bundle of murder books and trudged downstairs to his car. He tried hard not to think about the fact that Hart wouldn't be waiting for him, but couldn't help wishing for a glimpse of her smile, the healing touch of her hands, anything to take away this foreboding that had overcome him. This feeling that somewhere out there a killer was getting ready to strike again.

CASSIE'S ANKLE SCREAMED at her with each step she climbed as she walked back up the three flights to the PICU. But her nerves were much too jangled to consider taking an elevator. She hated the tiny metal boxes of doom even in the best of circumstances.

She crept into the ICU through the back door, feeling like a spy crossing into enemy territory. She wanted to warn Tammy Washington about the CYS referral before someone less sympathetic, like Sterling, did. Once at the nurses' station, she looked over at Charlie's bedside and was surprised to see him on a ventilator. What happened?

Cassie approached the nurse taking care of Charlie. "When did he go on the vent?"

The nurse looked up, annoyed by the interruption. "He had another seizure, went apneic."

"Was the mother here?"

"Of course she was. Virginia almost never leaves his bedside." The nurse bent to chart a set of vitals.

"Did you see the seizure? What kind was it?" Cassie pressed.

"Generalized tonic clonic. Now really, Dr. Hart, I have work to do."

"Did you see the start of it? Was it focal in the

beginning?"

"No, I didn't see it. Virginia was holding him and had the curtains closed. But she's an excellent observer, and she said that it was generalized." The nurse straightened and faced Cassie. "I understand your interest in Charlie, Dr. Hart. But we do know what we're doing up here—"

"I wasn't trying to imply that you didn't. I was curious because the seizure activity I saw in the ER was focal, that's all."

The nurse said nothing, merely turned her back and continued her work. Cassie wandered over to the nurses' station. Usually the PICU nurses were overprotective. Obviously they held no suspicions about Virginia Ulrich.

Cassie found Charlie's old charts stacked at the rack behind the desk. She didn't want to sit out in front, reading them where everyone could watch her, so she took them around the corner to the tiny break room. She poured herself a cup of coffee, sat, and began to read.

Charlie's course was a little less rocky, but even more perplexing than his brother's had been. Because of George's history, he was placed on the monitor immediately after birth. He had apparently thrived until he was four months old. The day after his four-month checkup, when he received his second set of immunizations, he had a cyanotic spell that required CPR.

Again the cycle of hospitalization, diagnostic testing, and discharge home began. Again the long list of medications that kept on growing, the failure to gain weight and then weight loss, special formula mixtures, and no diagnosis found.

George's downhill decline had been very rapid

over the two to three months before his death. Charlie's course seemed more of a roller coaster ride. Devastating setbacks followed by spectacular improvements.

Improvements, which, according to the nursing and social work notes, seemed wholly the product of Virginia Ulrich's dedication and untiring devotion to Charlie, rather than to any miracle of modern medicine. No wonder the nurses were so protective of Virginia.

Sterling's notes seemed to indicate that he had reached the conclusion that the affliction both Charlie and his brother endured was genetic in origin. He counseled against further pregnancies and Cassie was surprised to see in one clinic note an undercurrent of anger as he wrote that Virginia was pregnant again.

Charlie was hospitalized afterwards for unrelenting vomiting and dehydration. Even in the hospital he continued to have problems and exploratory surgery was done to look for a malrotation of his intestines.

She read the nursing notes from after the surgery. The surgeon had found no abnormalities but had removed his appendix anyway. Charlie had an uneventful recovery. They were able to feed him once more and weaned him from his medications. But Cassie noted that the nurses commented that his mother was not present for the week after Charlie's surgery. A social work note explained why. Mrs. Ulrich had suffered a miscarriage.

Charlie continued to improve and was able to go home. At his next clinic visit, Sterling's tone was optimistic, and he commented that Mr. Ulrich was planning to undergo a vasectomy.

Obviously not soon enough, given Virginia Ulrich's current advanced state of pregnancy. And, if

Cassie was right, until another child replaced him, Charlie remained valuable to his mother. Her hands tightened into fists and she rolled her shoulders to try to ease the tension there. Even for a cynic like her, it felt unnatural to be thinking these thoughts about a mother.

She closed the chart. There was still nothing that gave her any proof, but now it was more critical than ever that she do something to protect Charlie. But what?

She was returning the chart to the nurses' station when she turned the corner and almost ran over Virginia Ulrich. Cassie fumbled for words, trying to keep her expression neutral.

"Dr. Hart." Virginia looked at the chart in Cassie's hands. "What are you doing with Charlie's old records?"

"I came up to see how he was doing," Cassie said, returning the chart to its rightful place. "I was sorry to hear he had another seizure."

Virginia pursed her lips and stared at Cassie. "Dr. Sterling is on his way. I'm certain he'll get to the bottom of all this. Have you read any of his work?"

"No, I haven't."

"Well, he's the expert in this field," Virginia continued, dismissing any skills that Cassie may have. "He left some copies of his articles. Here." She rounded the nurses' desk with an air of familiarity and superiority, as if this was her rightful place, took a stack of reprinted journal articles from an empty slot in the chart rack and thrust them at Cassie. "Maybe you'll find them enlightening."

"Thanks," Cassie mumbled, still amazed by the woman's audacity. The chart rack and nurses' station were strictly off limits to non-medical personnel. Cassie picked up Antwan Washington's chart. "Guess I'd better check on my other patient up here." She tried to sound casual.

"I appreciate your interest in Charlie's case," Virginia went on. "I understand that he holds some fascination as a diagnostic dilemma, but in the future please direct your questions to Dr. Sterling instead of going through confidential medical records." Her tone had hardened and Cassie looked up, surprised. "I'm sure you agree that you are the last person who should be treating my son. Given my relationship with your ex-husband, I'm sure it is difficult for you to remain objective, isn't it, Dr. Hart?"

"I don't have any idea what you're talking about."

"Richard is a very close friend of mine. My husband works with his brother. I'm sure you can appreciate how dismayed they were when they heard you were involved in Charlie's case. Richard's brother went so far as to suggest that we have Dr. Sterling ban you from further contact with Charlie, said you were unstable, might even try to harm Charlie."

Cassie felt her face flush with anger. "How dare you. I would never—"

"Exactly what I told him. That you would never allow your personal emotions interfere with the care of a patient. I told him it wasn't your fault that you couldn't start a simple IV in Charlie, that you had to resort to a painful and potentially dangerous procedure."

"His veins were collapsed, the seizure—"

"Of course it was your first day back," Virginia continued, ignoring Cassie's protests. "You were rusty after taking all that time off. I'm sure it had nothing to do with who I am or the fact that I'm a friend of Richard's."

"Richard has nothing to do with me any longer. I don't care who his friends are." Cassie's voice emerged louder than she intended, drawing stares from several nurses nearby.

"I guess that explains why you never visited him while he was in the ICU, fighting for his life. After you put him there."

Cassie straightened to her full height, engaging Virginia head on. Virginia's face was placid, her voice low and steady as if she were discussing the latest summer fashion trends. Cassie's fists tightened and she rammed them into the pockets of her lab coat. "I didn't give Richard those drugs, he took them by accident. They were intended to kill me. And the reason I didn't visit him was because his brother forbid it. All of which has absolutely nothing to do with how I treated your son, Mrs. Ulrich. I treated Charlie with the same dedication and care I give to any of my patients."

Virginia smiled placidly at her as one of the nurses approached. "I guess that explains why there's another little boy in a coma, fighting for his life. Your track record speaks for itself, Dr. Hart."

"Can I get you anything, Virginia?" the nurse asked before Cassie could answer.

"Oh, no thanks, Gail. I was just wondering if Dr. Sterling would be here soon."

"He said he'd be right in. I'm getting coffee if you want any."

Cassie took the opportunity to escape before her temper got the better of her, opening Antwan's chart and turning her back on the two of them. Her hands shook with anger. She had to fight to keep the words before her in focus. It was even harder to silence the nagging voice in her mind that Virginia had spoken the truth, that she was to blame for missing something on

Monday when she first cared for Antwan.

And if she missed something then, what else had she messed up?

She swallowed hard and stilled her trembling hands. Scanning Antwan's chart, she hoped to find that he had made some progress since she saw him two hours ago. There was nothing substantial, she noted with a frown. They had almost weaned him from the ventilator, but he was still unconscious. The neurologists planned to repeat the EEG in the morning.

She went over to his cubicle. Tammy Washington was on the phone, talking angrily to someone, but hung up when she saw Cassie.

"Hi, I just wanted to see how everything's going," Cassie said, moving to Antwan's side.

"How do you think?" Tammy demanded. "I can't believe you're here, showing your face! They're trying to take my baby from me!" The mother's anger hit Cassie like a gale force blast.

"I tried to—"

"I don't care what you tried," Tammy interrupted. "This is my baby. I ain't got anyone to help me, but I've raised him the best I can. I don't need the likes of you coming around and telling me I done it all wrong!"

"Tammy," Cassie tried to calm her. "I'm certain that they only want what's best for Antwan, just like you do."

"Like hell they do! Is it best for my baby that he go and live with strangers? You know who that was on the phone? My work saying don't bother to come back! I never took nothing from nobody my whole life and now thanks to you—" she seemed to run out of words as her rage reached a crescendo. She stood and pushed Cassie's hand away from Antwan.

"I'm sorry. If there's anything I can do—"

"Ain't you done enough? Just get out, I don't want you anywhere near my baby! You all can just go to hell!" She was crying now.

Cassie left, the mother's anger a tsunami sweeping her from the room. She turned to leave the PICU, but not before she saw Virginia Ulrich smiling at her.

Out in the corridor, she added Sterling's journal articles to the stack of notes bulging out of her lab coat pockets. She lowered her head and headed down the hall to the stairwell, not wanting to make eye contact with anyone.

Better work on your bedside manner, the cynic in her whispered. Cassie felt awful about Tammy Washington. This was just what she'd been trying to avoid. The woman had terrific strength and a lot of pride. Take that away and what resources would she have left to help her son through this?

And somehow she was certain Virginia wouldn't let things rest. She had the feeling Charlie's mother had read her intentions and suspicions and would be making her life hell unless she backed off.

She returned to her office and found the number for Children and Youth. Too bad Virginia Ulrich didn't know her better. Then she'd know that being a pigheaded, stubborn, hyper-driven, pain in the ass was Cassie's most endearing quality. One of the few things that Cassie surpassed even her grandmother, Rosa, in. And it had nothing to do with the Ulrichs being friends with Richard. Well, maybe it did—but only in the sense that she refused to let Richard or his powerful family and friends intimidate her.

"Childline, how may I help you?"

"I'd like to report a suspected case of abuse."

CHAPTER 12

"Pardon my French, but you look like shit," Jimmy Dolan told his partner when Drake dragged himself through the doorway at the top of the steps the next morning. The Major Case Squad's office was on the fourth floor, and Drake looked like he'd felt every one of those steps. It didn't help that he was hauling about twelve pounds worth of murder books.

Jimmy handed his partner a cup of fresh coffee and gestured to the bag of Krispy Kremes on his desk. To hell with stereotypes. Ever since his wife, Denise, had banned donuts and other "junk food" from their home, calling them a Madison Avenue conspiracy to cripple the nation, work was his only chance to indulge.

"Hope you look so ragged out because you got some make up sex last night," Jimmy went on. Everyone in the House had heard about Hart and Morris—and Drake's reaction in the ER.

Personally, Jimmy liked Hart's style. The girl had guts even if she did sometimes lack finesse. He had to admit, she'd gotten the job done without bloodshed. He wouldn't necessarily have trusted Spanos to do the same—but his opinion was definitely in the minority. Last thing the cops needed was the civilian populace trying to do their job for them.

Drake hung his head low and didn't answer. So, still fighting with Hart. Which meant no tales of bedroom calisthenics. He sighed. Denise would be upset to hear that Drake was having relationship problems. Again. And she'd somehow manage to blame it on Jimmy. God forbid Drake ever take responsibility for his own actions.

Jimmy munched on a honey-glazed still warm from the ovens. Drake was almost thirty-five but every woman Jimmy'd ever seen him with seemed to either want to baby him or fuck him. Or both.

Except Hart. Which was probably why Jimmy liked the doctor so much—she seemed the perfect match for his wayward partner. Even if Denise didn't approve of her. Not after Hart almost got Drake killed six weeks ago.

But Denise probably would never accept any woman as being good enough for Drake.

"I thought we'd start with Regina Eades' husband and son," Jimmy said.

Drake nodded, his eyes brightening somewhat after the coffee. "I already set us up for nine o'clock. I ran everyone last night when the computer was free," he explained when Jimmy looked at him in surprise. He pulled a sheet of paper from his notebook and slid it across the desk. "Here are the current addresses. The Kents are divorced. I could only find the wife. The Frantzs are still in the same house over on the Northside, and the Clearys moved to Plum."

Jimmy nodded in satisfaction. One thing about DJ—once he was on board, he put his heart and soul into closing a case. A lot like his dad that way. "Nice work. Let's roll."

·⦿·

CLINTON EADES HAD moved from the city proper to an upscale neighborhood just outside of Murrysville. Once they passed the brick arch guarding the entrance of the development, the streets became meandering narrow lanes that threatened to curve back on themselves. They crossed Bear Meadow Lane, turned off Deer Leap onto Fox Hollow Road and finally made their way to Possum Path.

The houses were large monstrosities of brick and stone placed on too-small lots with manicured squares of lawns. Despite the size of the houses, it seemed as if children were as extinct as the wildlife in this suburban oasis. There were no sidewalks, no evidence of bikes, trikes, or toys and none of the chalk graffiti that littered Jimmy's neighborhood.

He found the Eades house and pulled the white Intrepid into the driveway. As he closed the driver's door and waited for Drake, he saw that theirs was the only car exposed to the light of day.

"If one of the Stepford wives answers the door, I'm outta here," he told Drake.

He remembered the man, Eades, as mid-thirties, a short, skinny man with bony hands that Jimmy had worried about crushing when he shook them. A CPA in one of the firms downtown, Eades specialized in managing pro-athletes' money, rolling short-term millions into long-term security. That had been Jimmy's lead in, their common ground. Denise was a financial planner, worked with most of the guys at the House, helping them to eke mortgage payments or tuition savings out of a city employee's take home pay.

While they waited for the door to be answered, Jimmy wondered how Eades had changed in the eight years since he'd lost his wife. He'd guessed that he'd somehow recovered from his grief, probably by immersing himself in his work. This house was a definite step up from the Bloomfield duplex he'd last interviewed the CPA in.

The door opened. A gaunt man with thinning red hair wearing jeans, a Pitt sweatshirt, and Fruit Loops in his mustache answered the door.

"Detective Dolan," he greeted them with a smile that came a few beats too late. "Come in, come in." Clinton Eades stepped aside, and they joined him inside the slate-floored foyer.

"I didn't realize it was so late," Eades continued, rambling on in breakneck fashion. He wiped the cereal from his mustache and grinned. "Food fight with the two year old—you know how it goes. Stella," he called out to the rear of the house, the kitchen presumably, "I'll be in my study."

Without waiting for an answer, he led the way into a large room paneled in knotty pine with a hunter green hobnail sofa and a desk that would rival a pool table for square footage. Eades took the seat behind the desk, barricading himself from them.

"This is Detective Drake," Jimmy introduced DJ. "If you don't mind, he'll just take some notes. And I'll record us, so in case I have to refresh my memory later I won't need to bother you again." Eades agreed readily to the prospect of not having to see the policemen again.

"Has there been—have you found—" His voice broke.

"No sir, I'm sorry to say. Periodically we try to

revisit these cases. We don't want to ever give up on them."

Eades nodded, but the look in his face said that he'd already given up on finding his wife's killer. "I appreciate that."

"Is Stella your new wife?" Jimmy asked, moving to perch on a windowsill to one side of the desk, leaving Drake unobtrusive in the background.

"No, our housekeeper." Eades reached for a framed photo that sat on his desk and passed it to Jimmy. "That's Cynthia, my wife. We got married three, no . . . four years ago. She's a realtor. And that's Billy, our son. He was only eight months when that was taken."

"And your older son, Mitchell? How is he doing? He'd be what, sixteen now?"

The father's face blanched, and the skin around his eyes tightened, revealing deeply etched lines there.

"Mitchell," the name seemed painful for him to speak, "was never the same, after—" He paused and looked past Jimmy, out the window. "I tried to get him help, counseling, kept him in school as long as I could—they said the routine would be good for him. But things just kept getting worse. Fights, bullying the other kids. Stealing things from teacher's desks, lying. Then, when he was in sixth grade a teacher found him in the boys room, smoking pot, and forcing some third graders to strip naked and urinate in front of him."

Jimmy said nothing, allowing the father to collect his memories of the painful past. "Mitch was thirteen then," Eades continued after a moment, still not making eye contact. "We had to go to court. They ordered him into a residential treatment program—out near Latrobe. I was only allowed to visit him on weekends. I thought it was just a phase, a result of everything he'd been through, but when he came home, things only got worse. He beat up a teacher—broke the man's arm with a baseball bat, and the judge sent him to juvenile detention. But he got into trouble there—went on a rampage one night, right before he was due to be released, and they sent him to another residential facility—this one with higher security. He's still there. They said next time he does anything he'll be charged as an adult.

"He won't talk to me or see me anymore. I send him letters, pictures of his brother, but the envelopes come back unopened. This is the last thing he sent me." Eades slid open the desk drawer and pulled out a thin sheet of lined notebook paper. The painfully printed pencil strokes were marred by erasures and smudged fingerprints. "See for yourself."

Jimmy glanced at the note.

"Dad," it read, "don't send no more pictures especially of Billy. I can't see him or you no more, so don't come here or call. It's the only way I can take care of you all. Good bye. PS: when you see Mom tell her I'm sorry, sorry." He passed the note to Drake.

Eades hadn't moved, still staring out the window, silent tears sliding from his eyes. "The day he wrote that, Mitchell tried to kill himself," he told them. "That bastard took everything from me—Regina, Mitchell. God, I wish he'd come after me instead."

The father swiped a hand across his cheeks, finally turning to face Jimmy. "Even if you caught him now, it would be too late, wouldn't it, Detective?"

"Maybe not for someone else's family," was the best Jimmy could offer. Eades nodded slowly. "When Mitch said 'when you see Mom', he wasn't talking about your new wife, was he?"

"No. After Regina was—died—we used to pray

together every night, talk to her, in a way. Mitch used to always whisper things for me to tell her when I saw her, he couldn't talk to her himself. Poor kid was always thinking I was going to end up dead too, I guess. I don't think he ever had a full night's sleep since that day—he never felt safe again."

"It must have been difficult for you to try to be both mother and father to him. While suffering your loss as well."

Eades shrugged. "To tell the truth, those bedtime prayers were about the only time we ever talked. I mean, more than please pass the ketchup, and Mitch gave up on those a few months later. It was like he locked me out of his world. I kept food on the table and clothes on his back but no matter how much I was there for him, it wasn't enough. I just didn't have what he needed."

"I'm sure you did the best you could," Drake put in as he returned Mitchell's letter to Eades. Jimmy knew his partner was getting impatient. DJ hated the emotional stuff, always wanted to cut to the chase.

The father shrugged and deposited the evidence of his failure back into the depths of the desk drawer.

"If you could just think a moment, remember back to the day of your wife's murder," Jimmy went on after giving Eades a moment to collect himself. "What was the routine for Mitchell supposed to be?"

"The same as always for a Tuesday or Thursday. Regina would drop him at school on her way to open the studio. He had school, and then met with his speech therapist until four o'clock when he'd walk over to the studio and wait for Regina to drive him home. I worked seven to three, so the rest of the week, I'd pick him up from school myself."

"And besides you and your wife and the therapist,

who else would have known Mitchell's schedule? A babysitter? Neighbors? Did he mention his therapy sessions to anyone else?"

Eades shook his head. "No one knew except the school. Mitch was very upset about needing speech therapy, and refused to do it during the regular classroom session that the school offered. Said it made him feel like a dummy, so he told all his friends he was working on a special extra credit project." He frowned. "Why all these questions about Mitch? You spoke with the therapist, you know all this already."

"We think the killer—" Jimmy lowered his voice, although he knew there was no way to soften the blow. "Might have known your son's schedule, might have purposely arranged things so that Mitchell would be the one to find your wife's body."

Eades flinched at that. Jimmy could understand his discomfort at the idea. Bad enough that someone would want to kill your wife in a horrible fashion. But also to plan it so your only child would be tortured, and haunted by the display was a grotesque thought.

One that only a cop who'd seen too much of the evil people could do would think of. Jimmy calculated how long he'd have until his time toward a full pension was in. Eight years. Days like today, that seemed for-fucking-ever.

⁘⦿⁘

"Dr. Hart, stat to Trauma One."

Cassie rushed to the trauma room. Once there she found a pair of college-aged boys hovering over a gurney bearing a little old lady wearing only a thin flannel nightgown.

"What's the story?" she asked, pulling on her

gloves.

"She's our landlady," one of the students answered. "We just found her like this, she'd left her back door open and we saw it when we were leaving for class this morning—"

"Seventy-two year old found cold and unresponsive on her kitchen floor," Rachel translated. "Brought in by private vehicle, history of angina and hypertension, on nitro and Lasix. No other meds, no allergies." As she spoke, two other nurses cut the nightgown from the woman and began to get her vital signs. Cassie moved to assess her patient.

"Bag her, she's not breathing. She's cold—someone grab a core temp." Cassie slid her fingers to the woman's carotid pulse and waited a full minute. The monitor showed a slow, irregular heartbeat, but she felt no pulse. "Start chest compressions. Warmed IV fluid, two lines, make sure the oxygen is heated too." She barked out the commands as she completed her examination.

The patient had an obvious fractured left hip and from the imprint on her skin, had been lying on the tile floor overnight. She was now hypothermic to the point where her heart had slowed and no oxygen could reach her brain. If Cassie could restart her heart and warm her, she had a fair prognosis. Big if, especially given her age and underlying heart disease.

Just one problem. Hypothermic victims were notoriously susceptible to fatal heart arrhythmias. Any action Cassie took might trigger a lethal heart rhythm.

She followed the ALS algorithm and instilled warmed fluid into the abdominal cavity where it could diffuse its heat to her patient's organs. Despite her efforts, the patient's heart rhythm deteriorated into ventricular fibrillation, exactly what Cassie feared would happen.

"Charge the paddles." She gave three shocks in rapid succession, hoping to restart the patient's heart. No result. "Another epi."

Cassie looked over through the open door as a nurse rushed in with the lab results. Virginia Ulrich stood at the nurses' station talking with Rachel. Probably trying to find out if Cassie was the one who called Children and Youth.

"Epi's in."

"Again three-sixty," she said. "Clear!" She hit the button to send the electricity to the monitor pads.

A strange man in a business suit came to the open doorway. "Dr. Hart. Cassandra Hart?" he called out as if he were a bellhop with a telegram. Beyond him Cassie could see that Richard had joined Virginia Ulrich and Rachel and that they all watched her with anticipation.

"Out! We're in the middle of a resuscitation," she snapped.

Instead of being intimidated or leaving, the man entered and approached her. "Are you Dr. Cassandra Hart?"

"Yes, and this lady is trying her best to die, so whatever you want it can wait." She turned her back on him.

Then she felt something slide into the back pocket of her scrubs. She whirled around, amazed at the man's rudeness only to see him give her a quick wave.

"Consider yourself served, Dr. Hart." He walked out.

Cassie looked past him to see both Richard and Virginia Ulrich smiling at her. Rachel's customary dour look had deepened. Then she realized that everyone in the trauma room was staring at her.

"Focus, people," she directed her team. "Any pulse?"

"No pulse."

"Repeat the epi. Shock again at three-sixty. What's her temp?"

"Rectal temp is ninety-six."

Damn, that was almost normal, definitely warm enough that the patient should have responded to their treatment. She quickly re-assessed the patient. She didn't see anything that they had overlooked.

Cassie sighed, one hand on the woman's neck, her fingers searching in vain for a pulse. "Anyone have any ideas?" she asked. Sometimes as leader of a code you became too focused and could miss something.

"It's been almost forty minutes," one of the nurses said quietly, her eyes downcast.

The rest of the team remained silent, each looking at the other professionals in the room.

"Anyone object to calling it?" Again silence. "Okay, time of death is eleven twenty-two am. Thank you everyone. You all did good work."

She left her team to go search for the college students and see if any next of kin had arrived.

Only afterwards did she remember the paper the man had shoved into her pocket. She pulled it out and quickly scanned it. Her eyes widened. It was a restraining order issued by Judge Franklin forbidding her from coming anywhere within fifty feet of Charles Ulrich. What the hell?

She started back toward the nurses' station but neither Rachel or Virginia Ulrich were there. Instead she found her boss, Ed Castro.

"I was just getting ready to call you. A man came into the middle of a resuscitation and gave me this." She stopped when she saw the look on Ed's face. He was furious. At her.

"Not here. My office."

He strode back down the corridor to his office. It wasn't until he ushered her inside and shut the door that Cassie became worried. She was in trouble, big trouble. Ed Castro was one of the most agreeable men she'd ever met—easy going was an understatement for his managerial style. He never conducted business behind closed doors.

Then she saw who was seated in the chair in front of the desk. Karl Sterling, a frown marring his Norman Rockwell features.

"What the hell's going on?" Ed placed his hands on his desk and leaned forward. "I leave for two days-"

Cassie held up the restraining order. "I have no idea. I don't understand."

"Which is exactly the problem," Sterling put in. "Dr. Hart seems unable to follow simple departmental procedures, much less—"

"I'll handle this, Karl," Ed snapped. Cassie could see that much of his anger was due to Sterling's presence.

"Actually, the Executive Committee will be handling it. I am certain that they will recommend an immediate suspension."

"Suspension! But I haven't done anything wrong," Cassie protested.

"As if interfering with my patient and ignoring protocol isn't enough, don't you think that being the object of two malpractice suits warrants some action, Dr. Hart?" the pediatrician asked in an icy tone.

"Malpractice suits?" she managed to choke out.

"Ms. Tammy Washington is claiming medical neglect and failure to diagnose the illness of her son. While Mr. and Mrs. Ulrich are claiming medical battery," Sterling informed her.

"Battery?"

"They state you did not receive informed consent prior to performing the invasive, painful and dangerous procedure of inserting an IO line into their son."

"That's ridiculous!" She not only had obtained Virginia Ulrich's consent, she had it documented on videotape.

"You'll be able to tell your side of the story to the Executive Committee Friday morning at eight o'clock. And, I explained to Children and Youth that your report of suspected neglect was the result of ignorance about the complexities of Charlie Ulrich's disease. Not that they'd take you seriously after today."

"That's enough, Karl," Ed put in.

"Very well then." The department chairman rose, his posture rigid. He stood in front of Cassie for a long moment, shaking his head as he stared at her. "I tried to help you, Dr. Hart. Believe me, I regret that it has come to this. Such a waste." He departed from the office, the elder statesman delegating his deputy to perform the dirty work.

"You won't believe who sat beside me on the shuttle from Washington," Ed began. "Senator George Ulrich—the same senator who canceled his appointment with me about the clinic funding. So, good political opportunist that I am, I'm thinking this is fate. I've got the entire flight with him as a captive audience."

His eyes narrowed, and he leaned forward, steepling his fingers. Cassie cringed, she knew that look all too well. The same look that Ed had given her when she and Maria, his middle daughter, had stolen Ed's prized El Dorado to go joyriding and had smashed the fender. The look that said—have you any idea what your impulsive, thoughtless actions have cost those around you?

She chewed her lower lip and looked down at the floor. It had been a long time since she had earned that look of disappointment from him. Ed was like a second father to her, and Cassie knew that in the past he'd defended her actions to administrators and others in the hospital hierarchy.

"I'm sure you can guess that I never had a chance," Ed continued, his glare not softening. "Instead I got an earful about an irresponsible ER physician who was intent on wrecking the Senator's family, turning their private tragedy into a public spectacle, and who wanted to take a gravely ill child away from his adoring mother. Seems this doctor is young, ambitious, and refuses to trust the judgment of our own Chairman of Pediatrics who has practiced for over thirty years and has won numerous awards."

Cassie looked up when he paused, bravely meeting his glare. "Ready to hear my side of it?"

"I don't care about your side or the Senator's or Sterling's. All I care about is what is best for our patients. Do you really think having the staff in an uproar, watching you and Sterling squabble is going to help Charlie Ulrich?"

"Of course not. But it's not my fault if Sterling lectured me where everyone could overhear it."

He raised an eyebrow at that. "From my understanding of it, you started things by not following procedure down here in the ER. And then you accused Virginia Ulrich of abusing her child right at the nurses' station in the ICU. My God, Cassie, why didn't you just announce it over the loudspeakers?"

"I had no intention of accusing anyone of anything." She faltered, remembering how smoothly

Virginia Ulrich had countered all her concerns. The mother had manipulated her into looking like a fool in front of the entire ICU.

"Let me guess," she went on the offensive, "Senator Ulrich said he'd give you the money for the clinic if I back down?"

"No, in fact he refused to discuss the clinic at all—said it would be a conflict of interest. And that, as a grandfather myself, I could understand how his mind wasn't focused on such matters while his grandson was so gravely ill."

"Oh." Hardly the underhanded diabolic machinations she'd expected from the Ulrich family.

"Then I return here to find these." He flung the malpractice notices onto the desktop. "Not to mention a complaint by Rachel Lloyd stating that you endangered the life of both a patient and one of our own nurses!"

The veins in his neck began to bulge—a definite danger sign. The ER staff was like family to Ed. No one messed with them, not even his goddaughter.

"I was trying to—" she stammered, taken aback by Ed's uncustomary outburst of anger. Ed often regaled her with stories of the explosive tempers of his Cuban father and Jewish mother, but he always prided himself on his own even temperament.

"You were trying to do the police's job for them," Ed cut in, his voice deceptively soft and level, "again. I seem to recall you doing the same thing two months ago—getting yourself and Drake almost killed in the process."

"But—"

"No buts! You don't carry a badge, you carry a stethoscope. You have no business interfering with the police or their handling of a potentially violent situation in my ER."

She cringed. Ed's disapproval hurt almost as much as Drake's had. Ed always supported her choices when it came to her patients and their care, he had always trusted her judgment. Until now.

"It doesn't help matters that the woman you're accusing was having an affair with your ex-husband while you were married. Makes it look like you're out for payback, targeting her."

Cassie shook her head in confusion. "Richard and Virginia had an affair?"

"You didn't know? I've been back less than half a day and several people made a point of mentioning it to me—"

"No, I didn't know. He never—I never—" She stood, planted her palms on his desk top and leaned forward, meeting his gaze. "Ed, you have to believe me. I had no idea who Virginia Ulrich was when I met her. Maybe she looked a little familiar, but after I heard her husband works with Richard's brother, I thought I must have seen her somewhere socially."

He pursed his lips but finally acknowledged his acceptance of her statement with a slight nod. "Still, it looks bad. Very bad."

"What are you going to do?"

He sighed. "I don't have any choice. As of now, you're on vacation until the Executive Committee renders their verdict."

She was silent. The Executive Committee was composed of department heads and had the power to suspend, or even revoke her privileges. Which basically translated to a huge blemish on her career, one which would follow her everywhere she went.

The only thing worse would be actually being found guilty of malpractice. She swallowed hard and nodded.

"Have you thought that maybe you came back to work too soon?" Ed asked, his voice lower now, his anger spent. "Maybe your judgment is impaired because of everything that happened—"

"I'm not crazy!" The words came out strident, harsher than she had intended and so carried with them the opposite connotation. Cassie tried again. "Really Ed, I'm fine."

He looked away, and she knew he was not convinced. She got to her feet and started to leave, then turned back. "You said we should focus on what's best for our patients. Have you thought about what would be best for Charlie Ulrich if I am right? Would you at least look at what I've found?"

She held out the papers that had accumulated in the pockets of her lab coat, a peace offering.

"All right," he said, taking the stack from her. "But this really is more a matter of investigating, not diagnosing—what does Drake say? He's got good instincts about these things."

Cassie looked down. Drake and Ed were friends, partners in the community clinic.

"You haven't told him, have you?" Ed asked.

"We're kind of taking things easy right now," Cassie tried to sound nonchalant and failed. "He needs some space." Why did it sound so reasonable when Adeena said it and so weak coming from her?

Ed frowned, then nodded. "Do you want me to talk to him about Charlie's case? I'd trust his judgment, even take it to the Executive Committee as an objective evaluation if you'd like."

It was an offer that was generous—and one she couldn't accept. Drake was her problem, her responsibility—as was Charlie Ulrich. "No, that's okay, I'll talk to him myself."

"Richard, I need you to do something for me." Virginia leaned forward across the cafeteria table and gently brushed a breadcrumb from his cheek.

Richard King reveled in the warmth of her touch. Ever since his accident, Virginia seemed the only person willing to touch him, to treat him as a man. Why couldn't his Ella touch him like that? He looked away, his vision blurring as he remembered Cassandra in his arms, her face lit up with a smile meant solely for him. Her hand in his, her body beneath his . . .

"This is important." Virginia's voice returned his attention to the crowded hospital cafeteria. "Important to me, to the baby."

His gaze dropped to her swollen belly. A baby. Something he'd always wanted with Cassandra, but they'd never had. Maybe if they had, things would have been different, so very different.

"Is there a problem with the baby?" His words slurred with concern. He reached an unsteady hand out to cover Virginia's. Their on-again, off-again affair had begun while he and Ella were still married, and had deepened into friendship. At least, that's how he remembered it.

"I'm afraid that filing suit against Dr. Hart isn't enough. I'm afraid that she'll manage to convince Children and Youth to take Charlie from me." Virginia didn't bother to hide her tears from him. He squeezed her hand, wished there was more comfort he could offer her. "Maybe Samantha as well, after she's born. Oh, Richard. What can I do? All I've wanted in my entire life is to be a mother, to have a family of my own."

He knew. Family was everything to Virginia. She'd been guilt-stricken over their affair, over the way he had seduced her away from Paul Ulrich. But the passion they had was overwhelming, irresistible for either of them. Virginia once told him that without Richard's love, she'd never have had the courage to survive Charlie's illness.

Once upon a time, Richard had been her strength, her hero. He'd never been that for Cassandra—she never needed rescuing, never needed anything from him. And he had so much he was desperate to give her.

"What can I do?" he asked, uncertain what to make of the anger that surged through him. It was Cassandra's fault that Virginia was in this position. Now he was the one who would have to make things right again. How could the one woman he loved more than anything also be the cause of such pain?

"Would you meet with the Senator? Tell him everything you know about Dr. Hart? Help him find a way to convince her that I haven't done anything wrong."

Richard blinked. Tell the Senator about Cassandra? All he remembered were fragments, blurry bits, and pieces of memories. What he held on to were the feelings, the overwhelming rapture she stirred in his soul every time he caught sight of her, heard her voice. And the hope, that tiny, secret spark of hope that one day she would be his again.

"I don't know," he started.

Virginia gripped his hand with a strength that was surprising. "You have to. I could lose my children because of her." Her eyes met his, their grey depths the color of winter storm clouds. "Please. The Senator's a powerful man, he can help you."

"Help me get my Ella back?"

He saw her cringe at his nickname for Cassandra. A cloud of sorrow crossed Virginia's features. He was sorry he couldn't remember more about their time together. A kaleidoscope of images: hands, bare flesh, rumpled clothes, panting in dark corners was the best he could do—although Virginia assured him there had been much more to their relationship than mere sex. Still, it paled in comparison to the love he had for Cassandra.

Virginia looked down at their hands and nodded. "Yes, Richard." Her voice lowered to a soft whisper that fanned the embers of his hope. "If that's what you want."

Richard felt his mouth stretch into a smile, even the side that was still dead to touch lifted higher at the thought of Cassandra Hart returning to him. This time it would be for forever, he vowed.

CHAPTER 13

AN HOUR LATER, Drake and Jimmy were back in the car, weaving along the curved streets leading away from Eades' house. Drake remembered now why everyone hated working cold cases. Facing victims and their families, ripping the scabs from never-healing wounds.

It was hard enough working with families freshly grief-stricken. At least then you could offer some hope that you'd find justice for their loved ones. But these interviews—remote from the immediate yearning for retribution, knowing that a loved one died in vain, a death meaningless even of protecting others by incarcerating the perpetrator—these interviews seemed only to remind a survivor that sometimes there was no justice in this world.

Eades had given them nothing new except a glimpse into his and his son's own private hell. And a handful of reports from Mitchell's school—both before and after his mother's murder. The papers had been haphazardly filed together in the dim recesses of a drawer. Eades had offered them to Jimmy, security against further visits from the detectives, the ghosts of the past.

As Jimmy drove, Drake skimmed over the detritus of Mitchell's third grade. The teachers initially described the boy as painfully shy and withdrawn, blaming his speech impediment. They said he was diligent in his work, but kept himself isolated and apart from the other children. At one point the school psychologist began to work with Mitchell, hoping to quell some of his social anxieties. He also tested the boy for any learning disorders that could be addressed.

"Anything good?" Jimmy asked.

"Kid was miserable even before he found his mother's body," Drake told him. "Real loner. The teachers describe him as quiet but sweet-tempered. But—"

"What?"

"The school psychologist said he saw signs of repressed anger, warned that the kid was aggressive, would be a bully, could potentially become violent."

"Sounds like the shrink was right on the money."

Drake didn't answer. He'd found the class photo and was staring at it, searching out the boy whose life was about to take a tragic turn. Mitchell was in the second row, on the end, closest to his teacher. He had his father's gaunt looks and red hair. The smile he flashed the camera seemed timid but wide, full of hope.

He compared the photo with the family photo in the murder book. The family shot was taken after the school one, probably at Eades' own studio, he thought, looking at the glossy Christmas card. Regina and Eades had their arms around each other's waists and one on each of Mitchell's shoulders, a circle of family unity. Their smiles were warm, and they looked into the camera with eyes set on the future.

Not their son. Mitchell's face wore what could be best described as a grimace. His lips were pressed together, his face pale, eyes hooded, looking down at his feet as if frightened that the camera might steal his soul if he faced it straight on.

Scared, Drake decided. The kid looked scared.

The Christmas shot was taken months before Regina Eades was found strangled in the dumpster behind her studio. What could have spooked the kid? When they stopped at the light on Route 22 he showed Jimmy the Christmas photo. "What do you think of the kid?"

"Cute, skinny. Fidgeting—probably pissed his parents made him dress up and put the tie on," Jimmy summarized, handing it back to Drake. "Why?"

Drake frowned and looked again. Jimmy was the expert—he had six-year-old twins, one boy, one girl. What did Drake know about kids? He was just letting his imagination run wild, trying to find some fresh trail to go down, he decided.

"Nothing."

But still, it nagged at the artist in him. The mother was a commercial photographer. Was this the best photo of her family that she could compose?

※◎※

SO THIS WAS what it felt like to be on vacation, Cassie thought as she slumped in her office chair. A dull throbbing echoed from her Achilles to the headache beginning behind her eyes. Richard and Virginia? Her marriage to Richard had been such a rollercoaster ride between euphoria and despair that she'd never had a chance to even imagine that he might be having an affair.

When things were good, he was extraordinarily attentive. They'd been virtually inseparable. And when things went sour she'd blamed his absences on the drugs and her own inability to help him.

How blind and stupid she had been. She grimaced and turned on her computer. Why was it that Richard and his world kept colliding with hers? All she wanted was to do her job, live her life, have a little peace and quiet. Was that too much to ask?

A few calls and e-mails later and her calendar was cleared, as was her desk. Cassie looked at the crystal Waterford clock in the shape of a flattened globe, the continents etched and frosted against a pale blue of water. A present from the senior residents last year. It was engraved : TO THE BEST TEACHER IN THE ER, THANKS FOR GETTING US READY FOR THE REAL WORLD.

Not even three thirty. On vacation for less than forty minutes and she was already bored out of her mind.

She stood and stretched. She'd love to go over to the dojo and see if Mr. Christean thought she was ready to return to her Kempo training, but she knew better. She had to get her timing back, regain her power before continuing to work on her brown belt. And she didn't want anyone at Mr. Christean's to see her until she was back at her fighting best. They all knew what had happened in February, and she refused to give them the chance to show any pity.

She wondered how Antwan and Charlie were doing upstairs in the PICU. As *persona non grata*, it was now off limits. Still, she could pull up their charts in the computer. She leaned over the back of her chair and began typing. Antwan was no better—but no worse either. And Charlie was enduring another round of consultations and tests, all with no answers. At least he was off the ventilator and clinically stable. Maybe her call to CYS had done some good, convinced Virginia Ulrich to keep her hands off her son for the time being.

Hang in there kid, I'm not giving up on you.

Cassie stared at the blank cinder block walls of her small broom closet of an office. She should ask Drake to paint her something, a *trompe l'oeil*, a window on the world beyond the cement walls with their institutional puke green paint.

If Drake ever spoke to her again after the way she treated him yesterday. She regretted the stubborn impulse that had caused her to refuse Ed Castro's offer of intervening with Drake. She was scared to face him; she could admit that. Was she more afraid that Drake would not agree with her about Virginia Ulrich or that he would take on Charlie's cause, but not take her back as well? Was there any way she could make it a package deal?

All or nothing—her and Charlie. How would Drake respond to that?

Cassie frowned. She knew how she would. She'd hate it, being forced, cornered—she couldn't do that to Drake.

So what could she do to help Charlie? Maybe find some convincing evidence to present to Drake and Ed. She thought about the notes she'd given Ed. There were a few gaps she'd hoped to fill in. Like Sheila Kaminsky and her suspicions that had led her to call CYS about Charlie's brother, George. And the medication error that had almost killed George and effectively ended that first CYS investigation. Sheila Kaminsky had been fired over that incident.

Where was the ex-nurse now? A few minutes with the computer, and Cassie had the answer:

Swissvale.

· ◎ ·

KAMINSKY SOUNDED EAGER to talk when Cassie called her. Cassie followed the ex-nurse's instructions and arrived at her apartment building half an hour later. The parking lot was rutted with potholes and the lines demarcating spaces had faded to invisibility, creating a working model for the chaos theory.

Cars were parked haphazardly. Some seemed purposely aimed at thwarting other's escape routes. None was newer than Cassie's own four-year-old Subaru and all sported dents and scraped paint—casualties of the parking wars.

The April sky was a brilliant blue that seemed to scoff at the paint peeling from the building, once upon a time a robin egg blue. Now the color had faded to a bilious shade etched with streaks of oxidation from acid rain. Once white trim around grimy windows and doorframes had yellowed like a smoker's teeth.

Cassie passed several people of indeterminate age sitting on the curb and steps leading to the front door of the two-story building. They were a mix of sexes, races, and the only thing they seemed to share were the cigarettes that hung between their limp fingers and a fascination with the parking lot. None of them raised their gaze from the mesmerizing asphalt to glance at Cassie as she zigzagged around them on the steps and entered.

Halfway house for psych patients? She noted the identical blank expressions that the residents all wore. A few had small blobs of dried spittle that they wiped absently with the back of their hands, hands that shook with the distinct tremor of tardive dyskinesia—a side effect of powerful anti-psychotics.

She made her way down the steps to Kaminsky's "garden" apartment in the rear of the building and rang the buzzer. Silence. As broken as the rest of the building and its residents.

Cassie raised her hand to knock but was surprised by the snap of a peephole sliding open. A watery brown eye, enlarged to grotesque proportions of the peephole, swam before her, darting in random directions before settling on Cassie.

"I'm Dr. Hart," she told the eye. "I called earlier."

The peephole slammed shut. The sound of several locks clicked and clanged before the door opened. A skinny hand squirreled out to grasp Cassie's arm and pull her inside. The door slammed shut behind her.

On the other side Cassie found herself in another world. What little furniture there was—two metal folding chairs with the name of a funeral home stenciled on the back, a upside down milk crate between them and a black and white thirteen inch TV with rabbit ears extended by a precarious arrangement of coat hangers and tin foil—was gathered into the middle of the room. The walls were covered with religious icons, prayer cards, crucifixes, even a black velvet Jesus whose sorrowful eyes followed her.

In between the religious mementoes someone was penciling and inking Bible verses in a random fashion—Job interwoven with the Song of Solomon, Psalms interrupted by letters to the Corinthians. The floor below was littered with votive candles, figurines of saints, and statues of the Virgin Mary draped with rosaries.

Cassie pulled her eyes away from the biblical feast to look upon its artist. Sheila Kaminsky was nothing like she'd pictured. Instead of a stocky, broad shouldered Polish matron, Cassie found herself looking upon the face of a saint. Thin, painfully so, and almost six foot tall, Kaminsky had long hair so blonde it glowed in a white halo around her. She carried herself with the posture and grace of a dancer, turning from the door while her fingers still twisted the locks, creating musical rhythm with their clicking and sliding. After a long moment, the woman seemed satisfied and gave a small nod.

The collection of locks was uniformly cheap, flimsy and poorly installed. They'd never stop any serious thief. But they were polished to a high sheen. Kaminsky's final movements were to wipe them all clean of her fingerprints with the corner of her flannel shirt. Cassie noted that she'd ended up with most of the locks open. Maybe it was the rhythm that was soothing rather than the thought of security?

"Thank you for coming, Dr. Hart," Kaminsky told her in the sweet voice of a choirgirl. She gestured to the folding chairs as if she were royalty granting an audience. "Can I get you anything?"

"No thank you," Cassie said as she took a seat. Kaminsky nodded and folded her long body into the seat opposite, crossing her ankles, not her knees, like a proper lady.

A proper lady whose blue jeans were worn to the point of allowing bony knees to protrude and who didn't seem to notice the incessant jiggling of one foot.

Or the cockroach climbing the chair leg, Cassie noted, quickly scanning her own space for any similar insect companions.

"You were interested in my career at Three Rivers?" Kaminsky went on, sliding a crumpled pack of generic brand cigarettes from the pocket of her flannel shirt. She spoke as if she were interviewing Cassie instead of the other way around.

Cassie watched the trembling hands light the cigarette. "Yes. I understand you were concerned about a mother named Virginia Ulrich, and reported her to CYS?"

Kaminsky took a deep drag of the unfiltered cigarette and exhaled. She nodded eagerly. "Virginia Ulrich, now there's a name I haven't heard in a long time. She's a wicked, evil woman," she told Cassie, her inflection never changing. "I tried to save her son, George, but Satan intervened and I was defeated."

"What made you suspect that Virginia wanted to hurt her son?"

"I see things," Kaminsky assured her. "I see everything. Virginia couldn't hide, not from me. No one can."

Cassie fought the desire to squirm in her seat and instead nodded gravely. "What did you see?"

"I saw her opening his central line, dripping his blood into a cup." Kaminsky drew on her cigarette, draining it of life. "She didn't think anyone was watching, but I saw how she looked at him—poor baby, he had the face of an angel." Her voice became a singsong croon as she looked past Cassie to a world faraway. "And Virginia hated him—loathed him. He would cry, and she would cover his mouth and nose to make him stop. When no one was around, she'd totally ignore him, treat him like he wasn't even there, no part of her life. But if anyone came near she'd get all sweet and sugary—butter wouldn't melt in her mouth and you'd believe anything she said. Well, everyone but me. They were all under her spell, but I was immune." She pulled a jangle of religious medals from under her shirt.

"I have protection." Kaminsky ran her fingers over the embossed profiles of saints and martyrs, and then abruptly brought her wandering eyes back to Cassie. "Do you?" she demanded, leaning forward, her face mere inches from Cassie's, ash-blonde hair billowing around her face.

Her brown eyes searched Cassie's as she exhaled an effluvium of tobacco, cheap wine, and rotting teeth. Cassie leaned back, trying to escape the rancid cloud of oppressive odors. Kaminsky hadn't bathed in a long while, nor washed her clothes, it seemed. Cassie wondered how many doses of her medication she'd missed, because it was obvious that the eyes locked onto hers were lit by insanity.

Paranoid schizophrenia was her first impression. Maybe bipolar in a manic phase. Kaminsky's bony fingers latched onto Cassie's arm once more, pulling Cassie back into her sphere of influence.

"You need protection to fight evil." She abruptly released Cassie and began untangling her medallions, her fingers frantically searching. "You know she put the potassium into George's IV fluids, don't you?" she continued as her eyes left Cassie's to join her fingers in scrutinizing her clanging medals. One after another, the saints were rejected. "There was a vial missing from the medication room—potassium wasn't locked up, not back then when we used to mix our own IV fluids. She must have done it right after I left the room, maybe flushed the vial down the toilet. It was small enough. Then she sat back and watched her son begin to die."

Kaminsky quieted, her body becoming still, eyes muted until the only signs of life were the jangling rhythm of her foot and the shallow rise of her chest. Her fingers tightened on one of the nickel medallions. She held this pose for several minutes.

Cassie shifted in her seat, reluctant to break the madwoman's reverie. Despite her mental illness,

Kaminsky was still lucid enough to be giving her some valuable information—even if it was nothing she could prove as fact.

Kaminsky's awareness returned, shuddering through her body as if she were possessed by an alien spirit.

"This one," she said, looking down at the face of the saint imbedded into the flesh of her palm. "This one for you, to protect, to shield." She slid the chain over her head, tousling feathery strands of hair as she did, and reached over to place it around Cassie's neck.

Cassie noticed that the ex-nurse's hands were no longer trembling and wondered at that. Then she looked into the face on the medal. St. Jude, patron of lost causes.

"I knew her—knew where she came from, what she really was," Kaminsky continued, lighting another cigarette, her hands shaking once more. "Jurassic, that was her real name. She's killed before. In West Virginia, Wheeling, West Virginia. Poor souls, they were old and worn out, never had a chance. Ask about her at the Golden Crest, ask about how many patients died while she worked there." Again the thousand-mile stare took an abrupt detour to land on Cassie's face. "You go there, see for yourself."

"Golden Crest?"

"Old folks home. Virginia impressed everyone. Told them she was planning to go to medical school soon as she earned the money." Kaminsky's gaze went out of focus once more. "She worked as a nurse's aide. But they wouldn't see the truth, even when I showed it to them. I took a job there—after what she did to me here—went undercover, to discover, to unveil the evil they had invited. I found the proof, but they wouldn't believe it, cast me out, accused me . . ."

"What happened?"

"They said I was sick, incompetent. Said they'd throw me in jail for going through their records. Called Virginia." She ducked her face down as if trying to hide. "She came in all of her glory, her facade, glittering and glistening, fool's gold. Fooled them all. And I—" She shrugged. "I tried, but they sent me away, shot me up, forced pills down my throat. Fixed me up right." A shudder shook her body and she blinked, returning to the present. "And no matter what I said, no one believed me. Said I was the one who almost killed Georgie, said I was the one who was dangerous. No one ever cared—not till you came along." She swept her shirtsleeve over her face, mopping up silent tears.

"You're going to tell everyone the truth, aren't you? The truth is the only weapon against Satan. Promise me you'll be careful. She's going to come after you, but someone has to shine the Light on the Truth!" Her voice rose into a singsong cadence, and she dropped to her knees, head bowed, torso weaving back and forth.

Cassie got to her feet as Kaminsky began to speak in guttural syllables that were like no earthly language. She edged away from the ex-nurse, but Kaminsky grabbed her legs, holding her fast.

"Watch out!" she yelled up into Cassie's face. "You're marked now, she'll find you." Kaminsky clutched her medallions, jangling them as if to ward off evil spirits. "I'll take care of you," she assured Cassie who cautiously backed away, toward the door. "I promise, I won't fail again!"

CHAPTER 14

TANYA KENT'S MOTHER was next on their list. Drake wasn't certain how much help she'd be. When he spoke to her on the phone last night, she'd seemed eager to talk to them, almost effusive, even though he'd explained that they still had no suspect.

"That's no matter," she'd assured him. "Y'all come on by, tell me all about my baby."

When they knocked on the door of Marion Kent's Homewood apartment, a teenaged girl answered. She gave Drake and Jimmy a dirty look and blocked their entrance.

"What'cha mean bothering my mother?" She said in a low voice, doing her best to usher them back into the hallway. "She's been through enough."

"Who's that, Tanesha?" came a woman's voice from inside the apartment. "Is that the policemen about Tanya?"

Tanesha Kent sighed and shook her head as her mother appeared. Drake was surprised by Marion Kent's appearance. Although he knew from the file that she was only thirty-four, his age, she appeared decades older. Her hair was sparse, brittle, pulled back tight, making her face appear pinched. Her cheekbones were hollow, her dark skin sagging over them as if she were a famine victim. Yet the apartment seemed neat, well kept, with the scent of cookies baking tantalizing them from the kitchen.

"Smells good, Mrs. Kent," Jimmy said after making introductions.

"Chocolate chip. They're Tanya's favorites," Mrs. Kent said, perching on the edge of an ultra suede sofa, hands clasped together.

"Maybe this isn't a good idea," Tanesha said, standing beside her mother, one hand hovering near the older woman's shoulder. "You know what the doctor said about getting excited."

"Hush now. I told you it was only a matter of time before the police found the truth."

Drake exchanged a glance with Jimmy. "Ma'am, we don't have any new evidence in your daughter's case," he told her. "But we haven't given up. We just wanted to clear up a few details."

The woman nodded eagerly, her eyes locked on his with the intensity of a laser. "Of course, of course. Have to do everything proper and right. I understand."

Her voice had taken on a singsong quality, and Drake wondered exactly what the doctor was treating her for. She was much too thin, her hands trembled, and she kept licking her lips as if parched. The woman was teetering on the edge—or had she already passed it?

"We can come back later," Jimmy said, obviously having come to the same conclusion.

"That would be a good idea." Tanesha grabbed onto his suggestion, and took a step toward the door before her mother reached out to stop her.

"No sir. I've got it all here," Mrs. Kent insisted. She opened a thick photo album that sat on the table between them. "Got all my proof and certification, you can take a look, decree anything. Tanya's my baby, it's all here."

She leafed through the album. The first section was crammed with photos of a beautiful baby girl who, with the flip of a few pages, transformed into a beaming toddler with a crooked grin and spark in her eye. Drake's stomach lurched. He hated this part, the reminiscing part. It seemed so cruel to see the possibilities that could never be, to re-live the short life, knowing that there was no way he could change the ultimate outcome.

Many of the photos revealed a grinning school-aged boy, obviously enchanted with his baby sister. A few had a younger Tanesha as well.

"Is that Tonio?" he asked, pointing to the boy, hoping to steer the mother back to the discussion of the case. "He was scheduled to go on a class field trip that day, wasn't he?"

"Tonio didn't go," Tanesha answered. "Because of the baby. One of the school people came and talked to him, tried to help him." Her voice trailed off. "Never did any good."

"My Tonio, Tonio," Mrs. Kent crooned, her fingers rubbing at the photo as if she stroked her son's face. "He's gone now, far away. How he loved his little Tanya. Used to read to her when he got home from school, would make up songs just for her—he had a beautiful voice." A long sigh escaped her, emptying her of whatever strength she possessed, releasing tears in its wake. "I miss that boy's voice."

Drake looked to Tanesha who had joined her mother on the sofa. "What happened to Tonio?"

"He lives with my father now," Tanesha answered. "He couldn't take all—" She gestured to her mother and the collection of memories. "This. They separated almost three years ago now. Tonio don't come back or call, he gets too upset by it all."

"So you take care of your mother?" Jimmy asked. Tanesha nodded.

Mrs. Kent's sobs quieted, and she straightened once more. "Wait, wait," she cried out, her hands rapidly turning pages of the over-stuffed album. "Got to show you my proof so you'll give me my baby back."

Drake almost groaned as he saw the remainder of the mother's collection. Four years of magazine clippings of pretty girls slowly aging, just as Tanya would have if she had lived. The smell of burnt cookies added to the twisting in his gut as he realized that Mrs. Kent believed Tanya was still alive.

His fears were confirmed when she pulled a stack of newspaper clippings from the back of the album.

"I documented everything," she told them. "The lady in Philly. They said her baby died in a fire, but really she was taken, living not a mile away. Can you believe that?" She looked up, her eyes gleaming with hope. "The baby in Florida, she was stolen from her bed like my Tanya. Five years later her mother saw her walking down the street and called her name and she came back. Five years . . . and Tanya's only been gone four. And even on that TV show, they talked about how maybe one person's genes can fool the scientists, not be who they say he is—a chimera, they called it. That's what happened to my Tanya, she got her genes mixed, so those people at the lab said it was her dead and it wasn't—"

Clippings from *The National Enquirer, TV Guide, The Watchtower,* even *The New Republic* swirled through her fingers. Her gaze locked with Drake's again, her face filled with expectancy and joy. "There's all my proof and certification. You going to give me back my girl now, aren't ya? Please, you got to give me back my Tanya. I'm lost without my little girl."

She stood, her bony frame shaking as she pled her case. Smoke began to billow from the kitchen. Tanesha moved behind her mother, pulling the other woman into a wordless embrace, tears streaming down her cheeks as she tried to sooth Marion Kent. Jimmy handed her a clean handkerchief.

Drake fled the storm of emotions. He moved into the kitchen, turned the oven off, and removed the charred remains of Tanya's welcome home cookies.

Cookies as dead as the little girl they were baked for, and as lifeless as the look of despair in her mother's eyes.

CHAPTER 15

"I NEED YOUR HELP," Cassie spoke into the plastic intercom speaker after she buzzed Drake's apartment. There was no reply except for the click of the door release. She grabbed the door handle, but almost ran away instead of opening it.

She gathered her strength and began climbing the three flights of stairs. Each step jarred her healing tendon. Drake was the last person she wanted to bother with her troubles, but there was nowhere else to turn. Ed Castro couldn't help her without compromising his own position; and, as he had said, this required more investigating than diagnosing.

Why was it then, that with each step, she felt like she was shedding precious bits and pieces of her pride?

He would tell her that she was wrong about Virginia Ulrich, her judgment impaired by the trauma she'd been through—like Adeena had, like Sterling had—especially since her only witness was a raving lunatic with a personal grievance against Virginia. Then what would she do? Would she continue to jeopardize her career, Ed's clinic, and her professional reputation to follow her instincts?

Cassie paused on the second floor landing. With a boy's life at stake—yes, the answer had to be yes.

And what if everyone was right and she was wrong? What if she was being foolish, seeing conspiracies where none existed, playing the crusader to fight an imaginary foe—what then? Her hand caught at the St. Jude medal, rubbing it like a talisman. She could lose everything.

Drake had been right about one thing yesterday. She didn't like to talk about things, it made her feel uncomfortable, nervous. And so very often what she said didn't come out with the same meaning that she intended. It was so much better just to take care of things herself. It was more difficult to misconstrue actions than flimsy words.

This was a mistake. She should go home, come up with a plan of action, and not drag Drake into the middle of all this. Things could get very ugly—especially with Richard and a Senator involved.

"Have you decided yet?" His voice came from above her. She looked up and realized that he'd been watching her slow progress from his doorway. He wore jeans and a Rolling Stone's T-shirt smeared with paint.

And a serious, half-smile on his face that told her he knew just what she was thinking. The man was irritating that way.

"I'll come back later," she told him.

"Then you'll miss my etoufee. They had fresh scallops and crawfish at the Strip. Jimmy and me knocked off early, so I had time to shop."

Damn, he did know her weaknesses. He sweetened the pot. "Andouille sausage. Chocolate for dessert."

Cassie took a reluctant step up. "Milk or dark?"

He met her halfway and took her hand in his. "Dark, of course."

"All right. But this was your idea. I need to salvage some of my pride."

They were at his doorway. Led Zeppelin's "Black Dog" and the aroma of Cajun spices swirled around them. He turned her against the threshold, his hands resting on her shoulders as he looked down on her.

"Been lonely around here without you." He kissed her gently on the forehead.

Cassie met his gaze and knew that he meant what he said. God, was it only yesterday that she'd had a future? How could she let everything slip away? Careless. She needed to take control of events.

Gram Rosa would totally disagree. Rosa believed in fate, destiny, kismet, and could forecast the future in someone's palm with more accuracy than meteorologists predicted the weather. *You can't outrun God's plan*, she'd tell Cassie. *What's meant to be, is.*

Cassie inhaled the aroma wafting from Drake's kitchen and pushed aside all thoughts of gypsy fortunes.

"I'm sorry about yesterday," she said. Drake moved into the well-appointed kitchen and began to pull plates down from the cabinets. "When I—"

She couldn't bring herself to say it, flushed with embarrassment when his hand went to his cheek as if it still burnt from her slap.

"I only said what I did because I was worried about you," he told her, passing the dishes and silver across the bar to her.

Cassie shook her head and said nothing, setting the table and pouring a glass of Merlot for herself, and a Yuengling Black and Tan for him.

"Are you going to tell me or do I have to guess?" he said when the seafood stew was half eaten in silence. "What do you need help with?"

"I think one of my patients might be in danger."

Drake looked up at that, his spoon halfway to his mouth. "Really?" She nodded, biting her lip, daring him to laugh. He set his spoon down and turned his full attention on her. "Tell me about it."

And she did. About Charlie and the intraosseus, and her confrontation with Virginia Ulrich and Sterling in the PICU. About the grandfather, the Senator, who could ruin Drake and Ed Castro's plans for the free clinic. About the first son who'd died so close to the second one's birth. About everything except Virginia's supposed affair with Richard—Drake hated anything to do with Richard and she wanted him to judge her case on its own merits.

"And she's seven months pregnant now," she finished with a rush. He remained silent, taking a long swallow of his beer. Cassie bowed her head and concentrated on her food. It did sound foolish when said aloud. Then why wouldn't this gnawing in her gut go away?

She mopped up the remnants of the stew with a piece of corn bread. Still he was silent. Finally, she looked up to see his eyes resting on her, watching her with curious attention. As if he was judging her rather than the merits of her argument. Cassie felt the color rise to her cheeks under the weight of his gaze.

"I'm not going crazy," she blurted out, breaking the silence. "There have been cases like this one before. It's a rare form of child abuse called Munchausen Syndrome by Proxy. The perpetrator, usually the mother, sees her child's illness as a way of manipulating others, of getting attention or some other need satisfied."

He pushed back his chair and moved over to stand beside her. Lowering his frame so that his face was level with hers, he placed a hand beneath her chin and raised her mouth to his.

The kiss took Cassie by surprise. Its passion was quiet and intense, a smoldering heat that spread from him to her.

She circled her arms around his neck, pulled him closer, opened herself to him. Forty-three days, she'd yearned for this.

He lifted her to her feet, shoving the chair aside as their bodies met. Cassie drank him in, savoring his taste—spicy sausage, barley and hops—and swallowed all her fears and doubts. Who needed food? The giddy thought made her smile. This was all she needed.

Her hands tugged at his shirt, sliding under the cotton to glide over his sweat slicked skin. He'd lost weight. His muscles, always strong and firm, now felt chiseled, in sharp relief. Her fingers danced over his back, reading the changes in his body. Then they came to the heaped-up scar under his right arm.

The exit wound from a thirty-eight caliber bullet. She knew because she was the one who'd patched the sucking chest wound.

Drake froze at her touch. Cassie immediately withdrew her fingers from the scar. Too late. He was gone. He gently disengaged himself from her, and she felt as if she'd lost something precious.

Give him time, Adeena had counseled. How much did he need? Or maybe what he really needed was distance—to be far away from her.

Cassie hung her head, refusing to say anything for fear she'd pour forth her doubts and worries, and speaking them aloud might crystallize them into a terrible reality.

He moved his hands from her face down to her shoulders, but his touch was now that of a neutral observer, there was no heat in it.

"Tell me more about this Munchausen's by Proxy." His voice came from light-years away. He slipped his hands from her body and began to gather the dishes, taking them into the kitchen.

She swallowed her anger, although it burned her to do so. Why wouldn't he accept what she wanted to give to him?

※

DRAKE RINSED THE dishes with a clatter. God, he couldn't resist her—not when she practically glowed with passion. But passion could burn. He'd learned that the hard way two months ago. Hart might be immune to its effects. He knew from painful experience that he wasn't. And he wasn't certain he could live through the fire twice.

His gut churned, and his heart pounded hard enough to jump through his skin—feelings that brought with them the overwhelming memory of that night six weeks ago. He took a deep breath and let it out, trying to collect his wits once more.

They had to find another way. For his sanity if not hers. A middle ground, safer ground.

He left the dishes and rejoined her at the table, keeping a safe distance. "I've heard about the woman in New York who smothered her babies, but they called it Sudden Infant Death."

"And there was a woman in Philadelphia, and another in California who poisoned her children with salt and baking soda. I found one article written by a survivor as an adult. She described her mother repeatedly breaking the same bone with a hammer. The mother told the child it was therapy."

"We both know there are sick people out there," he acknowledged, thinking of his day spent with families tormented by a predator with a taste for children's blood. What a world the two of them lived in.

For a moment he imagined leaving all thoughts of dead children behind, escaping with Hart to the bedroom, and locking the door and burrowing into the warm comfort of her arms.

No, he had a job to do. So did she. He regained his train of thought. "Why are you so certain that Virginia Ulrich is one of these? And if she is, would she dare abuse the grandchild of a United States Senator?"

"Part of the compulsion is the need to outwit anyone who might discover the abuse—physicians, nurses, family members. It reinforces the perpetrator's belief that they're superior to those around them. As they manipulate everyone, they're creating their own little narcissistic paradise where they are not only the center of attention but also the only person in control."

"Isn't Munchausen very rare? And haven't people been accused of it who were actually innocent? Over in England, they're overturning hundreds of cases, saying doctors were overzealous in their attempts to find a reason for children dying."

"Yes, I know," she admitted. "But Munchausen's is extraordinarily difficult to diagnose, and even harder to prove. There are several types of inborn errors of metabolism that can mimic abuse. In fact, Karl Sterling made his reputation by disproving allegations of child abuse against one Amish family. But all those things have already been tested for in Charlie's case. And each test narrows down the list of possibilities until the unthinkable becomes the probable, the only thing likely."

Drake still avoided her glance. No sense risking another lapse of judgment. But damn, she'd felt so good in his arms. He wrapped his hand around his beer glass, and drained the last dregs. "And you think you're there—you have a medical certainty of abuse? Because, if so, then you know you need to report it to Children and Youth."

"I called Childline yesterday. I think that's why the Ulrichs served me with a restraining order today."

He looked up at that. "Restraining order?"

"They're also going to sue me for assault and battery, and they've convinced another family to sue me for malpractice."

He listened with dismay as she explained about her patient with meningitis. "How can it be your fault if a mother doesn't give her child the medication you prescribe?"

"Tell that to the Executive Committee. I'm on a leave of absence until they meet on Friday. They may revoke my privileges."

Drake stared at her. She was talking about more than losing her job. Revoking her privileges would be a permanent blot on her career. And Hart didn't just love her job—it was her life.

He had the sudden image of her huddled alone in the darkness of her house, a recluse, shutting him out, shutting out the world—that's what stripping Hart of her career would do to her. Like Marion Kent, he could see her dwindling away, slowly fading from this world, not quite ready for the next.

No, not Hart. She was stronger than that—she was the strongest person he knew.

"I could lose everything," she whispered, and he

wanted nothing more than to hold her, comfort her. Drake clamped his hands on the table edge to prevent himself from doing just that. Keep talking, just keep talking. There would be time for the other later. Much later.

"And you can't prove any of this." The words came out cold, sterile. She jerked up at the sound of them. Drake saw the movement and softened his tone. "If I look into Ulrich, check out her background, would that help?" She nodded. "But you have to promise that if I don't find anything substantial, if I feel the case has no merit, then you'll drop it. All right?"

She looked down at the table, sliding her wine glass along the polished cherry, not answering him.

"I won't do this unless I can trust you not to interfere," he said.

That got her attention. Her eyes caught his and held them with an intensity that sparked across the table.

"Did you consider for an instant that I might have been right yesterday?" she asked, her voice level, but her hands clenched the stem of the wine glass in a stranglehold. "Trust that I did the right thing about Morris?"

"Hart—" he said, keeping his tone patient despite his irritation. "That was a police matter."

"It happened in my ER, with my patient and my nurse's lives at stake. That makes it mine—my responsibility, my obligation to see that things are done right."

"No, it still makes it a police matter. Which means you back down and trust them to do their jobs. No questions asked."

She set her glass down with a bang, slopping liquid onto the table's finish. "Even when they're acting like morons, about to get my nurse and my patient killed?" She pushed herself upright, leaned against the table, both hands fisted under her weight. "Why can't you trust me to do the right thing? I can't believe you'd trust an imbecile like Spanos' judgment over mine."

"Because he's a cop and he knows what he's doing!" Drake rose to his feet. Suddenly, the table between them seemed very insubstantial.

"And I don't? Do you even know what really happened?"

"I don't need to. It was a dangerous, violent man with a hostage and you should have let us do our job."

"Excuse me for not sitting on my hands when there are lives at stake!"

"You could have been killed!" His words echoed through the high-ceilinged room and circled back to hover between them in silence.

She looked up at him, eyes narrowed. "You can't lock me away, Drake. You can't even to keep me safe. If you try, you'll smother me. I don't care how good your intentions may be. You can't do that to me. I wouldn't let Richard and I won't let you."

Ouch, that hurt. King had isolated her, overwhelmed her in order to bludgeon her into submission. All Drake wanted was to protect her.

"It almost killed me to escape Richard," she went on heartlessly, "I'm not going through that again."

Anger flared in Drake. "You think I'm like King? Do you really believe that's the kind of man I am?"

She held his gaze for a long moment. "Maybe neither of us knows who we really are." She took a step toward the door. "I don't want to talk about this anymore."

A flash of fear colored his fury. He was going to lose her. For good.

His hand shot out without conscious control. It landed on her arm, on the puckered seam of scar tissue there.

The roar of rage and terror that he'd felt that night six weeks ago returned in full force. It flooded his vision, filled his mind with the pounding of his heartbeat, surging with adrenalin.

"Less talk, more action. If that's what you want, Cassie, then by God, that's what you'll get." Drake reached for her other arm before she could wrench away, pulled her off her feet and propelled her into the living room, up against the back of the leather sofa.

His body trembled with desire fueled by fear and anger. He bent her forward over the couch, standing behind her, one hand under her shirt, the other unzipping her jeans and pushing the cloth away until his fingers reached skin. Hart knew how to render him helpless with desire—but he knew her as well, where to touch, how to stroke her passion.

Drake took control of her body, not the mutual gift that lovemaking had been for them before, but pure animal passion. Sex as a primal force.

"I'm not in the mood," she protested, struggling from her position beneath his body. Then his hand found that sweet spot and her body sagged against his.

A shudder rippled through her as he brought her to a rapid climax.

"Drake," she started, but her words were swallowed as he brought her to the peak again, too quickly for her to savor any pleasure, more a release than fulfillment.

He pressed against her. Her skin was flushed and slicked with sweat. His tongue licked the base of her neck. There was none of the sweet vanilla and apple flavor he usually relished. Instead she tasted of raw sex, an animal in heat, musk seasoned with acrid fear.

A small, feral cry escaped her lips. He taunted her by moving his fingers over her, teasing, giving her what she desired for a fleeting moment, then abandoning her once more.

Hart squirmed beneath his weight. "Please," she moaned, urging him to continue. "Don't stop."

He lowered his jeans. Her hips rocked against him, the touch of her flesh exciting him even further.

As his hand continued to taunt her, he reached across her body, stretched toward the end table drawer. Before he could reach the condoms inside he knocked over a wrought iron lamp and sent the TV remote spinning across the floor.

He drove her with cruel abandon, then left her bereft once more. This time she cried out in desperation. "Drake, please!"

He lifted her hips up against his, entered her from behind. Her body responded with a shudder of passion that tore through both of them. He thrust himself inside her, pounding himself into her body as she urged him on.

When he'd finished, when his fury was released with a final groan of pain and pleasure, he slumped forward, pinning her enervated body beneath him.

***

HER FACE BURIED in the soft leather of the couch. Cassie breathed in its essence of animal, could taste its coarse earthiness as the grain rubbed against her skin. Her body ached for more of what Drake offered her. She wanted more, needed more, demanded more.

She twisted her sweaty body so that she faced him. The crimson of anger and pleasure filled her mind.

She was infuriated by how much she craved his touch, by her own response as she'd surrendered; riding the wave of ecstasy he gave her. Damn it, she hated him — the way he knew her every vulnerability, the way he could bring her to places she'd never dreamed of before. No one else knew her like Drake did, could drive her as crazy with lust, desire, and frustration.

Conflicting emotions constricted her throat and left her mouth dry. She resisted the urge to smile, she didn't want to encourage him. As irritated as she was, she had to admit that it was a hell of a way to end an argument. A big improvement over yesterday.

He said nothing but planted his mouth on hers, forcing his tongue past her teeth, devouring her. Her body answered once more with a hunger she was desperate to control.

She pulled her shirt down, some small barrier between them. Once she had her feet planted back on the ground and her hands against his chest, she pushed against him. If he wanted to play games, she could give as good as she took. She knew how to make him beg. She knew his weaknesses as well. He'd had his turn with randy jungle sex, now it was hers.

He resisted for an infuriating moment as if still intent on demonstrating his power over her.

Then, without warning, Cassie was suffocating, unable to draw air. She panicked. For one blinding instant it was Richard on top of her, not Drake.

"Get off of me!" Her shout startled them both.

CHAPTER 16

HART'S EYES BLAZED and Drake's desire rose once more. Then she broke eye contact, her gaze darting past him, a wounded animal desperate for escape. Her breath quickened and all thoughts of passion fled from him.

This was what King had done to her.

He lurched back, eager to give her the space she needed. Her pupils grew wide with terror, her chest heaved as she gasped for air.

He had hurt her. Just like King.

The realization left a sinking in the pit of his stomach. He'd given into his own anger and fear and because of it had made a terrible mistake.

CASSIE KEPT HER head down as she adjusted her clothing, edging farther away from Drake, eyes focused on the exit, her avenue of escape.

Once she passed through the threshold and slammed the door behind her, the panic attack eased and she could breathe once more. She raced down the steps without a backward glance.

She made it to her car, her head sagging against the steering wheel as she collapsed into the driver's seat.

As angry and irritated as she was by Drake usurping control, she had to admit: she'd liked it. Some small—or not so small—part of her enjoyed his touch, she thought as the memory of the waves of pleasure he'd given her returned. Wasn't it that touch what she'd been craving for the past six weeks?

She'd gotten exactly what she asked for, hadn't she?

Then why had she confused Drake and Richard for the split second that had sent her reeling into panic? Had she somehow asked for the treatment Richard had given her as well? Was she in some way responsible?

"No," Cassie said the word aloud once, and then repeated it louder, filling the Impreza with its echo. "No!" She'd fought Richard, escaped him and his warped ideas of love. She'd never allow herself to enter another relationship like that. Never again.

She thought about the victims of domestic violence that came through her ER. Wasn't that exactly what they said as they entered one abusive relationship after another? It won't happen again, this time is different, this man is different.

Despite the warmth of the night, she shivered. What if Drake wasn't so different? Worse yet, what if she herself hadn't changed—would she always be attracted to men who would fight her for control, and win? Maybe this was all her fault. Maybe everything was.

Cassie clenched the steering wheel, trying to bury those thoughts, doubts that shook the core of her being. Things that affected her even more than Drake's passionate touch had.

·◈·

DRAKE WATCHED HER go. Her eyes were dark and wide as a deer caught in headlights. She ran away almost as fast.

He pulled his jeans back up, fastened them, and sank to the floor, his back against the couch. How could he have done that to her? Treated her like that? He was as bad as King. His fingers tugged at his hair as he tried to understand his actions.

He couldn't. Something in him had snapped, some primitive beast broke loose of its chains. No excuse. He knew what King had done to her, how any confinement or loss of control panicked her—she wouldn't even ride an elevator, for chrissakes.

And he had held her, forced her—God, what was wrong with him? He'd never done anything like that, not even back in the days when Jack Daniels had been his best friend.

He had to talk to her, explain. Apologize. Pray that she would forgive him.

Drake climbed back to his feet, grabbed his car keys, and left.

He parked in front of her house. The lights were on upstairs. Good, she was still up. Hart's fat tortoiseshell cat, Hennessy, was silhouetted in the windowsill. He gathered his courage and got out of the car. He had no idea what he'd say to her. He hoped the right words would come.

The steps to her porch seemed to have grown steeper since he was last here, weeks ago. By the time he reached the top he was breathing hard and fast. He moved across the porch, his legs feeling heavy, and reached a hand toward her door. His arm grew numb, and he had the sudden feeling of being pushed back. A heavy weight pressed on his chest, threatening to suffocate him, and he broke out in a cold sweat.

Drake tried to move forward. His vision darkened. He fought for air as an overwhelming sense of doom and terror filled him. He stumbled backwards down the steps.

Hanging his head between his knees, he leaned against the Mustang's bumper and caught his breath. It was several minutes before he was able to raise his head and look up at the house looming over him. Slowly the numbness and sense of terror receded, leaving him feeling limp, powerless.

Adeena Coleman had once told him Cassie's house was haunted. Not by ghosts, but by memories. Shivering in the warm spring night, he wrapped his arms around chest, unable to ward off the memories of the last time he'd crossed the threshold into Hart's house.

His vision filled with a kaleidoscope of images. Bright roses flying through the air, scattered in all directions. The cold touch of a gun muzzle. Hart's body sprawled on the floor, bloody, maybe dead. Fear and rage and grief churning through him as he surrendered to a killer.

Drake shook his head. Ridiculous. He dealt with scenes of violence all the time. He was used to it, it was part of the job. There was no killer waiting inside the door tonight—only Hart.

He started toward the house twice more but couldn't make it past the first step before the pounding in his head and chest stopped him.

He returned to the safe haven of the Mustang. He bent over, racked with dry heaves, swallowing hard to keep his dinner down, drumming a fist on the still warm hood. Tomorrow, he told himself once he could breathe again. He'd talk to Hart tomorrow.

Far away from this house and whatever demons inhabited it.

CHAPTER 17

CASSIE WOKE REALIZING that she had nowhere to go, nothing to do. The thought paralyzed her. Then she remembered the way she'd left Drake last night and a feeling of dread overwhelmed her. What if she'd lost him as well?

It'd been weeks since she'd had a panic attack like that. And for Drake to see it. No wonder he was hesitant about getting seriously involved with her—who wanted to get involved with a nut case?

At first she'd been angry with him about the sex, the way he'd taken control. But, she had to admit, that kind of passion was exactly what she'd been wanting. It had been exciting, letting go like that—jungle sex, primal passion, call it what you will. It had been good.

So good. Until the end. Somehow Richard seemed to invade everything she touched, poisoning even the things she cherished—like her relationship with Drake.

Cassie hurled a Rom curse into the air, a weapon aimed at her ex-husband. Hennessy jumped and looked at her in reproach. Cassie clamped her hand over her mouth in chagrin, hearing Rosa's voice warning her about the power and danger of curses. What you send out in this world always comes back sooner or later.

"Sorry Gram," Cassie whispered. Then smiled. She'd never get Drake back this way. Talking to herself like a crazy woman, spewing gypsy curses, and half believing they might work.

She huddled beneath Rosa's quilt, despondent, blocking out the morning sun. Until Hennessy's plaintive meows forced her to lower the covers. The cat jumped lightly onto Cassie's chest, kneading the quilt back farther until she could butt her head against her owner's.

Empty food bowls must take priority. The cat punctuated her message with a tap of a paw against Cassie's nose.

"All right, already," Cassie muttered, sliding free from the warmth of her bed and grabbing her robe. Why bother getting dressed? She padded downstairs in bare feet and fed the cat. Who would see her? Would even care?

The house was quiet except for the sound of the cat gulping down her food.

Maybe she should get a TV. Let it hypnotize her, placate her until she didn't notice the passing of the days. Morphine for the masses.

That thought did it. She ran upstairs, threw on shorts and a T-shirt, and then went down to the basement where she spent an hour working with her heavy bag and weights. Her reaction time was off, her kicks lacked power, but it was satisfying imagining Virginia Ulrich's face on the bag. Then Richard's. Slamming one punch after another into them until her knuckles were red and raw when she took the gloves off.

She sat on the edge of the weight bench, head sagging as she caught her breath. Where had she gone wrong? All she wanted was to protect one little boy—was that so awful? Now she had nothing. Humiliated in front of her coworkers, facing disciplinary action. And Drake—what was she going to do about Drake?

"Why do anything?" she asked the cat who sat watching her from the top of the dryer. "Maybe it's better this way."

Hennessy looked up at that. Yeah right, her expression seemed to say. Then she rolled back on her haunches and began to clean herself, ignoring Cassie.

Cassie threw her gloves at the dryer, but the cat studiously ignored the bang. "Maybe what I need is another cat."

Later, in the shower, she remembered Drake's hands and the way they knew every secret of her body. Where did men learn that? She could live without him, she resolved. In fact, life would be so much easier without men in general.

Of course, she'd never been one to settle for easy. A short while later, she locked her front door. Rain was threatening, a cold front moving in, so instead of walking, she took the Subaru over to the Blarney Stone. Drake's favorite lunchtime haunt. It was neutral territory, well, more neutral than either of their houses. She could talk to him there.

He might tell her to go to hell. She wouldn't blame him either, after the way she'd fled last night, without a word of explanation. And she'd been the one trying all week to seduce him—he must have thought her crazy, or at the very least fickle.

DRAKE DRAGGED HIMSELF up the steps to the Major Case Squad, leaving Jimmy downstairs socializing with some of the uniforms. Another morning of playing grim reaper, forcing people to relive a nightmare they'd prefer to leave buried. They'd spoken with the speech therapist and both bus drivers. No one had anything significant to contribute.

After lunch they were scheduled to meet with Sophia Frantz's parents. Drake thought he might just skip lunch—this case had taken away his appetite—and bury himself in the murder books. Again. There had to be something he was overlooking.

As if he'd find something his father had missed. Fat chance.

He had also started the ball rolling on Hart's case, he'd begun a background check on the nurse she'd mentioned, Sheila Kaminsky, and the Ulrich family. It was the least he could do after last night. Maybe he could find something to help her patient, and take it to her as a peace offering of sorts.

His extension rang. He made the mistake of picking it up, acknowledging his existence. His hope that it might be Hart was instantly crushed.

"I understand that you are interested in one of my cases." Commander Sarah Miller's voice reverberated through the handset. "My office. Now."

She hung up. Drake didn't waste effort on a groan. Should've known Miller would get prickly about his and Jimmy re-opening a case she'd failed to solve. Miller much preferred her mistakes buried and forgotten. Sometimes he wondered if she kept him on the squad, under her immediate supervision, because she considered Drake one of those mistakes as well.

His leg hurt more today than it had yesterday. It

looked like rain. If he ever left the force, maybe he could get a job as a weather forecaster. He re-traced his steps back down the stairs to Miller's office on the third floor.

"I had a phone call from Clinton Eades. He wasn't too happy about your visit yesterday. Neither was Tanesha Kent," Miller said as soon as he entered her office. She didn't ask him to sit, so he leaned against the back of one of the chairs situated in front of her bleached oak desk. "She's requesting that we cease from interviewing her mother anymore. Apparently Mrs. Kent was so upset after your visit that her physician has her under heavy sedation."

Drake wasn't too surprised to hear this. The woman was in a fragile state before they arrived to burst her delusions. He stayed silent as Miller scrutinized him. She was dressed in a conservative charcoal grey suit, her blonde hair pulled back into a tight roll at the nape of her neck.

What was he supposed to say? He wished Jimmy was here, he was much better at playing Miller's games than Drake was.

"I'm sorry to hear that," he ventured.

"You look awful," she continued, her eyes raking him over, head to toe. "I think you need more time off."

Drake straightened, despite the protest from his aching leg. "I'm fine."

"So fine that you forgot your meeting with Dr. White this morning?"

Aw hell. What the hell was wrong with him? First behaving like a baboon with Hart last night, now blowing off an appointment with the man who held his future as a cop in his hands?

"Sorry," he muttered, his gaze focused on the view of Our Lady of Sorrows through the window behind her.

"I heard about what happened with Hart and Spanos. You know, DJ, you were one of my best detectives before you met that woman."

He wanted to protest that Hart had nothing to do with the state he was in, but knew it was a lie. Hart had everything to do with the state he was in. Last night after he'd fled her house and returned home, he'd been unable to concentrate on the re-opened cases, had tried to paint, but the pigment turned to mud in his hands.

He'd been unable to do anything except a few frenzied sketches of Hart and Marion Kent surrounded by the faces of Tanya Kent, Regina Eades, Adam Cleary, and Sophia Frantz. As if somehow four dead victims and two women who had survived their worst nightmares were linked together.

"I'll re-schedule with White," he said, hating the idea. The shrink would have a field day with what happened between him and Hart last night.

"I already did. He'll see you at one this afternoon."

"We've got—"

"Let Dolan handle anything you have scheduled. I understand how important these cases are to you, but we're talking your career here. Either White certifies you fit for duty by next week, or we're going to have to discuss more permanent arrangements."

She meant disability. Like he was nuts or something. Drake remembered the red haze of fury and fear that had blindsided him last night with Hart, and then again at her house, and wondered if maybe Miller wasn't on the right track.

He blew his breath out, sagged against the back of the chair, not caring that she noticed. What would he be if he couldn't be a cop?

Guilt twisted inside him. Hart was facing the

same problem. And instead of a sympathetic ear or comforting embrace, what had he offered her? An out of control lout. How could he face her again, even to apologize? How could he face anyone if they drummed him off the force?

· ⚅ ·

"I THOUGHT YOU said this was finished." Senator George Ulrich hung up his cell phone with a bang and turned to his son.

"It is. Dr. Hart is on leave, Sterling told me last night. Dad, why are you getting so upset—you know Virginia's done nothing wrong. I think it's wrong to push Hart too far, it'll only put her on the defensive." Paul Ulrich began to butter his croissant.

His father yanked the roll away from him and hurled it against the dining room wall. "How many times do I have to tell you! All it takes is the appearance of impropriety. Damn it, Paul, I'm in the fight of my life here. Welsch's campaign is gaining momentum, even right here in my hometown."

"And my son might be dying!" Paul said.

The Senator stared at his son, surprised by the outburst. Why had Paul picked now to finally grow a backbone?

"You've gotten rid of Hart—" his son continued. "Your problem's solved. So just go back to your campaign, Dad. Leave us alone. That's what you're good at."

"Paul, you know I'd lay down my life for Charlie—you know that. If there was anything I could do to help him, I'd move heaven and earth to get it for him. He's my only living grandchild. My chance at a legacy—"

"I thought I was your chance for a legacy. Isn't

that what you've been grooming me for all these years?"

"Son, you're a damned fine lawyer. You are. But you just don't have what it takes for the political life. You'd have to leave Virginia and Charlie and the new baby behind—for months at a time. Missed birthdays, holidays, school plays. Could you do that to them?"

"No. No I couldn't, I wouldn't want to."

The Senator assumed as much. Paul didn't have what it took to get the job done. Never would. He couldn't even get rid of one irritating bitch. It was Scott Thayer, Paul's assistant, who had taken care of gathering the background on Hart, putting a bug in Judge Franklin's ear—and put a hefty campaign contribution into his pocket. "It seems the good doctor is still a thorn in our side. That was Thayer. She's convinced her boyfriend to look into Virginia's previous CYS investigation."

"Those files are confidential—he can't get to them. Besides, Children and Youth said Virginia is innocent, so what does it matter? He'll just tell Hart that she was wrong."

George Ulrich shook his head. How could he have raised such a naive man? It was Paul's mother's fault, she'd coddled the boy too much, protected him from the realities of life. "Even so, it's still not something we want on the eleven o'clock news, now is it? Thayer's bringing Richard King here later."

He didn't add that he'd instructed Thayer to dig up more dirt on Hart and to spread the rumors about King's affair with Virginia. A long dead affair he could handle, especially if it added to the public perception of Hart as unstable and unreliable. He had to erase any doubt of Virginia's innocence before the primaries.

"Richard? Why?"

"He was married to Hart. He'll know her weak

spots. Then we can finish this once and for all."

Paul got to his feet, frowning. "You deal with King. I have to get to the hospital and see my wife and son."

"Hart, I need to talk to you."

Cassie spun around at the sound of Tony Spanos' voice. The Neanderthal patrolman was the last thing she needed. This corridor outside the Blarney Stone's restrooms was where he'd cornered her when they first met.

"What do you want?" she asked, planting her feet and facing him straight on.

To her surprise he stopped and looked down at the floor. "I got something—look, we got off on the wrong foot, and I was thinking about what happened, and I just wanted—" When he looked up his face was flushed. "It wasn't you—it was Drake I was mad at." He went on. "I should've never taken it out on you. Anyway, what happened with Morris, I just wanted to apologize. That should've never happened, I should've been watching what Johnson did more closely."

It wasn't elegant, but it was more of an apology than she'd ever expected to hear from Spanos. Maybe he wasn't such a Neanderthal after all.

"Drake told me about what happened last summer with Pamela," she told him. "I can understand why you'd be upset."

Spanos straightened to his full height, his broad shoulders almost brushing the walls of the narrow corridor. "Pamela—she was really something. I don't know what Drake told you about her and me, but we really clicked. I thought we had something going but then he came along—" He shrugged. "I don't know what women see in a jerk like him. If you know about what he did to Pamela, using her and throwing her away like she was nothing, how come you stay with him?"

Spanos' version of Pamela's death sounded very different than Drake's. Cassie could understand why he blamed Drake for her suicide.

"Anyway, I just wanted to say sorry for how I acted toward you. Maybe someday, we could—"

The door to the back room opened and Drake emerged. Both men bristled, the waves of antipathy palpable in the narrow confines of the corridor.

"What's going on?" Drake asked, his gaze skimmed over Cassie to rest on Spanos as if the other cop was a threat.

The two men squared off, fists clenched at their side. Idiots. It would serve them right if she left them to slug it out on their own.

But then she wouldn't have the chance to apologize to Drake. And the longer she let that go, the harder it would be.

"Nothing," Cassie said.

"We were just talking. You got a problem with that?" Spanos took a step toward Drake.

Drake's face hardened into a blank slate. Without another word, he spun on his heel and returned to the back room.

"Like I said." Spanos nodded to the closed door. "Complete jerk." Cassie could hear the sounds of pool balls hit forcefully, *clack, clack clack*, like the ricochet of bullets. "So, we square, doc?"

She nodded and put her hand on the brass doorknob. Spanos shook his head once more at the foolish ways of women and returned to the main room.

Cassie took a deep breath. Grace and poise, she coached herself. Then wrinkled her nose—the words were as foreign to her as the lunar surface. At least she could study the moon, even if from afar. How did you learn to be charming, alluring?

She turned the knob and went in. The back room was large enough to hold two old-fashioned billiard tables, a battered leather couch, and a jukebox currently belting Stevie Ray Vaughan. A sign on the wall said the maximum capacity of the oak paneled room was thirty. But it felt crowded with her and Drake as its sole occupants.

"YOU TWO DONE with your *tete a tete*?" Drake lined up a double bank shot and gave the cue ball a powerful slam.

He barely noticed when it hit its mark, sinking the three ball into the corner and going on to hurtle the four ball against the far bank and into the side pocket. He was much too occupied with squelching the surge of jealousy and anger that had ambushed him when he'd seen Hart with Spanos. This morning he wanted nothing more than the opportunity to apologize. Now this riot of emotion threatened to overcome his carefully rehearsed speech.

"Nice shot," she said, moving into the periphery of his vision. Suddenly he couldn't focus on the cue ball in front of him.

Drake grunted, moving away from her intoxicating, infuriating presence, and hit an easy power shot, line driving the seven across the table and into the side pocket. Who cared about the rotation, or the beautiful bank shot he'd so carefully set up for the five ball? Fuck the rules.

It wasn't like Hart ever followed them, so why should he?

Then he remembered last night. When he was the one who'd broken every rule of decent conduct. He stood, gripping the stick with sweaty hands and turned to face her.

"You here to see me or chat up Spanos?" Ouch, that hadn't been what he wanted to say. She colored, a pale crimson that shaded her cheekbones ever so slightly, but a red flag to Drake. He had to tread lightly or he would lose her. He took a breath, trying to swallow the bilious anger that had sparked in him.

She turned her face up, meeting his eyes, and he could see he'd hurt her again. "I came to apologize. For last night," she said, her voice barely audible over the crooning of Stevie Ray. "I should never have run away like that. I'm sorry."

Drake blinked, completely undone by her words. The anger vanished, replaced with shame. The pool cue slid from his hands, falling to the floor with a clatter.

"You're sorry?" He cleared his throat and tried again. "I acted like a barbarian. I should have never—" he stumbled. This had been so easy when he rehearsed it in the shower this morning. Without her large brown eyes soaking up every word, staring at him, seeing through him, knowing him for the lout he was.

She frowned, and Drake knew he'd blown it.

"You thought I was upset about the sex?" she asked.

He winced at her bluntness. Leave it to Hart to not mince words. He nodded.

"The sex was fine. In case you hadn't noticed I've been trying to get you to jump my bones for days. I was irritated by the timing—at first. But then I had other things to distract me." She grinned up at him, taking his hand in hers and tracing a finger over his palm.

Her touch made Drake's heart race. She brought his wrist to her lips and kissed the throbbing pulse point there. Her eyes remained locked onto his.

"Then why—" He tugged his hand from her and looked away. "I thought maybe I'd forced you—like Richard. Done something to hurt you."

"It wasn't you. It was me. I don't know what triggered it. Honestly, it wasn't anything you did. I just had this flash of Richard and I got scared." She gave a short, derisive laugh. "Actually it was a full-blown panic attack. I couldn't breathe, felt like I was being smothered, head pounding, hyperventilating—the whole nine yards. Guess you didn't know you were getting involved with a crazy woman, did you?"

She turned away from him, leaning over the pool table, spinning the cue ball against the velvet. But Drake wasn't fooled by her casual tone. Hart was extremely poor at hiding her emotions, especially from him. He saw the color in her face rise, the tension hunch her shoulders, and the muscle spasm in her jaw, marring that exquisite profile.

She'd described almost the same symptoms he'd had at her house and at the station parking lot yesterday. Was that what it was, a panic attack? Maybe they were both crazy.

Then he smiled. If so, there was no one he'd rather share a bed at Western Psych with. He moved toward her, encircling her waist, pulling her back against him. She fit just right, his chin resting on the top of her head, cushioned by masses of dark curls. He sighed. The scent of springtime filled each breath as he lay his cheek against her hair.

"I guess we're both a couple of fools," he

whispered. She nodded and turned within his arms.

She reached up, fisting her fingers in his hair and dragging his face down to hers. The kiss was long and deep, a tantalizing appetizer. Drake knew she had much more to offer, and he was greedy to savor all of her.

What was wrong with him, avoiding this for so long?

They parted for air. Hart hiked her hips onto the table. She reached for the buttons of her denim shirt and with a wicked grin, began to slowly undo them. Drake reached out to speed the process, but she batted his fingers away.

"I wore this for you," she told him, slipping the shirt off her shoulders and dancing her fingers over satin and lace, a surprising change from her usual cotton sports bras.

"You shouldn't have bothered," Drake said, his hands taking possession of her.

She arched with pleasure and leaned back on her elbows as he released her breasts from their silky confinement and his mouth moved over them.

"You know, Spanos apologized for what happened with Morris," she said, her voice dreamy and faraway.

Spanos, he thought with irritation. Spanos was the last name he wanted to hear right now. He slid his hands between the legs of her jeans, caressing, feeling her heat through the denim.

"Spanos is a jerk," he murmured, and then nipped at the skin between her breasts.

"But at least he's a polite jerk."

Drake's hands stopped their motion, and she squirmed against them. He drew back, just out of reach. "You want me to apologize for telling you that you were reckless and should have let the police do their job?"

She balanced on one arm and reached to tug him back to her. "You could start by going back to what you were doing."

He yanked his hand away and straightened, looking down on her. "I'm not going to apologize when I was right."

He saw the flash in her eyes. Then she sighed, acknowledging that this was an argument neither would win.

"All right then, I'll apologize to you," she said, grabbing his lapels and pulling him to her once more. "Come to dinner tonight."

He allowed her to nuzzle his neck. "Will you wear this?" he asked, his fingers flicking the satin bra that hung open from her shoulders.

"If you promise more jungle sex."

A pounding on the door interrupted his response.

"Everything all right in there?" came Jimmy's shout followed by a laugh. "Ah, yunz need anything?"

Drake cursed and stood up. "My idiot partner." He tucked his shirt back into his slacks and straightened his tie. She sat up, quickly re-fastening her bra and arranging her clothing.

She slid off the pool table, tucking in her own shirt. He put his hands on her hips and pulled her close one last time, his kiss a promise of things to come.

"Got to go." Another wave of pounding shook the door. "I'm coming!" Drake shouted in annoyance and was rewarded with another laugh from the other side.

"Go," she told him, pushing him toward the door.

Jimmy rushed inside as soon as Drake opened it, obviously hoping for a glimpse of something provocative.

"Good afternoon, Detective Dolan." Cassie greeted

him with a gracious smile and calm facade.

Drake was certain Jimmy didn't miss the blush that colored her face, or her rumbled hair.

"Hey ya, Cassie," was all Jimmy said even as his eyes raked over the scene. "How's it going?"

"I'm fine. How are Denise and the kids?"

Jimmy's eyes brightened at the mention of his kids—twins, just turned six and the light of his life. "Great. Soccer starts next week and they're psyched."

"Don't you have a witness waiting?" Drake put in, amused by how easily Hart turned the tide of the conversation.

"Oh. Yeah, let's go or you'll be late, too." They moved down the corridor.

Jimmy muttered, "On the fucking pool table, no less."

Drake couldn't help but grin.

Jungle sex? Finally something to look forward to.

CHAPTER 18

CASSIE DROVE CAREFULLY through the rain-slicked streets. She'd decided to start at the beginning. Virginia Ulrich's hometown was Wheeling, West Virginia, also the location of Golden Crest Nursing Home. Directory assistance had two listings for Jurassics, her maiden name.

The administrators at Golden Crest refused to give her any information over the phone about Virginia. All they would tell her about Sheila Kaminsky was that she had left their employ "because of illness."

There was no answer at either Jurassic residence, so Cassie decided to try her luck in person. Why not? She didn't have anything else to do except to sit at home and worry about little things like impending malpractice suits.

Once in Wheeling she pulled over for gas and a cup of coffee. She thought she'd try the private residences first. She bought a local map and found that they were only a few blocks apart, and not very far from the service station where she was now.

The neighborhood was crowded with row houses and small, gray shingled houses. It was difficult to tell their age given the uniform layer of soot covering them. The first address belonged to a small Cape Cod remarkable only for the sparse icicle shaped Christmas lights dangling from the porch roof, tangled by the wind. Cassie had the feeling they'd been there longer than the four months since the holiday, years even. She pulled the Impreza up to the curb and approached the house.

There was no doorbell, so she opened the storm door and knocked on the wooden door beyond. She waited several moments. Just as she was preparing to knock again she heard movement, and the door was opened by an older woman wearing a dingy pink sweat suit frayed by repeated washing.

"Stella Jurassic?" Cassie asked. Damn, she should have thought this through more. She had no idea what to say next.

"Yeah, who're you? Whatever you're selling, I don't want none."

"I'm not selling anything. My name is Cassandra Hart."

"You one those religion freaks? I already got my own, don't need no one elses."

"No ma'am. I'm a doctor in Pittsburgh. Do you know a Virginia Jurassic? She's Virginia Ulrich now."

The woman squinted her eyes, looking Cassie up and down. She clicked her dentures together, then sighed and took a step back.

"You'd best come in," she said walking away from the door.

Cassie hesitated, and then followed the old woman inside to the living room. Mrs. Jurassic sat down in a tweed recliner, using a remote control to mute the daytime talk show on her large screen television. Cassie perched on the couch beside her.

"Who's she killed now?" the old woman demanded to Cassie's astonishment.

"She killed someone?"

"My brother, her father. Can't prove nothing, but I know it. Who'd you say you were again? A doctor?"

"Yes. I took care of Virginia's son. He's very ill, in our hospital. I was hoping I could get some information about the family's health, anything to help us figure out what's causing Charlie's illness."

There was silence as she digested that. She looked at Cassie again, one eye squinted, head tilted. Cassie noticed a grey film over her left eye; the old woman probably couldn't see much at all from it.

"Why dinna ya ask Virginia herself?"

Good question. One that she had no answer for. When she didn't answer right away, the old woman nodded her head.

"You don't trust her either, do you?"

"No, I don't," Cassie said slowly. When in doubt, go for the truth. "Actually, I'm concerned that Virginia might have something to do with Charlie's illness as well as the death of her first son."

"Didn't know she had more children," Virginia's aunt said. "But then I don't talk with Mary anymore, not since my brother died. And I certainly don't keep track of that girl's doings. But I can tell you she's a snake in the grass. Look around you, think I want to spend the rest of my life here? I had money set aside, good money. But no, Mary and Sam talked me into helping out their little girl with her education. What good did all that learning do when her pa needed her the most? And let me tell you, most of the money didn't end up going to the school, it went straight into her pockets."

"How did her father die?"

"Had himself a stroke, was only fifty but it weren't no surprise the way he lived. Was like a baby. He couldn't talk, couldn't do nothing for hisself. Anyway, Virginia dropped out of school to take care of him, but then all sorts of weird things started to happen. He kept getting sicker and sicker and no doctor she took him to could figure out why. First it was throwing up. He was wasting away to nothing even though she said he was eating okay. Then he started to have broken bones, even though he couldn't do more than take a step or two at most. Then the broken bones got to be infected and they hooked him up to IV's and gadgets." She rolled her eyes, obviously not impressed with medical science. "That was the beginning of the end. A month later he was dead in his sleep, but no one could say why for sure."

"And you blame Virginia?" Cassie asked. The old lady nodded emphatically. "Was an autopsy performed?"

"No, course not. Can't go round cutting up dead bodies, ain't proper. Mary gave Virginia all the insurance money to finish her education, but instead Virginia ran off and got married. Never did pay me back any of the money she owed me, course." She shook her head. "I always did tell Sam he was marrying a fool, and that girl is the spittin' image of her mother. I don't have nothing to do with them no more."

"What was Virginia like as a child?"

"She was their only child. Ran around and did whatever she damned well pleased. Spoiled rotten, but always wanting more. She had to be the center of attention. If she didn't get what she wanted with her temper tantrums, she'd make out like she was faint or sick. Learned that from her mom, she did. I swear to God, Mary's spent more of her days on earth in bed than out, but I tell you there ain't anything wrong with her. Delicate, is what Sam always said."

"So Virginia was sick a lot?"

"Always complaining of one thing or another, always wearing one of those— whatchamacallit—Ace bandages on her wrist or leg. I'd a liked to wrap one around her throat to shut her whining."

Sounded like tendencies to fabricate illness ran in the family. Only in Virginia it had evolved into something more deadly. "What school did she go to?"

"Community college, was gonna be a nurse but never finished. She did have a job for a while at Golden Crest—that's the nursing home out on Springdale. She was married—conned poor ole Michael Stainsby into giving her a ring."

"Did anything unusual happen while Virginia worked at Golden Crest?"

Stella looked at her shrewdly. "Those folks, they called her a hero. Said she saved a few people who were fixin to die. Me, I think, maybe she put 'em there in the first place."

"What happened to Michael, her first husband?"

"Tried to kill hisself after their little girl died. Now he lives downtown, drunk more days than not. Every time I open the paper I expect to find his name in the obituaries."

"Virginia had a little girl?" This was news.

"Cute thing." She shook her head. "You should talk to Michael about her. Elizabeth was her name."

"Is there anything else you can tell me about Virginia?"

She pressed her lips together until they blanched. "She left after Elizabeth died. And that's the last I know of her. Except for Mary constantly running her mouth off 'bout how successful Virginia is now."

Stella Jurassic wrinkled her mouth as if talking about her niece left a bad taste in it. She picked up the remote and turned the sound back on. Jerry Springer was comforting a teenager above the caption: Cross-dressing teens undergoing LIVE exorcisms.

Cassie got to her feet, obviously the interview was over. "Thanks for your help, Ms. Jurassic." The old lady grunted, and Cassie found her own way out of the house.

• ◉ •

"VIRGINIA TOLD ME what you want." Richard King bounced his wheelchair's front wheels against the terrazzo of the sunroom. The Senator swallowed his irritation, forced himself to remain calm when King continued. "I'm not certain I like it."

As if this had anything to do with what King liked or didn't like. The Senator's family was threatened and everything came second to that. "You said yourself that Hart can be subject to fits of despondency. What if she's gotten to the point where she's become delusional? She might even be dangerous to her patients."

King seemed disinterested in the welfare of patients. "You've already sued her for malpractice, humiliated her in front of her colleagues—surely that's enough."

Ex-drug user, the Senator remembered King's background that Thayer had provided. Lost his career as a surgeon because of Hart. Rumors were that during their marriage King beat Hart. Possessive, jealous, narcissistic. Play on that.

"Apparently not. Hart has convinced her new

paramour—" King's eyes narrowed at that, the politician noted. "To look into my daughter in law's past. He won't find anything, of course, but still, the damage will be done. What kind of man is this Rembrandt Michael Drake?"

"Drake?" King scoffed. "An idiot, romantic fool. He's totally smitten by Cassandra, but he'll never have her."

"Why not?"

"Because she's my wife. She belongs to me."

"So you agree that Drake and Hart must be stopped?" King considered that and nodded. Halfway there. The Senator tried another tact. "Have you ever considered the possibility that Hart might be using drugs?"

King laughed. "That's crazy. Cassandra would never—"

"Ah, but you're in that wheelchair because of drugs found in her possession. Isn't that true? Because of Hart you were crippled by those drugs. Maybe there were other times—maybe she played a part in your own addiction." Typical addict, King would place blame for his own weaknesses on anyone except himself.

"Maybe that would explain some of her irrational behaviors," the Senator continued. "Like leaving a happy marriage to a successful surgeon like yourself, for instance."

King's face lit up like a beacon at the fantasy that his marriage to Hart had been happy. What a deluded idiot. But he was an idiot that he needed.

"Maybe. Someone using drugs certainly could act in a self-destructive way like that," King said, dropping into clinical jargon.

Too bad the splatter of spittle destroyed the

image. But they could take care of little details like that. The Senator saw his mistake now. He'd thought of this as a personal problem, best left to the medical and legal professionals. Now he realized that they had to win this battle in the only venue that counted, the court of public opinion. And there was no one better at convincing the masses of what they should believe than the Senator.

"Would you consider making a public plea to your wife, to stop her persecution of Virginia? To seek help for her addiction, just as you have? It might be an important first step to bringing her back home to you." His voice was soothing, trying to coax King to take that final step.

King cut his eyes at the Senator and for a moment he thought he'd lost his prey. But then he saw a look of cunning cross the surgeon's face.

"That would strip Ella of everything that matters to her," King said slowly, as if tasting each word, considering their palatability.

"Not everything. She'd still have you."

King nodded his agreement. "Then she'd see. We're destined to be together, forever."

⁘⦿⁘

CASSIE DROVE BACK to the gas station. Still no answer at the second Jurassic home, probably Virginia's mother, she realized. From what Stella said, Mary Jurassic probably wouldn't be very helpful.

She looked up Michael Stainsby's address, a hotel downtown, and got directions from the attendant. The hotel was a five-story brick building that exuded an oppressive atmosphere. The smell of decay, alcohol, and urine all mingled together to assault her senses as she entered the lobby. The desk clerk didn't look up when she asked for Stainsby, just gestured toward the stairs and muttered, "Three-oh-two."

The stairs were slippery with rainwater combined with decades of grime. She climbed to the third floor and knocked on Michael Stainsby's door.

After a few moments the door was opened by a grey-haired man bent over with a wracking cough. He straightened, and she saw that through the grey stubble and alcoholic flush the man wasn't as old as he first appeared.

"Mr. Stainsby?" He nodded with uncomprehending eyes. "My name is Cassandra Hart. Could we talk for a few minutes?"

Stainsby blinked several times. His eyes were bloodshot and a bright yellow trail of mucus oozed from their inner corners. Cassie didn't touch anything as the man gestured for her to follow him into the room. She edged just inside the door, ensuring a speedy exit if she needed one.

Stainsby stumbled onto the bed, reaching over to the nightstand for a can of Schlitz. Cassie guessed that it wasn't happy hour yet, happy hour being whenever the hard stuff came out.

"It's about your daughter, Elizabeth, and your wife, Virginia."

Stainsby said nothing, merely hung his head. When he looked up, tears were leaking from his eyes. He sniffed loudly and wiped his face on his sleeve.

"My poor little girl," he mumbled, his voice barely audible.

"How'd she die, Mr. Stainsby?" She tried to guide the man into some coherent path of conversation.

"Lizzy was the sweetest little baby. She never cried, always had this big smile for me when I came home from work." He looked up, his roving eyes finally focusing on Cassie. "I stopped drinking right before she was born, got a job, didn't miss a day, didn't touch a drop—" His voice trailed off. "But it didn't do no good. She still died. And it was all my fault."

"What happened?"

"God, that was the worse night of my life." More tears and sniffs. "Lizzy was a sweet baby, but she was always sick. Virginia was forever taking her to doctors. Twice we almost lost her. Would have, if it wasn't for Virginia. She saved Lizzy's life, gave her mouth to mouth. Virginia was always the smart one. It was just too bad for her that she married a loser like me." He hung his head again. Cassie decided to take a new approach.

"How did you and Virginia meet?"

"Virginia Jurassic she was then. Asked me out to her folks house to build a wheelchair ramp." He straightened up. "I was a carpenter, a damned good one. She'd had to leave nursing school to take care of her pa once he had his stroke. She'd keep me company while I worked on the ramp. Talked about finishing college, maybe even going to medical school, and become a doctor. She had a whole house full of medical books. Virginia would've made a good doctor. But she knew her mother wouldn't ever let her go, not with her father needing so much." He stopped for a moment, caught up in faraway memories.

"Funny, they only used that ramp the once after I finished it. And that was to take his body down to the funeral home." Stainsby shook his head. "Guess Virginia's luck was as bad as mine. She ran away after her father died, and we got married. She was going to try to finish school, but Lizzy came along and needed so much of her attention. She was the most beautiful little baby." His sigh echoed through the barren cell of a room.

"Tell me about the night Lizzy died," she coaxed him.

Stainsby finished his can of beer and added it to the stack by the bed. "Virginia had her at the doctors for a real bad cough—croup she said. The baby woke up coughing, and Virginia was 'bout worn out, so I said I'd give her her medicine. Virginia said she told me to read the label and give half a teaspoon, but I never did read too good."

His body began to shake and his voice broke. "I guess, I didn't even grab the right bottle or measure it right—I don't know." He was silent for a minute. "Virginia found Lizzy dead in the morning. They told me I gave her the wrong medicine and way too much, so she stopped breathing. It was all my fault," he wailed, his voice cracking like an adolescent's.

Cassie looked down at the remnants of a man before him. She had an idea who was behind Elizabeth's death and doubted that it was this poor, ignorant wretch. How hard would it be for Virginia to get up either before or after Stainsby and give the baby more medicine? Maybe she even mixed it in the baby's bottle.

"Mr. Stainsby, did the doctor's examine Lizzy's body after she died?"

"Yeah, they took her away and cut her up. They cut up my little girl!"

"Can I have your permission to look at Lizzy's medical records?" Cassie risked contamination by grabbing a sheet of yellowed stationary from the pad beside the telephone and wrote a quick authorization. She held it before Stainsby and watched him sign it with a shaky hand.

"You gonna lock me up for what I did?" the father

asked. "You gonna give me my just punishment?"

All she could do was shake her head. "No, Mr. Stainsby. I'm not with the police." She left Stainsby to the purgatory he'd created for himself.

※

VIRGINIA CHANGED THE dressing on Charlie's leg and applied the tape to it. The site where Cassandra Hart had drilled the needle into Charlie's bone was getting infected, just as she had told the doctors it would. She pulled off her gloves and tossed them into the trash can, then went over to the nurses' station to wash her hands.

The baby was kicking a lot and her back was sore from sitting for so long. Virginia walked around the corner to the side hallway that contained the isolation cubicles. As she passed Antwan Washington's room, she noticed that Tammy Washington sat alone by her son's side.

She was always alone. Other than Virginia, no one seemed to talk to Antwan's mother. The nurses blamed Tammy for Antwan's illness. And Tammy certainly had done nothing to earn anyone's friendship. She hadn't even thanked Virginia for the work Scott Thayer had done on her behalf in bringing suit against Hart—all pro bono. In fact, Tammy seemed to be having second thoughts about suing Hart at all.

The woman didn't seem to understand how to survive in this environment. Tammy was totally out of her element here. She just sat there, rocking with her comatose child, instead of fighting for him, gaining allies from among the staff or asserting her rights as a parent.

Virginia shook her head. She'd done everything

she could to help Tammy Washington, but Tammy seemed content to allow the doctors to have their way with her son.

Virginia had more important things to worry about.

She knew Charlie would be gone soon; she had come to accept that fact. And who knew how long Samantha would live?

Children lived and children died—that was the reality of her life. Paul didn't understand, but what would he know, spending all day in that office of his? He didn't appreciate how hard she worked, how difficult her life was.

Thank goodness for Dr. Sterling and his staff. They seemed to understand.

Virginia completed her circuit around the PICU and ended back at the nurses' station. The desk clerk came over and smiled at her.

"Mrs. Ulrich?"

"Virginia, please." The girl looked barely old enough to be out of high school, Virginia thought. But she was good at keeping things organized and helped Virginia when she needed to reach Dr. Sterling or one of the other specialists to discuss Charlie's case.

"There's a phone call for you on line two."

"Thanks Marina." Virginia crossed behind the barrier and took a seat behind the desk at the doctor's dictation area. No one else was there—the doctors were hardly ever around, it seemed.

"Hello?"

"Virginia dear? This is your mother. How are you?"

"I'm fine, Mom. Why are you calling me here? You know how busy I am whenever Charlie's sick."

"I know, I'm sorry. I just wish I was well enough to

come visit in person."

"Did you want something, Mom?"

"Oh yes. I just had the strangest phone call from your aunt."

"Stella? Whatever did she want?"

"That's what was so strange. She said she heard about Charlie being so sick. I didn't understand all of it, but it seems that some lady doctor from Three Rivers came by to visit Stella and was asking about you."

Virginia clenched her teeth. It had to be Hart, no one else would have the audacity to be prying into her private affairs.

"Stella seemed to think that you were in some sort of trouble," Mary Jurassic continued, oblivious to her daughter's distress. "Said the doctor talked with Sheila Kaminsky, too."

Sheila—she thought that idiot was locked up in a psych unit for good. Nobody, not even Hart could consider her a reliable witness. Not after Sheila tried to poison George.

"Virginia, you still there?"

"Yes, Mom, I'm here. Don't worry, I'm not in any trouble. Aunt Stella's got it all mixed up, is all."

"That's what I figured, dear. I just thought I'd better call and let you know."

"Thanks, Mom. Bye." Virginia hung up the phone before her mother could begin to prattle on with one of her stories. She didn't have time to listen to them, she had a sick child to attend to.

She drummed her fingers on the desk. Should she call Paul? This had to be a violation of the court order. No. She didn't want him to have to deal with Stella or the rest of her family.

She'd take care of Cassandra Hart herself.

CHAPTER 19

———

THE RECEPTIONIST AT the City Hall records office didn't need the scribbled note of release. She was happy to give Cassie a copy of Elisabeth Stainsby's autopsy report and death certificate—they were matters of public record, after all. All Cassie had to do was write a check to the city for twenty dollars and add an extra ten for copying fees.

Finally Cassie carried her hard won stack of papers over to a wooden bench in the marble waiting area. It was almost three o'clock, and she hadn't eaten lunch yet, but she wanted to read them before she hit the road again. Rain coated the large window beside her in a sheet of grime. People were rushing in, shaking their umbrellas and filling the high-vaulted area with giddy laughter.

She looked up from the dry details marking of the end of a child's life to see what was causing all the commotion. Then she realized the couples were lined up before the marriage office. A sign in front proclaimed that marriages were held between three and five every day except Monday and Friday. She watched as a man with trembling fingers dropped the corsage he was trying to pin to his bride-to-be's red satin dress. He bent down but not before a heavyset man stepped on the carnations, crushing them as he rushed over to traffic court.

The man held the ruined flowers in his hand, staring at them in incomprehension, but the woman just laughed and hauled him back up onto his feet, linking her arm with his.

Cassie smiled as the two of them crossed the marble lobby to the marrying judge. Her cell phone chirped, and she snared it from her jacket pocket.

"It's me," Drake's voice sang over the line, widening her smile. "Have you already started dinner?"

She blinked and looked at her watch again. She'd totally forgotten Drake was coming to dinner tonight. Thank God for take out. "No."

"Good. Would you mind terribly if I brought a guest?" He went on without giving her a chance to answer. "I forgot, my mom's flying in this afternoon. I promised her she could meet you—it's okay, isn't it?" he finished in a rush.

His mother? She made a small noise of panic and exasperation, but Verizon somehow mis-conveyed it as assent, because Drake began to thank her. "Great, I knew you wouldn't mind. We'll be there at seven. I've got to go."

Cassie stared at her phone. All the fancy options it boasted, but she still couldn't crawl through it and throttle the person on the other end. If she could, it would be justifiable homicide. No jury with any women on it would ever convict her.

As it was, she had to be satisfied with a muttered curse as she thrust the evil device into her pocket. She turned her attention back to Elizabeth's autopsy findings.

The Wheeling coroner had done a good job of documenting everything; even did a death scene visit. The bottle with the liquid codeine in it was Virginia's. She had gotten it refilled that week after a trip to the dentist. But it was almost empty when they searched the medicine cabinet.

The amount of codeine they found in Elizabeth meant the baby must have been given almost the entire bottle. Even if Michael Stainsby accidentally used a tablespoon instead of a teaspoon, it wouldn't have been enough to generate such a high of blood level.

But once again she had no proof—and Stainsby already admitted that any mistake was his.

Where to go next with this? Cassie could gather all the circumstantial evidence and innuendos in the world, but it wouldn't fly in a court of law. She needed some solid, tangible evidence.

She didn't care about the Executive Committee or her career anymore. She just wanted something that would force CYS to take Charlie into protective custody.

Then she could sleep soundly, knowing he was safe.

COOKING FOR DRAKE was bad enough, the man was practically a gourmet chef, but meeting his mother too? And the trip to Wheeling had her running late.

Cassie opened her freezer door and eyed the contents. There, a package of frozen chicken breasts. She dumped it in the sink, running hot water over it. To hell with FDA rules for food safety, if they got salmonella, she'd apologize later.

Maybe Drake was right, she should enter the twenty-first century, break down and buy a microwave. Truth was, she hated shopping for things like that, all those salespeople asking you what you wanted when you had no idea. Not to mention the noise the damn things made.

What else? She rummaged through the rest of her foodstuffs. Olives, she had fresh basil growing on the windowsill, have to use canned tomatoes, sorry Rosa, and capers—where'd she put the capers?—there.

Rosa's chicken and saffron rice. The only wine she had was a pinot grigio, shouldn't go too badly. Dessert? She wrinkled her nose, slowly turning around her kitchen, hoping for inspiration. Of course, Ed's wife had sent over some of her delicious Cuban pastries. Cassie smiled. This dinner was definitely taking on an international flavor.

She fled up to the bathroom, eager to shower off the stench of Wheeling. Hopefully Mrs. Drake wasn't made violently ill by capers, didn't detest white wine and wasn't on a strict diet. Because about the only other thing Cassie would have to offer her would be the choice of a peanut butter and jelly sandwich made with the remnants of a moldy loaf of bread or Hennessy's cat food.

Cassie rushed through her shower, then faced the question of what to wear. Again the decision was made easier from a lack of choices. She slid into a sleeveless sheath of peacock green silk. It had been the first nice thing she'd bought for herself after leaving Richard. She twisted from side to side in the mirror liking how the dark color shimmered.

The nickel religious medallion Sheila Kaminsky had bestowed on her was the only flaw. She reached a hand to slip it over her head and was surprised by a surge of heat that seemed to radiate from the cheap medal.

From the shower, idiot. She tugged it off. Still, unease flip-flopped her stomach as she tossed Sheila's charm onto the dresser.

Through the open window she heard a car pull up across the street. Damn, they were early. Cassie slid bare feet into her black leather all-occasion flats and ran down the steps. Her hair was still damp, but there was nothing to do about it.

Music—she should've put on music, she thought as she opened the front door. Oh well, she'd let Mrs. Drake chose. And the table still needed to be set. As soon as she got the chicken into the oven, she'd deal with that.

She stepped out onto the porch, waving to Drake as he emerged from the driver's side of his Mustang. At least the rain had slowed to a drizzle. She danced down the steps and crossed the street, skirting the puddles in the pavement.

Drake moved around to the passenger side of the car, opening the door for a slender woman with sleek dark hair and a graceful carriage. Cassie moved to join them, well aware of the lace curtains being drawn aside in Mrs. Ferraro's front window across the street.

"Hello, Mrs. Drake. I'm Cassie Hart." She held out her hand, suddenly feeling uncertain of herself. What if Drake's mother hated her? After all, Cassie was responsible for her son getting shot.

She was rewarded with a warm smile that lit up Mrs. Drake's dazzling blue eyes. "Muriel, please dear. Mrs. Drake was my mother in law." Muriel took Cassie's hand, then pulled her into a hug. "I'm so happy to meet you at last."

Raindrops began to splatter them. "Come inside,

dinner will be ready soon."

Up the hill a car started its engine. They were half way across the street when Drake stopped.

"Wait, I forgot something." He turned and ran back to the car, moving around to the curbside.

She paused for a moment to watch as he ducked his body into the back seat of the car and emerged, holding a bright bouquet of roses and a bottle of wine. He raised them aloft in a gesture of victory.

Muriel continued on, but stopped short of the curb. "Is everything okay?"

Cassie laughed. Mrs. Drake had no reason to know how difficult it had been for her son to bring her roses. The last time he'd done that, he'd been greeted by a killer.

"Fine, Mom. Go on inside," Drake called out, bundling the flowers under his suit coat as he started around the car once more.

Cassie waited for him. A little rain didn't bother her, not when it brought her Drake and a nice, normal night together. A night blissfully free of murder, mayhem and madness.

As she watched, Drake's smile faded and his gaze left hers to jerk up the street. "Look out!"

She heard the car just as he called out. A black van, no headlights on, gunning its engine as it hurtled down the hill. She pivoted and sprinted for the curb. The van sped up, swerving toward her.

Muriel stood directly in its path, her mouth open in surprise. Cassie leapt, tackling the older woman. They slammed into the hood of a parked Ford Taurus just as the van careened off the side of the Ford, propelling the two women into the air.

Cassie heard the squeal of tires and Drake's voice yelling in a kaleidoscope of sound as she and Muriel hurtled across the hood of the Taurus, finally bouncing onto the sidewalk with a sickening thud.

Muriel hit headfirst. Cassie threw her arms out, trying not to land on top of Muriel as she collided against the cement.

She ignored her own pain, rolling over to check on Muriel. The older woman's gaze met Cassie's, her eyes filled with confusion.

"So happy," she said, her words slurred. "You two. Remy—" Her mouth went slack.

Drake was there, shouting into his cell phone. "That's right, Gettysburg Street. Medics and a patrol car. Now!" He put the phone down and knelt beside Muriel, taking her hand. "Mom, you're going to be all right—you hear me? The ambulance is on its way. You're going to be fine."

Cassie moved to Muriel's head, immobilizing the woman's neck and swiftly checking her breathing. Mrs. Ferraro was the first neighbor out onto the street, but not the last. Soon there was a small crowd gathered around Muriel's still form.

Blood from the left ear canal, Cassie noted. Probable basilar skull fracture. Breathing good, pulse steady—should be faster though. Pupils? Damn, the left was bigger than the right.

She looked up, wiping the rain from her face, and met Drake's eyes.

"She's going to be all right," he told her firmly.

"We need to get her to Three Rivers."

The ambulance siren drowned out the rest of her words. As the crowd parted, she spotted the vibrant color of crushed roses scattered across the black pavement.

She looked down, unable to face Drake. So much for a nice, quiet evening in the Hart household.

CHAPTER 20

THE PARAMEDICS KNEW Cassie and were glad of her assistance. "Basilar skull fracture, left pupil blown," she told them, moving aside so that they could secure the cervical collar. "We need to scoop and run. I'll tube her en route."

With practiced hands they slid Muriel onto the backboard and loaded her onto the gurney. Drake started to climb into the ambulance with them.

"No," Cassie told him, echoing what the medics had already said. "Let me do my job. Trust me."

The look in his eyes almost broke her resolve. Fierce and pleading at the same time.

"She's in good hands," one of the medics told Drake as he closed the rear doors of the rig. "Doc Hart's the best."

The door slammed shut, locking out Drake and his lost expression. Cassie shook her head, banishing all thoughts but those of her patient from her mind.

"Seven-oh ET tube, suction. Do you have that IV started yet? Fluids at KVO, head injury protocol," she instructed the medics as she worked. "All right, tube's in. How're her vitals?"

The trip to Three Rivers passed like a carnival ride complete with lurching twists and turns, accompanied by the scream of the siren and horn when recalcitrant drivers failed to yield and punctuated by a snarl of fear that stabbed and twisted into Cassie's gut.

Every time she took her eyes off Muriel, her vision was filled with the sight of the black hulk of metal hurtling toward her with menacing intent.

Someone had just tried to kill her.

The ambulance lurched to a stop, and the rear doors opened once more. She jumped out and accompanied Muriel into the trauma room, her hands squeezing the bag that forced oxygen into her patient's lungs. Muriel was hers now and Cassie wasn't about to leave her in the hands of some green-horned resident.

To her relief, it was Ed Castro waiting for them, gowned and ready for action in the trauma room.

"Pedestrian versus van, hit her head on a sidewalk, probable skull fracture with blown pupil, improved now," she gave him the bullet.

"Neurosurg is waiting up in CT," Ed told her as he finished his exam and concurred with her diagnosis. They'd cut Muriel's clothing from her, inserted nasogastric and Foley catheters, started another IV line and shot X-rays of her spine, chest, abdomen and pelvis. "Let's get her upstairs," he commanded, and the nurses began to push the gurney from the trauma room now littered with debris.

Cassie started to follow, but Ed grabbed her arm. "You're bleeding," he told her. "We need to check you out."

"I'm fine," she argued. "I need to stay with her. I promised Drake."

The door burst open and Drake, followed by Tony Spanos, ran in. "Where is she? How's my mother?" His words came in a breathless frenzy.

"She's all right," Ed assured him. "She's upstairs in CAT scan. Dr. Park, the neurosurgeon is with her."

"Neurosurgeon?" He glared at Cassie. "You said everything would be all right."

Cassie flinched from his accusation. Who could blame him—his mother lay comatose because of her.

Ed looked from one of them to the other and took over. "She will be. But she's showing signs of some swelling in her brain—probably caused by a blood clot. Dr. Park can tell you more once he sees the CT scan."

"A blood clot? People die from that." Drake's voice had dropped to a low monotone.

"Not if they're treated quickly like your mother was. If it is a blood clot, Dr. Park can operate and remove it."

"And afterwards she'll be all right? Everything will be back to normal?"

Ed was silent. Cassie cleared her throat, trying to find the courage to break the news to him.

"Most people do well," she started. "But there can be a long recovery process. Sometimes there are residual defects."

His eyes hardened, and she knew he was thinking of Richard and his brain damage.

"Where's this Park? I need to hear it from him," he asked Ed, dismissing Cassie with a flick of his eyes.

"Jason will take you up to him." Ed waved to the clerk.

She watched as Drake left without a glance for her, his back rigid, his hands fisted at his sides.

The door shut behind him.

Spanos cleared his throat. "He's just upset, doc,"

he said, clearly uncomfortable defending Drake to her. He shifted his weight and retrieved his notebook from his pocket. "I was first on scene. I saw—no one could have done anything more than what you did."

"Dr. Hart needs attention," Ed told him, leading Cassie by the arm down the hall.

"That's okay, I've just got a few questions." Spanos trailed behind them.

Cassie was shivering. She wrapped her arms around her, realizing that her precious dress had been torn and stained beyond repair. Blood covered her arms and legs and somewhere along the way she'd lost a shoe. Water and blood dripped from her clothing and hair. As Ed led her down to an exam room she saw the ER personnel stop what they were doing to stare at her. They quickly looked away once more, not making eye contact, and she knew that the hospital rumor mill would be working overtime. Again.

Ed scowled at the other medical professionals. "Back to work, people," he told them, ushering Cassie into an exam room and closing the door. He handed her a gown. "Get changed and I'll examine you."

She stalled. There was nothing worse than being a patient—unless it was having your godfather, who was also your boss, being the one to see you naked. "Ed, I'm fine. Really, it's just some road rash."

"Then where's all the blood running down your face coming from?" He glowered at her, the same look he'd used when she was a girl and he'd caught her lying. It still worked. "You change, and I'll check on Mrs. Drake's CT."

He left, and Cassie kicked off her lonely shoe and stripped the remnants of her dress away. It wasn't like Ed hadn't seen her as a patient before. He was the one who'd flown through a snowstorm to transport her and

Drake after the shooting.

She tied the flimsy gown around her, glad that at least she was wearing her good underwear. Gram Rosa had been right about that.

Ed and Spanos returned, the policeman carrying a Polaroid camera. "Need it for the report, doc," he told Cassie, blushing as she hiked up her gown to reveal the scrapes on her legs.

Being a patient was so damned embarrassing.

"How was the CT?" she asked.

"Left epidural with mild cerebral edema and a right contusion."

"So she's in the OR?"

"Yes." Ed made quick work of the road rash, gently plucking pieces of gravel from the deeper abrasions and cleaning the wounds. Cassie didn't remember hitting her head, but she must have because her scalp was split open above her right ear. Ed numbed and cleaned that, finally stapling it shut as Cassie answered Spanos' questions.

"I never saw the driver's face," she told him. "It could have been a man or a tall woman. They were wearing a hat and a scarf was wrapped around their face."

She fidgeted as Ed kept poking and prodding at her various injuries, checking for fractures or other occult trauma that could come back to haunt her later. "Would you hurry up?" she snapped. "I want to see how Muriel's doing."

"Almost done," Ed said, applying a vaseline-gauze dressing to her forearm.

"Get me a pair of scrubs, I'm going up there." She started to get up, but he placed a restraining hand on her arm.

"You can go up when I'm done," he told her. "But

Park's just gonna toss you out on your butt and you know it, so hold still." He spoke as if to a recalcitrant child, but Cassie saw the fear in his eyes.

He was afraid—for her. Funny, she wasn't scared at all, not for herself. Not yet. Although that would come sooner or later. Instead all she felt was a growing fury that was flaring to uncontrollable proportions.

"Ed, she was almost killed because of me."

"You don't know that," he snapped. "Isn't that right, Spanos?"

"We don't know who the intended target was," the policeman said. "But all witness accounts confirm that it appeared deliberate. The van followed Hart onto the curb."

Ed shot him a look that shut him up.

"You know it was Virginia Ulrich," Cassie said.

"No, I don't and neither do you. Maybe it was Morris or one of his associates," Ed suggested. "It's not like you've been making a lot of friends around here lately."

She ignored him. Virginia Ulrich. Or her powerful lawyer husband or his powerful senator father. Out to get her—why? Had they heard about her trip to Wheeling? What she'd found supported her theory that Virginia was deliberately hurting her child, but it was hardly proof.

Jason, the ward clerk, opened the door. "Call for you, Cassie," he said. "Line two."

"Thanks." She hopped off the table, holding the loose flutter of gauze that Ed had been about to tape, and grabbed the receiver. "Dr. Hart here." She kept her fingers crossed, hoping it was the OR with good news.

"Dr. Hart? It's Virginia Ulrich. I just heard about your tragic accident and I wanted to call—"

"You've got some nerve!" The fury that had been

building in Cassie exploded. "Where are you? Do you have any idea what you've done?"

Ed and Spanos joined her at the phone.

"I'm up in the ICU with my son," Virginia continued in that same calm voice. "Where I've been all evening. Really, Cassandra, I know how upsetting this must be for you—"

"You don't know shit! I'm going to make certain that you can never hurt anyone again, do you hear me?" Cassie was shouting now, but she couldn't help herself. "Say goodbye to Charlie. If I have anything to do with it, you're never going to be allowed near him again!" She hung up the phone so hard it bounced off the hook and flew to the floor.

"Who was it?" Ed asked.

"Virginia Ulrich," Cassie spat the name as if it were a curse. "Calling to gloat."

"Did she confess to any involvement?" Spanos asked eagerly.

She shook her head, anger pounding through her head, knotting her gut. "No, she said she was in the ICU with Charlie all night."

"That's easy enough to check."

"Good, then go do it." She opened the door and started down the hall toward the women's locker room. Her gown flew open behind her as her legs carried her in a furious stride, but she didn't care.

"Cassie, remember the court order," Ed's voice followed her. "You can't go anywhere near Charlie Ulrich."

"Maybe not," she flung over her shoulder, startling an old man clenching a container full of urine. "But I can call CYS and convince them to put him in protective custody. At least I can keep one person safe around here."

Too bad it was too late for Muriel Drake, a small voice whispered. The voice that would keep her up tonight with repeated recriminations.

She pushed open the door to the locker room and grabbed a pair of scrubs. Time to get back to work.

Cassie stripped free of the gown and slipped into scrubs and a spare pair of Reeboks from her locker. She looked in the mirror. The dressings on her arms were already slipping, making her look like a poorly costumed extra from *The Mummy*. She stripped off the bandages Ed had so carefully applied. There, at least she could move. But the angry red skin was no more appealing. She grabbed her white lab coat from her locker and tried again. Better, at least she looked like she belonged in the hospital. If only she could do something with her hair. But that was a losing battle. She quit while she was ahead.

It took ten minutes before she reached a caseworker at CYS. Cassie quickly explained what she'd found in Wheeling and what happened tonight.

"Do you have any proof that the child in is imminent danger?"

"No. But there's no way to protect him with his mother at his bedside. I think temporary custody and close monitoring is warranted."

The worker was silent, obviously hesitant about yanking the grandchild of a US Senator into protective custody. "I'll talk with my supervisor," she finally promised.

"Tonight?" Cassie pressed.

"Tonight."

She hung up. It was the best she could do for now. She climbed the steps to radiology and reviewed Muriel Drake's head CT for herself. Ed had been right, serious injuries, but nothing that was necessarily life threatening with prompt intervention. She went up to the fourth floor where the operating rooms and ICUs were located. Passed the PICU where Charlie Ulrich was hopefully resting comfortably and sent a prayer in his direction. Thought about her other patient, Antwan Washington, and said another prayer for him and his mother, Tammy.

She sped past the family room, avoiding an encounter with Drake. She couldn't face him. Not yet. Not until she had some good news to offer him. Shedding her lab coat once inside the OR area, she donned a mask, hat and shoe covers and entered Nathan Park's operating room.

Cassie was silent, nodding to the circulating nurse who dutifully recorded her name on the log, and sidled behind Park at the head of the bed. David Allman, the anesthesiologist, looked up at her, and she could see the smile crinkle his eyes above his mask.

"Out!" Park barked without looking away from his work. "Now," the diminutive Korean-American continued, his hands moving swiftly under the operating microscope that he buried his head in.

"I just wanted—" Cassie started.

"Don't make me throw something!" The surgeon never glanced up from the eyepieces that offered him an up close and personal view of Muriel's brain.

Cassie took a step back and remained silent. She could see the vitals flashed on David's monitoring equipment: everything looked good. David gave her a thumbs up and an encouraging wink.

"Are you still here?" Park sighed dramatically. "All right then, you can look through the teaching head. I'm about done anyway."

Cassie moved closer, swiveling the non-sterile arm attached to a monocular lens. Through it she could see everything Park did, although not with the same depth of field. She watched as the surgeon's graceful hands deftly repaired a lacerated vein, using thread thinner than human hair.

"The clot wasn't too bad," he commented as he sewed. "But I'm a bit worried about the contrecoup injury—bit of a contusion and swelling there. Not much I can do about it, only time will tell." He finished tying the last suture and patted the field dry, watching to be sure that his work held. When he was satisfied, he stepped back from the microscope and folded his arms around his chest, keeping them sterile.

"All right, we're ready to close here. Tell the ICU we'll be there in about twenty." He turned and glowered at Cassie. "I suppose you could go hold hands with the family—give them a heads up so they won't have so many questions for me."

"Thanks, Nathan." Although the neurosurgeon was short on people skills, he had talent and knew his business. Cassie respected that. She knew Park felt the same way about her. She'd salvaged some pretty tenuous patients, kept them alive long enough so that he could use those finely honed skills on them.

"Yeah, yeah. C'mon people, I've got dinner waiting."

·⚙·

DRAKE HAD PACED and made his phone calls and snapped at the hospital minister who stopped by to comfort him and paced some more. Finally he came to rest in the chair by the window, looking out over the cemetery with its marble angel shrouded in misty rain.

What a stupid place to put a cemetery. His fingers found a pharmaceutical company pen and a discarded reprint from the *British Medical Journal* with the backs of the pages blank. Without conscious thought his hands began to sketch. Slowly the angel came to life as his pen scratched across the paper.

It was all his fault, the words echoed through his mind accompanied by a pang of guilt and anger.

He remembered grabbing the wine and roses, taking a whiff of their heady fragrance as he stood and waved at Hart. She'd turned, and he'd been captured by that three-quarter profile.

Then Hart had smiled. Her face lit up, eyes sparkling, the corners of her mouth crinkled. God, he loved that smile—saw it too rarely. Once he'd thought he'd give anything, do anything to make her look at him like that.

He'd been caught, off guard, helpless against the feeling that had made his heart skip a few beats as his joy turned to terror. Hart in the middle of the street, rain making her skin glisten. Her house looming behind her, its front door open like a goddamned monster's maw ready to devour anyone foolish enough to enter. The smell of roses and the sound of an engine roared through his mind.

He'd dropped the bottle, never noticing its crash on the pavement. His head was engulfed in a roar as loud as a thirty-eight caliber revolver being fired in the close confines of a cellar. His mouth filled with the taste of blood.

Suddenly he was simultaneously standing on Gettysburg Street and lying on a cold, hard floor, waiting to die. He froze, trapped in time and memory. The fist that gripped his chest did not allow him to breathe or move or call out a warning. He was drowning in blood and the smell of copper salt. Down to his last breath.

And Hart had stood there, smiling at him.

It only lasted a moment, less than a second, but it was a moment too long before he could call out a warning to his mother and Hart. In that time the van had rushed toward the women with the ferocity of a charging bull.

He took a step forward, watching as Hart did his job for him, turning, pulling his mother out of danger.

His hand reached for his off duty Glock at the small of his back, but found — nothing. Nothing but air.

The van closed in. The black bull snickered as it obscured his view, blocking him from the place he needed to be, concealing the fate it had rendered. Then it was gone, its brakes squealing in laughter as it rounded the corner at the bottom of the hill.

All he could see through the red haze and pounding that filled his brain were two women laying sprawled on the sidewalk.

The pen slipped from Drake's numb fingers. He buried his face in his hands. He couldn't feel anything except the steel bands that encircled his chest. Each breath was a fight as he tried to suck in enough air to sustain him.

What had Hart called it? A panic attack? Good name. Because Drake sure as hell was panicked. He was scared to fucking death by this ambush of emotion that hijacked his body and mind.

He finally got his breathing under control. The feeling that he was about to die receded. Only to return — when?

He opened his eyes. An angel stared up at him from the paper. An angel with Hart's face, Hart's smile.

Drake reached for the paper and shredded it until all that remained was a small mountain of ash-sized flakes.

"Mickey?" Hart's voice startled him. She was the only one who called him Mickey, and usually only when her emotions ran high.

The frisson of fear clamped its cold fingers around his chest once more. Had something gone wrong? Was she here to tell him Muriel had died?

She moved into the room, dressed in surgical scrubs, a ridiculous paper cap struggling to contain her hair.

"Everything's going to be all right," she assured him. The cap surrendered, slid to the ground, and her hair flew free. She perched on the coffee table in front of him, scattering the ashes of his creation. "Dr. Park is just finishing. Your mother is doing fine. You'll be able to see her soon."

Drake stared at her. Her face was out of focus and her voice came from a very far distance. His gaze wandered over her, then halted when he noticed the gleam of metal in her scalp. There was a small area of shorn hair at her right temple, the skin stained burnt umber. Seven shiny staples surrounded by dried blood sat there. His hand reached out to touch the wound. It was boggy, swollen.

Hart took his hand in hers. She shook her head and the wound was immediately covered by falling locks of thick, chestnut curls.

"You can see her soon," she continued, squeezing his hand and suddenly everything was back in focus, as if he'd awakened from a nightmare.

"When?" he asked, jerking his hand away from hers. Her touch brought too many memories. He shook away the sudden vision of his hand reaching desperately for hers, sliding across a cellar floor covered in his own blood.

Hart looked down at her empty hand for a

moment, then folded it into her other hand, closing them both into a tight grip. "It will be awhile. Dr. Park has to finish, then he'll take her to the ICU. He'll be by to talk to you soon. But everything went well. They evacuated the blood clot. That relieved most of the pressure on her brain."

Drake rose to his feet and turned toward the window. It was too difficult to look at her, to sit so close to her, smell her scent of April showers and apple blossoms.

The pounding of the blood haze began to sneak up on him, but he took a deep breath and clenched his fists. Not now, you bastard.

He forced himself to breathe deeply, to prove to himself that he could. That he was in control.

"Most of the pressure?" he echoed her words, a not-so-instant play back.

She stood and moved behind him. Don't touch, don't touch, the words shuddered through his hunched shoulders. He kept his back to her. His fingernails bit into his palms as he squeezed his fists tighter, welcoming the pain that kept the red haze at bay.

"There's still some swelling. That's normal," she rushed to assure him, her voice thankfully growing distant as she stepped away from him again. "It might even get worse over the next twenty-four to forty-eight hours. They'll be monitoring her very closely. That's also normal."

In what warped universe was it "normal" to have your mother's fate hanging in the balance for two fucking days? Drake didn't want to be a part of that world. Yet here he was. Again.

Only last time it was his life that hung in the balance.

He shoved his fists into the pockets of his mud-splattered jacket and encountered a small bunch of keys. Hart's. Spanos had grabbed them at the scene, brought them to Drake before he went back to the House. The memory was already dim, as if it had happened years ago. His fingers clenched the tiny bits of metal like they were a lifeline.

Hart had saved him. And now, because of her, his mother was still alive. The surgeon had told him before the operation that Muriel was lucky Hart was there, that if everything right hadn't been done quickly, she might not have made it to the OR alive.

He turned away from the view of the angel guarding her dead and faced Hart. "Thank you."

She colored and looked away. "I'm sorry," she said. "You know it had to have been because of Charlie Ulrich."

He was silent. The cop in him had figured that out a long time ago—after Spanos had told him about Hart's extracurricular activities researching Ulrich's past.

"Something you dug up must have struck a nerve," he said, his voice flat.

She looked up at that. "You know about that?"

"Spanos." She nodded. "I told you I'd look into Charlie's case," he said, the words rushing out, propelled by his anger. "Why couldn't you trust me? Just because I'm not carrying a gun, doesn't make me any less of a cop." Liar—look what happened tonight because you couldn't act like a cop. Not a real cop anyway.

But if she'd only trusted him, then none of this would have happened in the first place. His anger at her grew—and so did the rage and humiliation he felt for himself.

He would have been carrying a gun if she hadn't

gotten him shot. Wouldn't have gotten shot if he hadn't gone to her house that February night, hadn't fantasized about seeing that damned smile of hers. Wouldn't have known about that bewitching smile if she hadn't gotten involved in what didn't concern her in the first place.

The chain of logic was inevitable, cemented in stone. Everything was Hart's fault.

Leaving Drake totally out of control and at her mercy. Which only infuriated him further, and the cycle started all over.

That crimson tide rolled closer, closing in all around him. Threatening to drown him in blood once more.

"I did trust you." Her protests were barely audible over the roar in his head. "But after talking to Sheila Kaminsky—"

"Kaminsky is a goddamned nut case!" he shouted, whirling on her. "She's been arrested twice for stalking Virginia Ulrich after she lost her job, been in and out of Western Psych like it has a fucking revolving door! Paranoid schizophrenic. Does that sound like someone you'd trust your child's life to? Ulrich was right in getting her fired."

"But Kaminsky told me about Virginia's past, and I found—"

"You found shit!" The words reverberated through the small room like the sound of gunshots. "A drunk of an ex who admitted to poisoning his own baby. A jealous aunt who gossips about her niece. Tell me what you found, Hart. Anything worth my mother lying in the OR with her brain sliced open? Tell me!"

All color fled from her face. She backed away from his fury.

That surprised him. He'd never seen Hart back

away from a fight—agree to disagree, yes. But back down, give up—never.

Then he saw the fear in her eyes. And that hit him like a wave of cold water.

He collapsed in the chair, his hands dangling between his knees, head hung low. "Shit," he muttered, barely finding the energy to tug his fingers through his hair, trying to make sense of all this.

"I'm sorry," she whispered. Then she turned and ran away, her footsteps a dim echo.

Drake was crushed. The only thing Hart had ever run from in her life was her ex-husband. And now him—twice in two nights, in fact.

Used to be a good cop. Used to think he was a good person. Now he wasn't sure about anything.

Except this aching void where he knew Hart's hand should be, wrapped in his, sharing her strength. But they seemed to both be running on empty. Running away, running scared.

He covered his face with his hands, kneaded the tears from his eyes as the red haze consumed him.

CHAPTER 21

JIMMY DOLAN OPENED the door of the ICU waiting room and flinched from the naked pain ravaging his partner's face.

"Muriel?" he asked as Denise moved past him to take Drake's hands into hers.

"They say she'll be all right," Drake said.

"DJ, I'm so sorry," Denise crooned. Jimmy watched as she gathered Drake's limp body against hers, in full-blown mothering mode. "What has she gotten you into now?"

No need to specify who "she" was. Denise still held Hart responsible for Drake almost dying two months ago. Some of her resentment of the younger woman came from a fear of being supplanted in his partner's affections. Denise was DJ's surrogate mother: providing food, clean clothes, shelter, a sympathetic ear whenever needed.

Jimmy shook his head. His wife wasn't the only one who treated DJ like the kid was her own personal redemption project. Even Miller, hard-assed cop that she was, had a soft spot for Drake.

Maybe that's why Jimmy liked Hart so much—she didn't let Drake get away with shit, stood toe to toe with him, not giving an inch. Hart reminded Jimmy of Drake Senior. Same passion for her work. Ornery, stubborn as hell, needing to control everything, occasionally sullen and withdrawn. But also dependable and fiercely loyal—the highest praise a cop could give.

All qualities he'd tried to instill in Drake Jr. with mixed success. The kid was bright, resourceful, but also rambunctious and foolhardy. He could read a crime scene like a book, but seemed blind sometimes when it came to understanding people.

The kid. Jimmy grimaced, looking down on his distraught partner.

"Where is Hart?" he asked.

The anguish on DJ's face as he disentangled himself from Denise's embrace made Jimmy think maybe the kid was finally growing up after all.

"I don't know," Drake told him. His face blanked, but his voice was choked. Jimmy knew his hands would be bunched into tight fists as well.

Jimmy pursed his lips. "Spanos said the actor was aiming for her. Don't you think she needs watching over?"

Denise looked up at that. "Jimmy, he's been through enough. He's worried about his mother. Hart can take care of herself." Her tone was stern, suggesting that Hart would be luckier to tangle with the hit and run driver than with Denise.

"How could she let this happen?" she continued. "What has she gotten herself mixed up with now? More drugs?"

Drake looked down at the floor. "She's trying to

protect a little boy," he said. "Hart thinks he might have been abused."

"Oh," Denise said, sinking back into the vinyl cushions of the couch. Her finger reached up to twirl a lock of her blonde hair, and Jimmy knew she was thinking hard. Hopefully about cutting Hart a break.

"So who we looking at?" Jimmy asked, trying to get DJ's mind off his mother.

It worked. Drake stood and began pacing, ticking off possible suspects as he went. "We need to check into Virginia Ulrich, her husband, Paul, and the grandfather."

Jimmy arched an eyebrow at the last. "You mean the Senator."

"Yes. And Sheila Kaminsky—she's a nurse Virginia Ulrich got fired. I checked her out this morning and found out she's also a nut case, paranoid schizophrenic. She has a history of stalking Virginia Ulrich, maybe she became obsessed with Hart."

"What's she have to do with Hart?"

"She's the one who sent Hart to Wheeling, got her to dive into Virginia Ulrich's past. I'm guessing she was looking for Hart to vindicate her somehow, maybe help her get revenge on Ulrich." He paused and shook his head, his fingers raking through his hair. "I don't know."

"Is Hart asking for protection?"

"No. And she wouldn't take it if we offered."

A cloud passed over Drake's face, giving Jimmy some idea of how things now stood between his partner and Hart. This was going to be harder than he thought.

Before he could say anything, the door opened once more and a short, Asian man accompanied by Adeena Coleman entered.

"Ed Castro called me," Adeena said, moving to

take Drake's hand. "I'm sorry to hear about your mother. Dr. Park wanted to talk to you about her surgery."

Drake turned to the surgeon. "Is she all right?"

"She's out of surgery, on her way to the ICU," the surgeon told him, motioning for them to sit down. His gaze moved from Drake to Jimmy.

"This is my partner and his wife," Drake said, sitting on the couch. Adeena and Denise joined him, one on either side while Jimmy moved to the corner of the room, leaning against the wall where he could watch everyone. "When can I see her?"

"In a few minutes. Everything went well," Park assured them. "But the next few days are very important. We'll keep her under sedation tonight and repeat a CT scan in the morning. I've also placed a pressure monitor so that we can keep an eye on the swelling."

"Swelling?" Denise breathed the word

Park nodded. "It's normal to have swelling after an injury—any injury. But the brain is within a closed cavity, so there's very little spare room. If the swelling becomes excessive—"

"You can treat that, right?" Drake asked.

"Yes, to some extent. It's much better to prevent it in the first place, which is why we have her paralyzed on the ventilator."

"You mean she's not breathing, she's in a coma?" Denise asked, squeezing DJ's hand.

"It's normal procedure," Adeena interjected, translating for them. "So the patient doesn't have to work so hard."

"And we can control things better," Park added.

"She's going to be all right?" Drake asked again.

"Odds are very much in her favor. I'll be able to

tell you more after the CT tomorrow." His beeper sounded, and he looked at the display. "I have to get down to the ER. Adeena, can you take Mr. Drake in to see his mother?"

The four of them sat there in silence for a moment as they digested the neurosurgeon's words. Jimmy cleared his throat. "I'll get to work on checking the Ulrichs," he said, moving toward the door.

Adeena looked up. "The Ulrichs? Why? I thought this was an accident."

"The van was aiming for Hart," Drake told her. "My mother just happened to be in the way."

"And you think the Ulrich family is behind this?" the social worker asked.

"Hart spent the day in Virginia's hometown, digging up her past. Who else would have a reason to go after her?"

"They couldn't have had anything to do with it," she told them. "I was with them all evening."

"All evening?" Jimmy asked.

"From about five o'clock until past eight. Virginia, her husband, and father-in-law. Dr. Sterling was there also. We went over Charlie's case, preparing a defense for the CYS investigation Cassie started."

Drake looked up at that. "You think Virginia Ulrich is innocent?"

"I know she is. I've worked with her and Charlie since he was born, worked with her first son as well."

"So Hart was wrong? All this happened for nothing?"

"I don't know what happened tonight, but I'm certain it had nothing to do with the Ulrichs," Adeena told him. "Cassie has been under a lot of stress since she came back to work. You know what happened with Morris?" Drake nodded. "I think she came back to work too soon. I think," she paused, "she needs help."

Denise opened her mouth to say something at that, but Jimmy shook his head. DJ's fists were clenched over his knees, fingers digging into the fabric of his slacks like claws.

"If Hart's wrong about the Ulrichs, then why was someone trying to kill her tonight?" Jimmy asked.

No one seemed to have the answer to that.

※

DRAKE FOLLOWED ADEENA into the surgical intensive care unit where she left him at Muriel's bedside. Here the lights were dim as if to shield visitors from the flurry of activity surrounding them. Men and women in pale green scrubs gathered around patients, busy attending to beeping alarms and strange-looking apparatus. There were several people at Muriel's bedside. Her head was bandaged and there were tubes in each nostril. Drake looked down and saw a plastic bag with urine draining into it. He winced and pulled his gaze away.

Muriel's chest rose and fell in time with the ventilator. Her heartbeat, blood pressure and other measurements were outlined in bright tracings on the monitor above the bed. The worst thing was the clear tubing that snaked under the swath of bandages around her head. A wire ran alongside the tubing and then connected into the monitor—this must be the device measuring the pressure in her brain.

A nurse who looked too young to be out of high school explained everything to Drake in a well-rehearsed monologue. He couldn't pay attention to what she was saying, his mind wandering as he looked around the ICU to the other patients. This place was worse than the morgue. No one here was human, it was all depersonalized. To them his mother was merely the head injury in bed four.

Suddenly he was very angry at these people who had the power to save lives, who had such awesome talents at their command, but who would treat Muriel as they would any anonymous Jane Doe.

He tore his eyes away from Muriel's swollen face framed in white gauze. Hart wasn't like these others. She saw each patient as a person, had the compassion—or was it just simple passion?—to battle any obstacle that stood in her way of caring for them.

Once he'd accused her of caring too much, risking too much to help a patient. He remembered the angry set of her jaw as she stared up at him then, the slight arch of her eyebrows and the angry splotches of crimson that had blossomed on her cheeks as she had defended herself.

I'm just doing what needs to be done, she'd told him.

He wished she was here now, caring for his mother with that same fierce possessiveness.

He turned to take the chair the nurse was offering him and saw her. She was huddled over a chart, Muriel's he assumed, half hidden by the drapes gathered around the other side of the bed.

Hart's teeth worried at her lower lip in that gesture that he found so endearing. Finally, she nodded her head in satisfaction, flipping a page. Drake allowed himself to relax as the look of concern faded from her face. He took his mother's hand in his, surprised and relieved at its warmth.

"Everything's going to be all right," he whispered to Muriel's still form.

Drake watched as Hart closed the chart, saw her

hesitate. "Hart," he called softly. She turned to face him. A mere six feet separated them, but it felt like an ocean of desolation.

Then she stepped toward him, stopping on the opposite side of the bed, Muriel's body between them. She raised Muriel's other hand, her fingers automatically going to the pulse at the wrist.

"Everything looks good," she told him. He watched her stroke Muriel's arm in a soothing motion, as if the unconscious woman could feel it. "There won't be any news until tomorrow after the CT scan. You might want to go home, get some rest while you can."

He shook his head. "My aunt and uncle are on their way from Cleveland. I'll wait until they get here."

She nodded.

"I'm sorry about yelling at you earlier," he said. She shrugged, her attention focused on Muriel, almost as if she didn't hear him. He dug in his pocket for her keys. "Here," he handed them across the bed to her. "Spanos locked your place for you."

"Thanks."

Her fingers brushed his before closing over the keys. He wanted to take her hand, hold it, hold her. But Muriel was between them.

"I guess I'll go home and get cleaned up," she said after a long moment of silence. She looked down at Muriel's face, then back up, meeting his eyes for the first time. "Would it be all right if I came back? Sat with her a while?"

"Yes, of course." Another awkward moment of silence. He cleared his throat. "Jimmy's here. He can take you home, make certain everything's okay."

She looked up at that. A shadow of fear crossed her face, quickly chased away by a flush of anger. She clenched her jaw—he knew that look, all too well.

"Don't worry about me," she said, releasing Muriel's hand and turning away.

Drake watched her negotiate the maze of equipment and personnel that spanned the ICU.

"I can't help it," he whispered as the doors swished shut behind her.

•☙•

"I DON'T CARE if they were having dinner with the president," Cassie told Jimmy as he drove her back to her house. "Maybe they hired someone."

"A US Senator or one of his family members just happened to have the connections to hire a hit man?" he said, doubt evident in his voice. "It's not that easy in real life. What about Morris? He'd be more likely to have cohorts who could do his dirty work for him."

"If Morris wanted to hurt me, he'd do it in person." And take his time about it, she thought with a shudder, remembering the crazed look in the crack addict's eyes as the succinylcholine took effect.

Jimmy grunted his agreement. He pulled up in front of her house.

"I'll get working on it," he assured her. "You going back? Want me to wait for you?" His unspoken question was clear: was she going back to Drake?

"I'm just going to get cleaned up, then I'll take my car back."

He escorted her up to the front door. She waited there as he quickly scoured the house for any signs of intruders. Cassie couldn't believe that someone actually wanted to kill her. Maybe tonight's events had been more designed to frighten and intimidate her. After all, wouldn't that further Virginia Ulrich's cause more? To have Cassie drop her allegations, maybe even resign in disgrace.

Jimmy returned. "All clear," he told her. He surprised her with a quick kiss on the cheek. "Take care now. I'd better get to work sorting all this out."

Cassie watched him go, one hand on her cheek where he'd kissed her. At least one cop was on her side.

But what to do about the other?

·⚙·

THE NURSES KICKED Drake out after half an hour. Denise waited in the family room, leafing through a year-old *Newsweek*. "How is she?" she asked when he sank into the chair across from her.

"Stable," he quoted the nurse. "I think I hate that word. What the hell does stable mean when she's anything but? She could stay in a coma, she might need more surgery, she could wake up like Richard King did—missing bits and pieces of her memory and God knows what else!"

Denise moved to perch on the arm of the chair. "It's going to be all right."

He frowned. Coming from her, the assurances didn't mean very much. He wished Hart was here with him. She'd know the right questions to ask the doctors and nurses, how to interpret their jargon—she would tell him the truth instead of pointless platitudes.

"I can't believe Hart got you into this," Denise went on. "I swear that woman can cause more trouble without even trying—"

"Don't," he snapped, jumping to his feet and moving to the window. "Don't blame her. It's my fault. I froze out there."

"What could you have done? You're still on inactive duty. You don't even have your gun."

And that was the point, wasn't it? Drake stared into the night. The angel glowed in the light of a spotlight aimed up at her face. Please God, don't let anything bad happen to her, he prayed for both his mother and Hart.

"I believe Hart," he said, the words coming slowly, but they felt right, felt true. For the first time that evening the knot between his shoulder blades began to loosen.

Denise opened her mouth, then closed it again, staring at him. Finally she nodded. "She couldn't do better."

He saw her smile, and he frowned. What the hell was she so happy about?

"All right, then. Charlie Ulrich's mother is trying to hurt him. What do we do now?"

Her sudden change of mind surprised him. Then he realized her choice of pronouns and had to smile himself. Hart, like it or not, wasn't going to fight this battle alone.

He returned to sit across from her, knees brushing the coffee table between them as he outlined strategy. "Jimmy's looking into anyone who could have been involved with tonight. But we have to think of a way to convince Children and Youth to place Charlie into protective custody until we can get this all straightened out one way or the other."

"Can't a police officer take a child into custody if he thinks he's at risk?"

Drake shook his head. "Not unless the danger is clear and imminent. We need someone to put pressure on Children and Youth." He thought for a moment. "I think I know just the people."

"Who?"

"How about a Pulitzer prize winning journalist

and her husband, the former managing editor of the Cleveland *Plain Dealer?*"

"Your Aunt Nellie?"

"And Uncle Jake. They should be here soon. They both have friends at the *Post-Gazette*. And there's nothing the bureaucrats at Children and Youth would hate more than to be the object of media scrutiny."

⋆◉⋆

SCOTT THAYER TOOK his sweet time to answer the phone, knowing who was on the other end. A little suspense was good for the soul, he told himself.

"It's me. Did you take care of everything?" Virginia's words were clipped, impatient.

"Of course." Wasn't that what he did? Solve everyone else's problems for them. "But Hart—"

"I heard. That's all right, I'm sure she learned her lesson. And better yet, it seems like this has alienated her from Drake. From the way he was yelling at her, I doubt he'll be rushing to help her anytime soon."

"Do you still want Richard King at the Executive Committee in the morning? Would it be overkill? Hart's career was already in shambles. But King's testimony against her would be the final nail in the coffin."

She made a humming noise as she thought. He could almost see her hand stroking the handset, imagined her touching him. "Yes. Tell him to be there bright and early."

"Don't worry. He's looking forward to it. Thinks he has a shot at getting Hart back if she loses everything. Thinks she'll be desperate enough to come running back to him." He thought of the former surgeon whose fashion accessories now consisted of drool bibs instead of Italian silk ties and smiled. Hard to imagine Virginia had ever seen anything in Richard King. But she was his now—and his alone.

"They deserve each other," she said in a frosty tone.

There was a long pause. "I miss you," he finally said. "When can I see you again?"

"Not until this is all over and Hart is taken care of."

"Everything's all right with the baby?" Even after all these months, he still felt a rush at the thought of her carrying his baby. Their little girl might start out with Paul Ulrich's name and all the money and prestige that went with it, but it wouldn't be long before he and Virginia and their baby would be together forever. He just had to be patient.

Be patient and watch for the right opportunity. Two things Scott excelled at.

CHAPTER 22

Cassie stripped free of the remainder of the gauze bandages Ed Castro had encased her legs in. They made her feel like a victim. And she refused to play that role. Not after what it had cost her to leave Richard. Never again.

She took a warm shower, wincing as the jets of water beat against her battered skin and scalp. Gingerly, she washed mud and street grime from her hair, careful to avoid the laceration with its staples. She stepped from the shower, grabbing a towel, and tried to convince herself that the damage didn't appear as bad as the mirror reflected.

Long sleeves and jeans covered the worst of it. She left her hair down—pulling it back hurt too much, besides it would do what it damned well pleased, anyway.

Her fingers brushed against the St. Jude medallion sitting on her dresser. A shiver raced over her as she remembered Sheila Kaminsky's warning. Silly superstition, what good could a cheap nickel medal do?

But she put it back on, tucking it under the shirt. And felt better wearing it.

She sat on her bed, tying her Reeboks. Damn, she was sore already—would be worse in the morning. She ran her hand over Rosa's quilt and thought for a moment.

Then she smiled and bundled the heavy collection of velvet and silks into her arms. It was the least she could do for Muriel. And who knew? It might help.

At least it would make Cassie feel better knowing that Rosa's quilt guarded Muriel from further harm. Just as good—no, better—than the St. Jude medallion she wore. Because she knew Rosa's quilt had magic, it had saved Rosa's life.

•◉•

DRAKE LOOKED UP as the waiting room door was flung open. A striking woman with black hair and fierce dark eyes rushed in.

"What happened? Is she all right?" Muriel's older sister, Eleanor DeAngelo Steadman, wasn't one to mince words.

"She's fine, Nellie," Drake assured her, getting to his feet and embracing his aunt.

She still smelled of Jean Nate. He remembered the fragrance from summers spent at their house on the shore of Lake Erie. Nellie may have won the Pulitzer, not once but twice, but she'd won his heart at an early age with her ability to bait a hook and almost effortlessly pull bluegills from the Lake. It seemed like magic to a four year old. Then, when Drake was older, Nellie had given him his first sailing lessons on an old Snark, Uncle Jake looking on from his lawn chair while he'd proofed galleys.

Nellie gave him a peck on the cheek, holding him at arms' length, scrutinizing his face, as if doubting his words. Then she nodded. An older man, taller than Drake, but with thinning hair and a slight build came in behind her.

"She's going to be all right, Jacob," Nellie told him, taking his hand.

Jacob Steadman nodded, and his face relaxed into a smile. Drake looked at the two of them. They'd gotten older, he realized with a pang. When had that happened? Suddenly there were glints of silver in his aunt's dark hair, fashioned as always into a French knot. And Jacob's blonde hair, usually cut short, allowing pink sunburned scalp to peak through, was almost gone, replaced by leathery skin mottled with brown splotches.

"They say only one visitor at a time," he told them. "Don't expect much. She's being kept under heavy sedation. They've hooked her up to a ventilator because they want to control her breathing, and her face looks pretty swollen and beat up. The surgeon says this is all very normal," he reassured them, repeating the spiel the nurses had given him.

Nellie blanched as she gripped Jacob's hand tighter. This was the woman who had single handedly brought down the Cleveland Mafia when it tried to take over the local unions? Drake wondered. All his life he'd heard stories about Nellie's fearlessness: her tangle with the KKK in the early sixties during a Freedom Ride, her unflinching exposure of corrupt public officials. He'd never seen his aunt frightened before.

Jacob placed an arm around her and squeezed her tight. "It's going to be all right," he promised, his lips grazing the top of her head. Nellie closed her eyes for a second. Drake watched her take comfort from his uncle and his stomach clenched. They'd been married for forty-one years and still needed each other desperately. He could only hope for a love like that.

Nellie straightened and reluctantly disengaged herself from Jacob's embrace. "I'm ready," she told Drake. He led her to the ICU and waited until Muriel's nurse came to escort her. He saw her swipe at tears before she reached the bed space. Drake sighed and returned to the waiting room.

"Denise had to get home to the kids," Jacob told him, handing Drake a cup of coffee and taking one for himself as well. "She said you needed my help."

Drake nodded, draining the cup without tasting it. He quickly explained to Jacob about Charlie Ulrich and Hart's crusade to protect the boy. To his surprise, Jacob merely arched an eyebrow and nodded when he detailed Hart's suspicions of Virginia Ulrich.

"Munchausen's by Proxy. We did a story on that a few years back," the former editor said, closing his eyes as his almost encyclopedic memory roamed. "Lady in Toledo killed three of five kids before the doctors could prove anything. She killed herself before the trial started. Another in Parma, a babysitter, no a foster mother, was poisoning the kids she was supposed to be taking care of. And there was the lady in Philadelphia—I think nine or ten kids died. Called it SIDS but it wasn't."

He opened his eyes and looked up at Drake. "Of course, the big controversy now is that a lot of doctors are saying that it really doesn't exist. In England, they've overturned hundreds of convictions of women accused of Munchausen's. Nasty business. Your lady friend certain?"

"She can't prove it, but she's certain."

"And you? This could get ugly—case in Toledo

polarized the entire city. Some said the doctors and prosecutors drove the mom to suicide, others said she was a homicidal maniac. You up for that?" His eyes darted to the door, and Drake knew he was thinking of Muriel.

"If someone was trying to kill Hart because of her suspicions, then the only way to keep her safe is to prove them." Drake frowned. Making this public was also a good way to put Hart back in the sights as a target. Someone's sights. He would just have to find out who before anything happened. Anything more, that was. "And the only way to keep Charlie safe is to get him away from his mother."

Jacob nodded. "I'll bet that's where I come in, right?"

"Right. I thought you might be able to put some pressure on Children and Youth, convince them to place Charlie into protective custody until we get to the bottom of this."

His uncle considered. "Would a sympathetic judge help?"

Drake inclined his head. Uncle Jake was better connected than even he imagined. "Yes."

"Let me make some calls." Jacob moved to the corner of the room and pulled out his Blackberry.

Drake sat down, then bounced to his feet once more. What was he supposed to do now? He couldn't sit here all night. He quickly discovered that the room was twenty-seven paces by thirty-two. There was no reading material newer than nine months old, and the free coffee was designed to erode the stomach lining in the most efficient way possible.

Jacob's glares soon chased him out into the hallway where he continued his pacing. He rounded the corner and came up short in front of a set of sliding doors labeled "Pediatric ICU".

Once he entered, he really understood why he hated hospitals. All those kids, surrounded by beeping machines and plastic tubing going in and out of their bodies. Drake shuddered and looked around the windowless room. He recognized Virginia Ulrich from Hart's description. She hovered over a small boy, dwarfed by the large ICU bed, his leg swathed in bandages.

Two nurses talking at the desk looked up when he entered. "Can we help you?" one of them, Gail Robbins her nametag read, asked.

Drake joined them and produced his credentials.

"Detective Drake," the other nurse said in a melodic Island accent. "You probably don't remember me, I'm Rachel Lloyd. I'm a charge nurse down in the ER."

Drake looked again at the woman with the dark complexion, her ebony hair pulled back in an elaborate configuration of braids. "Yes, I do remember. How are you?"

"Dr. Sterling warned us about Charlie, but I didn't know the police were involved as well," Gail continued. "We've been watching him closely. Dr. Hart hasn't even been up here today."

"You don't have to worry about her," Rachel put in. "I heard that she'll be suspended. Tomorrow there's an Executive Committee hearing about her."

Drake tried to hide his surprise at the nurses' condemnation of Hart. "Has Dr. Hart been a problem?"

The nurses exchanged glances. "She's an excellent doctor, always has our patients stabilized before sending them up," Gail said hesitantly.

"But that's her problem," Rachel interjected. "She's too good in some ways. Never asks for help, doesn't trust anyone—has to do everything her way. That's how she got into this trouble in the first place. I told her that protocol on pediatric patients was to call Peds to place difficult lines, but she insisted that there was no time, that he needed fluids immediately. So she placed the intraosseus line and now it's infected."

"You should have seen Dr. Sterling's reaction to that," Gail said. "I thought he was going to hit the roof. But, I have to admit, by the time Charlie got up here, his perfusion was much better and we were able to place a femoral line without any problems."

Drake wasn't certain that he understood all of the medical subtleties. "So Dr. Hart did the right thing and it helped Charlie?"

"Well, yeah, but you have to understand that an IO is a very painful procedure. And Dr. Sterling is very protective of his patients—especially the Ulrichs, they've been through a lot."

"And Dr. Hart's other patient?"

"Antwan? He's a sad case. Dr. Hart saw him a few days ago and diagnosed an ear infection. Apparently the mother never gave him the antibiotic, and he came back with meningitis. Dr. Sterling called CYS to report the mom's neglect, but Dr. Hart came up here and talked to the mother. She told her it wasn't her fault, that she hadn't done anything wrong because no oral antibiotic could have treated the bacteria that was growing."

"Was she right?"

"Yes, but that's beside the point. She's always coming up here, following her patients she calls it, but it seems more like she doesn't trust us to take care of them after they leave the ER. None of the other ER docs do that, they realize that when it comes to kids, we've got the best doctors in the city."

"Like Dr. Sterling?"

"Oh yes. He's the best. It's too bad he doesn't see as many patients now that he's chairman of the department. He's devoted to his patients."

"That's why he was so upset about the way Dr. Hart treated Charlie," Rachel said. "And Virginia is so nice, she'd never complain unless it was really bad. She even came down to the ER after Charlie was admitted to thank me and to express her concerns about the way Dr. Hart interacted with her and Charlie. She said she was so happy when Dr. Sterling arrived and took over—that she got the idea that Dr. Hart thought she was lying about what happened."

Gail shook her head. "Virginia is one of the best mothers we have. It's so helpful that she has a medical background and can understand better what the doctors are doing. She probably just intimidated Dr. Hart because she is so assertive and knows what the proper care for Charlie is."

Rachel nodded her agreement. Drake looked past them to Charlie's bed space and was surprised to see Virginia Ulrich nonchalantly reach up and turn off the monitor connected to Charlie. Then she began to rummage through his bedside table, pulling out various medical supplies.

"Should she be doing that?" he asked the nurses.

"Yes, it's time for Charlie's dressing change. Virginia likes to do it herself, it comforts her and it's a big help to us. You see, Detective, we treat entire families here, not just the patient."

"So I see. Well, thank you for your help, ladies, I'd better be going."

"Don't you want to meet Virginia?"

"Not right now, she looks busy. I'll be back later when she has more time to talk."

"Don't worry, Detective. We'll keep a close eye on Charlie for you," Gail said.

Drake nodded and left the ICU. He paused outside the doors, thinking about the small boy who had set all this in motion. What if Hart was wrong, and he was yanking a sick child away from his loving mother?

He moved into the stairwell, Hart's favorite thinking spot, and sat down on the top step.

Footsteps echoed up the stairwell and a few moments later Hart appeared, carrying a bulging garbage bag. She stopped on the landing below him, tilted her chin up at him. "Everything all right?"

He nodded and patted the step beside him. She joined him. "What's in the bag?" he asked.

"A surprise for your mother."

"She's still sedated, you know."

She smiled. "I know. You want to come see?"

He nodded and helped her to her feet. She kept hold of his hand, and he took a deep breath. There was no red haze now, just a tingling deep inside—the same feeling he'd felt when he watched Nellie and Jacob together.

Drake gathered her into his arms and held her there, his head bowed over hers, inhaling her scent. Allowed himself to be transported to a place where all his loved ones were safe, and he had no worries of mothers harming their sons.

"It's going to be all right, Mickey," she whispered. "Everything will be all right. I promise."

Now Drake believed. A weight dropped from his heart. Hart never made a promise she couldn't keep. He swallowed back tears of relief and clung to her, able to relax for the first time in weeks.

Finally, after long moments where the only sound

in the stairwell was their breathing, he moved back far enough to look at her. Why had he waited so long to let her get close again? Careless—might have lost her for good.

She smiled and raised his hand to her lips. "Want me to read your palm?" she asked. "Rosa taught me how when I was a kid."

"Only if it's good news."

She nodded and kissed his hand once more before lowering it to rest over her heart. She held it there until her pulse and his had synchronized, as if their blood flowed through one heart. Then she turned his hand palm up and lightly traced the lines in it, staring with deep concentration.

"Your life line is long," she intoned. "But with several forks. You'll meet many challenges and overcome them all, have several careers—"

"Gee, that's a surprise," he laughed. She already knew about his art and his working with Ed Castro on the community clinic. "Tell me something I don't know. How's my love line?"

"I see sadness early on, but then it proceeds in a deep, straight furrow—no straying," she said, her face hovering mere inches over his hand.

"Is that my future or your command?"

She nipped at the flesh at the base of his thumb and turned to smile wickedly at him. "Better be both."

"I see. Guess I'd better start working on finding my soul mate, then." She slapped his hand away. "I have a surprise for you, too."

"What?"

"I'm working to get Charlie Ulrich placed in protective custody."

"Really? How?"

"I've a few journalist contacts who are nudging

Children and Youth to take action. With any luck, I'll have a court order by morning."

Her eyes widened as her face lit up. "That's the best news I could have gotten." She flung her arms around him. "Thank you," she whispered. "After everything that's happened because of me—thank you."

Drake held her for an exquisite moment, reveling in her warmth, loving the way her enthusiasm erased all his doubts.

"Come on, I want to see what you brought my mother." He held the door open for her, and they walked hand in hand down to the ICU.

DRAKE WATCHED AS Hart slid her Grandmother Rosa's quilt from the bag and clasped it tight against her chest. She buried her face in its rich velvets and inhaled as if she could smell the memories embedded in the fabrics.

"This quilt saved my grandmother's life," she whispered to Muriel as she smoothed the fabric over his mother's motionless body. "This," she traced her fingers over the intricate, thick stitching that joined the kaleidoscope of fabrics together, "this quilt is magic."

She reached for Muriel's hands and lightly lay them beneath one of hers, moving them with the light touch of a Ouija board, fingertips caressing the soft textures of the textiles. Drake's breathing became shallow.

All he could see was the woman before him. *Are you casting a spell on me, Cassandra Hart?* he wondered, powerless to resist the hypnotic allure of her voice. He leaned forward, adding his hand to the two women's. A tingle of energy shot through him as Hart linked her free hand with his, completing the circle.

"My grandmother Rosa made this *perina* when she was a young girl. Her mother and her grandmother helped her, contributing pieces, some of them going back three, four generations." Hart's voice took on a cadence in synch with their hands moving back and forth along the stitches.

"A *perina*?" Drake asked, his own voice subdued.

"The gypsy version of a bedroll. A heavy blanket to lie on under the stars or roll up in when it grew cold. The women would sew small treasures into the squares—pieces of gold and silver, bits of jewelry. Insurance for when times got bad. It was 1936 and Hitler was already rounding up the gypsies—or anyone that didn't conform to his idea of Aryan. Rosa and her clan as well as several other families thought by traveling together they could protect each other, move outside of Hitler's sphere of influence. Instead all they offered was a tempting target.

"It was the middle of a warm spring night when the soldiers came. The gypsies fought. All of them— men, women and children—but what good are knifes and rocks against machine guns?"

Hart's hand clenched around Drake's. Her eyes had a dreamy, unfocused look as if she'd passed beyond him to another time.

"See that rust-colored spot?" She pointed to a stained piece of ivory silk. "That's the blood of a Nazi soldier Rosa killed with her knife. Then someone clubbed her over the head. When she woke, she was on the back of a truck filled with other women. She was the only one there from her own family. The other women told her the men were mostly killed or taken elsewhere. They wouldn't tell Rosa what happened to the children, not at first at least."

"What happened? Did they take her to a camp?"

"Some ended at Dachau. Others ended up slave labor for local industries or government projects to aid Hitler's glorious Four Year Plan. Rosa was taken to a farm that needed labor to help with the spring tilling and planting. The army had taken his mules and oxen, so they substituted a dozen or so terrified women instead."

As she spoke of a distant land and time, the sights and sounds of the ICU seemed to fade away. He felt his mother's pulse strong and steady beneath his fingers, beating almost in rhythm with Hart's words.

"Rosa kept to herself, not complaining as they were worked from sunup to late into the night. She clung to her *perina*—the only possession she had. The Germans had taken all her skirts, her jewelry, even her shoes, and given her rags to wear. But they laughed when they saw her clutching the bloody, filthy and torn blanket, and called her crazy. Rosa let them think that. Everyday her *perina* grew more covered in mud and slime from the barn where the women were housed. She refused to clean it or to be parted from it, wearing it around her waist or shoulders as she worked in the fields each day.

"Then, one night, coming back from sowing a field, Rosa took a step off the path and was never seen again."

"What happened?" Drake asked, right on cue. He could almost feel the chill of the spring night, clouds masking a sliver of moon, the scent of peat fires mixed with a rich, earthy smell.

"The guards searched for her, but no trace was found. They took the rest of the women back to the barn and spent the night debating whether to send for more troops to aid in the search. In the morning they decided that they would be ridiculed by their compatriots and the better part of valor was to forget that Rosa ever existed."

"And Rosa?"

"By morning she was already far away, headed toward Budapest. She stole clothes from a nearby village, shoes from a train passenger's luggage and bought a rail ticket with gold that had been hidden inside her now clean *perina*."

"But how? How did they not find her?"

She smiled. "The *perina*. Everyday Rosa ground more dirt into it and also grass seed, moss, whatever she could find. Her body heat helped the seed to germinate until finally she had a blanket that was alive."

"The perfect camouflage," Drake said.

Hart nodded. "She stepped off the path into a weed-filled ditch, spread the blanket overtop of her and voila, she was gone."

Drake looked at her, a smile creasing the corners of his mouth. "Magic."

His cellphone gave a raucous chirp, and they jumped apart. He frowned at the number flashing on the screen.

"I'd better see who this is," he told Hart, raising her hand to his lips before releasing her. He leaned down and kissed Muriel on the forehead, trying his best to avoid the bandages swathed around her.

The family room was empty. Drake stared out the window as he dialed the unfamiliar number. He yawned as the phone on the other end rang. The angel continued her vigil, her face smiling serenely, hinting at untold secrets.

"Hello?" came a tentative voice from the phone.

"Drake here." No response. "Someone there called me," he continued, more than a little irritated. If this was a wrong number from some punk, he was going to rip them a new one.

"Thank you for calling back, Detective Drake." The voice was lower now as if the speaker were trying hard not to wake anyone. Drake could understand why, it was after midnight. "It's John Trevasian. We spoke yesterday—"

"Nate's father." Drake sat upright. "Has something happened? Is he all right?" He wasn't certain why he assumed that the boy was in danger, just the kid had seemed so vulnerable. Lately Drake's world had been filled with too many wounded kids—like Mitchell Eades. Not to mention Sophia Frantz, Adam Cleary and Tanya Kent. And Hart's patient, Charlie Ulrich.

"Nate's fine," Trevasian assured him. "But something has happened. I was going to handle it myself, but something didn't feel right and I'd appreciate your advice—I'm just not sure—"

Drake cut the rambling father off. "What happened?"

"It's the dog, Snickers. He's out on my front lawn."

"I'm glad he got home all right," Drake said, stifling another yawn. What did the father want—him to come out and give the dog a scolding? Or check the mutt for rabies before the kids played with him?

"You don't understand. He's—" the man's voice caught. "He's dead. He's been butchered—hacked to pieces."

CHAPTER 23

DRAKE JUMPED TO his feet, choking on his yawn. "Could you repeat that?"

"You heard me. Someone killed the dog and dumped him on my front lawn."

"Call the Zone Seven Station House, have them send a squad car over."

"I have. They said it would probably be a few hours before anyone was available. I covered him with a blanket, but—" Now the father's voice held a definite tremble.

Drake remembered the steady way Trevasian had handled his kids on their mission at the House. He didn't seem the type to scare easily.

"Look, I can't explain over the phone. Is there anyway you could come over yourself?"

Drake was silent. Of course he couldn't go. But how was he supposed to explain to Trevasian that he had to sit with his sick mother? Or that since he wasn't on active duty he wasn't supposed to respond to any calls—Miller would nail his ass to the wall.

Hart's reflection appeared in the window. Drake spun around. She was watching him from the doorway. "Hold on a second," he told Trevasian and covered the phone. "Everything all right?"

She nodded. "The nurses kicked me out. They're doing a procedure on the patient beside Muriel. After that it will be awhile before anyone can go back in, they'll be taking some X-rays. I'll stay and wait if you want to go home and get some sleep. Or," she nodded at the phone, "whatever."

Sleep was not an option, but Drake liked the way she read his mind. Better to be doing something than sitting here slowly going crazy with worry. To hell with Miller and her rules.

"Give me your address again. I'll be right over," he told Trevasian.

·⚙·

TREVASIAN WAS SITTING on the porch, his front door ajar, head cocked, listening for any sounds from inside the house. There was no sign of a patrol car. Drake parked in the driveway, and Trevasian met him as he got out of the Mustang.

The man wore powder blue cotton pajamas with white piping and his feet were bare. Drake hadn't seen pajamas like that since his father died. They were the kind wives picked out for kids to give for Father's Day.

Trevasian held a large flashlight while Drake grabbed his Maglite from the car. "My wife's out of town," he said in a low voice. "I'm trying not to wake the kids—especially Nate. It would kill him to see this."

He led the way across a dew-covered lawn. Well-mulched beds surrounded the house. Crocuses, daffodils and a few of the tiny irises that Hart loved were blooming, adding color to the night. "That's why I was tempted just to clean it up myself, but I have to tell you, Detective, this scares the crap out of me."

They crossed to the opposite end of the porch where a clump of boxwoods blocked the view from the driveway. Beyond the bushes, beneath the still-barren limbs of a small weeping cherry lay a form covered in a blanket bearing the Steelers' logo.

"Whose window is that?" Drake whispered.

"Nate's. First thing he does when he gets up in the morning is open his drapes. He loves getting up early, sometimes he sketches the birds." Trevasian gestured to the bird feeders hanging from the eaves above Nate's window.

Drake crouched next to the blanket, taking care to aim his flashlight beam away from the sleeping boy's window. He noticed that Trevasian stayed well back. He raised a corner of the blanket and shone the flashlight on Snickers—or what remained of the once beautiful dog.

Trevasian had been accurate when he said the dog was butchered. The animal's neck had been slit, deep enough so that his head sprawled to one side leaving the gaping wound wide open like a second, bloody mouth. The poor creature had been gutted as well, its internal organs pulled out to form some kind of warped anatomy display.

Drake could hear Trevasian retching behind him. He took one last quick look and replaced the blanket. He spent a moment shining his light around the area of the body but saw nothing except a faint impression of a drag mark in the mulch.

He climbed to his feet. He hadn't expected to find anything. Whoever had done this had planned it carefully, trying to maximize the terror with minimal effort or risk to himself. He moved to the edge of the lawn farthest from the house and beckoned Trevasian to join him.

"How did you find it?"

"When Marcia's gone, the kids like to bunk together. And I don't sleep well when my wife's away." Trevasian blushed. "Sometimes I'll crawl into bed with the kids. I tell myself it's to keep them from waking up scared, but—" He shrugged. "We were all in Nate's room, and I heard something like a flag or banner flapping in the breeze. I went to the window. Was just checking to see if a storm was coming, the wind picking up—and I saw a car drive off. Then I looked down." He shuddered.

"What if it had been Nate?" he asked. "Why would anyone do that to a kid? Why didn't they just come after me, pick on someone their own size?"

Drake was silent. Bullies never fought fair and neither would anyone capable of this degree of violence.

"Any ideas? You or your wife run into any trouble lately?" he asked the question as neutrally as he could. Most people took offense at the thought that they might have done something to warrant a personal attack. Everyone wanted it to be "some crazy" out there—as if every violent act were the work of some anonymous madman. But Drake knew that the overwhelming odds were that this had been done by someone the Trevasians knew, someone familiar with the family and their routines.

Trevasian didn't take offense, which impressed Drake. The man had obviously been thinking hard about the possibilities. "I'm an attorney," he told Drake. "But I specialize in estate law, hardly the kind of thing to promote animosity. Most people are happy to hear from me—it means they've come into an inheritance of some sort."

"And your wife?"

"She's a flight attendant for Southwest. As far as I know she hasn't had any problems, no run ins with obnoxious passengers, no friction with her coworkers. They usually work the same crews, so they're all pretty close. And," he went on when Drake looked at him with narrowed eyes, "we're happily married. There's no spurned lover hiding in the wings."

"How about the kids? Either of them having any trouble—fights at school?" Not that this was the work of a eight or ten year old. Maybe a parent?

Trevasian shook his head. "Other than Nate's refusing to talk and starting the medication for ADD, everything's been fine. And believe me, Katie Jean would have told us if any of the other kids were bullying her brother. After she slugged them herself," he added with obvious pride at the way the older sister defended her brother.

"When did Nate stop talking?" Mitchell Eades had a speech disorder as well. Why was this case reminding him of a murder eight years old? "Was he seeing a therapist?"

"He was fine until Snickers disappeared. Then he went all quiet. Marcia called the school psychologist who had tested him for the ADD, and he told her it was a normal reaction. Said Nate was scared by the realization that the world was not a permanent place and that he was worried either Marcia or myself might disappear next. Classic fear of abandonment, he said. So no, we haven't taken him to see anyone about it. If he'd seen that," he jerked his chin at the blanket, "we'd all need therapy."

Drake nodded. What the blanket hid was enough

to give any kid nightmares for the rest of his life. He thought about what the Eades kid had seen when he found his mother and was struck again by the similarities between the two cases. Not in the actual crime—killing a dog was hardly the same as murdering a woman—but more in the emotional subtext.

How many actors out there would go to so much trouble to terrify a couple of kids? It could be the same actor, but after four years of silence, why start with killing a dog? Wouldn't he get more gratification from stalking and killing a human?

Drake shook his head. Something wasn't adding up. He pulled out his cell phone and called Jimmy. When it came to the psychology and people stuff, Jimmy was much better than Drake was. Give Drake a crime scene to read anytime—so much easier than people and the warped fantasies that drove them.

Jimmy arrived a short time later. "No luck with the Ulrichs or Kaminsky," he told Drake as they approached the dog's body. "I'll try Kaminsky's place again when we're done here." He crouched and peeked under the blanket, giving a low, almost soundless, whistle.

"Someone's pissed off, right?" Drake said as they moved away from the house.

Jimmy shook his head. "No, just the opposite. There's little blood—the dog was killed elsewhere and brought here to be posed. That rustling noise Trevasian heard was probably the actor dumping the dog out of a plastic garbage bag or drop cloth. And you can see how the body's been arranged just so. This isn't anger. This was very deliberate."

Drake was almost disappointed to hear that Jimmy's thoughts ran in the same direction as his own. "Think it has anything to do with our cold case?"

"I hope not," Jimmy said after a long pause and a frown. "But I'm not sure, it feels—"

"The same, I know." Drake leaned back against the Mustang and ran his fingers through his hair. "Were any of the other families subjected to anything like this?" He gestured toward the dog.

Jimmy thought for a moment. "The Eades didn't have any pets. Kent and Frantz I'm not sure about, but Cleary's mother mentioned their cat was found dead on their porch a week or so before the murder. Said the older brother found it, really freaked him out, but Adam never saw it."

"Still, we should check with Kent and Frantz. I've got a bad feeling about this."

"You and me both."

※

JIMMY YAWNED AS he steered the departmental Dodge into Sheila Kaminsky's parking lot, narrowly avoiding taking off the open door of a beat up Pontiac that was sprawled diagonally across the main entrance lane. Thank God he'd picked up the city vehicle and sent Denise home with the Sienna—she'd have a fit if he'd driven her pride and joy here.

There were no readily discernible parking spaces, cars were left randomly, it appeared, so Jimmy did a three point and double parked in front of the entrance. Well, triple parked, actually. There was already a Jetta perpendicular to the curb and an ancient Datsun wagon blocking it in.

Jimmy got out, his attention drawn to a rusting black Econoline van jumped over the curb, halfway into the grass at the far end of the lot. Kaminsky had a '81 black Econoline registered to her. The van hadn't been here when he'd come by earlier.

Technically the investigation belonged to Jo Anderson over in Traffic, but she understood why Jimmy wanted on board. As long as Jimmy didn't do anything to tank her case when it came to trial, she didn't mind.

He walked over to the old van and used his light to examine the front grill. There was what appeared to be a fresh dent on the passenger corner. The headlight was shattered and a streak of green paint was visible along the passenger side door, highlighted by naked steel where the van's paint had been scraped clean by the impact.

Jimmy gave a low whistle. Jo said the Taurus that had been hit was green. Looked like he'd might have hit the jackpot.

Jimmy called Anderson on her cell. "Sorry to get you out of bed," he started when she answered. Then he heard the roar of an eighteen-wheeler and the honk of an air horn.

"You didn't," she told him when the background noise died down. He heard a car door slam and suddenly her voice was much clearer. "Major pile-up on the Parkway did," she continued. "What's up?"

"Think I found your van from the Drake hit and skip."

"Yeah?" He heard the interest in her voice. "Dumped?"

"No. Parked in front of a suspect's building. I was calling to see if you wanted to talk to her—"

"I'm stuck out here for the next few hours. Why don't you do the initial, get the van impounded and the boys working on it? I'll meet you back at the House."

"I don't want to take your collar—"

"Jimmy, you know that's not how I work," she

said. And she was right. Anderson had one of the highest clearance rates in the Bureau, despite the fact that her chosen specialty was often one of the more unrewarding areas of police work. She had nothing to prove and as she put it, no male bullshit to get in her way. "If you've got enough to bring your suspect in, do it, take the collar. It'll be good for Drake to have this closed."

He smiled at that. Once upon a time a few years ago Anderson and Drake had been a short-lived item. Before Anderson met her dream man in the form of an auto-mechanic who shared her passion for amateur stock car racing.

"Yes, ma'am. I'll see you back at the House."

He picked his way past empty beer cans and cigarette butts to the open front door of the building. Odors of marijuana and burnt Mexican food mixed with the stench of vomit, urine and unwashed bodies in a malodorous goulash that he barely registered.

His steps down the stairs were accompanied by pounding hip-hop mixed with the melodious strains of a woman yelling at a worthless piece of shit named Frank. As he passed the apartment in the front of the building where the screaming was coming from he heard the sound of breaking glass. He hoped Frank had ducked.

Kaminsky's apartment was quiet. He knew from his previous visit that the buzzer didn't work, so he knocked loudly. No answer. He tried the doorknob, and it turned.

Shit. Should've waited for the uniforms. Still could. But he'd already alerted anyone inside that he was here. Should have gotten Anderson out here. Or brought Drake—who was at the House fighting with the computer system, trying to track down other cases with dead pets.

Kaminsky was a nutjob, but nothing in her file said she'd ever been violent. Yet. There was always a first time. Jimmy drew his gun, stayed to one side of the door and gingerly pushed it open.

He crouched low and looked around the door jam, sighting his gun to follow his gaze as he visually cleared the room of any potential danger.

The lights were on but no one was home, he saw immediately. At least no one living.

Sheila Kaminsky's body sprawled over a rickety folding chair, her jeans wet with urine and vomit, her face the dusky grey of death.

Jimmy quickly walked through the apartment, ensuring that he and Kaminsky were the only occupants. No bogeymen under the bed or hiding behind closed doors. He used his cell phone to call it in and then approached the body, noting the scrambled heap of empty pill bottles that littered the carpet beside Kaminsky's right hand. He took care not to touch anything until the photographers and other crime scene techs arrived.

Men and women whose business was death. Like Jimmy's. Anderson was off the hook. This wasn't a traffic case anymore.

CHAPTER 24

VIRGINIA ULRICH WATCHED as the ICU team made their morning rounds. They came in waves. First, the nurses gathered their information and gave report to their replacements on the day shift. Then the residents came and copied the information from the nurses' records at the bedside and did brief examinations on their patients. Virginia knew better than to ask anything of the residents. She had learned from experience that they were powerless.

The fellow on call that day would quickly sweep through the unit discussing any troublesome cases with the physician he was relieving. Then, in the grand finale, would come attending rounds with everyone following the physician in charge of the PICU like a gaggle of white-coated geese in formation.

Virginia always made certain that she was up and ready for the attendings. Dr. Sterling had several patients in the PICU and so he would usually join attending rounds as the unofficial monarch to the PICU attending's prime minister. As chairman of the department, everyone deferred to him.

And he usually listened to Virginia. Especially if she broached her suggestions and concerns in front of the audience of other physicians present during rounds. This way she could ensure that her voice was heard, and that Charlie received the care he needed.

It was an inefficient way of running things, but after so much practice, she'd actually learned to enjoy the spectacle of attending rounds.

The trick was to never embarrass the attendings and to make them feel as if her suggestions were indeed their own ideas. Sometimes she wondered why doctors always seemed to think they were smarter than everyone else. She knew as much about medicine as any of them, more than some, and she had taught herself without the benefit of any fancy medical school.

This morning she was disappointed to see that Dr. Sterling wasn't present for rounds. She wanted to discuss the idea of a possible PET scan for Charlie. She'd read several articles about the procedure and thought it might be helpful. Also, he'd had a fever last night, and she didn't think that they had him on the proper antibiotics to cover the infection caused by the intraosseus needle.

Virginia settled back into her chair. She'd just have to catch Dr. Sterling after they moved Charlie downstairs to Pediatrics later this morning.

The flock of white coats was two bed spaces away from her when a tall, black-haired man accompanied by an overweight woman with curly brown hair entered the PICU. Virginia watched as they approached the desk clerk who immediately rushed to get the charge nurse. The charge nurse, Beth, frowned as she looked over some papers that the man gave her, then turned to look at Virginia.

Virginia felt a surge of alarm. The man's face was a blank mask, unreadable, but Virginia saw storm warnings in his dark blue eyes. She sat up straight, straining to hear what they were talking about.

Then, just as the team of physicians arrived, Beth and the two strangers came over.

"I'm sorry to interrupt," the man said with an air of authority as the woman moved to the head of Charlie's bed, placing herself between Virginia and Charlie.

"Who are you?" Virginia demanded, trying to pull the woman away from the bed. "Get away from my son!" Her voice was frantic and every head swiveled to stare at her.

"I'm Detective Drake," the man continued, unperturbed.

Drake—of course, Hart's lover. The good doctor obviously thought Virginia was responsible for what had happened at her house last night. And wasn't it Drake's mother that had been injured?

He handed Virginia some papers. "This is official notification that Children and Youth is taking protective custody of one Charles Ulrich."

Virginia looked at them, stunned. How could the police allow an obviously biased officer to do this to her? She clutched at the bed rail. "No, you can't!"

"I'm in charge here," Dr. Marchant, the PICU attending, said. "On what grounds—"

"This will not interfere with the patient's medical care," Drake interrupted. "I understand that transfer orders have already been written. Ms. Caulfield and I will accompany Charlie to his new room on the Pediatric floor. Mrs. Ulrich," he turned back to Virginia, "visitation by you and your husband can be arranged with advance notice to CYS and will be supervised."

Virginia glared at the police officer. How dare he do this to her? And in front of all these people? They had no right, Charlie was her son, damn it!

"You can't take Charlie away from me!" she wailed, flinging herself toward the bed. "Dr. Marchant, what's going on here?" Virginia pleaded, tears streaming down her face. "Don't let them take my son!"

By now the entire ICU was in an uproar. Medical staff and family members were all crowding around, watching. Virginia clutched at the bed rail.

"Please, someone call Dr. Sterling," she begged. "He'll fix all this."

Dr. Marchant and one of the residents came to Virginia and tried to calm her. "It'll be all right, Virginia. We'll get to the bottom of this."

Charlie's monitors began to alarm as the toddler woke up crying.

"Charlie, what's wrong?" Virginia screamed. "See what you've done, you're hurting him!"

"Mrs. Ulrich, the boy's upset by your yelling," Drake said coldly. "Please step away from the bed. Ms. Caulfield and I will accompany Charlie's nurse and help move him down to Pediatrics."

Virginia felt the policeman's eyes on her and despised his calm acceptance of her distress. He and the CYS worker seemed utterly oblivious to the torment they were causing her. In fact, she could swear that Drake was almost smiling at her.

She wanted to slap the man, spit in his face for what he was doing to her. But instead, she took a deep, ragged breath and attempted to compose herself. She grasped Dr. Marchant's arm, leaning heavily on him.

"Please, will someone go with him, a familiar

face?" she begged the medical personnel who surrounded her.

"I'll go with Charlie." Beth came forward. "I'll watch over him and make sure that he's settled in. He'll be fine, honest."

"Thank you." Virginia used her free hand to wipe her tears. "Thank you so much, Beth. Please don't let anyone give him any medicine until Dr. Sterling comes. You know what's happened before when he got the wrong medicine."

"Of course, Virginia. Don't worry, everything will be all right."

Virginia took another deep breath and pulled herself upright, releasing Dr. Marchant's arm. "Please, can I just say goodbye?" she asked in a low voice.

Drake looked at the CYS caseworker who nodded and moved aside enough for Virginia to approach Charlie. Charlie was wide awake now, he had stopped crying and was looking around in silence at the adults who had gathered above him. He must be terrified, Virginia thought, reaching forward to brush his hair back.

"It's okay, Charlie. These people are going to take you to a new room, that's all. Mommy will come visit you soon," she whispered, then leaned forward to kiss him.

He was so scared that at first he pulled back away from her. Virginia held his head with one hand and steadied it in place so that she could plant her lips on his. She felt Charlie tense, resisting momentarily against her grasp, then he relaxed, accepting her embrace.

"Goodbye, Charlie. Mommy loves you," she called as Drake and the woman helped Beth push the bed toward the door.

Virginia rushed forward as the PICU doors slid shut behind them, then stopped, tears flowing freely down her cheeks.

"Charlie," she cried out as physicians and nurses surrounded her. Then she couldn't bear it any longer and collapsed to the floor.

•❦•

HART WAS SLUMPED over Muriel's bed, her hand over his mother's.

"Wake up." Drake nudged her gently. She jerked upright, and he could tell from the dark swelling below her eyes that she'd probably just fallen asleep. "I need to ask you a favor."

She combed her fingers through her thick hair, wincing as she grazed the area with the staples. She glanced at Muriel's monitor. "She'll be going down for her CT in a short while," she told him. "Dr. Park was already here, said things looked good."

Drake nodded his thanks at her update. "What time is your meeting?"

Hart looked up at the clock. "In about twenty minutes. What do you need?"

"I just took Charlie into protective custody. He's safe in the monitored room on Peds. But his mother—she freaked. I'd feel better if someone stayed with Mom," he paused, "just in case."

She nodded her understanding. "Of course. I'll come right up after the meeting."

"It's this cold case—I have a few things to track down this morning, then I'll be back," he assured her. "I know you have better things to do—"

"No, I don't. But if I'm suspended, then I might have to charge you." The joke fell flat. They both knew how devastating it would be for Hart to be suspended from her job.

Drake reached for her hand and squeezed it in his. "Good luck," he told her. She rose to her feet and gave him her seat.

"Thanks. I've a feeling I'm going to need it."

※

CASSIE CAUGHT UP with Sterling at his office. If she could make the pediatric chairman see reason, maybe they could work together. "Dr. Sterling, I think you and I should talk."

He paused, his hand on the door to his office. "Why? So you can use me to help spread more vicious rumors regarding Virginia Ulrich?"

"No. Actually I thought you might help me to discover the truth. After all, you know this case better than anyone."

Sterling sighed and opened his door, motioning her inside. "Very well. Maybe I can help you come to your senses."

Cassie ignored his comment and took the opportunity to start going through everything, presenting it as unbiased as possible. She had barely started when Sterling slammed a hand down on top of his desk.

"Enough! I know all this—I was there for George and Charlie's admissions, remember?"

"But Virginia was the only person present at all of these incidents."

"She's a very caring and diligent mother who spends probably 99% of her sons' hospital stays at their bedsides. She would have a much higher chance of noticing anything abnormal than any of our medical personnel. Surely you're not suggesting that it is a crime to be a good mother?"

Cassie was starting to lose her patience. "Did she tell you about her first child, Elizabeth?"

"Of course she did. I just wish that I'd been involved in the case back then. It's too bad those yokels in West Virginia never did an autopsy, that tissue might have the answer I'm looking for. I could search for genetic markers, comparisons between her and the two boys, and narrow down the gene locus that is causing all of this." His voice grew distant.

Cassie imagined that he was dreaming of a future Nobel Prize, or the like. Obviously Sterling was as obsessed with this case as she was, but for different reasons.

"They did do an autopsy," she told him.

He turned to stare at her. "What?"

"The Wheeling coroner followed the suspected Sudden Infant Death protocol, so they did an autopsy. Here's a copy of the findings." She drew out the autopsy protocol.

"I'm certain Virginia told me that they ruled it a SIDS, without an autopsy," he muttered. And for the first time, Cassie heard a trace of uncertainty in his voice.

"I never told you about it because I was so ashamed," came a voice from the doorway. Cassie looked up to see Virginia Ulrich glaring at her. "My first husband was a drunk, and he poisoned our beautiful little girl. If I'd known it was so important, I would have told you, Dr. Sterling." She was choking on her tears now. Cassie marveled at the woman's performance.

"It's all right, Virginia." Sterling moved to guide her to a chair. Virginia kept hold of his hand even after she sat down.

"It's just that I was trying so hard to start a new life here. I wanted to put all that behind me. And I had—" She looked up at him. "Until now. Now, they've come to take Charlie away from me." The last came in a mournful wail.

"What? That's nonsense!" Sterling thundered.

"Dr. Sterling, can't you tell them that it's all a mistake? I would never hurt my own child!"

Cassie watched the theatrics, amazed at just how convincing Virginia was. If she didn't know better, she would start to doubt also. Sterling looked up at her from where he was comforting the distraught mother.

"I'm certain that you're behind this, Dr. Hart," he snapped. "You'd better pack your belongings and be prepared to leave this hospital permanently, because I guarantee you'll never practice medicine here again!"

Cassie gathered her papers and started out. Virginia Ulrich looked up, taking a break from her sobbing. Cassie searched her face for any trace of a smirk or smile. If she'd seen one, she probably would have been unable to resist the temptation to slap it off. But instead, all the mother did was to wipe her tears and grip Sterling's arm.

"What are we going to do about Charlie?"

"I'll tell you what we're going to do," Sterling said, his eyes still on Cassie. "We're going to call the media and inform them that you've been the victim of persecution by CYS and one misguided physician. We'll rally so much support for you, Virginia, that they'll have to return Charlie to your custody."

Cassie left without a word. She'd heard more than enough already. And the worst thing was if a man like Karl Sterling was convinced of Virginia Ulrich's innocence, then she was certain most of the uninformed public would be as well.

She wouldn't be able to tell her side of it, not without violating patient confidentiality—which Virginia knew damned well Cassie would never do.

It seemed that Cassie had just attended the preview to her own public lynching as orchestrated by Virginia Ulrich.

※◎※

DRAKE PULLED INTO the Trevasian driveway for the second time in eight hours. As he approached the front door, he glanced past the boxwoods and was relieved to see that the dog was gone. There was no way he could justify the complete forensic exam he wanted, but he'd called in a favor and convinced one of the crime scene investigators to join the patrolmen. At least the scene was documented, and any evidence preserved.

Hopefully it would be a long time before Miller saw the bill for that, he thought, as he rang the doorbell. Especially since this technically wasn't even a case yet.

A case that didn't exist, investigated by a cop who wasn't one right now, because he thought it might tie into murders going back eleven years? He shook his head, hoping he wasn't making a fool out of himself.

Sometimes you just gotta go with your gut, Hart always said. Usually when he was arguing with her to think a problem through logically instead of jumping into action.

Maybe she had a point. When had Drake started following rules and procedure anyway? He must be getting old—or finally growing up, like Jimmy and Andy kept telling him to.

The door opened, and the sounds of Bugs Bunny

filled the air. "Mom!" Katie Jean yelled back into the house. "Mr. Detective is here! The one who's helping us find Snickers!"

She didn't wait for any parental approval but grabbed his arm and tugged him over the threshold. She poked her head out the door, looking past him to his car.

"No Snickers?" she asked, her voice mournful, making him want nothing more than to run out and find another dog identical to the lost Snickers.

"I'm sorry, Katie Jean."

She bit her lip, and Drake knew why he found her so endearing—she was a miniature Hart done over in freckles and blonde hair. The same impulsive, reckless energy, the same worry about her responsibilities.

Now those worries bowed her skinny shoulders with their weight. Her eyes cut down the hallway. "Are you going to tell Nate? I've got to be there if you are— he may cry."

Drake restrained his impulse to lift her into a bear hug, and instead merely tousled her hair, earning a stern look of disapproval from Katie Jean. "All right. Let's get your mother too."

"She's in the kitchen with Nate."

Katie Jean led Drake on a roundabout path through a family room, the source of the TV sounds, past an empty dog bed surrounded by brand new chew toys and bones that were destined never to be enjoyed, and into a well lit eat-in kitchen.

Still in his Rescue Hero PJ's, Nate sat at a breakfast bar, his head bent over a sketch book, a bowl of soggy Cap'n Crunch beside him. Mrs. Trevasian was on the phone, obviously to the kids' school.

"So you understand why they won't be in today? Oh yes, they'll be fine. Why thank you. Yes, I'll tell him.

Thanks, you too."

She hung up and turned to Drake, outstretching her arm. "Detective Drake, I'm Marcia Trevasian. John has told me how helpful you've been."

He took her hand, a firm grip, he noted. Marcia Trevasian was in her mid-thirties, thin, but in a healthy way, her reddish-blonde hair cut in a well-mannered bob that swept to her shoulders. She was wearing a Southwest Air T-shirt and black jeans that mirrored the circles of fatigue her faded make up revealed. Her lipstick had feathered into fine lines around her mouth. Drake doubted that she'd been to bed at all—probably just arrived home a few hours ago.

What a thing to come home to. He hoped the guys had removed the dog's remains before she got there.

"You're all Katie Jean's been talking about the last two days," Mrs Trevasian continued as Katie Jean tugged Drake over to the bar and pulled out the stool beside Nate for him to perch on. "Nate." She scooped up the untouched cereal bowl. "I wish you wouldn't ask for food you're not going to eat." She emptied the bowl into the sink. "Mr. Mendelsohn says he hopes you feel better. Coffee, Detective?"

Drake felt the boy go rigid at his mother's words. Sensitive, he thought, watching Nate's pencil bore into the paper until the point snapped.

Katie Jean immediately slipped the broken pencil from Nate's clenched fist and whispered something into the boy's ear that relaxed him. She scampered over to a pencil sharpener mounted on the wall beside the refrigerator and returned with a freshly sharpened pencil, climbing onto the stool on the other side of Nate.

"Thank you," Drake told their mother. "Black, please."

Drake examined Nate's work in progress. A series

of sketches, a boy and his dog. Fluid, lacking in detail, but with an advanced sense of perspective and proportion. The kid definitely had something.

Now if he could only get him to talk.

"You're pretty talented," Drake told Nate. "I like your drawings."

He accepted the coffee with a smile. Marcia Trevasian stepped back to lean on the counter, cradling her own cup with a worried expression as she watched Drake with her children.

Drake felt beads of sweat pool at the base of his spine and wished Jimmy was here. Jimmy knew how to talk to kids. He decided to take the easy way out and just tell the truth.

"We found Snickers last night," he began.

Katie Jean looked up at that, but her smile faded when she caught Drake's eyes. Her arm immediately went around her brother's thin body. Nate dropped his pencil but didn't look at Drake, his body slumped, hands falling into his lap.

"Snickers died," Drake continued. "I know how much you both loved him, so I wanted you to know right away."

"He was a good puppy," Katie Jean said, her voice breaking as tears overwhelmed her. Her mother grabbed a box of tissues and joined them.

Nate said nothing, only flinched as his mother tried to embrace him. He shrugged away from Katie Jean's touch and stared down at his drawing pad, an island remote from any human contact.

And he was breaking Drake's heart. Tears he could understand—but this? It was as if Nate was afraid to take comfort from his family. Why? Did he blame himself for Snickers' death? Or was he afraid that if something bad happened to his beloved dog, then something bad could also take someone else he loved away from him?

"Nate," Drake continued in a low voice. "Has anything scary happened to you? Besides Snickers getting lost?"

The boy was silent, biting his lip. Not in worry, Drake thought, but to prevent him from opening his mouth.

"I'm a policeman—you can tell me. Then maybe I can find out who hurt Snickers. Make it so he doesn't hurt anyone else. Would that be a good idea?"

A quick, infinitesimal nod of the head was all the response he got. Progress. Drake slid the drawing pad and turned to a fresh page. "Do you think you could draw the scary thing for me?"

Nothing.

"Are you afraid?" Another quick jerk of the head. "Is it something here, something around your house?" A vigorous shaking in the negative. "Something at school?" Nothing. "Did someone at school scare you?" Nothing.

Drake lifted his head to find Marcia Trevasian staring at him, her gaze intense with worry. He shrugged, wishing he knew how to get a response from her silent son. Then he saw that Nate had taken his pencil up and was slowly sketching something. His grip on the Ticonderoga was white knuckled, and his face was screwed tight with intent.

John Trevasian shuffled into the kitchen, running his hands over sleep deprived eyes. "Drake? You back already? Sorry, I fell asleep. Any news?" He looked over at the tableau in confusion. Katie Jean, tears now spent, was whispering encouragement to her brother as Nate continued to move the pencil across the page. "What's going on?" he asked, accepting a mug of coffee from his wife.

"Nate's trying to tell us something," his wife whispered, as if she was afraid to break the spell.

"Nate's talking?"

Drake shook his head, quickly quelling the look of relief that filled Trevasian's face.

Then Nate straightened, revealing his masterpiece to the adults. The blank sheet of paper was now filled with the outline of a giant hand, palm up, fingers spilling over the edges of the paper as if the hand belonged to an alien creature. Nate looked from one adult to another in anticipation and expectation at his disclosure. His parents nodded encouragement.

"That's really good work, Nate."

"You even filled in the tiny lines that cross the palm."

Nate's eyebrows drew together in a scowl and he turned to Drake, his last hope, the one adult who seemed to appreciate his work for what it was.

Drake looked at the over-scaled palm print with confusion. What the hell did it mean? Why wouldn't the kid just talk, for chrissake?

He lifted blank eyes to meet Nate's and felt crushed by the eight year old's face as it filled with disappointment. He didn't know what to do or say.

Katie Jean did though. She slid off her stool and tugged at Nate's arm. "C'mon, Nate. Road Runner's on next."

Nate nodded. Hand in hand, the two abandoned the adults for the Technicolor world of cartoon land, where dogs and people alike could fall off a cliff or be hit by an anvil and still shake it off, coming back to life.

CHAPTER 25

"My name is Dr. Richard King. I'm an alcoholic," he said turning his face full onto the Executive Committee.

Cassie sat on her hands and wrapped her foot around the base of her chair to keep from jumping up. She'd already protested Richard's presence here with no success. Of course, it didn't hurt that Richard's father was the Chief of Orthopedic Surgery and Vice-chair of the committee.

"And recovering from an addiction to pain relievers," he added, lifting a hand to dab at a small spray of spittle.

Pain relievers, Ecstasy, methamphetamine—whatever happy pill he could get his hands on. What the hell was Richard doing here, talking about his past problems? They had nothing to do with the charges against her.

"I received the treatment I needed. And with the grace of God and the help of my friends and family, I've been sober for a long time now." Meaning that it was a long time since breakfast, Cassie translated. "But I have a confession to make." He paused and looked away as if needing to compose himself. Jesus, he was good. He even had her half-believing him.

"While I was addicted, I was married to another physician, Dr. Cassandra Hart. She was aware of my addiction, in fact she shared in it."

What the hell? Cassie leapt to her feet. Richard's pronouncement had an equally energizing effect on the other physicians, who as one turned to glare at Cassie. "That's a lie! I never—"

"Sit down, Dr. Hart," the chairman told her, banging his fist on the table when the others began to talk at once. "You'll have your turn. Go ahead, Dr. King."

"Cassandra never received the help she needed for her drug use. She refused my pleas to attend therapy, to go into rehab. Like many addicts, especially impaired physicians, she felt that she could handle it, that she was above human frailties.

"Last month Cassandra was involved in the investigation of a narcotics ring that operated out of Three Rivers. She was on the scene of several homicides and even admitted to killing a man."

"How dare you!" Cassie raged. One of the deaths he mentioned was her best friend, who had died in her arms. The other received his injuries while he was trying to kill Cassie and Drake.

"The police filed no charges against her. Maybe in part because Cassandra was having an affair with the lead detective on the case."

More uproar from the others on the committee.

"What does this have to do with Dr. Hart accusing Mrs. Ulrich of child abuse?" a lone voice was heard over the melee.

Ed Castro. Cassie appreciated his help, but hoped

that he didn't bring the wrath of the others down on him in the process.

"I now believe that my ex-wife is suffering from paranoid delusions, possibly brought on by past drug use, and that her illness has caused her to falsely accuse Mrs. Ulrich. It is with a heavy heart that I make these feelings known. Only the possibility of an extreme miscarriage of justice could make me do it." He turned to Cassie. "Cassandra, I beg of you, please, get the help you need."

Cassie raged with impotence as her anger surged through her. The bastard. And he'd done it without the slightest hint of a smile. But she knew that someone else had written the script for him—in his current condition she doubted that Richard could concentrate long enough to compose such a statement. Probably his brother, Alan. Or maybe even the Senator himself.

Richard slumped back in his wheelchair, apparently exhausted from his recital. His father left his seat to join him.

"I hope you all realize how much this has cost my son to come here today and speak to you," the orthopedic surgeon said in his careful, precise speech.

"We do," the chairman said. "Thank you for your time, Dr. King. The committee appreciates your efforts."

Richard's father wheeled his son from the room, and then returned to his seat. The chairman consulted his notes.

"I think we should now address the matter of Ms. Rachel Lloyd's complaint against Dr. Hart," he intoned. "Apparently Dr. Hart took matters into her own hands when a patient became violent and threatened harm to a staff member. Dr. Hart refused police intervention and arranged for the patient to be injected with a potentially lethal dose of succinylcholine."

"Why did you assume you were better equipped to deal with the situation than the police officers on the scene?" the head of internal medicine fired at Cassie.

Cassie didn't answer at first, still preoccupied by Richard's litany of lies. She could tell the committee about his own bias, about the affair with Virginia, but it would only make her look jealous and desperate. She felt the others staring at her and tried to focus. "The police weren't doing anything and I had a plan—"

"Yes, the famous succinylcholine switch. Just what made you so certain that you weren't sending that man out onto the street with a lethal drug? How do you know he wouldn't have injected someone else with the succinylcholine?"

"Morris was coming down from a crack binge," she tried to keep the frustration from her voice. Why couldn't they see that she'd done the only thing possible? "I knew he'd want to take the edge off, shoot up with something right away."

"You knew? Based on what your personal experience?" Richard's father flung the last at her.

She snapped her head up. "I assumed," she emphasized the last word, "based on Morris' past history."

"So you risked lives based on the predictability of a homeless drug addict high on crack cocaine?" Cassie remained silent as the internist continued. "Tell us, Dr. Hart. What evidence do we have that your husband's allegations aren't correct? That you haven't abused drugs."

"I'll take any test—"

"Ah, but what good would a negative test do us now? What proof can you offer us besides your word?" This last came from Sterling, the first he'd spoken since the meeting began.

Cassie stared at him. "What proof do we have that you're not a drug user—besides your word, Dr. Sterling?"

Silence settled over the room as all eyes turned on Cassie. She knew immediately that she'd gone too far.

"Dr. Hart," the chairman snapped, "please try to conduct yourself in some semblance of a professional manner."

She took a deep breath. "I'm sorry. What I meant is, there is nothing beyond our word, our honor to prove any of this."

"So you're saying we should simply believe you and leave it at that?"

"Why is this suddenly a trial of my morals?" she demanded. "What about Charlie Ulrich? Aren't we supposed to be discussing the facts of his case instead of listening to a known drug addict?"

"Tell us. What would Dr. King have to gain by lying to us about such a thing? What could possibly motivate such actions?"

She floundered. How could she explain that the shrunken man in the wheelchair still harbored a deceitful, willful purpose when it came to Cassie? How to explain that when Richard King had lost everything valuable to him he was driven to decimate her to similar circumstances?

She looked around at their closed faces. They wouldn't believe her even if she tried. They'd already made up their minds about her. This whole thing was a sham.

Sterling was the only one at the table who met her eyes. At least he didn't smile as he nodded to her, accepting her silent surrender.

CHAPTER 26

CASSIE WALKED BACK toward the ER, clutching the small bundle of files on Charlie Ulrich, her anger growing with each step. Other than Richard's accusations that she was deluded, Charlie's case had not been mentioned. No one seemed to care; everyone had their own agenda.

At least Charlie was safely in protective custody. She could stop worrying about him.

The cause of her new worries glided up to her on silent wheels.

"I'm sorry, I had to do it," Richard said, his voice earnest.

"I'm not having this conversation." Cassie kept on walking, but he kept pace with her.

"Please, Ella, let me explain."

Richard's voice held a note of pleading she'd never heard before. She shrugged, what did she have to lose by listening?

"I know how you feel," he began, his words emerging in a slow, precise way as if he had practiced this speech. "You've lost everything important to you — just like I have." To her surprise, he reached out his strong hand and clasped hers. "I was wrong to blame you. I was angry, hurt."

Cassie snatched her hand away. She took a step back. The Armani suit, despite its lapel smeared with saliva, the polished Italian leather shoes—he almost looked like the old Richard.

"Don't you see, Ella? Now that we've both hit bottom we can climb back. Together. This is our chance to rebuild our lives." He caressed her ring finger. The one where his ring used to live. "You and me—just like it was always meant to be."

"No." The single word echoed through the small space of the hallway. "Never."

"Why?" He looked down, his face hidden from her and she wondered if he was crying. "Don't you understand? I love you, Ella. I need you." He wiped his face on his sleeve and looked back up. "You need me. Especially now. Drake can't help you."

"This has nothing to do with Drake. You think I've lost everything today? You're wrong, Richard. You say that I've hit bottom just like you—"

"You'll never get another job practicing medicine, not after today—"

"Not after your lies, you mean!"

"But," the word emerged a stuttered slur, "I did it for you, for us—"

"You did it for you, Richard. And because Virginia Ulrich or someone in her family got hold of you and convinced you that I'd come back to you, or I deserved it or whatever." The wheelchair rocked back and forth, a witness to his agitation, and she knew she was right.

"Not Virginia." He shook his head, tiny bubbles of saliva splattering the air as he did. "Alan said, and

Scott Thayer, and the Senator, he said—"

"He told you to destroy my career to save his own reputation."

"No. That's not why I did it. We're the same now, we've both lost everything—" His eyes clouded with confusion as he repeated his mantra.

Cassie felt sorry for him. He'd done terrible things, awful things. He was narcissistic, sociopathic even—but once upon a time she had loved the man. And he had lost everything important to him.

"They were wrong, Richard." She crouched down so that their eyes were level. "I did lose everything once. My pride, my integrity, my self respect—I lost it all once, but not today."

"Not today?"

She shook her head. "Not today. I lost it all that last night with you. You finished with me, left me in a bloody mess on the floor, and I got to my feet. I hurt all over, but I couldn't really feel it. As if everything you'd done hadn't really happened to me. I looked in the mirror and I thought—that's not me. Not that woman with the black eye and split lip. Who is that?"

His hand covered hers on the arm of his chair. "It'll be different now, I promise."

"You don't understand. I might have just stayed, let you keep separating me from my soul until I forgot who I really was. But then the phone rang."

He frowned. "The phone?"

"You were supposed to be on call. A patient needed you. And you were passed out, drunk." She stopped, looked down at the floor, stomach clenched as she remembered the shameful thing she'd done. "I lied for you, Richard. I told the hospital you had a bad case of food poisoning. I could barely talk, I got blood all over the phone, couldn't even look at myself in the mirror—but I still loved you enough to lie for you, to protect you."

"You love me." His hand tightened over hers as if she'd offered him a lifeline.

"I did. Once. But when I hung up, and thought about what I did, what you did—that was when I knew I had lost everything. That was when I hit bottom, Richard."

"That was when you left me."

"I built a new life, just like you will now. It won't be easy. But it can be done."

"But, I need you, Ella. Can't do it without you—"

She pulled her hand from his grasp and stood. "You will." She swiped errant tears from her eyes. "I did."

She moved toward the ER's door, and knew what she had to do now. First thing was to protect Ed Castro from any fallout. He'd risked a lot coming to her defense.

Then she'd talk to Drake. Together, they'd think of something.

❦

NELLIE STEADMAN SAT in the family waiting room, hoping Muriel would return from the CAT scan soon. The TV was tuned to a local news station covering an event at the front steps of Three Rivers Medical Center. She heard a familiar name and her attention perked.

"Has the hospital begun an investigation into Dr. Hart's misconduct?"

"Have any other patients or their families complained about Dr. Hart?"

"What legal action are you taking, Mr. Ulrich?"

The questions were fired in a staccato fashion.

Paul Ulrich, one arm comforting his wife, raised a hand to quiet the reporters. Nellie looked up as Jacob roused from his nap on the couch and joined her, sitting on the arm of her chair, one arm automatically going around her shoulder.

"We are working with both the hospital administration as well as the legal system to rectify this miscarriage of justice." Mr. Ulrich's was the voice of reason, not that of an upset or hysterical parent. "In fact, Judge Flory and the Deputy Secretary of Children and Youth Services are meeting with us tomorrow. We can only pray that our son remains safe until then. Virginia and I would also like to thank Dr. Sterling for his excellent medical care as well as his compassion in coming forward to help us get our child back where he belongs, with his parents. Thank you, that is all."

With a dramatic flourish, he dismissed the reporters. The camera zoomed in on the station's correspondent, a pretty young blonde in a perky red hat.

"And that concludes the press conference convened by local attorney, Paul Ulrich. In summary, the Ulrichs claim that they are the targets of an unwarranted attack by a physician here at Three Rivers, Dr. Cassandra Hart. They claim that she has reported malicious and unfounded accusations, which have resulted in CYS taking their child, who lies critically ill in the pediatric ward of Three Rivers, into protective custody.

"Our thoughts go out to this family, and we hope that their son will recover. It remains to be seen what emotional ramifications these accusations will bring to this family. Pennsylvania law currently protects physicians who report suspicions of child abuse, however more cases of false accusations are being brought to the public attention daily. Some are lobbying for a change in that law in order to protect people such as the Ulrichs from this type of tragedy."

Jacob clicked the TV off before the reporter could continue. "I especially liked the way they immediately presumed Hart's guilt without ever hearing her side of the story."

They both knew that none of his reporters would have gotten away with coverage like that. Nellie nodded but said nothing, still staring at the darkened TV screen.

"Of course, who couldn't help but sympathize with the distraught but brave parents that the Ulrichs portrayed themselves as."

"You think we should have jumped in so fast?" Nellie asked, feeling doubt for the first time. She was a reporter, damn it. She should've questioned Hart more, investigated herself.

"We're not reporting a story here. When it's family, you don't have to be objective," he assured her, effortlessly following her thoughts. "You just do what needs to be done."

"Hart's not family," she reminded him.

"Not yet," he said with a smile. "And Remy is."

"Remy is." She still was uncertain.

"What do you think we should do?"

"For starters, as soon as Muriel gets back, one of us stays with her. Always. We can't take any chances until we learn what the truth is."

·⊙·

CASSIE MADE HER way back to Ed Castro's office and found him waiting for her.

"I'm sorry. I did everything I could," he told her,

gesturing for her to take the chair across from him. "They decided to wait for a final vote until the Medical Board can investigate the allegations of drug use. Until then, you're on indefinite leave."

In answer, Cassie dumped the stack of files onto his desk, watching as they cascaded over the surface, not bothering to pick up the ones that slid to the floor. She was so angry, so tired. She felt close to either tears or laughter, and she had no idea which. It was as if her body was no longer hers to control. Why not? She'd lost control of every other aspect of her life. She slumped into the chair.

"We'll appeal," Ed said, straightening the files.

"Sterling and the Ulrichs are holding a press conference denouncing me as some mad fanatic who forced CYS to take Charlie away. Virginia is already practicing her martyred mother routine, and Sterling has the pompous ass role nailed."

"We'll get through this," Ed said softly.

"No." The syllable came out with a force she hadn't expected. She rose to her feet and stood again. "I'm out of it. Virginia Ulrich and the rest can go to hell."

She started out, feeling giddy, lighter somehow.

"Cassie—"

"If they want my resignation, give it to them," she told him.

With Drake protecting Charlie, she was free to escape the tangled mess of lies and accusations her life had become. She could trust Drake to get to the heart of things, and keep Charlie safe. Virginia Ulrich may have won the battle, but she hadn't won the war.

Cassie closed the door behind her. Time for her to get back to Muriel, and keep her promise to Drake.

Paul had a deposition, so Virginia stayed after the press conference to talk to the reporters and answer their questions. Dr. Sterling remained with her, giving her moral support.

"If there aren't any further questions," he finally said, "Mrs. Ulrich needs her rest. This has been a grueling ordeal for her." With that, he wrapped his arm around Virginia and escorted her inside the hospital.

"I don't know how to thank you," she told him once the sliding doors closed behind them. "I'm certain that you must have other, more important things to do."

"Nonsense. Until we get this straightened out, you and Charlie are my top priority."

"Dr. Sterling, I just don't know what to do." Her voice broke, but she couldn't control herself. "It's hard enough to be a parent and be forced to sit by and do nothing—but at least I was there for Charlie, I could comfort him. I could at least do that. But now—" Sobs overcame her, and she turned away so that he wouldn't be embarrassed.

"It will be all right, Virginia," he told her, guiding her to an empty couch near the information desk and handing her his handkerchief. "I promise, I won't let you down."

"But you've done so much, already," she protested. "Without you, Charlie would be dead—" Her voice broke once more, and she looked up at him, anguished. "You will still be his doctor, won't you?" She gripped his hands tightly, ignoring the tear-stained handkerchief. "Promise me, you won't let them take you off the case and give it to some stranger who doesn't even know Charlie or what he's been through—I couldn't bear it!"

"That will never happen, Virginia. You know

better than that."

"It's just that Dr. Hart has convinced everyone else that I'm a monster of some sort. Do you know she even accused me of trying to run her down with my car? And she's saying I had some kind of affair with her husband."

"The woman is delusional. I'm certain she won't be practicing medicine here much longer."

"Scott told me her boyfriend's family was instrumental in getting Judge Flory to issue the protection order. Do you think talking to them, giving them my side of the story would help?"

He considered this. "That might not be a bad idea, Virginia. Maybe they could convince Hart to withdraw her allegations against you."

Virginia straightened in her seat. "Would that mean that I could be with Charlie?"

"It would be the first step."

She wiped her face with the handkerchief, took a deep breath, and stood. "Let's go."

They found the Steadmans in the ICU waiting room. Virginia knew right away that the tall, dark-haired woman was related to Muriel Drake by the way the woman tensed and glared at her as soon as she and Dr. Sterling entered.

"Mr. and Mrs. Steadman?" Virginia was glad of Dr. Sterling's reassuring presence behind her as she moved forward to introduce herself. "I'm Virginia Ulrich and this is Dr. Karl Sterling, the Chief of Pediatrics. Dr. Sterling is my son's doctor."

The husband remained silent, letting his wife take the lead.

"We know who you are," Mrs. Steadman said, nodding at the television.

"I just wanted to offer my condolences about your

sister. I know how terrible it is to have a loved one so critically ill." Silence as Mrs. Steadman continued the staring match.

"I don't know what Dr. Hart has told you about Virginia," Dr. Sterling put in, "but I assure you that Mrs. Ulrich would never harm any of her children. I've been involved in their care since they were born, and I have over thirty years of expertise and experience in Pediatrics. Dr. Hart hasn't been practicing very long, yet she's already facing possible suspension and a review of her license by the Medical Board. She has many serious problems and when I met with her this morning she appeared to be emotionally unbalanced."

Mr. Steadman spoke up at that. "You met with Cassie this morning?"

"She came to me, wanting my support for yet another ridiculous theory about how Virginia hurt her first child. As before, she offered no proof, only vague innuendos. Of course, I didn't fully understand why she's been so obsessed with this until her ex-husband explained to us that she has a history of drug use and is suffering from paranoid delusions as a result. You knew that he was hospitalized and is still recovering from an accidental drug overdose that he received because of Hart, don't you? In any case, it's perfectly obvious that young lady needs a great deal of help."

He didn't wait for their answer, turning to Virginia as if his statement should be enough to convince any reasonable party. "Virginia, shall I leave you to it, then?"

"Of course, Dr. Sterling. Thank you for your help." The pediatrician left the room. Virginia rubbed her belly and took another step toward the Steadmans. "May I sit down?"

She took a seat in the chair across from them. "I

wanted you to see for yourselves that I'm not a monster. Actually, I'm quite worried about Dr. Hart. I'm good friends with Richard King, and I know he's been trying desperately to reach out to her, to get her help. I don't understand what I did to make her dislike me so, but she even has it in her head that I'm somehow responsible for your sister's accident. And that's impossible, because I was here all last night. You can ask anyone down the hall in the PICU.

"So," she took a deep breath, "I need your help. Because of Dr. Hart, they took my child away from me. I'm asking you to help me get him back." She leaned forward, returning Mrs. Steadman's gaze without flinching.

"What do you want us to do?" Mr. Steadman asked.

Virginia was surprised. She'd assumed that the wife would be the one making the decisions. She took her time answering, rubbing her swollen belly in a slow, rhythmic pattern.

"I thought if you could talk to Dr. Hart, maybe convince her to work with Dr. Sterling if she's really interested in helping Charlie, instead of going behind his back—" Virginia brightened, deciding that she was on the right track. "After all, he's been working with cases like Charlie's for years. Although he says that our case is the biggest challenge of his career, he promised me that we'd get some answers in time to help Samantha." She patted her belly. "That's Charlie's new sister.

"Dr. Sterling assures me that this isn't the first time allegations of child abuse have been made in difficult cases like ours, so I totally understand why a naive young doctor who doesn't specialize in these complex areas could assume the worse. I'm even grateful that Dr. Hart has so much passion when it comes to protecting her patients. But," her voice choked with tears and she swallowed, "I need to be with my son. Can you imagine him locked in a room all alone, no one to take care of him or comfort him? That's another form of abuse in my mind."

Virginia opened her purse and removed the bundle of snapshots that she always carried. "Most of these were taken while Charlie was in the hospital." She spread them out on the tabletop so that the Steadmans could view them.

"That one was just three months ago." She pointed to an image with Charlie, surrounded by balloons and smiling nurses. "We were going home after his G-tube was placed. Then we were back a week later—there was a mix up with his medications and he had a severe reaction." Her voice dropped. "I almost lost him then."

"What about all this Munchausen's business?" Mrs. Steadman spoke up. "Maybe Cassie is right."

"It's true, I probably do fit the profile for Munchausen's," Virginia admitted. She met the wife's gaze without flinching. "But, I'll bet you do also, Mrs. Steadman."

"Me?" The wife straightened at that.

"Don't you watch your sister closely—even though you know your doctors have her best interests at heart? Don't you ask them questions to make sure they're giving her the best possible treatment? Do you ask the nurses to double check before they give her any medication or perform a procedure—just to avoid any mistakes?"

Mrs. Steadman nodded her head slowly.

"And haven't you educated yourself about her expected course of treatment?" Virginia continued. "Of course you have. Look, we all know that being a helpless patient in a hospital as busy as this one is dangerous. Mistakes are made, ignorant residents and interns don't appreciate the subtle changes in a patient's condition that someone who really knows him can see. Anyone who is at all protective of their loved ones fits the Munchausen profile. And I'll be the first to admit it—I am an over-protective mother. I've already lost two children—I can't, I won't—go through that again!" Virginia's voice rose in indignation as she pled her case.

When she finished there was only the sound of the photos being shuffled as the Steadmans looked at them. Finally, Mr. Steadman stacked the pictures together and handed them back to Virginia.

"You keep this." Virginia gave them the top photo, one of her and Charlie on a swing together. "I want you to put a face with the name of the child. A child who right now is being denied the comfort of his mother's presence. Think about this, please. What if something happens, what if," her voice caught, "Charlie dies and he's all alone? Is there anything that could be worse for a child?"

CHAPTER 27

Cassie saw Muriel safely back to her bed space after her CT, then called Drake with the results. He answered right away, but she heard the faint sound of a TV in the background, and he kept his voice muted.

"It looks good," she told him, happy to have something go right today. It was only ten-thirty, but she felt as if weeks had passed since she'd seen him. "Dr. Park will probably allow her to wake up later today."

"She's doing all right, then?" His voice was strained with exhaustion and worry.

"She's fine," she assured him, hoping to ease some of his fears.

"I'm not sure how much longer I'll be—"

"Don't worry. I'll stay with her." She heard his answering sigh resonate over the line. He had to be close to catching the man who killed those children Jimmy had told her about—nothing less would keep him away from his mother. "I promise, nothing will happen to her."

"All right, then. Call me if anything changes."

He hung up, and she went to tell Nellie and Jacob about the CT results. They sat together on the couch, heads bowed together in earnest discussion when she entered the family lounge.

"Good news," she said. "The CT shows improvement. Dr. Park is cutting back on the sedation, and will probably take her off the ventilator this afternoon once she's awake."

Instead of the smiles she'd expected, they both turned to her with grim expressions.

"What is it?"

Nellie answered her. "We've decided—" She cut her husband a look, but he remained silent. "That is, we thought it would be better if one of us stays with Muriel from now on. I'm certain you need your rest after being up all night."

"I'm fine—" she started, and then realized that this had nothing to do with her beauty sleep. "Who have you been talking to? Karl Sterling?"

Nellie nodded. "And Virginia Ulrich. They mentioned your husband's accusations and an investigation from the Medical Board. There was also a news conference on TV that said you might be suspended."

"It's not that we believe any of this—" Jacob put in.

"I promised Drake I'd stay with her," she protested.

"I have to protect my sister's best interests," Nellie continued in a firm tone. "You understand, I'm sure."

Cassie glanced down; she saw the photo of Charlie Ulrich on the table between them. Virginia Ulrich's trump card.

"We understand you only wanted to help," Jacob said, trying to soften the blow. "Thank you. But it really is for the best."

"Don't forget your quilt," Nellie added. "We wouldn't want to be responsible for a family heirloom."

They were tying up loose ends, giving her no excuse to return. How could she keep her promise to Drake if they wouldn't let her near Muriel? Cassie's jaw clenched in frustration, and she didn't trust her voice. She nodded her understanding, spun on her heel, and left.

She wasn't surprised when Nellie followed her into the ICU and watched her as she gathered Rosa's *perina* into her arms. The quilt's colors appeared faded and dull in the bright lights, as if all the magic had been drained from it. Cassie bent over the bedrail, took Muriel's hand in hers and gave it a small squeeze. She saw Nellie approach, but didn't let go.

"You take care," she whispered to the comatose woman. "I'll be back. Somehow."

"Please leave now," Nellie said. Cassie saw the determined expression on her face. "Don't force me to call security."

Cassie backed away from the bed. At least Nellie and Jacob would be watching over Muriel.

She clutched the *perina* to her chest and walked away. She couldn't help but stop and look back. Nellie stood beside her sister, one hand protectively on her shoulder, staring at Cassie. Muriel appeared pale, otherworldly, in the glare of the lights reflected from the crisp white sheets and bandages surrounding her. Then Nellie yanked the curtain closed around the bed, blocking Muriel from view.

• ❀ •

DRAKE NOW KNEW more about the Trevasian family

than their parish priest. He'd gone over the family routines, friends, families, and acquaintances in tedious detail until all of them were frustrated. Nothing seemed to have any connection to the attack on Snickers. An attack Drake was convinced was aimed at the children.

He was just leaving when his cell phone rang again.

"I've got Lucas to move the Kaminsky PM up," Jimmy said by way of greeting. "He's getting ready to start now."

"I'm on my way." Drake said farewell to the parents, then stopped by the family room where Katie Jean and Nate sat Indian-style on the floor, mesmerized by the cartoons flickering on the TV. Bugs Bunny had been replaced by Scooby Doo.

Katie Jean scrambled to her feet and ran to Drake, almost bowling him over with a hug. She tugged his arm until he squatted to meet her gaze. "You find the bad man," she whispered to him. "Put him in jail for hurting Snickers."

It wasn't a question, he understood, but a command. A single, silent tear slipped from her eye as she looked over her shoulder at Nate, who stared blankly at the TV as if he'd escaped into his own private world. Own private hell, more like it.

"I'll do my best," he assured the ten-year-old. She held his hand as he moved into the room and squatted down beside Nate. "Draw me some pictures, all right Nate? Anything you're worried about, you just draw it and I'll come take a look at it. Maybe bring you some paints and art books next time I come, all right?"

Nate's gaze never wavered from the point fixed just below the TV screen. He didn't even blink, merely rocked back and forth as if an unseen wind was pushing at him. Drake gave up, reached out and patted the boy's head, and left.

Lucas Steward, the Assistant Medical Examiner, was noted for his attention to detail and strict adherence to his routines. Which is why Drake wondered what Jimmy had done to get him to bump his scheduled cases to perform Kaminsky's autopsy. When he arrived at the autopsy suite, he found Lucas had already begun the external exam, but hadn't yet made the Y-shaped incision.

Jimmy was dressed in a white Tyvek coverall and had his protective mask on. Another break in routine—Jimmy hated post mortems—usually it was Drake's territory. Drake didn't mind. He was fascinated by the endless variety of the human form.

"What's the big deal?" he asked after changing into his own protective gear and joining them in the well-lit autopsy suite. "Kaminsky killed herself after trying to kill Hart. Case closed, right?"

"Not quite," Jimmy replied. He and Lucas were bent over the naked woman's face, huddled together as they peered through the large round illuminated magnifying lens.

"Look here," Lucas instructed, holding Kaminsky's mouth open. "Petechiae and contusions on the upper gingiva and frenulum."

"Someone held her mouth closed so hard that it caused bruising inside her lip," Jimmy translated. "Probably while they were force feeding her the pills and booze."

"Couldn't she have injured herself?" Drake asked. "Maybe trying not to vomit after she took everything? Because if she did, she'd have to start all over again."

Jimmy and Lucas exchanged glances.

"Show him Exhibit One," Jimmy said.

Lucas pulled out an Alternate Light Source and

handed both of them tinted goggles. He nodded to his assistant who turned off the room lights. A moment later the darkness was broken by the gleam of the ALS, revealing faint markings on Kaminsky's neck and face. Drake leaned forward, held his hand out as a gauge. The markings lined up almost perfectly.

"A hand, probably a man's," he said.

"Bingo," Jimmy replied. "Our suicide just became a homicide."

⁘

NELLIE STEADMAN FOUND Paul Ulrich alone in his office at King, King, and Ulrich. It was a corner office, spacious enough to hold several large and expensive Navajo rugs, a leather sofa, coffee table and two club chairs as well as a rough-hewn desk with two chairs in front of it, both upholstered in a western motif. The only personal item in the room was a framed photo of Ulrich with his wife and son.

Nellie had done her research. Ulrich had a reputation as a fierce divorce attorney whose motto was: take no prisoners and leave no asset untouched. He was a man who'd made many enemies during his fight to ensure his clients walked away from the bargaining table with their pockets brimming over.

The man who stood before her, head bowed low as he stared at the family portrait on his desk, was not the man she'd expected to find.

"Thank you for seeing me," she told him, standing a small distance away, giving him time to collect himself. "I know this is a bad time for you."

He pinched the bridge of his nose and nodded. "I just got back from the hospital. The social worker took me in to see Charlie. Virginia—she broke down, she couldn't bear to go in there knowing that she'd have to abandon him, leave him—" his voice caught, and he cleared his throat.

"How's he doing?" Nellie asked. She knew how she'd felt when the nurses told her she couldn't stay by Muriel's side. How much worse for a parent forced to leave their child?

"Actually, he seems much better," he said. "He smiled at me, and laughed at the video we watched. Veggie Tales, his favorite." He took a deep, ragged breath, and then turned to face Nellie. "So what can I possibly do for you, Mrs. Steadman?"

"You know what happened to my sister?"

"Of course. And surely you also know that Dr. Hart's accusations against my wife are preposterous. Virginia, my father, and myself were all with Dr. Sterling and several other medical professionals discussing Charlie's case."

"I know. Apparently the van that hit my sister belonged to a nurse who accused your wife of abusing your first son."

"Sheila Kaminsky. I don't think I ever met her myself, but Scott—Scott Thayer, my assistant—he told me how unstable she was. I believe she was even hospitalized for psychiatric reasons."

"Did you know she lost her job because Virginia accused her of giving George an overdose of potassium?"

Ulrich looked up at that, surprised. Nellie wondered how much the man actually knew about either of his sons' illnesses, or what went on when they were in the hospital.

"Virginia deals with all the medical details," he explained. "I used to try to go as much as possible, but with work—" He gestured at his affluent office as if it explained everything.

"And I admit, I get nervous in hospitals. Virginia says I only make things worse for the boys—for Charlie," he amended with a catch in his voice. "Just the other night when I was holding him, I almost pulled his IV line out. Virginia caught it in time, thank God. So I try to concentrate on providing her and Charlie with everything she needs to focus on getting him better." He shrugged. "It's what works for us."

"Did you know about the first CYS investigation while George was alive?"

A shadow crossed his face. "That nurse, Kaminsky, said she'd seen Virginia do something—I can't remember what. But when they looked through the notes they realized that a lot of times George would get worse while I was there. Virginia said if I wasn't careful, they'd start investigating me. That's when I stopped going as often." He glanced down at the intricately woven rug beneath his feet. "I have to confess, it was a relief, in a way. I felt so helpless, overwhelmed, every time I saw him. And the look in Virginia's eyes whenever things would get worse—"

His gaze drifted up to his family's photo again. He straightened, and seemed to take strength from the images of his loved ones. "You have no idea how brave my wife is. She's given her heart and soul to those boys and somehow even found the time to help the Children's Coalition. Everyday I think how lucky I was to have found her."

Nellie watched as his shoulders shook and realized that the attorney was weeping. Sleep deprivation and the emotional strain of everything Charlie and his family were going through had no doubt taken their toll. The woman in her felt guilty about taking advantage of his emotional vulnerability.

The reporter in her recognized a golden opportunity to get to unspoken truths.

"I think your wife is very lucky to have you, Mr. Ulrich," she offered. "Without your support, where would she have found the strength to make it through George and Charlie's illnesses?"

He shook his head, one hand raised as if warding off her praise. "The only thing Virginia has ever wanted in this life was a healthy child. I've failed, I haven't been able to give her—God, she deserves so much better than me." He sank into his desk chair and stared unseeing at the panoramic view of Point Park. "At least with Samantha everything will be all right. Virginia can finally have a healthy child and live the life she deserves."

Nellie looked up at that. "What makes you so certain that Samantha will be healthy?"

He seemed oblivious to her blunt intrusion into his personal life. Nellie usually had to work to relax a subject to the point where they lowered their guard. The stress that Paul Ulrich had been under lately had done that for her.

"Samantha isn't mine." He stated the fact as if commenting on the weather. Then he looked up at her, making direct eye contact for the first time. "I see every kind of marriage and relationship come through here, Mrs. Steadman. I see what breaks the vows and pledges once given out of love. I understand that what drives most divorces is the need to take control, to selfishly deprive the partner of whatever it is that they cherish. Often this is done in an attempt to refocus their attention back on their spouse, but it always backfires.

"I have learned over the years that the key to a successful marriage is the willingness to do whatever is necessary, no matter the personal cost, to ensure that your spouse is given what they most desire and need. Virginia has done that for me—given unselfishly of herself to care for our children, to create a wonderful home, and allow me to focus on my career. When Dr. Sterling suggested that our sons' illness could be hereditary, I decided to—" he hesitated, searching for a word, "encourage Virginia to seek pleasure outside of our bedroom."

Nellie found herself holding her breath, afraid to disturb the spell that had loosened the lawyer's tongue. Paul Ulrich spoke as if he were unburdening his soul in an act of confession.

"I was never a very satisfying lover to her, never devoted the attention or time to her that she deserved. It was hard, probably the most painful thing I've ever done, but she's carrying a healthy child. After Samantha is born, we can be the family that Virginia always dreamed of."

Nellie stared at him dumbfounded. "Why are you telling me this?"

Ulrich looked up at her with red-rimmed and weary eyes. "Because Virginia had an affair with Richard King. I believe he's the father of the baby she's carrying."

Nellie took a step back. King, Cassie's ex-husband—the one who had accused her of using drugs. And Cassie was the reason King was in that wheelchair to start with.

The possibilities swirled in her mind. Was Muriel lying in the ICU, fighting for her life because of some kind of warped tug of war between Richard King and his ex-wife? Had this whole awful situation evolved out of the wretched remnants of a marriage gone bad?

She'd overheard Remy mention that King was obsessed with Cassie—could the reverse be true as well?

"I'm sure you understand now why it's so important that Charlie be returned to us. And why I had to take such extreme measures to ensure that Dr. Hart never goes near him again," Ulrich finished.

His voice now sounded calm and professional, while Nellie was the one reeling.

Was Hart responsible for this entire tragedy? she wondered as she left Ulrich's office. The same woman that she'd almost trusted with Muriel's life? The woman Remy was falling in love with?

Nellie stabbed at the elevator button, cursing its slowness. She had to find Remy, and tell him the truth about Cassandra Hart.

CHAPTER 28

Morning clouds had given way to brilliant afternoon sunshine. The temperature was a balmy seventy-four. Great for the farmers and gardeners, but torture for school children trapped behind windows and closed doors.

It hadn't done the raw chicken Cassie had set out last night any favors either.

What more could go wrong? she thought as she moved through the house opening all the windows.

The morning had been frustrating enough. After Drake's aunt had kicked her out, she'd decided if she couldn't stay with Muriel, she would follow Virginia Ulrich. Cassie had spent most of the day watching Virginia hold court in the Pediatric family room while her husband visited Charlie. Nurses, aides, even a few other parents had come to see Virginia, to offer their sympathy and support.

And to voice their uniform condemnation of Cassie's actions. She'd stayed out of sight, but she was certain Virginia knew she was there. Finally, Virginia had gone home to get some rest, and Cassie had followed suit.

She held her breath as she double-bagged the ruined meat and walked it out to the trashcan in the alley behind her house. The way her job prospects were looking, it probably wasn't a good idea to be so wasteful with food.

Cassie began to scour the sink. She'd spent too many hours under Rosa's sharp eyes and had worked her way through college as a hotel housekeeper, which made cleaning a chore she often rebelled against, procrastinating it until the dishes overflowed or her shoes stuck to grimy floors.

Or until strong emotions drove her to pick up the sponge and bucket. Almost as good as time on the heavy bag or Kempo sparring.

Once started, it was hard to stop—the sink now shone brightly, making the counter tops look dingy in comparison. Cassie turned up the volume on her father's LP, James Lee Hooker, rolled up her sleeves, and went on a cleaning frenzy. The mindless activity drove all thoughts of the Ulrichs, Sterling, and Richard from her mind.

But not Drake. She wished he was there, imagined his strong arms around her waist, his laughter as he transformed her dour mood into hope for the future that was now spread before her like a blank canvas.

The doorbell rang just as she finished with the oven several hours later. Cassie rinsed the abrasive cleaner from her hands—as usual she'd forgotten to put gloves on and now her hands were raw, red, and wrinkled. She dried them on the backs of her jeans and went to the front room, hoping to find Drake waiting for her.

It was Adeena. Cassie opened the door and

looked out at her friend. Adeena shifted her weight self-consciously, just like she used to do whenever they were called to the principal's office at Our Lady of Sorrows.

"Hi," she said, her face turned down, but her eyes angled up to meet Cassie's. She scuffed her immaculate shoes on the welcome mat. "Can I come in?"

Cassie moved aside and gestured for her to enter. Adeena took two steps into the living room and wrinkled her nose.

"What crawled in here to die?" she asked.

"That's my dinner you're talking about," Cassie protested.

"Smells like the time we snuck the goat cheese under the radiator in Sister Paula's room so we wouldn't have to take the math test." She looked over at Cassie and offered a smile.

Cassie returned it. She'd missed Adeena, and not being able to talk to her because of their differences about the Ulrich case. "Come on out back, to the garden."

Adeena covered her mouth with her hand as they walked through the house and out to the back yard. Azaleas, rhododendrons, irises, hyacinths, and tulips all competed for attention. A wrought iron table and two chairs sat on a tiled patio in the middle of the riot of color. Cassie slid into one chair and motioned for Adeena to join her.

"I wanted to apologize," Adeena started. "I feel like I let you down. I should have paid more attention."

A frisson of fear straightened Cassie's spine. "Did something happen to Charlie?"

Adeena frowned. "No, of course not. Charlie's fine. I'm talking about you. I heard about the Executive Committee meeting this morning."

"For a confidential meeting, it seems like a lot of people already know what happened. Except for my side of the story, of course. Pretty smart of Sterling to move that the committee defer any decision. Let the media and court of public opinion crucify me first." She sounded bitter and she knew it. Guess all that cleaning hadn't totally purged her anger.

"Cassie, I'm sorry," Adeena said, laying one hand over hers.

She shrugged. "There was nothing you could have done about it."

"Yes, there was. I should have seen this coming, somehow got you to listen to reason—this is all my fault. I'm trained to recognize people in crisis, but you're always so strong, have your own way of coping—I should have made you see reason sooner."

Cassie felt anger flood her face as she looked at her friend in astonishment. "Make me see reason?" she demanded. "You're the one with her head in the sand, Adeena! When are you going to realize that Virginia Ulrich is using you and everyone else at Three Rivers?"

She shoved the chair aside and stood, pacing around the patio, oblivious to the beauty around her. "I can't believe that woman. After all we've been through, she's still able to turn you against me."

"I'm not against you," Adeena spoke in the slow, measured voice she used with volatile patients, which only irritated Cassie further. "None of us are. We are all trying to help you before someone else gets hurt. Before you hurt yourself."

That was it. She didn't care how far back they went, Cassie wasn't going to allow anyone to come into her own house and accuse her of being crazy and self-destructive.

Okay, so she talked to her dead grandmother.

Every once in a while Rosa even talked back. So she believed in magic charms and destiny contained within the palm of a hand—it didn't mean she was wrong about Virginia Ulrich, and it sure as hell didn't mean she was crazy!

"I think you'd better leave. Now," she said through clenched teeth, her fingers wrapped around the back of the iron chair.

Adeena scrambled out of her chair, obviously frightened and alarmed by her friend's reaction to her offer of help. The look on her face angered Cassie further. And scared her—Adeena knew her so well, how could she possibly believe Cassie had gone off the deep end?

Unless it was true. After all, Adeena was the mental health professional.

She took a deep breath, and forced herself to calm. "I'm sorry. It's been a rough couple of days." Adeena nodded from her position across the patio, watching warily. "I know you came here because you're worried and you care about me, but please, you have to believe me. I'm not delusional, obsessed, or paranoid— Virginia Ulrich really is a monster. I don't know how, but I know she was responsible for hurting Drake's mother last night. She has to be stopped." The last came out as a plea, but Adeena's expression only hardened.

If Cassie couldn't convince her best friend, what hope was there?

At least Drake stood with her. She wasn't alone in this. His faith in her was the one bright light in this whole dark nightmare.

"Virginia had nothing to do with last night," Adeena said in that same clinical voice. Only now it held a trace of pity, which stabbed at Cassie like a knife in her gut. Adeena had seen her through a lot of tragedy, but she'd never pitied her before. "The police found the van that hit Mrs. Drake. It belonged to Sheila Kaminsky."

She felt her grip on the chair slip. "Sheila?"

Adeena nodded. "They found her body this morning as well. She killed herself. That's why—" the social worker stopped, as if uncertain Cassie could bear hearing anymore.

"What?" Cassie asked, forcing her feet to keep her upright despite the unsteady ground moving beneath her.

"Drake and his family talked to Virginia awhile ago. She told me that they're going to ask Judge Flory to reverse his decision and give Charlie back to Virginia."

Cassie tried to swallow, but couldn't. The earth was spinning out of control. There had to be a mistake. Drake wouldn't have done that, would never have betrayed her—

"You're lying," she whispered.

Adeena shook her head; her braids rattling with a happy noise that bombarded Cassie. "No, I'm not. I'm sorry—"

"Get out!" Cassie yelled as her last vestiges of control snapped. "Go now!"

Adeena backed up the steps leading into the house, staring at her friend like she would a rabid dog. "You need help Cassie," she tried one last time. "Let me help you—"

Cassie raced up the steps after her best friend. Adeena's shoes scuffed the hard wood floors in her hurry to flee. Cassie slammed the front door on her friend and listened as her footsteps clattered down the porch steps. She heard Adeena's car start, then pull away.

She leaned with her back against the solid oak

door, her breath coming in heaving gasps that left her starving for oxygen. She slid to the floor, pounding her fists on her thighs in an effort to feel something, feel anything. The last rays of the setting sun fell away from the porch, leaving the living room in shadow.

No one trusted her, no one believed her.

Her best friend thought she was insane, obsessed, delusional.

Drake had betrayed her. Leaving Charlie unprotected, vulnerable.

Slowly, cautiously, she worked to untangle her snarled emotions.

What did Rosa used to say? *Increde se inseala*, trust invites treason. Cassie threw her head back, banging it off the door and laughed. The sound echoed through the empty house like a jackal's call in the night.

Why did Rosa always have to be right?

CHAPTER 29

"It's me," Cassie said when Drake's intercom sounded.

"I'm busy right now." His voice was distant, cold even. What did she expect?

"Now or never. We need to talk." The ultimatum sounded shrill, but Cassie didn't care. She needed to get her world back in balance—with or without Drake. And try to convince him to stand with Charlie, if not with her.

The buzzer sounded, and the lock sprang open. She ignored the pain in her ankle as her anger propelled her up the steps.

"How could you?" she blurted out as soon as she stepped inside his apartment. He looked up from his seat at the dining table. "You're the one person I trusted. How could you do this to me?"

Her words echoed into silence as Drake stared at her. She knew how she must appear to him: flushed, hair straggled and wind blown, hunched forward in a fighting stance. She didn't care—she needed answers.

He got to his feet, slowly, too slowly. Then she

noticed the circles of fatigue that hung below his eyes. He still wore the same mud-splattered slacks as last night.

"I don't know what you're talking about," he said. "This isn't a good time—"

"It's good enough for me. You said you believed me, that you were on my side in all this, you said—" She choked on the words, swallowed back tears.

He drew up to his full height, taking a deep breath. His eyes had darkened with emotion despite the impassive set to his face.

"Not now," he stated. "We'll talk later."

"What's more important?" she asked, brushing past him and moving to the paper-strewn table. "I'm trying to save a boy's life here."

"So am I," he said quietly.

She looked down at the photos that covered the table, and her irritation faded. Although the anger and betrayal remained, smoldering just beneath the surface.

Cassie couldn't tear her gaze away from the crime scene photos, scrutinizing each in turn, feeling compelled to bear witness for the dead children, the dead woman thrown out like trash. Last night, Jimmy had told her about this case, how it had obsessed Drake Senior and now his son. He said he was sorry he'd ever brought Drake into it.

"This is your dad's case?" she asked, trailing her fingers over the reams of paper piled onto the table.

He joined her, flipping the photos upside down. "I told you I was busy. Why are you here? You got what you wanted—Charlie is in protective custody. I'm not doing any more of your dirty work for you."

"Dirty work? What the hell is that supposed to mean?"

"Nellie talked to Paul Ulrich. The baby Virginia is

carrying isn't his. He told her about Virginia's affair with Richard King." He shook his head. "I had no idea you could be so vindictive, so manipulative. I should have seen it coming. Every time we try to get close, King comes between us. You just can't give him up, can you?"

She stared at him, her stomach clenching as if warding off a blow.

"You believe that?" she whispered, leaning on a chair, uncertain if her legs could hold her up any longer.

※

"I KNOW YOU'RE obsessed with King," Drake began, but he was no longer as confident. Damn, it had all made so much sense when Nellie laid it out. But now he was beginning to wonder.

"Haunted would be a better description," she said, raising her face to meet his gaze. She looked so pale, so fragile that he wanted to gather her into his arms. "Why would I care who Richard was sleeping with? We aren't married anymore. Do you think I held a grudge all this time, waiting for Virginia Ulrich to come into my ER so that I could exact some warped revenge on her?"

"You've been acting so strange lately—" he stammered. He looked away, suddenly on shaky ground.

"I've been acting strange? You're the one who—"

"Sterling says there's an explanation—"

"Sterling can't face the fact that he's helped Virginia torture her children," she snapped.

Drake sank into his chair, grinding his palms into his eyes. God, he was so tired. "But you ran out—after you promised you'd stay with my mother. You left her."

"Nellie asked me to leave," Cassie said. "After she saw the press conference and talked to Virginia Ulrich. I guess she got an earful from Sterling as well because she knew about my impending suspension and Richard's accusations that I used drugs."

"That's crazy!" He looked up at that. "I could have told her not to trust anything King said."

"You could have, but you weren't there."

"No, I wasn't." He reached for her hand. "I'm sorry. I didn't know about the suspension."

She bit her lower lip, and then shrugged aside her problems. "Please don't ask Judge Flory to reverse Charlie's protective custody order."

"What are you talking about?" Now he finally understood the anger that drove her here tonight. "Who told you that?"

"Adeena—she heard it from Virginia Ulrich," she said with a wry twist to her mouth.

"We both need to check our sources better." He tugged on her hand, and she moved onto his lap. "I'm sorry I ever doubted you," he told her, encircling her with his arms. "Will you forgive me?"

She leaned her head against his shoulder. "Only if you forgive me. Sometimes I don't think before I act—or put my foot in my mouth."

He kissed the top of her head. "That's what I love most about you, Hart. You're never predictable."

She twisted in his lap so that he could kiss her more thoroughly. "Guess what I'm going to do next," she murmured as her fingers began to undo the buttons on his shirt.

Shivers of heat followed her fingers as they grazed over his skin. Her touch electrified him as she approached the sensitive area at his lower back. Her mouth moved from his down to his throat, her body humming with sexual tension.

Drake felt his own body respond and desperately wanted to give in to her unspoken demands. But he remembered how things had ended last time, and the pleasure he felt at her touch was suddenly clouded by the red haze of fear.

He caught his breath, pushing the fear back, holding it at bay as he straightened, dropping his hands from her body. She looked up, puzzled.

"I'm sorry," he said, and it was the truth. "I can't—not now." His gaze darted past her to the table laden with its tales of murder.

Hart sat up, sliding from his lap, but taking his hand in hers. "It's my fault. You said you had work. I should have realized that anything important enough to keep you from Muriel's side—"

"I think there's a killer out there getting ready to strike again," he said, his voice flat as he slipped his hand from her too-warm grasp and re-buttoned his shirt.

"Tell me about your case. You've listened enough about mine."

He looked up at that. He'd never talked about his cases to any of the women he'd been involved with before. But Hart was different—as he was constantly learning.

Drake hesitated, then took her hand once more, and walked her through the original murders. "And now there's this kid, Nate. I think he might be next."

"Why? After four years, the killer may not even still be around here."

"It's the dog," he said. "Cleary and Frantz both had pets that went missing several weeks prior to the murders. Eades and Kent didn't have any pets, but Kent's mother did mention a dead bird left on their stoop." He shook his head, it sounded so thin when spoken out loud. It was really just a feeling—an instinct.

Hart had risked everything on her instincts about Charlie Ulrich. Could he do less with another boy's life at stake?

He watched as she re-examined the photos of each of the victims with their families, the light revealing new hollows beneath her cheekbones. She'd lost weight, hadn't been taking care of herself. He frowned. Wasn't that his job? Or at least he wanted it to be—more than a job, a full time commitment.

"So all the victims with pets that were easily accessible lost them? Is there anyway to see if there have been other reports of animals killed?"

"There's no other links of family pets killed in association with murder victims."

She shook her head. "Not with victims. The deaths of the animals is a warning, it's designed to instill fear, to intimidate."

"Threatening the family pet would be good way to intimidate a kid," he allowed, still unsure where she was going.

Hart shuffled the photos back and forth, and then added the family photo of the Trevasians. He didn't think she knew where she was going either, but the frown of concentration that lined her face told him she was on the track of something.

"You think he's stalking these kids? He plays with them, terrorizing them, then kills them—and moves on to the next?"

Her hand became slick with sweat and began to tremble. The photos slipped away from her, fluttering to the tabletop.

"What is it?" he asked, pulling her to him, away

from the table and its gruesome visages.

"It's not the victims," she mumbled. She drew in a ragged breath and took a step back, looking up at him. "Does Nate have a sibling?"

"His sister, Katie Jean. Why?"

She didn't answer but turned back to the photos, reaching for his felt tip marker. "These are your victims, right?" She circled the faces of the dead children, Regina, Eades, and Nate.

"Yes." It was sad to see those faces, bright with smiles, distilled down to a single black circle.

"Wrong. These are your victims." She tapped the photos indicating Sofia's brother, Adam Cleary's brother, Regina Eades' son, and Tanya Kent's brother. Then, finally Nate Trevasian.

"Shit," Drake breathed out the expletive. Why hadn't he seen it before? He'd been so blind, stupidly blind. The boys were all about the same age, all in third grade, probably all in the same sporting leagues, cub scouts, and after school clubs.

"He used the murdered victims to ensure their silence," he said, remembering Nate's refusal to speak after his dog went missing. "There's probably a dozen more kids that he never escalated to this degree of violence, kids who he could keep quiet with less drastic measures."

It all made sense now. Like that moment of clarity when a painting came together. It wasn't the killing that drove this actor, the killing was only a means to protect himself.

It explained why the victims had nothing in common—different ages, different sexes. The actor had merely chosen the most easily controlled person closest to his victim.

His prey. Drake was looking for a sexual

predator, not a signature killer.

He looked up at Cassie and raised her hand to his lips. "Thank you," he said. "I think you may have just saved Katie Jean's life." He pulled her close for one too-brief moment, burying his face in her hair, inhaling enough of her scent to strengthen him until he was able to return to her.

"I guess you have work to do," she said when they parted.

"Thanks to you I know where to start," he told her, grabbing his phone. It was late, he'd have to call the shrink at home. He searched through his coat pockets for the card White had given him and dialed the number of the answering service.

"This is Detective Drake," he told the woman who answered. "I need to speak to Dr. White immediately. Yes, I'll hold."

A surge of energy filled him, the weight of his fatigue and worry dropping away. Hart blew him a kiss and started to leave. He looked up and put a hand over the phone. "Look after my mom, will you?"

"Of course."

"I love you," he called, as she disappeared down the steps, his voice echoing through the high-ceilinged room and down the staircase, following her. He felt a little light-headed as he realized that not only were the words the truth, but also that it was the first time he'd said them aloud.

• ⊙ •

DRAKE MET JIMMY at the doctor's office. White opened a conference room for their use, and they spread the murder books and photos over the table. Drake quickly walked them through Hart's theory of the crimes. As he spoke, everything seemed to fall into focus. Before he had finished, the doctor was nodding in agreement and Jimmy was diving into the murder books, dredging up the original family interviews.

"We've been asking the wrong questions all along," Jimmy said. "No wonder we never got anywhere."

"It's incredible that anyone ever linked the deaths in the first place," White replied.

"That was my dad's doing," Drake told him.

"But it's your persistence that will lead to the killer. I would focus on a man, probably white, who is in a position of authority over the boys."

"A teacher? Priest? Coach?"

The shrink pursed his lips. "Priest, maybe. The degree of coercion fits."

"They weren't all Catholic. And the boys lived in different parts of the city, how would he have access to all of them?" Jimmy argued. "The same with a teacher. They all went to different schools."

"The Cleary boy killed himself," Drake said, "and Frantz died in a car accident."

"I would guess that you'd find that was a single car accident," the shrink put in. "Probably suicide as well."

"Mitchell Eades is in jail, and refuses to talk to us or anyone. He tried to kill himself as well."

"What were the charges?"

"Gross sexual imposition, sexual assault on a minor," Jimmy supplied.

"Typical for a kid with a history of abuse who doesn't learn how to deal with his own feelings of rage and humiliation," White said.

"Not to mention the guilt at getting your mother killed," Drake added. The image of Muriel sprawled on the sidewalk shot through his mind. He was so lucky she was going to be all right. How would an eight-year-old kid deal with the knowledge that his mother was murdered because of him? No wonder Eades had turned into a head case.

"That leaves Kent, and we haven't been able to track him down. Parents are divorced, and the father has custody. I'll give the sister a call, see if she has a current number." Jimmy reached for the phone.

Drake turned back to the psychiatrist. "Our next victim is Nate Trevasian—and he isn't talking. To anyone."

"Elective mutism. A very difficult defense mechanism to overcome. But when it is, the subject tends to not hold back. If you can get him to talk, he'll tell you everything."

Drake frowned at that. "Do you think our actor knows that? Otherwise why escalate the reign of terror by killing the dog in such a brutal fashion? Nate had already clammed up after the dog went missing."

He thought about it. If what the doctor said was true, maybe the killer wouldn't stick with his old methods of intimidation. Maybe he'd go after Nate, and silence him for good.

"Our guy must have some kind of psychological training to know about elective mutism," Drake said. "A guidance counselor, maybe?"

"Different schools," the shrink pointed out. "Were any of the boys in private counseling—maybe they shared the same therapist?"

Drake held up his hand, thinking as he rustled through the notebooks strewn about the table. Jimmy hung up the phone and shook his head. "No answer." He looked at his partner. "What'cha got, kid?"

"Nate's father said he'd been placed on

medication for hyperactivity a few months ago. Don't you need to see a doctor for that?"

"A medical doctor, and usually a school psychologist," White supplied.

"Check the family doctors, pediatricians—any of them in common?"

Jimmy began turning pages in the thick binders. "I got one South Hills Peds, one goes to Forbes."

"Frantz used a family practice doc and Kent the clinic at Children's. Damn, thought I was on to something."

"How many school psychologists are there?" Jimmy asked. "Maybe they can help us."

"Actually," Dr. White put in, "I think the elementary school psychologist travels throughout the district. In fact, I remember meeting the man at one of the local APA dinners."

The two detectives looked up at that. "He travels—even to the private schools?" Drake asked.

"Oh yes, there's no way the school district could afford to base one at every school." The shrink was leafing through a membership directory labeled: American Psychological Association, Allegheny County Chapter. "Here he is," he turned the book so that they could see.

"Darin Mendelsohn," Jimmy read. "PhD from SUNY Rochester, specialty elementary school psychology, currently employed by Pittsburgh school district."

"Damn, that's him," Drake said, the pieces falling into place. "He's been treating Nate since he stopped talking. The sonofabitch actually called and talked with Nate's mom this morning. Told her to tell Nate he hoped he was feeling better—and that's when the kid froze up."

He stared at the black and white photo of a killer. Mendelsohn's features blurred into the background. He was so goddamned average that you had to look twice to notice him at all. Brown hair, brown eyes, weak chin, smooth, unlined face—no hint of the monster that lay beneath.

"Hold up," Jimmy cautioned. "Let me call Miller and the DA, make sure there's no problems with us bringing this guy in."

"We have to do it tonight," Drake insisted. "If we have to subpoena school records or any garbage like that, we'll spook him for sure."

"It'd help if we could get the Trevasian kid to open up." Jimmy raised an eyebrow at White.

"Bring him tomorrow," the doctor replied. "I'll arrange to have a colleague who specializes in children here."

"Thanks, doc." Jimmy returned to the phone. Drake paced the length of the conference table, anxious to get to work and nail Mendelsohn.

"Detective Drake," White said. "Could we speak in private for a moment?"

Drake looked up at that. He cut his eyes to Jimmy, who was laying out the case for Miller, then shrugged, following White down the hall to his office.

"You can't arrest Mendelsohn if you're still on inactive duty, can you?" White said, settling himself in his chair.

Drake stiffened, he hadn't thought that far ahead. "That's all right. Jimmy can take the collar." But damn, he wanted to be the one to take Mendelsohn down. Not for himself. For his father, for Nate Trevasian, and his family.

"Let me be blunt," White continued in his pedantic fashion. "You haven't been very forth coming during our sessions—"

"Hey, doc, that's not fair," Drake protested.

"Want to tell me about the panic attacks?"

Drake was silent. No, he did not.

"Or the nightmares?" White persisted. "Any sexual dysfunction? Blind rages you can't explain?" Drake raked his hands through his hair, looking down at the floor. "Any of this ringing a bell, Detective?" White's voice had taken on an edge, unlike his usual genial, soft-spoken manner.

Drake jerked his head up. "All of it. Happy now?"

White nodded. "Tell me about it."

And Drake did. He talked about the flash backs, the red haze, the panic attacks, even the other night when he'd jumped Hart, then couldn't go up the steps to her house to apologize. He spilled his guts like a perp rolling on a friend to get his own charges kicked.

And jeezit, it felt good. Once he started, he couldn't stop, it was like a dam had burst.

"How well do you know Hart?"

"What's to know?" Drake replied, surprised by the abrupt change of subject. "She's smart, beautiful, a good doctor—"

"I mean about her life. What has she told you?"

Drake squirmed in his seat. What did this have to do with him getting back on the streets? Or his panic attacks? "What's it matter what Hart tells me? She's entitled to her privacy."

The shrink nodded. "You said that she keeps her house—" He leafed back through his notes. "Like a museum to her family's memory. And she hid there for several weeks after the shooting, withdrew from the world?"

He felt a frisson of fear. "It's her way of coping when things become too much," he said, defending Hart and resenting that he even had to. "Look, where are you going with all this?"

"Just trying to get all the pieces. Where do you think Hart fits into everything?"

"She doesn't. This is about me getting shot."

"All right. Then let's talk about that night. What did you feel when the gunman confronted you?"

Drake was silent. He got up and began to move around the room.

"You'd just opened the door to Hart's house," the doctor prompted, "and he, what? Brandished a gun in your face? How exactly did he disarm you?"

Drake turned his back on the shrink and pretended to look out the window. The lights of PPG place blazed like a fairy tale castle in the distance.

"He was behind the door, I couldn't see him," he said, keeping his voice expressionless.

"And you felt?"

"Surprised, ashamed, angry, terrified—I don't know, it all happened so fast."

"Ashamed? Why ashamed?"

"Because I was helpless!" Drake flared, whirling to face the psychiatrist. "There I was, hands full of fucking candy and roses. What was I supposed to do? Bat him over the head with the flowers? Hart was down. I could see her body. I didn't know if she was dead or alive. All I could do was stand there while that bastard took my gun."

"You felt naked, vulnerable," the doctor suggested.

"Damned right. You try staring down the muzzle of a thirty-eight and tell me how you feel."

"Completely understandable. But let's go back in time. How did you feel when you first arrived at Hart's? As you climbed the steps, knocked at her door, anticipated her opening it?"

Drake stared at the shrink, opened his mouth, and then closed it again. How the hell should he know what he was feeling a given instant almost two months ago? Why was it important anyway?

"I don't know." He slumped back into the chair. "I can't remember," he muttered, bouncing his fist idly against the chair arm.

"Try. Just take a deep breath and picture yourself. You're in your car, it's snowing, you pull up in front of Hart's house. What are you thinking?"

The quiet, rhythmic tones relaxed Drake somewhat. He pictured that night once more, for the first time in weeks his mind's eye seemed panoramic, filling in the nuances of light and shadow that escaped him every other time he dreamed of that night.

"The snow is really coming down," he replied, his voice low and steady. "I grab the flowers and candy and hope I don't slip on the steps up to her porch. I imagine myself falling, sprawled on the sidewalk like an idiot and Hart having to rescue me."

"Is that thought upsetting?"

Drake closed his eyes, caught up in his reverie. "No," he replied, his mouth stretching into a smile. "I think it's hilarious. Everything that night seems funny, exciting—I can't stop grinning like an idiot. The only thing worrying me is what to do if Hart won't forgive me. But even that isn't too disturbing. I'm confident she'll accept my apology. I imagine the look she'll give me when she answers the door and sees my arms filled with bright roses just for her. I can hear her laugh and it thrills me to know I've made her happy, that she has that smile of delight because of me."

His eyes popped open. "Then the door opened."

The shrink nodded. "Then the door opened."

The clock ticked softly as Drake thought about

that. "I was so happy, then everything turned awful and I was powerless to stop it, to do anything." He looked up. "Is that why I haven't been able to touch Hart? I mean, not the way I really want to. It's because I've somehow tied up those feelings of pleasure with the terror and pain that followed."

"Is that what you think?"

He leaned forward, anxious to make himself clear. "It was because of her that I was there, that I was vulnerable. I've been blaming her, been swallowing my anger. But she didn't do anything—it was just my feelings and memories about that night all jumbled up."

The words came in a rush. Drake straightened up and inhaled deeper than he'd been able to in weeks. He got to his feet and stretched his arms out, relishing the simple act of breathing.

His hands weren't clenched in a death grip. He could feel the blood rushing to every part of his body as if his heart was finally free. He spun around, noting the luminescent dust motes that caught the light and danced it about the room. The doctor sat, impassive except for a slight twinkle in his eyes as he removed his glasses and polished them.

"There was nothing anyone could have done differently," Drake said. "And if I had done it differently, we'd both be dead. It was only because it was Hart and I together that we were able to survive."

He paused, looking down at the shrink with a grin. "Together, we're a force to be reckoned with—separate, we're each vulnerable. God, I've been such a fool, pushing her away like that!" He grabbed his jacket and started for the door. "Thanks a lot, doc," he said, and then called back over his shoulder. "When can I hit the streets again?"

"Tomorrow. I'll fax my report over to Commander

Miller tonight," the psychiatrist replied, but Drake was gone before he finished.

·⊙·

CASSIE STROKED HER fingers along Muriel's arm as the older woman roused herself into consciousness. A phone call from Drake had convinced Nellie and Jacob to go back to their hotel for a few hours. She wasn't exactly certain what he'd told them, they had been gone when she arrived. Denise Dolan had been waiting at Muriel's bedside instead. She had told Cassie that Muriel had been awake and talking before Nellie left.

"How do you feel?" Cassie asked Muriel as her eyelids fluttered open.

"Like someone's been using my head for a drum. Where's Remy?" Muriel's voice was a scratchy whisper. Cassie held a glass of water with a straw to her lips.

"He had to go out for a while. He'll be back soon." Cassie didn't want to worry her with the details, but Muriel saw through her evasion.

"On a case? He's with Jimmy, yes?"

"Yes. Don't worry, he said all he'd be doing is preparing a warrant."

Muriel tilted her head, regarded Cassie with skepticism. "And you believed him?"

Cassie smiled, remembering how exuberant Drake had sounded when he called her a short while ago. "Of course not—but I let him think I did."

Muriel patted her hand. "Good girl."

"Drake's closing one of his father's cases, one that he was working on when he died."

Muriel sank back onto the pillow. "I wouldn't know. Mickey never talked about his cases with me—it was the only part of his life I never shared. But," she sighed, "he always had to be in control of everything: his emotions, his work," she chuckled, "the kitchen."

"I think your son inherited that."

"Maybe, but he didn't get much else from his father—including the approval Remy always craved. Now you, on the other hand, I think you're a lot like my Mickey."

"Me?" Cassie thought a moment. "I am kind of a control freak," she admitted. "But I'm afraid I don't keep my emotions well controlled. I can't even tell a simple lie without it showing all over my face."

Muriel smiled. "Probably more healthy that way. And Remy needs someone to take the reins, so to speak. He's always been searching for a—" she searched for the right word, "counterpart, someone to bring balance to his life. He needs someone who he can share his life—all of it—with. Someone who won't hold back from him like his father did. Don't get me wrong, those two loved each other a great deal, but they could never expressed it. I think Remy is still trying to make his father proud."

It was Cassie's turn to smile. She knew all about clinging to the expectations of family members long gone. The weight of responsibility that never eased, it motivated every action.

"I'm afraid all I've brought to my relationship with your son is pain and hardship. And to you," she added. "I'm so sorry this happened."

"Nonsense, dear. I saw what you did. You had plenty of room to jump clear of that van but instead you turned to get me out of the way. You probably saved my life." Cassie looked away, silent. "Do you know why it happened? Was there something wrong with the driver or the car?"

"It happened because I was trying to save a little

boy's life," Cassie said. "And someone didn't want me to."

"Tried? Is he dead, then?" Muriel seemed more concerned about Charlie's safety than her own injuries. Cassie looked at her in admiration.

"No. He's all right for now."

"Then you can't give up. Not because of this." She gestured to her IV and the medical equipment surrounding her. "Tell me all about it. I'm certain we can think of something."

Cassie told her Charlie's story and her suspicions, leaving nothing, including the ambiguous medical facts and Sterling's and Adeena's doubts about her own mental health, out. Muriel was an excellent listener and despite her weakened state, she grasped the intricacies of the situation immediately.

"So you can't prove that Charlie's mother is going to do anything, but you believe he's in danger?"

"Yes, ma'am." Cassie sat in silence for a moment. She was ecstatic that Muriel was going to be all right, but felt like she was there under false pretenses. "Your sister and her husband don't agree with me, either."

"And my son?"

She couldn't stop her smile as she remembered Drake's last words to her at his apartment. Words she'd been too stunned to acknowledge. "He believes."

"Good enough for me." Muriel squeezed her hand. "I think I see what my son likes about you. You don't do anything half heartedly, do you?"

Cassie blushed. "That's a kind way to put it. I believe the words your sister used were: incorrigible, stubborn, and obstinate."

"That's Nellie. Once a journalist, always a journalist. Has to show how erudite she is. I would call it spunk—or better yet, passion. Zeal, zest, a crusading spirit. No wonder you and Nellie butted heads. She's the same when she's after a story. Poor Jacob would go about crazy with worry at times." She shook her head. "Young lady, you fit right in with our family, believe me."

Cassie gawked at her. Although she'd tried to make it clear that her actions were responsible for Muriel's injuries, it was obvious that Drake's mother hadn't heard.

"You don't understand. If it weren't for me, you wouldn't be lying there. And it was because of me that Mickey got hurt last month—"

"And because of you he's alive today, a murderer is dead, a dangerous drug epidemic was stopped, and a little boy is safe in protective custody. Have I missed anything?"

"No, but—"

She raised a finger to silence Cassie. "It's been obvious for quite sometime that my son is in love with you. And after meeting you, I heartily approve of his choice. So what's the problem? You do love him, don't you?"

"You just don't understand," Cassie stammered. "After last month, the shooting, nothing's been the same."

Muriel nodded. "I know. That's why I flew back so soon. I had to do something. I couldn't bear to watch Remy make another horrible mistake, to let you slip away. And I thought it was about time we met." She grinned. "My son turns thirty-five in October, and I think it's high time he grows up and enjoys a mature relationship with a woman."

"I'm afraid I don't have a very good track record in that department," Cassie admitted.

"Neither does he, so you're perfect for each other."

Muriel's eyes fluttered, and Cassie could see that she was getting tired.

"I'd better go now," she said.

"No, stay." Muriel took her hand. "I seem to remember you telling me a story about a woman named Rosa." She frowned. "Or was that a dream? These drugs, they give you such strange dreams."

"No, that was real. Rosa is my grandmother. Was. She's been dead three years now."

"Tell me another story. Tell me about your family." Her eyelids slid to half-mast.

Cassie stroked her hand rhythmically, feeling Muriel relax into sleep beneath her touch. "Rosa was Rom, a gypsy, of the Kalderasha clan," she began.

⁂

CASSIE AWOKE WITH a start when someone tapped on her shoulder. "Muriel?" she asked, looking around at the monitors. But everything was reading normal.

"She's fine, Dr. Hart," the ward clerk told her. "I just got a call from the Peds ICU for you. They were asking if you could come see a patient of theirs, a Tony Washington?"

Cassie shook her head to clear it. "Antwan Washington," she corrected the clerk. "I'll be right there. Thanks."

"Sure thing, Dr. Hart." The clerk headed back to her station near the phones. Cassie rubbed her eyes and looked around. There were no windows in the ICU, it could be noon for all she knew. She finally spotted the clock above the door. It was ten after two, she'd slept almost three hours. She felt like she needed about forty more.

Standing and stretching the kinks out of her neck,

she looked at the monitor readings more closely. If anything, they were improved.

"I'll be right back," Cassie whispered to Muriel and squeezed her shoulder.

The PICU was down the hall. She went in through the sliding doors and approached the desk clerk. "Someone called me about Antwan Washington?"

The clerk shrugged. No one else was around except for two nurses back in the medication room.

Cassie walked over to Antwan's cubicle. Tammy Washington was asleep, her head and arms slumped across her son's body. Cassie looked down for a moment, smiling at the domestic tranquility of the scene, despite the medical equipment looming all around the mother and child.

Then she noticed two large eyes staring at her. Antwan Washington was awake. Cassie took the chair on the other side of the bed, lowering herself to his height.

"Hi, I'm Cassie," she said. The little boy said nothing, merely stared. "You're Antwan, right?" He nodded, still silent. "How old are you, Antwan?"

He looked at her suspiciously, obviously he had learned not to trust anyone in this place, where they were just as likely to poke you with a needle as give you a hug.

Cassie just smiled and waited. Slowly, he withdrew a hand from under his mother's head and held up three fingers. Cassie nodded. "Three? You're a big boy." She spotted a stack of books on the counter. "Would you like to read a bedtime story?" He nodded.

She went through the books. They were all brightly colored with thick cardboard pages little fingers could turn easily. She had no idea which one to choose, so she picked out the most worn, thinking that it must be a favorite.

"*Goodnight Moon,*" she read the title to Antwan. "Is that okay?"

He nodded eagerly and guided her hand to position the book where he could reach it. He obviously had the book memorized because as Cassie read it, he turned the pages at the right places. Until about two thirds into the story, when she noticed his breathing was slower and his head had slumped over. She quietly finished the book, then kissed his forehead gently before replacing the book and leaving.

One success, at least. She stopped by the nurses' station and took Antwan's chart into the dictation area to review. She wanted to see what the neurologists thought his ultimate outcome would be.

Antwan's chart had grown as thick as a bible, filled with the cryptic scribbles of house staff and consultants. Apparently the meningitis had caused a small stroke that affected the muscles on his left side. Cassie deciphered the cramped scrawls with an ease that came with practice, but was frustrated to find no definite prognosis given. The neurologists were taking a "wait and see" attitude. At least they'd already ordered some physical therapy and a child life consult.

The lines of black ink began to blur and Cassie yawned. Just a few more pages and she'd go back to Muriel.

"Dr. Hart, wake up!" A rough pair of hands shook her. "We need you!"

"What?" Cassie jerked awake. She'd fallen asleep in the dictation area of the PICU, Antwan Washington's chart her pillow. "What?"

A nurse was shaking her. "It's Antwan Washington. He started to seize about five minutes ago. The fellow and Dr. Sterling are down in the ER with a patient that's crashing. Could you help?"

Cassie jumped to her feet and raced to Antwan's cubicle in the back hallway. The nurses had the crash cart in the room and had already placed an oxygen mask on the little boy as his body jerked mightily in all directions. Tammy Washington stood in one corner, tears streaming from her face.

"Help him, Dr. Hart, please help my boy," she cried.

Cassie grabbed a stethoscope from one of the nurses. "Get me one point five of Ativan," she ordered as she bent forward to listen. He was barely moving air, the seizure was preventing the oxygen from entering his lungs. Cassie looked up at the monitor. Antwan's oxygen level was falling.

"Ativan in."

She grabbed the anesthesia bag from the head of the bed. "Hyperventilate him. Let's set up for intubation. Give me a two blade and a number five tube." The seizures continued unabated despite the medication. "Another one point five of Ativan," Cassie ordered.

"But it's only been two minutes."

"Give it. I'm going to tube him anyway."

The nurse quickly gave the second dose. The seizure activity slowed somewhat, but so did Antwan's breathing and his heart rate. Cassie moved to the head of the bed and quickly intubated him. Once the tube was in place, his oxygen level and color improved dramatically.

"Damn it, why is his heart rate so low? Atropine point three and a fluid bolus."

The nurse gave the medication just as Carl Sterling arrived.

"What happened?"

"Generalized seizure, responded after a second dose of Ativan. Tubed for apnea, but he's bradycardic and hypotensive," the nurse reported.

"What meds is he on?" Cassie asked, checking the pupillary reflexes and trying to think of anything that could be triggering this constellation of symptoms.

"Only vancomycin and phenobarbital," the nurse answered her as Sterling moved to the bed and yanked the ophthalmoscope from Cassie's hand.

"What are you doing here?" he demanded.

Cassie ignored him and turned to the nurse. "Are his levels okay?"

"Yes, I checked them myself," Sterling replied. He listened to the breath sounds and looked up. "You can leave now, Dr. Hart. I have everything under control."

"Not with his pressure so low. Give him one and a half cc's of epinephrine," Cassie ordered. If they couldn't get his blood pressure higher, his body wouldn't get the oxygen it needed. "And set up for an epi drip." The nurses scrambled to get the medications from the crash cart.

"I'm in charge here," Sterling snapped.

The nurses froze at the crash cart looking from one physician to the other. The alarm blared as Antwan's blood pressure fell further. Sterling's eyes cut over to the monitor display.

"Do it," he finally conceded. "And hang the drip."

"What's this?" One of the nurses stooped over then rose with an empty syringe of lidocaine in her hand.

"Who gave him lidocaine?" Sterling demanded, his glare settling on Cassie.

"The crash cart was already here when I arrived," Cassie said. A lidocaine overdose could cause seizures, a slow heart rate, and low blood pressure. There was no specific treatment. It would wear off in a few hours if you could keep the patient alive for that long. "What is that? A hundred milligram vial?"

The nurses became even more hyperkinetic as they scrambled to discover where the lidocaine had come from. Antwan's heart rate and blood pressure improved with the epinephrine.

"Dr. Sterling, that lidocaine didn't come from our crash cart," a nurse spoke up. She held up two amps of the medication. "We have both of ours and the lot number is different."

"So, where the hell did that lidocaine come from?" Sterling demanded. The nurses all jumped at his tone and epithet. He quickly took control of the situation. "He's stable now, I want everyone out of here except Linda and his mother."

Cassie turned to Tammy Washington. "Do you remember anyone being in here?"

She shook her head. "I just woke up 'cause he was thrashing around. I called the nurse right away. Is he going to be all right? What happened?"

"He's going to be fine. We're still looking into what exactly caused this seizure."

"I said, everyone out, now. I'd like a note of what happened before I arrived, Dr. Hart." Sterling's tone was frosty, and Cassie was too tired to argue further. She went over to where she'd left Antwan's chart at the dictation station.

If only she hadn't fallen asleep, she might have seen something. Or someone. She felt certain that Virginia Ulrich was behind this latest incident. Antwan's cubicle was in the side hallway, close in proximity to the nurses' station, but not in a direct line of sight. It would be frightfully easy for anyone with knowledge of the PICU to walk in unseen.

And Virginia certainly was familiar with the

PICU.

Cassie finished dictating her part of Antwan's resuscitation. She called down to the Pediatric unit, but the nurses said that they hadn't seen Virginia Ulrich at all that night.

Sterling entered the dictation area. "The police are on their way."

"Good. How's Antwan?"

"Stable," he said in a grudging tone.

Cassie stood.

"Where are you going?" Sterling asked sharply.

"To see Antwan and talk to his mother. I'm sure she's frightened by all this."

"You can't do that."

"Why not?" Cassie looked around the nurses' station, realized that everyone was staring at her. And their looks were distinctly unfriendly.

"The charge nurse tracked down the lot number of the lidocaine vial," Sterling said. "It came from an ER crash cart."

CHAPTER 30

"Surely you don't think I had anything to do with this!" Cassie tried to keep her voice low, but failed.

Sterling glared at her. Cassie looked at him in disbelief, and then pushed past him. She'd left Muriel alone—she had to get back to her.

Two police officers and a hospital security guard blocked her way as she left the PICU and turned toward the SICU.

"Out of my way!" she flared, her patience exhausted.

"Dr. Hart, will you please come with us?" one of the uniformed officers said as his partner moved to her other side.

"I need to get to the Surgical ICU." She'd promised Drake she would protect his mother, and that everything would be all right. She needed to see Muriel, make certain that she was safe.

"We would prefer if you had no contact with any patients until this is cleared up," the hospital security guard told her.

"I need to see a patient there," she tried to explain. She couldn't keep the shrillness of her fear out of her voice.

"I don't think that's a good idea right now," the police officer said, taking her arm. "Why don't you come with us? We just want to talk to you."

She twisted away from his hand and tried to push past them to the SICU.

"Please, I just need a minute." She was almost in tears. Why couldn't they understand?

Both police officers took her arms, holding her in place. A small crowd had gathered, night shift workers from the ICU's as well as family members. Cassie looked up to see Jacob and Nellie Steadman emerge from the elevator. The security guard guided them to one side, as if they were in danger from her.

"Come along now, Dr. Hart. Let's go someplace quiet where you can calm down."

"Nellie," Cassie called out. "Stay with Muriel. Don't leave her alone."

Muriel's sister looked at Cassie with a mixture of horror and disbelief. "Please," she pleaded as the officers lead her past the Steadmans into the elevator.

The four of them rode down in silence. She looked up at the police officers and thought about how she looked in their eyes—a disheveled, tear-stained maniac, probably. If they thought she'd deliberately poisoned Antwan Washington, she didn't blame them for wanting to get her away from there as fast as possible.

In their minds she was a monster. How could she ever convince them that it was Virginia Ulrich who was the real monster?

"Where are we going?" she asked as the elevator doors opened on the first floor.

"That's up to you, doctor. We can take you down to the station and the detectives will talk to you there in private. If you refuse to go, then we'll have to make other arrangements."

Cassie didn't like the sound of that. Other arrangements probably meant getting a warrant for her arrest, having the hospital security expel her from the premises, and more publicity.

"I'll go to the station," she said quietly. "You need to call Detective Drake. He knows everything about this case."

"Detective Drake isn't on duty."

They walked her through the front lobby to where their cruiser sat in the circle at the doors. She was surprised that several reporters were waiting. The flash of their cameras blinded her as the policemen helped her into their car.

Cassie turned to look out the back window. She couldn't help but wonder if she'd ever be allowed to return to Three Rivers again.

THEY PLACED CASSIE in a room no larger than a linen closet, bare except for two scarred plastic chairs and a table. The table was bolted to the floor and had rings secured to its top, presumably for handcuffs. She had a lot of time to think about it and imagine herself wearing those handcuffs as she waited for the detectives. Her only companion and distraction in the room was a whistling steam radiator that would occasionally rattle and shake, forcing a disproportionately tiny amount of warm air into the already stuffy room.

If she'd just stayed calm up in the PICU, she was

certain she could have explained everything. Well, maybe. So now she was doing her best to be a model prisoner, not insisting on a telephone or a lawyer. After all, she had not done anything wrong, so she'd nothing to worry about, right?

Cassie paced back and forth, measuring the narrow confines of the room with her steps. The police had repeatedly told her that she was free to go at any time, a ploy to avoid any semblance of coercion. Only question was: where else could she go?

Finally she stopped moving and sat down on one of the two plastic chairs.

This was it. Time to give up. She'd been through a lot of fights in her life, but she'd met her match in Virginia Ulrich. She was more certain than ever that Virginia had killed her first two children and was trying to kill Charlie and Antwan. But how to prove it? Cassie couldn't even prove her own innocence right now.

She squeezed her eyes shut, wishing she could sleep for a million years, wake up, and this would all be behind her. But that wasn't going to happen.

It was all her fault. If she hadn't been so stubborn in the first place, Virginia Ulrich would have never have targeted her. Muriel would be at Drake's enjoying his company, Antwan would be on his way to recovery, and Cassie would still have a job and no threats of lawsuits, suspension, or jail time hanging over her head. If only she hadn't been so damned stubborn.

And what about Charlie Ulrich? And his soon-to-be-born sister? How many children would have to suffer at Virginia Ulrich's hands before someone stopped her?

"I can't, she's won," Cassie whispered, squeezing her eyes tighter, hoping to drown out the voice inside her. Her father's voice. His final words, *I need you to be strong, Cassie.* "I can't save anyone, not even myself."

"Excuse me, what did you say?" a woman's voice sliced through Cassie's soliloquy.

Cassie bolted upright. Janet Kwon smiled down at her. The detective had the same slight build, dark hair and eyes as Cassie, but there the resemblance ended. Cassie rarely smiled, but when she did it was with her entire face.

Kwon often smiled, the grin of a predator homing in on the kill, and never with her eyes. She sat a cup of coffee in front of Cassie and took the other chair.

"Dr. Hart," she said in a pleasant voice, sharp as a rapier, "it's been a while."

Cassie held the coffee to occupy her hands, she knew better than to drink the battery acid-flavored beverage. Best save it to dissolve the metal rings if it came to that.

"Detective Kwon." Cassie held the woman's gaze without flinching. Kwon was the detective who had almost arrested Cassie for attempted murder after Richard's overdose. "If you don't mind, could I give my statement to someone else? Detective Dolan, perhaps?"

Kwon made a clicking noise with her teeth, a sound that Cassie took as sympathy. "So sorry, but Detective Dolan is out executing a search warrant." She smiled again. "In fact, I doubt he even knows you're here. And unless he was in Antwan Washington's room tonight, I don't think he'll be able to help you much."

Cassie sighed. Might as well get down to it. "There's this woman, Virginia Ulrich—"

"I've heard all about your dealings with the Ulrich family, Dr. Hart. I've just gotten back from Three Rivers."

"Then you know she's tried to kill her own son

and there's a good chance she was responsible for Antwan's poisoning."

Kwon's eyes flicked over to the one-way mirror. Cassie had the sudden thought that she was playing right into their hands. Maybe a lawyer wasn't such a bad idea after all. But she hadn't done anything wrong.

"Has anyone read you your rights, Dr. Hart?" Kwon asked as if commenting on the weather.

"No."

"It's just a formality, but before we proceed, let's go over them." Kwon slid a piece of paper that outlined the Miranda rights in plain language across to Cassie. "I'm sure you remember them from the last time we talked." Again with the smile. "Now then, you have the right to remain silent. But I think you want to tell us about Virginia Ulrich and everything that has happened tonight. Of course, what you say will be on the record and could be used against you in a court of law if you've done anything wrong. You haven't done anything wrong, have you Dr. Hart?"

"No, of course not," Cassie blurted out, feeling more like a criminal than ever.

"Then, I guess you don't need an attorney either. But if you do, one can be appointed to you without cost. Do you understand all these rights?"

"Yes."

"All right then, please initial each one and sign there at the bottom." Kwon took a felt tip pen from her jacket pocket and handed it to her. Cassie scrawled her initials and name where indicated.

She knew that most criminals made the mistake of waiving their rights and talking too much, but she hadn't done anything. There was no way she was going to get an attorney involved with this—he'd just tell her to say nothing and this whole thing could drag on forever. Which was exactly what Virginia Ulrich wanted.

Outsmarted by a devious woman who had barely finished high school. She was certain Virginia Ulrich was loving every moment of her victory.

"What can you tell me about what happened tonight to Antwan Washington?" Kwon got right to the heart of the matter.

"Someone poisoned him."

"Someone? Do you have any idea who?"

"I suspect Virginia Ulrich," Cassie sounded bitter, but she didn't care.

"Virginia Ulrich wasn't seen in Antwan's room before he had the seizure, Dr. Hart. You were. Care to tell me how you came to be there?"

"I was in the surgical ICU with Muriel Drake—"

"Detective Drake's family told me that they had specifically requested that you stay away from his mother during her recovery."

"Drake asked me to stay with her. He was afraid Virginia might hurt her after he took Charlie into protective custody this morning."

"This morning, before you were suspended because of suspected drug use?" Kwon asked, her smile making it clear that she knew everything that had happened behind the closed doors of the confidential Executive Committee meeting.

"I haven't been officially suspended, not yet," Cassie protested. Kwon merely arched an eyebrow and nodded. "Anyway, I was at Muriel's bedside when the clerk told me someone in the Pediatric ICU had requested that I go there. She said it was about my patient, Antwan Washington."

"The Pediatric ICU is just down the hall from the Surgical ICU?"

"Yes."

"And do you know who the message came from?"

"The clerk didn't say. She barely got Antwan's name right."

"And Antwan Washington, he was your patient?"

Cassie was suddenly reminded of the old attorney adage: never ask a question that you don't already know the answer to. She had the feeling that Kwon knew all the answers already—at least the answers that Kwon wanted.

"He was."

"Was?"

"I took care of him in the ER when he was admitted."

"Did you not also care for Antwan a few days earlier? And isn't Mrs. Washington currently pursuing a malpractice suit regarding your treatment of Antwan that day?"

"You don't understand," she protested. "Virginia Ulrich put her up to that."

"Yes or no, Dr. Hart. Is Mrs. Washington suing you over Antwan's care?"

She hung her head. "Yes," she mumbled.

"Then what were you doing in his room? You weren't there as his physician, so why were you there, Dr. Hart?"

"I told you—someone called and asked me to go there."

"Right. Someone called and asked you to visit a patient you were being sued over. At two in the morning."

She raised her head at the note of challenge in Kwon's voice. The detective was staring at her, the disbelief evident in her eyes. Cassie held her stare and remained silent.

"Okay, let's put that aside for a moment. What did you do while you were in Antwan's room?"

This was going to sound crazy, they'd never believe her. "I read a book to him."

"It's two in the morning. He's a critically ill child and you've left the side of your equally ill," Kwon hesitated here, obviously uncertain how to describe Cassie's relationship with Muriel, "friend, to read a book to him?"

Cassie couldn't help but smile. She remembered Antwan's tentative grin and the look of trust he'd given her. Damn it, she wasn't going to give in to Kwon. And not to Virginia Ulrich, either. She'd find someway out of this. She had to if she wanted her life back.

"*Good Night Moon*," she told the detective, meeting her gaze unwaveringly. "After Antwan fell asleep, I went out to the dictation area to review his chart. I fell asleep. I was there when they called me to help with his seizure."

"How convenient," Kwon said.

"I'm not the one who poisoned him. Why aren't you checking where Virginia Ulrich was?"

"According to her husband, she was home in bed with him."

"Then he's lying!" Cassie took a deep breath and tried to calm down. "Look, I'm sorry. It's just that I've been through a lot lately. My life hasn't been the same ever since I met that woman."

"Virginia Ulrich?"

"Yes."

"Tell me about that. How did you come to suspect that she might be hurting her own child? Is that something you've ever accused any other parent of? This Munchausen by Proxy?"

"No. It's very rare. A caretaker, usually the

mother, induces or lies about symptoms in her child to manipulate medical professionals and other people's feelings about her. She becomes the center of attention while her child is subjected to unnecessary medical procedures."

"And you've never seen a case yourself?"

"No. I've read about them, and heard a lecture on it once."

"So why did you suspect Virginia Ulrich of having this rare disorder? It wouldn't have anything to do with the fact that she had an affair with your ex-husband and that the child she's carrying may be his?"

"No, of course not. I didn't know about Richard and Virginia, and if I did I wouldn't care. They deserve each other."

"So you met her for the first time that day in the ER? Had no idea who she was or what she meant to your ex? You didn't have any previous history to base your conclusion on, so what made you think of this rare disorder?"

Cassie shook her head. "I don't know, I just—" she stopped, remembering Charlie's resuscitation. "At first I was puzzled by Charlie's symptoms—his clinical picture didn't fit the story she gave us. But everyone else believed her."

"So what made you accuse this mother of such a heinous crime?"

"It wasn't until I saw the videotape—" She broke off. That was it! Finally, she had a chance of proving that Virginia Ulrich was the monster Cassie knew her to be.

"Videotape? Dr. Hart?" Kwon prodded her.

"They said the lidocaine came from the ER, right?"

Kwon nodded, puzzled by the abrupt change of topic.

"We have video cameras in all of the critical care rooms in the ER," Cassie rushed on, excited by the prospect of clearing her name. "Call over to hospital security, have them pull all the tapes for the last shift. You'll have proof who took the lidocaine used to poison Antwan."

Kwon raised an eyebrow. "And have you been in the ER lately, Dr. Hart?" she persisted.

"Not since two nights ago." Cassie didn't care, Kwon could ask all the questions in the world. She had Virginia Ulrich nailed. Then she realized a flaw in her plan. There were other crash carts besides the ones in the critical care rooms. If Virginia had used one of them, there would be no record of her on video. Plus, the tapes were just for teaching purposes so they were recorded over every few hours to save money.

If that had happened, then what would she do?

CHAPTER 31

It was fascinating to see how a pervert's mind worked, Drake thought as he thumbed through the books lining the shelves of Mendelsohn's inner sanctum. Jimmy had already left with a trunk full of evidence: computer, assorted flash drives, photo albums, and DVD's. None had appeared to be pornography or in anyway related to Mendelsohn's alleged extra-curricular activities, but Drake had worded the warrant so that they had the right to remove and examine any images found on the premises.

"Still nothing," one of the uniforms complained, climbing down the ladder from the overhead crawl space. "Thought you said these sickos always kept souvenirs."

Drake ignored him as he continued his perusal of the psychologist's collection. Mendelsohn's house was a split-level, dating back to the seventies. He hadn't changed much; it still boasted avocado green appliances, burnt orange shag carpeting and fake pine paneling. The only improvement was the large set of bookcases that stretched the entire length of one wall of the study.

Texts from Freud, Jung, Adler, Ericson—the founding fathers of psychology—lined the shelves. Drake ran his finger along their spines, letting his finger bounce, bounce over their embossed leather covers. He stopped halfway down and looked at his finger.

Clean. Not a speck of dust. He sat down behind the desk. Mendelsohn's chair was too short to be comfortable for Drake, but there were well-worn grooves in the rug testifying to the hours Mendelsohn sat here. There was an empty space on left corner of the desk where the computer had sat but no dust marks. The light sat behind him, also on the left.

Drake reached out a hand, and flicked it on. It's shaft of white glare sliced down to where the computer would have sat. He slumped down, trying to approach Mendelsohn's level.

No, he thought, flicking the light off once more. *You prefer the dark for your work.* They would find something buried in the computer's hard drive, he was certain. He placed his hands flat against the desktop. It was a fake burled wood veneer, polished smooth. The surface flowed beneath his hands like silk. *Or the touch of a young boy's flesh. Sweat-slicked from fear, soft, unmarred, compliant.*

He looked up once more. This actor would not have been content to confine himself to visual images. No, Mendelsohn would need something tactile, something he could handle, caress, fantasize over.

His gaze centered on a fat volume of Freud's collected works. It sat on the center of the lovingly crafted shelves, in the place of honor. He pushed up from the chair, and strolled over. The edges of the binding were frayed, as if a man had spent many hours simply gazing on the treasured volume, his fingers stroking it.

There was a shelf hidden below the ledge where the book sat. Drake pulled it out, it moved on well-oiled runners, the only sound a soft sigh as it emerged. There were no other shelves, he noted. He tilted the fat volume back. It was heavy, much heavier than he'd anticipated. He needed both hands to remove it from its spot and lay it onto the waiting shelf.

"He probably had a ritual," Drake murmured, his fingers suspended above the rich, blood red, leather.

"What's that?" Kirby asked, looking up from where he sat in a corner, thumbing through receipts.

"Nothing," Drake told the officer. He pulled back the book's cover. "Bingo."

Nestled inside the hole carved from the pages of Freud's wisdom were small, silk-covered boxes. They lined up like soldiers on parade, a dozen in all. Calligraphy in a bold hand spelled out names on parchment labels. Some he recognized: Frantz, Cleary, Eades, Kent. Five others interspersed between them were strangers. Then the box closest to the top: Trevasian.

What really got to Drake were the two boxes still blank. No way this actor would have stopped at twelve. His stomach tightened, wondering how many more boxes, how many more young lives would have been filled with the horrors wracked by Mendelsohn's warped mind.

His cell phone trilled, bringing him back from the abyss of a predator and into the present. "Drake."

"You got anything?" Jimmy asked.

"Jackpot. Don't worry, I'll have Kirby bag and tag.

As far as Miller or any defense attorney knows, I was never here."

"Good job, but that's not what I'm worried about. Hart's in trouble."

Drake felt his fist tighten around the phone. He threw the study door open and started down the stairs at a gallop. "What happened?"

KWON LEFT TO call the hospital. Cassie waited, something she did poorly even in the best of circumstances. But what other choice did she have?

After an hour, she was even tempted to drink the coffee. One sip dissuaded her. She could save it for a suicide attempt. Not funny, but anything to distract her was helpful.

She resumed pacing the tiny room. Then the door opened again. Jimmy Dolan entered.

"Is everything all right? Have you talked to Mickey? Nothing happened to Muriel, did it?" Her questions and anxieties spilled out at the sight of his welcome face.

"Muriel's fine. DJ's over at Three Rivers, reviewing the videotapes from the ER. He said," Jimmy smiled, "not to worry. And that Kwon's bark is worse than her bite."

Cassie couldn't resist, she moved forward and gave the burly detective a quick hug. "Thanks, Jimmy. Maybe we can finally put this mess behind us. I'm so tired."

"I know," he told her. "But it'll all be over soon. It's just that, in this case, what we know and what we can prove are very far apart."

She brightened at the plural pronoun, hoping that

it still included her. "So what's our next step?"

"First of all, how about some breakfast? I've got fresh Krispy Kremes."

She followed Jimmy out to the main squad room and grabbed a glazed donut from the green and white box. It vanished in an instant.

"Will you marry me?" she sighed in pleasure, licking the sugar from her lips, leaning back in Drake's chair. Janet Kwon looked up from her desk and shot her a glare. Cassie resisted the urge to wrinkle her nose at the high-strung detective.

"Even if we can prove Virginia Ulrich poisoned Antwan, there's still a few problems we have to contend with." Jimmy took a newspaper from his jacket pocket and slid it over to her. Cassie unfolded it. On the front page was a photo of the police helping her into their car. The headline read: *Local doctor questioned about child's poisoning.*

"Who called the paper?" she asked.

"An anonymous tip." Jimmy told her. "A tip, that according to their records was made almost ten minutes before the initial call to the police from Three Rivers."

"Before?" Cassie looked up. "Virginia Ulrich."

"That'd be my guess," he answered around a mouthful of donut.

"How is your other case?"

"We nailed him—thanks to you, from what I understand. He's cooling his heels, waiting on his lawyer." He jerked his head towards the interview room beside the one Kwon had questioned her in.

"Did he say anything?"

Jimmy rolled his eyes. "Pretended like he has no idea who any of these boys were, asked for a lawyer, and clammed up."

"There's something you both should see." Janet Kwon was smiling again.

Jimmy and Cassie moved over to where a small TV sat on an empty desk. The morning local news was playing and Cassie recognized the front steps of Three Rivers. Today they were filled with a group of people protesting something, carrying placards.

"Shit," she heard Jimmy say. Cassie moved closer. One of the signs had her name in a circle with a line drawn through it, another proclaimed: Let Her Baby Go! and there was more of the same. The news commentator was analyzing the outpouring of public sympathy and community support on behalf of Mrs. Virginia Ulrich.

She looked at Jimmy. "I don't believe it."

"Power of the press. If we ever do get this to trial, we're never going to find an impartial jury. Let's just hope that we get some solid evidence to back us."

His phone rang and he moved to snag it. "Hey, DJ," Jimmy said into the phone. He looked over at Cassie and smiled. "Yeah, she's here." He handed her the phone.

Cassie moved around to sit in Jimmy's seat as he lifted a carton of evidence from his desk. "I'm going to get this logged in. Hey Janet, keep an eye on my guy for me, will ya?"

The other detective waved her hand without looking up.

Cassie curled her finger around the phone cord, wishing for more privacy. "How's your mother?"

"Down for another CT," Drake told her. "But Park was by already, said she's doing 'better than expected'" he mimicked the neurosurgeon's clipped tones. "Says she ought to make a full recovery, probably go home in another day or two."

"That's great." She wanted to ask about the ER videos but was afraid to jinx herself.

"Three Rivers won't release the security tapes without a court order," he told her, and she sighed. More waiting. "I convinced them to dupe me a small segment. Summers is waiting for the court order to bring the original, but I'm on my way back to the House now." He paused.

She edged forward, almost leaving the chair. "Did you find anything?"

His chuckle resonated through the phone line. "Oh yeah, I think you'll find this very interesting."

"You found her?" Cassie felt her body bounce against the chair seat. "You've got Virginia on video taking the lidocaine from the ER?"

"Clear as daylight."

She didn't know what to say. Unable to sit still any longer, she pushed away from the chair and paced around behind it, as far as the phone cord would stretch. Finally solid proof that her instincts about Virginia Ulrich were valid. "Someone's watching Antwan?"

"Yes, and security is on the lookout for Virginia. We'll send some uniforms over to help them after shift change."

She saw Kwon move toward the interview room where Jimmy's prisoner waited for his attorney. The squad room was empty except for them. Kwon looked through the one-way glass of the room then stiffened, hurrying to unlock the door.

"Hart, get over here," she shouted. "He's choking on something!"

Kwon disappeared inside the room as Cassie dropped the phone and moved to join her. She could hear Drake's voice calling her name.

Kwon turned around in the doorway. "Hurry, he's turning colors," she urged, and then twisted back inside the room.

When Cassie reached the doorway, Kwon was on the ground face down. A brown-haired man held a gun. He whirled on Cassie.

"Don't move!" he shouted. "Who are you? You a cop?"

Cassie shook her head, her mouth too dry to find the words. The man sprang to his feet, his movements jittery with adrenalin, and grabbed Cassie's arm. "C'mon, we're getting out of here."

He dragged her into the squad room, backing toward the door while he looked around for any resistance. Kwon emerged from the interview room.

"Don't do this, Mendelsohn," she shouted at the man.

"Stop where you are!" His voice was high-pitched, choked with fear. He wrapped his arm around Cassie, using her as a shield, his right hand aiming the gun at her temple. "Keep your hands where I can see them!" He jumped as Kwon slowly brought her hands, palm up, in front of her.

"I'm not going to hurt you," Kwon said in a low voice. "I just want to talk. Your lawyer's on his way—he can straighten this all out. You have to let her go, that's all."

Mendelsohn tapped the gun against Cassie's head. She tried not to flinch as the cold metal touched her flesh. The hand that held the gun shook. Then she realized that his entire body was trembling. She closed her eyes and prayed his trigger finger was steady.

DRAKE HELD THE cell phone clenched close to his ear and steered one-handed. Damn it, what was going on? He heard shouted voices but couldn't make out the words.

He squealed into the Zone Seven parking lot and left the car running as he ran inside.

"What's the hurry, lover boy?" Spanos almost collided with Drake. The uniformed officer was already dressed for his shift.

"Something's wrong in the squad room," Drake told him, yanking open the stairwell door. "Get backup!"

"You don't even have a gun," Spanos reminded him.

"Hart's up there," Drake said by way of explanation. Footsteps pounded behind him. Spanos quickly caught up and passed Drake.

Drake's thigh muscles were screaming at him to slow down, but he stayed on the larger man's heels until they rounded the landing for the third floor. One more flight.

"Quiet now," Drake yanked on Spanos' belt to slow the younger cop down. Spanos nodded his agreement, and they climbed the rest of the way in a slow, silent crouch. Spanos had his gun drawn, aiming it up the stairs to where the unknown subject would have to exit the squad room.

They reached the squad room's open door. Across from them Kwon stood, hands spread wide. In between them a man stood, his back to them, a gun in his right hand. The man turned slightly, and Drake recognized Mendelsohn. But all of his attention was drawn to Hart and the gun pointed at her head.

Spanos held his gun in the regulation two-handed Weaver stance, but his hands trembled. He used one hand to wipe sweat from his eyes and resumed his position. Drake looked over at him and realized that the patrolman had never been in a hostage situation before—probably had never used his gun off the range.

It didn't help knowing that he and Spanos usually tied for the bottom of the rankings every time they had to re-certify. Jimmy and Kwon were the sharpshooters of the House.

"If you shoot me there, I won't be much good to you," Hart told Mendelsohn. Drake couldn't believe how calm she sounded. "I'll be dead and then the police will just kill you."

She turned her head the slightest bit, just enough to make eye contact with the gunman. *Good girl, let him see you as a person.* He wasn't certain if Hart could see him and Spanos, but he knew she was getting ready to do something.

He placed his hand out and after a moment's hesitation, Spanos gave Drake his forty caliber Glock.

"You're right," Mendelsohn said in grudging admiration.

"I want to get out of this alive, just like you," Hart continued as Drake strained to get a clear shot.

He could see why Spanos had hesitated. It was an impossible shot. Drake raised his hand, sighting the gun in line with his gaze, as if it was a brush and the tableau before him was a canvas. Suddenly he saw his shot clear as day. He twisted into position, and raised the Glock.

·⦿·

"WHY DON'T WE work together?" She paused. "My name is Cassie, what's yours?"

"Darin." His eyes darted away from her and back

to Kwon. "I told you not to move!" he screamed at Kwon.

Cassie saw that Kwon had edged toward them slightly. She knew the detective would be carrying a backup weapon. Drake usually kept his in an ankle holster when he was on duty—would Kwon do the same? She had to distract him long enough for Kwon to reach it.

"So how about down here?" Mendelsohn asked earnestly, moving his gun to aim at Cassie's belly. "This wouldn't kill you right away, would it?"

If he shot her there, she'd probably end up paralyzed. The muscles and flesh of her abdomen recoiled, pulling away from the gun and the hand that held it there.

"Not right away," she agreed through clenched teeth. His left arm held hers behind her back. Her right arm wasn't as restricted as he squeezed her in an unholy embrace.

"Good," he said, his voice breaking. "Then we're leaving now."

Cassie took a breath in, focusing on his gun hand. Now or never. He took a step back. She plunged all her weight forward, throwing him off balance. She grabbed for the gun hand, twisting it away from her body, leaning forward and sinking her teeth into his wrist. He yanked her left arm, wrenching it until she feared her shoulder would dislocate.

The gun went off, the explosion deafening in Cassie's ears. It was quickly followed by two more shots as she fought free and threw herself to the floor.

The coppery smell of blood and gunpowder rained down on her. She opened her eyes to see Kwon kicking Mendelsohn's gun away, straddling him and snapping on handcuffs. Cassie's ears filled with a deafening roar.

She pushed herself into a sitting position and suddenly Drake's arms were around her and she could breathe again. He turned her towards him, his hands searching her body for damage, his lips moving, but she couldn't hear what he was saying. He gathered her into his arms, holding her tight. His breath was jagged as it vibrated through his chest, and she felt his heart pounding when she lay her head down. After a few moments her hearing began to return, and she could hear him whispering her name.

"I'm fine," she said and realized her voice was too loud. "I'm fine," she tried again, this time there was no answering echo in her ears. She pushed back in his embrace, only enough to turn her head and look over at Mendelsohn.

"Is he? Can I—" She was ashamed that she really didn't want to help the child killer. She swallowed. "Is there anything I can do?"

Kwon rocked back on her heels, allowing Cassie a good look at the killer's body. "Pronounce him," she said with satisfaction. "That was good shooting, DJ."

Mendelsohn's upper face was obliterated and there was another wound in his left upper chest. She turned to Drake. "You shot him?"

"Spanos lent me his service piece. I saw you lunge forward, so I took the head shot, figured it was safest." He glowered at Kwon.

"Hey, I didn't hit her, did I?" the detective defended herself. "You should always go for the biggest target, the body shot, so I did."

The thunder of footsteps rang out as other cops filled the room. Cassie knew there would be interviews and statements and forms to fill out, but she ignored the swirl of activity around her, content to be cradled, safe in Drake's arms.

· ⚙ ·

WHEN MILLER ARRIVED a short time later, the noise level immediately dropped. She called Kwon to her office first, then after she'd dismissed her, summoned Drake and Jimmy Dolan. Drake held onto Hart's hand, and Miller nodded her acceptance of Hart's presence.

Jimmy and Hart sat in the two chairs in front of Miller's desk. Drake took his position behind Hart, one hand on her shoulder, the other still entwined with hers as she held it up to him.

"It's lucky for you that Dr. White's fax is timed hours before the shooting, otherwise we might have a mess on our hands," Miller began, addressing Drake. "I know you already spoke to the Officer Involved Team. But I'm interested in hearing exactly how you came to be using Officer Spanos' service weapon."

"Officer Spanos had something in his eye, obscuring his vision, so he gave me his weapon to use," Drake said, keeping his voice formal.

Miller cut him a look that said she didn't believe a word of it, but changed the subject. "What's Mendelsohn's story?"

Jimmy answered. "The whiz kids hit pay dirt with his computer. Seems he kept a journal for posterity. Documented how he'd spend all summer weeding through potential victims, then work to gain his special boy's trust. It was all a game to him, outwitting third graders," he said with disgust.

"He detailed various ways he'd manipulate the boys, and coerce them into silence. Even how disappointed he was when he finally had to resort to violence to ensure silence and cooperation. Like it was one big psychology experiment, research for a journal article or some shit like that. Oh and if that's not enough—" Jimmy smiled again. "He collected trophies from each boy and left detailed plans of each murder: time, place, method, and observation point so he could watch his kids find the victim. Whole nine yards."

"Too bad we couldn't have found him before he started killing. If just one of those boys had come forward—"

"Pretty unlikely," Jimmy told her. "Pedophiles are experts at manipulating kids—making them unwilling participants in their own abuse and too guilty and ashamed to speak of it later. This guy could've kept operating for years."

Drake felt a shiver race through Hart's body. "So, case closed on Mendelsohn, right?"

"Except for the shooting review. Kwon's in with IAD now. Three days inactive for both of you until Internal Affairs' and Dr. White's reports are completed."

"But, I just—"

Miller arched an eyebrow at him, and he shut up. Jimmy raised a hand to cover his grin, but not before Drake caught it.

"Take the holiday and don't argue, Detective," Miller told him, her glance settling on Hart for a moment. "I told Dr. White you'd be in to see him on Tuesday."

Drake opened his mouth to protest the delay and thought better of it. "Yes ma'am," he said meekly.

"Now get out of here, I've got a press conference to put together."

Jimmy started out the door, and Hart got to her feet. "Any word on Virginia Ulrich?" she asked Miller.

"No. Turns out she and her husband have

separate bedrooms so he didn't know she was missing. She could be anywhere."

"She'll go after Charlie, I'm certain of it. Is someone guarding him?"

"He's under video surveillance, and we've got someone on the floor," Miller told her. "Not that I expect her to get that far."

Drake watched as Hart chewed her lip, obviously not sharing Miller's optimism. He tugged at her hand, leading her to the door.

"Drake," Miller called him back. "Your father would have been proud."

He turned away to hide his smile. It was probably the nicest thing Miller had ever said to him.

※

IT WAS SO easy to lose yourself in the routine of a busy hospital, Virginia Ulrich thought as she sipped her coffee in the OR's nursing lounge. So many people coming and going, each too busy with their own affairs to notice anyone else. Especially if you looked and acted like you belonged there.

She turned the volume up on the TV. The camera crews hadn't gotten to Three Rivers in time to film Hart's arrest, but they made up for it by re-broadcasting highlights of the press conference from yesterday and discussing the doctor's detention, while flashing the photo that had appeared in the paper this morning.

The bitch got what she deserved. She had no right to try to take Charlie from her, to make people think Virginia had done anything wrong, to pry into Virginia's private life. Well, Cassandra Hart would think twice now, wouldn't she?

Virginia smiled. Almost time to end the charade. By now CYS should have backed down. She'd make sure things were all right on Peds, then change into her own clothes and go back to her own son, her own life. And if CYS hadn't dropped the charges, then she'd head outside instead and talk to those nice people in front of the cameras.

No one was going to stand between her and her son. Not now, not ever.

Virginia left the crushed coffee cup on the table behind her. She took the stairs down to Peds and was about to step triumphantly to the nurses' station when she almost ran into two police officers. She ducked back into the stairwell, leaving the door ajar so that she could hear what they were saying to the nurses at the desk.

"We need to find Mrs. Ulrich," one was saying.

"Why?" Carol, one of Virginia's friends, snapped. "You already took her son away, what more do you want?"

"Look lady, we need to take her in for questioning. Have you seen her?"

"Not today. What do you need to question Virginia about? She hasn't been allowed near Charlie since yesterday morning."

"Something happened last night. If you see her, call security right away, okay? There'll be a guard downstairs monitoring the video feed from her son's room as well."

"Yeah, right," Carol replied reluctantly.

Virginia pushed the door shut as the cops left the nurses' station. Damn it, how had they known? She'd been so careful. Everything should point to Cassandra Hart, not her.

CHAPTER 32

DRAKE TOOK A deep breath and opened the car door for Hart. Her house didn't look so bad in daylight. It looked like a nice, ordinary brick house dating from the nineteen-twenties. Friendly porch, complete with swing, big picture window, and solid oak door. Nothing to be afraid of, nothing at all.

He took Hart's hand, and she led him up the steps. This was nice. Like coming home. She opened the front door, and he made it to the threshold without a flutter of fear. No pounding in his head and chest, no feeling of suffocating.

"Sorry about the smell," she said. He was surprised that she sounded nervous.

There was nothing to be nervous about. Nothing at all. He laughed and scooped her up into his arms, carrying her over the threshold, delighted by how easy it was. Maybe that headshrinker knew what he was talking about after all. Or maybe it was having Hart back — with her at his side he could face anything.

"Put me down!" But her laughter joined his,

echoed through the room. It was good to see her happy again. It had been too long, much too long. He spun her around, ignoring her protests, then finally settled her back onto her feet.

"I want to see it all. Everything." The only other time he'd been inside it was only for a few moments. A few terrifying, gut-wrenching moments.

Drake traced his fingers over the lace antimacassars draped over the arms of the ivory damask, camel-backed sofa. One of the matching pillows flipped over, revealing the faint remnant of a purple stain.

"Did you do this?" he asked, showing her the stained pillow.

Hart blushed and took it from him, carefully returning it clean side up on the couch. "When I was four—grape juice. Dad and I tried every stain removal technique we could find, turned it into a kind of science experiment."

Drake moved over to the mantle, inspecting the photos there. Most were in black and white, a few aged to a sepia color. He lifted one in a heavy silver frame. A smiling woman with vibrant red hair and a tall, thin man wearing thick glasses staring out at the camera as if he were in shock. Hart's parents.

After he'd been shot and released from the hospital, he'd painted a picture of them for her. He was pleased to see she'd hung his small watercolor sketch over the mantle, a place of honor. Damn, had that only been a few weeks ago? It felt like he'd gone decades without color or light in his life since he'd finished that painting. As if without Hart in his life, his vision was darkened, lifeless.

He remembered White asking about Hart's life, how she never spoke of her past. But Drake had also never asked. She joined him at the mantle, her fingers stroking the top of the frame lovingly. "Tell me about your Mom."

"She's an angel," she whispered, her voice suddenly sounding like a child's. She looked up at him in surprise, her fingers touching her lips. "Sorry," she continued in her normal voice. "That was all my Dad ever said about her. He couldn't talk about her, it made him cry. But Rosa told me the story."

"What happened?"

"My mom died right after I was born."

"I'm sorry." He took her hand and wove his fingers between hers.

"She did it for me. When she was pregnant she found a swollen gland on her neck. It was lymphoma and had already begun to spread. But she refused to have any treatment that could hurt her baby, and she refused an abortion. The doctors told her that she'd never survive the pregnancy and that I never would either."

"Wow. How do you feel—I mean, knowing—"

"That I killed my mother, literally, just by existing? How do you ever repay a gift like that?"

He put his arm around her. "I'd say you've made a pretty good start. I think your mom would be really proud of her daughter, and the person she's become."

She looked down into the fireplace, silent, and he knew that it would take more than words for her to believe that. Hart had to prove it to herself, everyday. Finally Drake could understand some of that passion that drove her so hard.

"This is Rosa, right?" His hand moved to a sepia toned print of a man in an English naval uniform and a woman with bright eyes and untamed dark hair.

"That's her." Now she was smiling again. "And my

grandfather, Padraic Hart. He came from Ireland."

She'd once told him how Rosa had risked her life for Padraic, giving up everything to be with him. He turned her to face him, tracing his fingers over her face, loving the faint hint of Alizarian crimson that colored her cheeks, the way she trembled ever so slightly beneath his touch, as if she were afraid to break a spell.

God, he had missed her so much, he'd been such a fool to let so much time go by. What if he'd lost her this morning?

He shook the thought away and focused on Hart. "No more ghost stories," he told her, leaning down to plant a gentle kiss on her forehead. "I want to see upstairs." He raised her hand and kissed it. "Take me to your bedroom."

⁂

CASSIE LED HIM up the steps. Her face burnt with pleasure, embarrassment, and sudden shyness. She'd never brought a man here, not to this house, to the bed she'd inherited from Rosa, the bed carved by Padraic's hands. What would Rosa think?

She suppressed a giggle and clasped Drake's hand tighter as her grandmother's voice came to her: *Never pass up an opportunity for good old fashioned fun, girl. The kind where no one gets hurt and everyone's still friends in the morning. Why else would God have made so many men, when just a few could have gotten the job done?*

She stopped on the landing and turned to Drake in the dim light. His hand rested on her hip, snuggling her close. It felt so right, his warmth and strength beside her in this house. Like it was meant to be. All the pain they'd both been through, it had somehow led here. Led home. But her home had never felt this full of life. Drake's presence had banished the ghosts of the past.

She smiled up at him, suffused with a feeling of perfect contentment. Together they moved into her bedroom.

The morning breeze softly diffused the air, almost as if it came from a perfume atomizer. A rosy glow from the early morning sun shifted as the shadows cast by the lace curtains moved. The room was chilly, she'd left the windows open all night, but it didn't feel cold. Not with Drake beside her.

He turned her within the embrace of his arms. Cassie circled her hands around his neck and stood up on tiptoe, pulling his head to meet hers. The kiss was soft, a gentle symphony of tastes and perfumes, spiced by an undercurrent of desire. They moved slowly as if they had all the time in the world to explore, to pleasure.

Drake's fingers skimmed over her flesh in a delicate caress as he slid her shirt from her shoulders. There was no lacey push up bra this time, she thought with amusement, but they didn't need it. She could feel that he was already aroused.

Cassie stepped away from his clever hands and shrugged out of her bra. He looked down on her, watching as she shed her jeans, his mouth open like a schoolboy looking through the window of a candy store, knowing that the dollar in his pocket could buy him anything he wanted. Naked before him, Cassie raised his hand, placing it over her heart, holding it there, feeling their pulses synchronize into one steady rhythm. Then his hands and his mouth were on her, moving over her until she shivered with delight.

He lowered her onto the bed, and she sank into

the rich silks and velvets of Roas's quilt, floating in dreamy contentment. He stripped free from his clothes and joined her on the bed. She ran her fingers over his scars—the surgical incision that ran the length of his abdomen, the more ragged, stellate shapes of the entrance and exit wounds, the tiny puckers where the doctors had inserted tubes and drains. He didn't flinch from her touch as he lay beside her. Cassie leaned over him, kissing each one, delicately caressing them with her tongue, savoring each as proof that he was alive. She finished by lying on top of him, her finger tracing the v-shaped scar on his chin.

"This is the one that has me curious," she murmured, flicking her tongue over the smooth pucker of skin nestled below the stubble of his beard. He hadn't shaved in two days, and the growth was long enough to tickle and itch as she rubbed her face against it.

"Long story," he said, his fingers traveling the length of her spine, tantalizing her.

"We've time," she assured him.

He looked up at her, his eyes dark with emotion. "I've got better ideas of what to do with the time," he said with a lopsided grin. He flipped her over so that he was now astride her, and she laughed.

His face lowered to her breast and his hands began their movement once more. Her laugh was choked by a gasp of pleasure. She danced her fingers down to the sensitive area at the base of his spine and was rewarded with a shiver from him. Their bodies began to shine with sweat that glistened in the early morning light.

Drake continued to move slowly, tantalizing her with his tango of passion, arousing and rewarding simultaneously until Cassie felt herself thrumming with pleasure. She felt need but no urgency, trusting that he wouldn't disappoint.

Relaxed, surrendering all control, her only responsibility now was to enjoy the ecstasy that he so painstakingly built in her. And that was more than enough, she thought as languid warmth spread through her body. She curled her fingers in his hair, pulling his face to meet hers, their eyes locking, their bodies moving in perfect and absolute synchrony.

Together they rode the wave, higher than ever before and in the end when the final cry of release came, they sounded it together, with one voice.

It was some time later before Cassie could speak. Her body was floating on an ocean of rich velvet, her mind drifting in a similarly warm place. Her eyes were open, but all she could see was the gleam that had filled Drake's before he collapsed into her embrace—sunlight beamed through a prism of sapphire. A color she'd never seen before. She wished she had Drake's talent so that she could render that beautiful glow onto canvas, and immortalize it.

"We have to do that again," she whispered.

He raised his head from her chest, one eye open, the other squinted shut against the sunlight streaming through the window. "Right," he sighed, rolling off of her and collapsing onto the quilt. "Maybe next millennium when I get my strength back." He tangled his hand in her hair, gently pulling her head to rest on his shoulder. "That was pretty nice," he conceded.

Cassie lifted up on one arm to look down on him. "Nice?" she asked. "That's all you have to say—"

He opened both eyes now and grinned to let her know he was joking. "It was okay," he continued. "Not one of my best efforts—course if I had the right partner—" The last was smothered by the pillow Cassie buried him under.

"You know there is a way we could do this more often," he said, moving the pillow aside.

She tensed, hoping that he wasn't going to ask her to make a choice they both might regret. Neither had mentioned his declaration of love the other night, and she certainly wasn't going to bring it up. To do so would mean making her own feelings about him clear, and they were anything but.

What she felt for Drake—she wasn't certain if there were even any words to describe it. Was it love? After Richard, she was no longer sure she could recognize true love.

She closed her eyes for a moment, waiting for Drake's next words, hoping he wouldn't ask her for a commitment that she couldn't make. Not yet, anyway.

"You could move some of your things over to my place," he said, and she opened her eyes in relief. "And I could maybe bring a few things here?"

Cassie smiled. "I'd like that," she told him, her fingers stroking the scar on his chin that intrigued her so much. "I'd like that very much."

He raised his head to kiss her again and Cassie allowed herself to be pulled into his embrace. She might not be certain if what she felt for Drake was love—the real thing like what Rosa and Padraic and her parents had shared—but she was certain that he was her best chance to find it.

．◉．

VIRGINIA MEASURED A length of hair with her fingers before cutting it with the bandage scissors she'd liberated from a medication cart. She probably didn't need to be doing this. The police were so dumb, they had no idea how easy it was to hide in a hospital if you knew what you were doing and had an ounce of brains. There was no way they would catch her, not unless she wanted them too.

And she didn't, at least not yet, not until she could figure out what had gone wrong. She'd been so careful. Had someone seen her in the PICU? Maybe Tammy Washington hadn't been as sound asleep as she had seemed?

The baby kicked again, hard enough to make Virginia wince. Stop it, Samantha. You're no better than your brothers, never knowing when to be quiet so that your mother can think.

In response the baby shifted, this time putting pressure on Virginia's bladder. Virginia sighed, put down the scissors, and went into one of the toilet stalls. That was one of the nice things about hospitals, plenty of tiny bathrooms hidden in back hallways. All you had to do was find one, place an out of order sign on the door, and it might be weeks before anyone disturbed you.

Virginia sat there for a few minutes, thinking about her next move. She could run away, and start all over again in a new city. But it wouldn't be easy with a new baby and no money. And she couldn't leave Charlie behind—if he lived, they'd find someway to blame everything that had happened to him on her. No, Charlie was going to die. And none of these doctors would be able to stop that. It was just the way things had to be.

But what was she going to do about Samantha?

CHAPTER 33

Cassie held Drake's hand as they climbed the stairs to the ICU. "We could have taken the elevator," she told him as they rounded the second floor landing.

Drake paused and pulled her close, kissing her deeply. "Can't do that in an elevator."

She arched an eyebrow. "If you did, I probably wouldn't mind riding in them so much."

"I'll keep that in mind."

Cassie tugged at his hand. "C'mon, there's time for that later. I want to see your mom."

The clatter of feet galloping down the steps above them echoed through the concrete-walled space. As Cassie and Drake rounded the next landing, a woman in surgical scrubs bent her head over the railing from the flight above.

"If I was you," she called out in a sing-song voice, "I wouldn't waste any time."

Cassie looked up. Virginia Ulrich, her hair chopped in a haphazard pageboy, grinned at them. The gleam in her eye reminded Cassie of Morris, the crackhead.

"Not if you want to see your mother alive, Detective Drake."

Drake dropped Cassie's hand and charged up the steps. "What did you do?"

Cassie was close on his heels, but Virginia had the lead on them. She fled through the third floor door before they could reach her.

"She's going after Charlie," Cassie said.

Drake hesitated, torn between apprehending the fugitive and ensuring his mother's safety.

"Go," Cassie told him, wrenching open the door to Pediatrics. "I'll get the guard from Charlie's room."

"Have him call for back up," Drake shouted over his shoulder as he bounded up the steps two at a time.

Cassie raced through the third floor door, startling the clerk at the nurses' station just beyond. "Did you see her?"

"See who?" The clerk looked up from his computer screen in surprise.

"Virginia Ulrich. She came this way." Cassie looked up and down the corridor. No sign of Virginia.

"I don't know, I'm just covering."

The security alarm sounded on the computer console. The clerk looked at it and jerked his hands off of the keyboard as if it had electrocuted him. "What the hell?"

"Call security, have them get a police officer to Charlie Ulrich's room." The clerk looked at her like she was escaped from the psych floor. "Do it, now!"

Cassie ran down the hallway to the closed door of Room 303. She pushed it open, and then froze.

Inside, Virginia Ulrich was holding a needle and syringe at the port of Charlie's IV. She calmly sat with her son as if she was waiting for Cassie's arrival. Her eyes were wide and her gaze leapt around the room erratically. But the hand that held the syringe, poised to inject whatever poison was in it, remained steady. With her other hand she massaged her gravid belly.

Charlie was sleeping, peacefully oblivious to the danger.

"Come in, Dr. Hart," Virginia said in low tone. "Don't wake the baby."

"What have you given him?" She tried to keep her voice calm, edging into the room until she was at the foot of Charlie's bed.

Virginia smiled. She jerked her head at Cassie. "Right there is fine. I believe the camera has a good view of you." She raised her eyes to the ceiling where the video surveillance camera was hidden.

There were the sounds of running footsteps and a police officer appeared at the open doorway, his gun drawn. Cassie recognized Johnson, Spanos' partner.

"Step away from the child," he ordered Virginia.

Virginia's eyes darted to him. "Stay back," she replied calmly, gesturing with the syringe.

"You okay, doc?" Johnson asked in a low voice, holding his position just outside the room.

Cassie nodded. "I'm fine."

He lifted his radio from his belt and took several steps back before speaking into it. Cassie returned her attention to Virginia.

"Virginia, why don't you come with me? You really don't want to hurt Charlie," she said softly.

"Of course I don't want to hurt him!" Virginia stroked his hair with her free hand. "I love my son. But you drove me to this—you took him from me! Who will watch over him, guard him if I'm not around? I know you doctors. You'll poke and prod and torture him and what will come of it in the end? He'll die, just like his brother and sister before him."

"Virginia, Charlie is going to be just fine. As long as you put the syringe down and come with me."

"No!" she cried out, and Charlie stirred slightly under her hand. "No," she repeated in a lower tone. "I can't let him go through what his brother and sister did. Not without me here to protect him. I'm going to save him from you. You'll never take my son from me!"

"I'm just trying to help Charlie," Cassie told her. "You didn't really do anything to Muriel Drake, did you?" Keep her talking, she thought. Stall. Maybe she'll let her guard down.

"Tell them to give me my child back," Virginia instructed Cassie, nodding toward the hidden camera. "Tell them how you had it all wrong, that you were persecuting me—jealous of what I have because your own life is falling apart. Tell them how you almost killed Antwan Washington and how your incompetence has gotten you fired." The woman's voice rose, and her fingers clenched on the syringe. "Do it now!"

Cassie gritted her teeth, her eyes cutting over to the doorway. Johnson nodded encouragement to her.

"Don't look at him," Virginia yelled. "He doesn't know anything—about how you invaded my privacy, made up dirty lies about me, tried to tell Dr. Sterling I was a bad mother. Go on, say it!"

Cassie took a deep breath and focused her attention on Virginia and the hand holding the syringe. "I was wrong," she said. "Now, give me the syringe. Please, Virginia."

"That's right," Virginia raised her face to the camera. "The great Dr. Hart was wrong." She glanced over to the doorway as footsteps sounded down the hallway. "Did you all hear that?" she called out to Drake as he skidded to a stop in front of the door.

"You're a witness. Your good doctor just admitted her mistake—one of many, I'm sure."

Drake took a step into the room. "I heard her," he said, locking his gaze with Virginia's. "And it's on tape. So why don't we all leave here, let Charlie get his rest?" He took another step forward.

"Why don't you just go to hell?" Virginia answered sweetly. "Stop right there, Detective. You're the one who told them to take my boy from me, locked him up down here all alone."

"I'm sorry," Drake said, spreading his hands wide in apology.

"You sound so sincere," she scoffed, dismissing him. Virginia turned her smile on Cassie, chilling her to the bone. "You think of yourself as the great healer, the brilliant doctor," she said in a bitter tone. "Well, Dr. Hart, tell me, how much do you value life?"

"I don't understand what you're asking." She could hear more police and security arrive outside in the hallway, but she kept her eyes focused on Virginia.

"You'd do anything to save Charlie, wouldn't you?"

"Of course. So why don't you—"

"And my unborn child, would you try to save her if she were in trouble?"

Cassie looked down at Virginia's swollen belly. What was she getting at? Had she done something to hurt her fetus, maybe induce early labor?

"I would do everything in my power," she replied slowly.

"And if I were dying, would you try to save me?"

"Of course I would."

"Liar." Virginia spat the word out with venom.

"I'm trying to help you and your son right now, Virginia." She held out her hand. "Give me the syringe."

Virginia looked at Cassie for a long moment. Cassie released the breath that she'd been holding when Virginia removed the syringe and needle from the IV hub.

Before she could move forward to take it, Virginia plunged the needle into the large vein in her own forearm. Again her finger hovered over the plunger.

"Prove it, Doctor," she said. "Show me how important my life is to you. How important is the life of my baby?"

"What do you want me to do?" Cassie asked.

Her eyes darted from Cassie to Drake and back again. "You two make such a cute couple. But I wonder how Detective Drake will feel about you, Dr. Hart, after you're branded a murderer."

Before either of them could respond, Charlie's monitor began to alarm.

Cassie focused on the green lights tracing the boy's heartbeat. "Ventricular tachycardia. Get a code team here," she called out to Johnson. "Damn it, what did you give him?" She took another step toward Charlie.

"Come any closer and you'll be killing me and my unborn child in front of all these witnesses," Virginia said, her voice rose to carry out into the hallway where there was a crowd gathering. "Our deaths will be on your head. It's your choice: one life or two?"

Cassie looked at the unconscious child, his golden curls spread out on the pillow like an angel's halo. Then she met the gaze of the monster who was his mother. Would Virginia Ulrich do it? Actually kill herself and her baby just to prove herself better than Cassie according to her warped brand of logic?

Did it matter? Charlie was her patient, he was the one she knew to be in immediate danger. Was she really going to allow Virginia to manipulate her like this, with a little boy's life on the line?

Maybe Cassie had lied when she told Virginia that she'd save her life. Maybe she wasn't a good physician, maybe she didn't value all life as equal, because suddenly the choice was very clear and very easy to make.

"To hell with you," she muttered, lunging forward and pulling the IV line from Charlie's arm.

Drake rushed past her, tackling Virginia. He grabbed for Virginia's arm, shoving her away from Charlie and Cassie. When they separated, Drake held the syringe. Cassie stared in horror—it was empty, the plunger all the way down.

"My babies will always be with me," Virginia said, slumping against the wall. "You'll never take them from me now."

The pulse ox monitor blared as Charlie stopped breathing. Cassie fumbled for the bag valve mask at the bedside and began to pump oxygen into the boy.

"Potassium?" she shouted at Virginia, looking over her shoulder from where she worked on Charlie. "Was that it?"

Virginia didn't answer. Her eyes stared at Cassie with hatred.

"Bag that for evidence," Drake told Johnson, gingerly handing him the syringe, restraining Virginia with his other hand. "What should I do?" he asked Cassie.

"Get me a crash cart," Cassie ordered. "I need some help here! And someone stat page OB."

Several of the bystanders pushed past the police officers to enter the room. Two of the nurses went directly to Virginia. They turned and glared at Cassie.

"Check her pockets. See if you can find out what

she used," Cassie told Drake who looked on, helpless as Virginia Ulrich slumped, unconscious. The nurses cradled her body, easing it to the floor and checked her vital signs. They tried to push him away, but Drake ignored them as he scoured Virginia's lab coat.

The pediatric code team and crash cart arrived, adding to the crush of people crowded into the small room.

"Get the adult team here with another crash cart," Cassie ordered just as Charlie's heart went into fibrillation. "Someone start CPR on him. I think it's potassium," she told the bewildered pediatric resident who'd responded to the code.

The nurses began CPR, sliding a board under the boy's back to support his body.

"No pulse," someone announced, and Cassie saw that it was one of the nurses working on Virginia. They quickly began chest compressions and mouth to mask ventilation on Charlie's mother.

This was turning into Cassie's worst nightmare.

The resident seemed stunned, so Cassie took charge. As she worked on Charlie, she tried furiously to think about the effects of potassium on a fetus. How much time would they have before the drugs in Virginia's system circulated into the baby inside her?

"Give me twenty of bicarb, twenty cc's of D50, and one unit of insulin," she snapped, grabbing the defibrillator paddles. "Charge to twenty." Cassie shocked the boy.

"No response."

"She's got a lot of stuff in here." Drake had several empty vials in his hands. She heard the frustration in his voice but had no time to answer it. Was his mother all right? the thought sped through her mind even as she considered the next step to treat her patient. She looked down on the glistening vials Drake presented to her. Succinylcholine, vecuronium, atropine, and potassium chloride. Enough to kill a small army. Damn it, where was the adult team?

"Here's the bicarb and D50," the nurse handed Cassie the syringes, and she pushed the medications as the nurse drew up the epinephrine. "There's no insulin on the crash cart, Megan went to get it."

"Give me some calcium and another twenty of bicarb. Set up for intubation."

Cassie looked over to Virginia's body. There were so many people in the room that the two resuscitation teams were bumping into each other as they performed CPR on the woman.

She took the defibrillation paddles again just as a nurse was reaching for them, presumably to use on Virginia.

"I need those."

"So does her son," Cassie replied grimly.

She shocked Charlie again. *Come on, don't do this, don't die right here in front of me. Damn it, you have to live. After everything that's happened, you have to live!*

CHAPTER 34

"Repeat epi and push ten of lidocaine," Cassie ordered. "Charge to fifty and clear." Another shock without response. "Where the hell is that insulin?"

The doorway jammed with people as the nurse with the insulin tried to get through at the same time as the adult code team arrived with another crash cart.

"Stop!" Cassie shouted. This resuscitation was deteriorating into chaos.

"Get her out of here," she indicated Virginia Ulrich. "Take her to the treatment room where there's oxygen and a monitor. And someone get that insulin in here!"

The room became even more crowded momentarily as people surged forward to help carry Virginia's body out to the gurney waiting in the hallway. Cassie noticed several of the Peds nurses crying as they saw Virginia, remaining with their friend rather than helping her with Charlie. The police officers trailed out after their prisoner. Except Drake. He stayed with Cassie.

She felt as if she was finally able to breathe now that Virginia was gone and she had room to work on Charlie. She gave the insulin, her eyes glued to the monitor.

Without being told to, Drake relieved the nurse giving CPR to Charlie. His shoulders moved up and down in a steady rhythm, but his eyes never left Cassie's face.

"Hold CPR," she ordered.

Come on, come back, Charlie, she prayed.

They were rewarded with a definable heart rate on the monitor. Cassie bit her lip. "Pulse?" she asked, hoping for the right answer. It seemed an eternity while the nurse palpated the carotid artery.

"Yes. Faint, but it's there."

"Okay. Let's get a complete set of vitals, hang an lidocaine drip, and call the PICU to have a vent ready."

She looked up at the clock. It was hard to believe, but the elapsed time since Virginia Ulrich had poisoned her son was less than ten minutes. That was the way with codes, it was like being in a time warp. She could only pray that Charlie would pull through without serious brain damage from the hypoxia that occurred while his heart was stopped.

"Is he going to be all right?" Drake asked, his voice low. One of his hands gently stroked Charlie's arm as if he were reassuring the unconscious boy.

"I wish to hell I knew."

• ⚫ •

CASSIE WAS HELPING the nurses move Charlie to the PICU when she heard her name called.

"Dr. Hart!" It was the internal medicine resident who was in charge of Virginia's resuscitation. He waved to her from the open door of the treatment room. "We could use some help in here."

She wanted more than anything to pretend to not hear him, but she couldn't ignore the note of panic in his voice. She sighed and allowed the pediatric resident and nurses to continue without her.

Virginia's resuscitation was going worse than Charlie's had. For starters, more people had crowded into the tiny room, but very few were actually working on the patient. Cassie got to the doorway and had to push her way through the crowd to reach the patient.

"Everyone not touching the patient or a medication out! Now!" she commanded. "Drake, you don't let anyone in through that door unless I tell you." He nodded and began to usher people out of the room. Cassie could hear the snide comments directed at her, including several nurses who demanded to stay as witnesses to ensure Virginia's safety.

While Drake cleared the room, she conferred with the medical resident on what steps he'd already taken. Virginia was in full arrest, the monitor showing a ventricular fibrillation, just as her son had experienced. And Lord only knew what was going on with her unborn child.

Cassie grabbed a small doppler unit and tried to get fetal heart tones. They were there, but definitely too fast and too faint.

"We're not going to mess around in here," she decided after a moment's assessment. "Sally," she addressed the charge nurse. "Call OB, tell them we'll be there in five minutes and they'd better have a crash C-section ready to go. No excuses. And get someone from the ICU up to OB with a hemofiltration unit. That's our only chance at this point."

Sally nodded and got on the phone while the other

staff members scrambled to prepare the patient for transport. Minutes later they were rolling down the hallway to the elevator that would take them up to Obstetrics. Cassie tried to monitor the fetal heartbeat as they moved, but it was progressively slowing and becoming more difficult to pick up. She lost it just as they arrived at the OB operating room.

"Get her prepped," Cassie told the nurses as the OB resident emerged from the nurses' station with a puzzled and angry look on his face.

"Are you the one who keeps paging me to Peds?" he asked angrily. "I don't respond to codes down there—" He stopped as he saw the patient. "What the hell?"

"Potassium overdose, I just lost the baby's heart beat," Cassie snapped. "They're sending a hemofiltration team up from the ICU. I'll work on getting lines into the mom while you get the baby out."

The resident nodded and turned to a nurse. "Right—call neonatal, we need a full team here, now!"

He and Cassie rushed through a quick scrub. Through the windows into the C-section room she could see the nurses still giving Virginia chest compressions while the OR crew prepared for the stat C-section.

"How far along is she?" the resident asked.

"I don't know, anywhere from twenty-eight to thirty-six weeks."

"You realize that even if we get this baby out, he doesn't have a snowball's chance in hell," he told her as they entered the room.

"We have to try."

The neonatology team arrived and began to frantically gather their equipment, including some whole blood, Cassie saw. Smart thinking. It was actually possible in newborns to use the umbilical vessels to exchange the infant's entire blood volume. The old blood, with the dangerous levels of potassium, could be exchanged for fresh blood. It was a risky procedure, but probably the baby's best chance—if they could keep the baby alive long enough to undergo the exchange transfusion.

The room echoed with a cacophony of noise as each team tried to perform their job: the OB crew cutting the baby out, the neonatal team preparing to resuscitate it, while Cassie and the anesthesiologist, David Allman, tried to keep Virginia's heart pumping enough blood and oxygen to keep the baby alive.

Cassie, David, and his nurse developed a graceful pattern of pushing meds, defibrillating, and drawing up more meds. Another nurse had climbed onto a stool beside the table, a sterile sheet over top of her while she performed chest compressions. Cassie inserted a central venous line while David placed the arterial cannula and they started hemofiltration. Several minutes later, when Cassie looked up again, she saw that the baby was out and that the neonatal team was hard at work.

She looked at the clock. Virginia Ulrich had been in arrest for twenty-six minutes.

"Let's check a pulse." Cassie sighed. She heard the failure in her voice. David and his nurse looked at her. David nodded to halt the chest compressions. The room was silent as he held his fingers over the carotid artery.

"Nothing," he said. "Should we call it?"

The OB resident nodded. "She's gone."

Cassie agreed, they had done everything they could. "Time of death—"

"Stop!" A voice echoed into the tile-walled room. Everyone turned to look. "Dr. Hart, step away from that patient."

It was Karl Sterling, one hand holding a mask over his face, standing in the doorway of the OR. Beside him, at the scrub sinks, were Paul Ulrich and his assistant, Scott Thayer.

"There's nothing more we can do for her," Cassie protested. Ulrich turned away and Thayer paled as he looked through the window at the carnage in the operating room.

"I don't care. You all proceed with the resuscitation until I've had a chance to review the chart," Sterling ordered.

David Allman looked at the Pediatric Chairman. "Dr. Sterling, I'm in charge of any codes in my OR. There's nothing more we can do for this patient. Time of death is 1158." He extended a hand to help the nurse down.

Cassie looked over to where the neonatologists worked on the baby. Things didn't sound very promising. She turned to join them, see if she could help in any way, when Sterling grabbed her by the arm.

"Don't you dare touch that baby!"

The man was hysterical. Cassie could understand why as she surveyed the blood-bathed room. A crash C-section was no pretty sight even when the outcome was good. And Sterling was probably just now realizing how wrong he had been in supporting Virginia Ulrich.

"There's a police officer outside. I'm asking him to take you into custody until we get to the bottom of this," Sterling continued, tugging on Cassie's arm to pull her with him.

She batted away his hand. The entire OR crew was staring at her. She didn't want to disrupt the neonatology team's efforts, so she turned and left the room.

Outside the doorway she stopped. Paul Ulrich

was there, staring into the OR, at his wife's body. His face was ashen, but there was little emotion on it.

"I'm sorry, Mr. Ulrich," Cassie said. Ulrich looked at Cassie and she was chilled by the blankness in his face. She tried to reassure the man. "We did everything we could—"

He turned to her with uncomprehending eyes. It was his assistant who finally spoke.

"You're the woman—" Thayer whispered in a venom-filled voice. "You're the cause of all of this."

Cassie ignored him, more concerned with Ulrich. The man appeared ready to pass out. She reached out a hand to lead him away.

A low snarl came from Thayer's throat. Cassie turned in surprise just as he launched himself at her. "You killed Virginia and my baby!"

His weight propelled them both to the floor. His hands were around her throat, trying to choke the life from her, his eyes blazing down at her.

"I should have killed you when I had the chance! Run you down like the bitch you are," he screamed. "You took Virginia from me!"

Cassie rammed her knee into Thayer's groin. He jerked back, allowing her enough space to wrench one of his thumbs back. He howled in pain as the joint dislocated and she broke free. Johnson rushed in, gun drawn. He realized the weapon's futility in the crowded room, re-holstered it and grabbed Thayer, quickly handcuffing his hands behind him.

She caught her breath and climbed to her feet. Drake ran in, brushing past the nurse who tried to stop him.

"Get him out of here," he told Johnson. Sterling tried to protest, but Drake quieted him with a glare, taking Cassie's arm and escorting her from the room.

Johnson read Thayer his rights as other police officers arrived. "I heard him," he told Drake. "He confessed to trying to kill Hart." He shook his head, turned to Cassie. "That was the craziest thing I ever saw—that lady and what she did to her own children. Do you understand it?"

Cassie shook her head. "No, I don't."

Drake jerked his head at the younger officer. "They can take him in. I want a statement from you while everything's fresh. And get someone here to stand guard, this is a crime scene."

He ushered Cassie through the crowd of medical personnel, security and police to a quiet corner beside the vending machines. "How'd it go in there?"

"We lost Virginia," Cassie said. "I don't know about the baby. Is your mother all right?"

"She's fine—Ulrich never touched her. She only said that to separate us."

He pulled her into his arms for a long moment. Cassie reveled in his warmth, allowed the ebb tide of adrenalin and failure to rage through her. Finally, once she could control her breathing again, she looked up.

"Thank you."

He frowned, obviously upset by the events of the morning. "For what? I couldn't do anything." He sighed. "I felt so helpless—that poor kid."

"For just being here. For believing in me."

"You don't have to thank me for that. I'll always be here for you." He held her tight again. "You gonna be okay if I go take care of business?"

"I guess Virginia saved the taxpayers the expense of a trial," Cassie said, startling herself with the bitterness in her voice. "I'm sorry, I shouldn't talk like that—"

Drake looked down at her, one hand brushing her

hair away from her face. "You're tired. We all are." He started to leave, then turned back. "You know, you did the right thing. You made the right choice."

"I wish I could feel like that. I can't help thinking, she's dead, her baby's probably dead, and it's my fault."

"Ulrich made her own choice. You can't allow her to manipulate you now that she's gone. It's just as bad as the way she manipulated Sterling while she was alive."

Cassie thought about that. Typical of Drake to cut straight to the heart of the matter—no philosophical or ethical tightrope for him.

"You saved her son's life not once, but twice," he continued. "You got involved and risked everything to help that boy when no one else cared. You tried to save her and her baby's life. You did the right thing. I'm proud of you."

He kissed her on the top of her head and gave her shoulders an encouraging squeeze before leaving.

Trading one life for three, counting Sheila Kaminsky. Could it have been the right thing?

Most frightening of all was the fact that she wasn't sorry Virginia was dead. Only that the baby and Sheila had died.

She wasn't the person she'd thought she was, perhaps she never had been. But she knew the truth now—she could kill, she had killed, she might very well kill again.

She remembered Rachel Lloyd's accusations after she'd dealt with Morris. The nurse had been right, too right. Her oath to first do no harm, words she'd pledged her life to. They now seemed distant and meaningless.

As usual, the universe frustrated her attempts to understand it. It wasn't the first time. Cassie was certain it wouldn't be the last. Life would go on and she would learn to live with the consequences of her actions. But it was difficult to accept that so many people had been harmed by her desire to help one little boy.

※

DRAKE RETURNED TO where Ulrich's body lay in the operating room. He looked in through the windows. In the corner, a large blue sheet shrouded the warmer where the baby's body lay. Johnson and another patrolman stood guard outside the door, waiting for the coroner's unit to arrive.

Virginia Ulrich appeared less peaceful in death than she had in life. Her body was surrounded by blood-splattered drapes; there was a tube down her throat and a mass of IV lines hanging from her arms. Her eyes were wide open, staring at the ceiling.

Johnson stood with his back to the woman, hunched over his notebook. The patrol officer looked a little pale. Drake understood why. Even a veteran of street violence would have a difficult time accepting what Ulrich had done this evening. Or its aftermath. And he knew Johnson had a daughter almost Charlie's age.

"Need a minute?" Drake asked in a low voice.

The younger man shook his head, but there was a sheen of sweat on his upper lip. He sighed and straightened up. "No thanks, I think I've got everything straight."

"Let's go somewhere and talk. You okay in here, Rankin?" Drake asked over his shoulder as he led Johnson from the room.

Thank God, the press hadn't arrived yet. He'd told security not to allow them access to either the pediatric or OB floor, but in a building this size it wouldn't be long before someone found a way in. Miller should be here soon, then it'd all be her headache.

He and Johnson returned downstairs to room 303. Another uniformed officer stood outside the closed door, but waved them through.

Drake shut the door behind them and surveyed the room. It wasn't very large, space enough for a single bed, a rocking chair, and a fold out recliner. There was a large window opposite and a sink beside the door. A closet and the door into the bathroom lined the other wall.

No get well cards or balloons, no toys. A lonely place for a little kid. The bed was gone now, leaving a clear space amid the medical debris that cluttered the room. The crash cart stood to one side, its drawers open, syringes and vials of medicine littering its surface. Empty paper wrappings, boxes, and EKG paper were strewn across the floor like remnants of a New Year's celebration.

Except this had been no party.

"Do you have the video?" Drake asked.

"Rankin has it," Johnson answered.

"Okay, walk me through it."

"I was patrolling the floor and received a call at—" Johnson glanced at his notes. "1118. I arrived to find Ulrich at her son's bedside, holding a syringe containing an unknown substance at his IV. Dr. Hart was inside the room, attempting to calm Ulrich. Ulrich saw me and told me to stay outside the door, and given the imminent threat to her son, I remained where I was."

"You had a good view inside the room and could hear everything?"

"Yes sir. Ulrich was upset, saying Dr. Hart was trying to take her son away and that she would never let that happen. Then—" He frowned. "She took the syringe from her son's arm and put it into her own."

Drake nodded, wishing he could have just shot Ulrich instead of letting her play head games with Hart.

"Then the monitor alarms started to go crazy and Dr. Hart realized that Ulrich had poisoned the boy. Ulrich screamed something about Dr. Hart killing her, but the doctor ignored her and went to help the boy. Then you—" The patrol officer stumbled.

"Go ahead," Drake told him, bracing himself for the worse. He wasn't sure—had Ulrich pushed the plunger herself? Or had he done it when he rushed her? Had he killed that little baby?

Johnson cleared his throat. "Then you moved toward Ulrich. But before you could grab the syringe, she injected herself."

Drake stared at the officer. "You're certain about that? Absolutely certain?"

"Yes sir," Johnson asserted. "The camera caught it clear as day." He shook his head. "I'll never forget it to the day I die. Her son's dying, Hart goes to save him, and she has this look of," he searched for a word, "triumph. That smile—I don't ever want to see nothing like it again."

"She injected the drug? Before I touched her?"

"Oh yeah. No doubt about it."

"I see." Drake blew out his breath and his fists relaxed.

"Believe me, if I had known she had poisoned the boy, I would have taken her down right away. The syringe looked almost full. I don't think Dr. Hart realized what had happened either, not until the monitors started to alarm."

"Okay. You head back to the House and write it up." Drake looked around the room once more, then turned to leave.

Johnson remained in the center of the room, where Charlie's bed would have been. "I never would have dreamed—what would make a mother do that to her own son?" he asked, his voice filled with a mixture of wonder and disgust. "I mean, I've never seen anything like that."

Drake shook his head. "Me neither. Let's just hope that there's not many more like her out there."

CHAPTER 35

DRAKE KNOCKED ON the open door to White's office. The psychiatrist glanced up from the file he was dictating, and waved Drake inside. He couldn't help but notice the latest addition to White's decor: a framed Nate Trevasian original. Much nicer than the one Nate had drawn of Mendelsohn's hand over his face, stealing his words, his will.

This one was done with pastels—maybe from the set Drake had given Nate?—and depicted White as a roly-poly Santa Claus watching a boy play with his new puppy.

"Miller told me to report to you, even though you already cleared me," Drake said, lounging against the wall of windows beside the desk. He eyed the patient chair warily.

"That was before you killed a man," White reminded him. But his smile was warm as he swiveled his chair to face Drake, pulling back from his desk and forsaking his notepad and pen. "So, how've you been?"

"Great," Drake said. Then remembered the reason he was here and wiped the grin from his face. It was hard, though.

The last three days with Hart had been the best

three days he could remember. Waking in her bed, working side by side with her in her garden, sketching—he'd even begun to paint again—making love to her, it was as if they'd been granted a vacation from the real world and its problems. For the first time since February, he and Hart had talked, really, truly talked. About things he'd never expected to ever voice to another living soul.

"Hate to tell you, doc," he said, "but I think I've found another therapist. And she's a whole lot prettier than you."

White nodded thoughtfully, his shrink face back on. "No aftereffects from shooting Mendelsohn? Sleepless nights? Panic attacks?"

"Not about him. Face it, some creeps deserve what they get." Drake didn't mention the few bad dreams about what could have happened to Hart if he'd missed that shot, dreams that were quickly erased by her warm caress and soothing words.

White seemed to follow his thoughts effortlessly. "Dr. Hart is good for you. But I have one observation, Detective."

Drake resisted the urge to roll his eyes. He could afford to humor the man—after all, this was only a formality. IAD and the Officer Involved team had already cleared him, he had his gun and was scheduled to return to active duty tomorrow. "What's that?"

"I've been through your records and noted a pattern of behavior. Although you test very high, you were always a mediocre student. Never went out for competitive sports, only intramurals. And as a police officer, despite an excellent closure record and some fine work undercover, you've shown no interest in promotion and seem to almost invite a reputation as a screw-up."

Drake winced at that. "Don't sugar coat it, doc. Tell me what you really think, why don't you?"

"I am," White said in a serious tone.

Like he was Drake's father or something. Forget that, his dad would never be talking to him like this. "Go on."

"You barely even qualify on your weapons re-certification. Yet, the shot you made when you killed Mendelsohn was spectacular. I asked one of the Emergency Response snipers, he said he would have thought twice about it."

"I guess even screw-ups get lucky sometimes." Drake tried hard not to imagine what could have happened if he'd missed Mendelsohn, given the killer time to shoot Hart—or worse yet, what if he'd hit Hart by accident?

"How many times did your father win the Zone Seven marksman trophy?" White asked.

Drake jerked his head up, surprised by the question. "I dunno, why?"

"He won it every time he re-certified," White answered. "Set a new record."

Drake looked out the window, focused on the cerulean sky outside White's windows. No ball game today to distract him from the shrink's mumbojumbo.

"I think, in order to not compete with your father or his memory, you've learned to take the easy way out. You coast by, doing only what needs to be done, until something grabs your attention, and attracts your passion. Like the Trevasian family and their problems. Or Dr. Hart."

"Maybe I do," Drake replied, still staring out the window. "If that's what works for me—"

"Has it?" White interrupted. "Has it really worked for you, Detective?"

Drake whirled around, tired of the psychobabble. "What are you trying to say, doc? You're not going to let me go back to work? You gonna put a bad review in my jacket?"

White sighed and shook his head. "You need this job, just as you need Hart. I think you have the makings of an excellent police officer."

"But?"

To Drake's surprise, the shrink laughed. "No buts. That's the whole point. Stop holding back, Detective, waiting for your father's approval or judgment. Start living for you—use that passion Hart stirs in you. Don't run from it or try to control it." White stood, emerging from behind his desk to stand before Drake. "You've been granted a terrific gift, Detective. Don't let it go to waste."

White held out his hand. Drake took it.

"Go on, now," the shrink said in dismissal. "I've got real patients to treat." Drake started for the door. "But," White called after him, "don't let me hear about any more screw-ups or I'll call Hart and tell her to kick your butt!"

Drake grinned at the older man, thinking of the sparring session he'd had with Hart the day before. She had kicked his butt. Of course, then she'd eased the pain of defeat in a most pleasurable way. "Don't worry, doc. That's her specialty. No one slacks off around Hart."

※◎※

CASSIE WAS BUSY packing up her office when a knock came at her door. Before she could answer it, the door opened and Ed Castro filled the doorway.

"Hi."

She reached for the clock the residents had given her. Best teacher. Yeah, right.

Ed handed it to her, held it for both of them to look at for a moment. "I was so proud when they gave you this award," he said, relinquishing the crystal clock. She began to wrap it in newspaper. "I kept thinking how happy your father would be, if he could have been there."

She sucked her breath in. This was hard enough without him bringing up dreams that could never be. How many times over the years had she wished her parents were there to witness her accomplishments? How many times had she prayed for their guidance, and tried to live up to their expectations?

"Maybe it's a good thing he's not around to see what's happening now," she muttered. She gestured to a stack of mail on her desk. "Get a load of what was waiting for me when I got in today. Not to mention the websites memorializing Virginia as a fallen martyr. Or the news segment Sterling did today, claiming she suffered from pregnancy induced psychosis and that none of this would have happened if I hadn't accused her of Munchausen's."

Ed took the top letter from the stack and quickly read its message of hate. "This is awful. Did you ask Drake for protection?"

She shrugged. "I don't think any of them will actually do anything. Besides," she said with a scoffing laugh, "some of the things they suggest aren't even anatomically possible."

"Still, that's a lot of venom. Are they all like this?"

"Actually, no. Read this one." She reached for another letter. "This one is anonymous. She says her mother subjected her to numerous hospital admissions and procedures, even smearing feces in her wounds to cause infections. She survived because her mother turned her attention to her younger sister after she started kindergarten. Her sister died, and she's certain it was because of what her mother did."

"God, what a way for a child to grow up." Ed returned the letter. "At least she's grateful that you brought this Virginia Ulrich business into the public light. Maybe there are others out there that it will help, too."

"Maybe. Sure hasn't done your clinic any good. I heard The Senator is blocking any government funding for it. I'm sorry. I know how much the Liberty Center meant to you and Drake."

He moved a stack of books from where it threatened to topple from her desk and leaned against it. "Actually, that's what I came to talk to you about. The Liberty Center has been given a grant from an anonymous benefactor. Enough to get it opened by September."

"Really? That's fantastic. Any idea who the donor is?"

"No. It goes through a non-profit called The Riverstar Foundation. But, I need your help."

"Of course, anything. I've got nothing but time on my hands. Not since the Executive Committee accepted my resignation. At least the Medical Board found me innocent, so my medical record will be clear, even if no one around here will hire me."

"I want to hire you. Two jobs, actually. One as Special Projects Director of the clinic—hands on involvement with project development as well as clinical shifts. Maybe even making house calls if you're up to that."

She nodded, already envisioning the work that the Liberty Center could accomplish. Every time Drake and

Ed discussed it, they came up with new ideas to help the people of East Liberty and the surrounding neighborhoods. "Sounds great."

"It won't pay much, but with the addition of the second job, I think you'll make by."

"Second job?"

"You know how much I hate flying, doing any kind of transport."

Ed's fear of flying and tendency to get sick in the back of ambulances were legendary. She didn't enjoy flying either, but she still loved transports—the thrill of being on-scene, improvising, using only her hands and skills to make a diagnosis and save a life. "You'd like me to take over as Transport Director?"

"I won't have time, not with my job in the ER and being Medical Director of the Liberty Center. And, that way, you could also cover some shifts here in the ER, to keep your skills up."

She was speechless. He'd just described her perfect job. She dropped the clock she was wrapping into the box and threw her arms around him. "Thanks, Ed. You're my favorite fairy godfather!"

He returned her embrace. "I promised Rosa I'd look after you," he reminded her. "Wouldn't want the old witch to curse me from beyond the grave."

"There's just one catch," he continued.

Cassie broke away. Wasn't there always? "What?"

"Adeena is going to be heading social services for the Center. You'd be working closely together. Is that going to be a problem?"

She hesitated. Adeena had left several messages of apology on her answering machine, but Cassie hadn't found the time to return her calls. Who was she fooling? She didn't want to talk to Adeena. She was still too angry to face her.

"C'mon," Ed said. "You two have been friends for too long. Don't let Virginia Ulrich take that from you as well. You have to forgive her, Cassie. She made a mistake—but she was trying to do what was best for you and the Ulrich family."

"I know." She looked away, finished piling photos of the ER staff, medics she'd worked with, into her box. This was her home, her family. And she was being forced to leave it, to start over. She couldn't afford to lose another friend. Especially not one as important as Adeena. "I'll talk to her," she promised Ed. "It'll be all right."

"Good. Then, as your new boss, here's your first assignment."

She looked up at the tone of merriment in his voice. What was he up to now? Ed hated confrontation, any disruption in the emotional equanimity of those he was close to—he loved playing matchmaker, peacemaker, Santa Claus. Whatever it took to restore the balance.

"What?"

"You're going to let me finish in here while you go upstairs to Drake's mother's room. He's waiting for you."

"Ed, what's going on?"

"No questions, that's an order. Now, go!"

⁂

MURIEL HAD BEEN moved from the ICU and to a bed on the Neurology ward. Park said she'd be ready for discharge in another day or so. Cassie found Drake huddled over his mother's bed, his tall form blocking her view.

"Is everything all right?" she asked, joining him at

the bedside.

"How do you like my new hair do?" Muriel asked, moving a hand mirror away from her face. Ribbons of dark hair littered the bed as Drake brandished a pair of shears.

Cassie stopped and stared. Muriel's long hair had been replaced by a short, spiky cut that made her look a decade younger. She nodded in approval. "It's you. I like it."

Muriel combed her fingers through it. "Thanks. I do, too. You can still see the staples, but Dr. Park said those will come out soon. And the hair he shaved will grow in soon."

A knock on the door interrupted them. The door opened, and Antwan Washington limped inside, followed by his mother and Adeena.

"Can we come in?" Adeena asked Muriel, but her eyes were fixed on Cassie.

Should've known Ed wouldn't wait for Cassie to make the first move. He'd set her up.

"Sure," Muriel called out. "Who are you?"

Tammy approached, staying behind Adeena, not meeting anyone's gaze. Antwan wasn't as shy and marched up to Muriel, his left leg dragging slightly from his stroke, the white plastic of an ankle-foot orthotic visible above his sneaker.

"This is Tammy Washington and her son, Antwan," Cassie made introductions. "And this is Adeena Coleman." She saw Adeena stiffen at the sound of her name and realized that their estrangement was hurting her as much as Cassie. She wrapped an arm around Adeena's waist, drew her into the tableau of adults around the bed. "My best friend since third grade."

"Pleased to meet you," Muriel said, after

introducing herself and Drake.

Antwan was trying to climb onto the bed, but couldn't with his hands full of a large stuffed kitten with blue eyes and impossibly long whiskers. Muriel patted the mattress beside her, and Cassie raised him up, loving the vibrant grin he gave her. "And who is that cute little kitty cat?"

"This is Felix," Antwan told them, waving the kitten's paw in greeting. "He's only pretend. I can't have a real kitty."

"They said Antwan can go home today after his physical therapy, so I wanted to say good-bye," Tammy said in a shy voice. "Wanted to thank you for everything, Dr. Hart."

"No need to. I'm just happy to see Antwan looking so well. Do you have everything you need at home?"

"Oh yes. His exercise equipment is already there, and the therapists are set to come three times a week. He needs another week of antibiotics, but they have home nurses who can come and give it to him. And we get to stay together. CYS and Adeena are helping me with a tutor so I can find another job, a better job that will let me take care of Antwan like I should." The young mother beamed with pride as she watched her son and Muriel join in earnest conversation, Antwan tickling Muriel's cheek with the stuffed animal.

"Just don't forget to call us if you need anything," Cassie told her. Then she thought of a way to repay Ed. "Adeena, don't you think Tammy might be a great help at the Liberty Center? I'm sure Drake or Ed could find her a job there."

Drake picked up his cue and smiled at Tammy. "We'd be honored to have you join the team, Ms. Washington. But only if Antwan can come visit as well."

"You mean it? A job where Antwan could stay,

too?"

"Of course," Adeena said. "We're planning the best daycare facilities in the city."

Tammy was speechless, but the grin that filled her face and lit her eyes was thanks enough. Antwan's free hand reached up to tug at Cassie's hand, and she looked down at him.

"Look, we match!" Antwan pointed with excitement at the semi-circle of staples in Muriel's scalp to the line of them in Cassie's and then to the two that marked where his cerebral pressure monitor had been inserted. "Mom, look! We all got our brains fixed."

"See, he's a future doctor." Drake laughed. He glanced at his watch, then over at Adeena. "Isn't it about time for us to head out?"

Adeena nodded. Cassie looked to the two of them, what now?

"We'll be back tonight, Mom," he said, kissing his mother on the cheek and running his fingers through her newly shorn hair.

Muriel grinned up at him, and Cassie realized she was in on it as well. "Have fun."

"Where are we going?" she asked as Drake led her out, followed by Adeena, Antwan and Tammy.

He pulled four tickets from his back pocket and handed them to Antwan. "To the Pirate's game. Buccs versus the Reds. I'm going to catch Antwan a fly ball. But first, we need to take a little elevator ride." Drake's eyes were twinkling with excitement. He intertwined his fingers with hers. "Don't worry, I'll be right here."

"Drake—" He leaned forward and kissed her before she could say more. Antwan giggled despite his mother telling him to hush.

When they broke apart, she saw Adeena using an elevator call key to summon the patient transport elevator. Antwan rushed in, nimbly maneuvering his bad leg over the threshold, his mother and Adeena following. Cassie hesitated.

"Trust me," Drake whispered, leading her inside the steel box.

She tried to relax as the doors closed, trapping them inside. Drake ran his fingers over her tensed shoulder muscles, soothing her. He pulled her close as they lurched to a stop on the third floor and the doors opened again.

Cassie watched as one of the pediatric nurses who had helped her with Charlie's resuscitation wheeled a patient into the tiny space. Then she realized that the patient in the wheelchair was Charlie.

A remarkably changed Charlie Ulrich. He glanced around at the occupants of the elevator with animated interest, grinning at Antwan. Cassie exchanged glances with Adeena and the nurse who smiled and nodded.

"He's doing great. Eating, laughing, talking like I've never seen him before," the nurse told her.

"Where are you going?"

"His father is transferring him to a private care facility," Adeena answered. "But he's left the law firm, and is going to take him home himself. Said he'd never let Charlie be less than his top priority again."

Antwan was busy introducing Charlie to Felix. "This is my kitty cat."

Cassie crouched down beside the wheelchair. Drake's hand squeezed her shoulder in encouragement. "Hi, Charlie."

Charlie looked up and smiled at her. "Hi." He pointed to the stuffed animal. "Kit-cat."

"That's right. What's a kitty cat say?" she asked. Charlie was silent.

But Antwan knew the answer. "Meow," he gave a

credible impression of a cat. "That's what a cat says."

"Meow," Charlie parroted, clapping his hands in delight. He reached out to pet the cat's soft fur. "Meow." He giggled.

The elevator doors opened, and the nurse pushed the wheelchair out. Adeena turned the key to the Stop position.

"Bye, Charlie," Cassie called.

Charlie twisted in his chair so that he could see her. "Bye, bye," he waved at her. He giggled once more as she blew him kisses with a loud smacking noise. He imitated the gesture, then waved again.

"Bye, bye."

Adeena and the Washingtons followed. "See you guys later," Drake told them. Cassie started out, but Drake pulled her back, wrapping his arms around her, snuggling her tight against his chest. The doors closed, and they stood in silence.

"Thank you," she whispered when she could find her voice once more. She swallowed against a knot of tears and turned in his embrace, tilting her face up to his. He raised a hand to brush a tear from her cheek. "That was the best gift anyone could ever give me."

She stood on tiptoe and kissed him deeply. He responded immediately, shifting his body so that they fit just right, deepening the embrace as his strong arms circled her waist and lifted her. He twirled her, pinning her back against the wall, resting her weight on the large guide rail that ran across the length of the elevator.

"We can't, not here," she protested. He stole her breath with another kiss, his hands tugging at her shirt.

"Sure we can. I've got the key, this thing's not going anywhere until I say so," he assured her with a wicked gleam in his eye. "Besides, don't you know, every man's fantasy is to make love in an elevator?"

She wrapped her arms around him, laughing. It didn't matter that they were trapped in a steel cage. Not as long as they were together.

Want More Hart & Drake?

They Return in

FACE TO FACE

#1 NYT Bestseller Sandra Brown called NERVES OF STEEL, the first Hart and Drake novel, "A perfect blend of romance and suspense. My kind of read."

In the second book, SLEIGHT OF HAND, you saw Hart and Drake risk everything to save a child and you knew they were meant to be together.

Now, see what happens when they lose it all...

Drake hunts a stalker with deadly intentions. Hart fights for justice for one special victim while also fending off her ex and his family as they try to destroy everything she holds dear.

Neither realizes the real danger lies with an old enemy whose fury has grown and will not be satisfied with anything less than Hart and Drake's blood.

FACE TO FACE

Available Now!

About CJ

New York Times and *USA Today* bestselling author of twenty-seven novels, former pediatric ER doctor CJ Lyons has lived the life she writes about in her cutting edge Thrillers with Heart.

CJ has been called a "master within the genre" (Pittsburgh Magazine) and her work has been praised as "breathtakingly fast-paced" and "riveting" (Publishers Weekly) with "characters with beating hearts and three dimensions" (Newsday).

Her novels have won the International Thriller Writers' prestigious Thriller Award, the RT Reviewers' Choice Award, the Readers' Choice Award, the RT Seal of Excellence, and the Daphne du Maurier Award for Excellence in Mystery and Suspense.

Learn more about CJ's Thrillers with Heart at www.CJLyons.net

CPSIA information can be obtained at www.ICGtesting.com
Printed in the USA
LVOW11s1457070715

445280LV00005B/375/P